"You think I'm trash now, don't you?"

Her directness rendered him speechless.

"I didn't sleep with Tavio," she whispered, frantic for him to believe her.

"I don't care!"

"Okay. I don't know why I bothered to defend myself—to you, of all people."

She hated him for being able to compel her just by sitting across from her. "I hate you," she whispered in a low, seething tone. Then she instantly regretted saying anything.

"Good." He flashed her a ruthless white grin. "I wish to hell you'd figured that out before you seduced me and got yourself pregnant! Because now—for better or worse—we're stuck with each other!"

"You can leave, for all I care! I don't ever want anything from you again," she said.

"You want out of here, don't you?"

He took her silence to mean yes.

"You're not calling the shots anymore, darlin'. I am. Listen, because I'm only going to say this once. You have to do exactly what I say. Exactly. Your life and *mine* depend on it."

D0172810

Also by ANN MAJOR

THE GIRL WITH THE GOLDEN SPURS
THE HOT LADIES MURDER CLUB
MARRY A MAN WHO WILL DANCE
WILD ENOUGH FOR WILLA
INSEPARABLE

ANN MAJOR

THE GIRL
=== with the ===
GOLDEN GUN

MIRA®

If you purchased this book without a cover you should be aware
that this book is stolen property. It was reported as "unsold and
destroyed" to the publisher, and neither the author nor the
publisher has received any payment for this "stripped book."

ISBN 0-7783-2224-6

THE GIRL WITH THE GOLDEN GUN

Copyright © 2005 by Ann Major.

All rights reserved. Except for use in any review, the reproduction or
utilization of this work in whole or in part in any form by any electronic,
mechanical or other means, now known or hereafter invented, including
xerography, photocopying and recording, or in any information storage or
retrieval system, is forbidden without the written permission of the publisher,
MIRA Books, 225 Duncan Mill Road, Don Mills, Ontario, Canada M3B 3K9.

All characters in this book have no existence outside the imagination of the
author and have no relation whatsoever to anyone bearing the same name
or names. They are not even distantly inspired by any individual known or
unknown to the author, and all incidents are pure invention.

MIRA and the Star Colophon are trademarks used under license and registered
in Australia, New Zealand, Philippines, United States Patent and Trademark
Office and in other countries.

www.MIRABooks.com

Printed in U.S.A.

Nobody has time to write!

So many people support me in big and little ways so that I can get a few words down on paper.

Professionally, I want to thank Tara Gavin, Karen Solem, Nancy Berland and all the talented people they work with. I want to thank everybody at MIRA. I want to thank fans, especially those who have taken the time to send me encouraging letters.

Personally, I thank Ted and my mother, who go without things they need too often, so that I can get the work done. My children and grandchildren are wonderful, too. I must also thank all my friends, who understand when I forget to return their phone calls.

I dedicate this book in loving memory
to Sondra Stanford.

Smart Cowboy Saying:

When you lose, don't lose the lesson.

—From "Cowboy Quotes, Sayings and Wisdom"
www.Cowboyway.com

Prologue

"When I'm through with you, you'll have nothing and be nothin', boy! Mia will finally see what a lowlife you are!"

Rain slashed the windshield so hard Shanghai Knight could barely see to drive. He speeded up anyway, slamming his foot down on the gas pedal with such a vengeance his truck weaved recklessly through the slippery mud.

He couldn't get away from the Golden Spurs Ranch fast enough. Damn. He was such an idiot!

As if to knock some sense into himself, he hit his brow with the bottom edge of his fist. He'd give anything if Caesar Kemble's taunts would stop repeating themselves inside his head like a broken record.

When he rubbed his right cheek and jaw, he only aggravated the painful bruise that Caesar had caused when he punched him, so Shanghai clamped both hands back on the steering wheel. It galled him to remember what quick work Caesar had made of him in front of Mia.

A few punches in the ribs and a few more below the belt,

and all the fight had been knocked clean out of him long before Caesar's men had picked him up and shoved him down the ranch house steps into the mud.

Every time he thought about Caesar standing over him in his dining room with his fists raised and that nasty grin on his face, Shanghai wanted to wheel around and go back. Looking prettier than a picture, Mia had knelt beside Shanghai stroking his face. How he'd hated her, of all people, for being a witness to his humiliation.

The wealthy Kembles despised the lowly Knights, and the Knights held an ancient grudge against the Kembles for stealing their ranch. Shanghai and Mia never should have become involved with each other.

They wouldn't have if Caesar hadn't damn near backed over her at Old Man Pimbley's gas station when she'd been two. Shanghai had been twelve at the time and sneaking a smoke out back. At the risk of his own neck, not that he'd ever been one to mind that much, he'd thrown his smoke down and run screaming toward the truck. Not that Caesar had noticed. When he'd kept on backing, Shanghai had dived behind the truck and thrown her to safety. One of the big back tires had broken his leg.

When his cigarette butt had started a grass fire out back, Caesar and Old Man Pimbley had cussed him out for his trouble although Caesar had relented and paid to get his leg set. But the local gossips had made Shanghai into something of a hero, which had truly galled Caesar.

As Mia grew up she'd heard the story, and like the gossips, seen him as a hero, too. Thus, she'd developed a bad habit of following him around, her whiskey-colored eyes sparkling with adoration. He'd liked somebody admiring him, especially since it had rankled Caesar so much, until he'd started chasing girls his own age. Then her habit had gotten annoying since she was always watching him at the damnedest times.

Once when he'd been dating two girls at the same time, she'd called them both and told each one about the other. Mia knew how to make trouble, all right.

What did she think of him now?

Hell, why should he care?

Not many people admired the Knights much anymore. The Kembles were everything in Spur County—mainly 'cause they'd stolen from the Knights. Shanghai had grown up poor while Mia had been a princess from birth. If he worked for the rest of his life he'd never be able to earn a fraction of her wealth.

Everything about tonight was pure, raw hell. The weather was wild and wet, the road bad and Shanghai was breathing hard and driving way too fast. He'd made a fool out of himself, and tomorrow after Mia and Caesar got through bragging to all their friends, everybody in three counties would know.

If he had a fault, it was pride. He didn't like feeling like he was nothing. He realized now that it was too late, that maybe he shouldn't have gone alone to Caesar Kemble for a showdown on Kemble's vast Golden Spurs spread.

Suddenly up ahead Shanghai saw the dark, familiar outline of the small, hunting cabin where he'd spent many a night when his daddy was drunk or just plain too mean to live with. Shanghai stomped on the brakes, causing the big old truck to skid on its bald tires. It hurtled through the mud and rain at a frightening speed and slammed into the bottom step that led up to the porch.

Wood splintered. Cursing silently, he cut the engine. He didn't know what to do.

If he went home, his daddy might be drunk. If his old man saw his face, he'd figure out what had happened. Whether Shanghai confessed or not, his daddy would most likely start a fight. Caesar was going to do what he was going do.

He grabbed the steering wheel and laid his dark brow on

it, remembering how filled with pride he'd been when he'd boldly slapped those documents that proved his ancestors had as much right as Caesar's to the Golden Spurs Ranch onto Caesar Kemble's massive dining-room table in front of Caesar and his foreman, Kinky. He'd eyed the men cockily, feeling full of himself. Rubbing his brow, Kinky had frowned.

Caesar hadn't even bothered to read a single page. He'd said simply, "This don't mean nothin'! Hell, you're nothin', kid." Then he'd punched him in the jaw and knocked him out cold.

A girl's screams had startled him back to consciousness. He'd been sprawled flat on his back under the table when he'd felt little bits of shredded papers raining down on him and the tenderness of soft cool fingers brushing his face.

He'd said, "Ouch!"

Then she'd been yanked away by her father.

"Mia! I'll tan you, too, if you don't get back upstairs with Lizzy where you belong!" Caesar had yelled at her.

"You'd better not kill him!" she'd whispered fiercely, crossing her arms over her chest.

"I don't need your help, little girl. I'll be just fine!" Shanghai had muttered, feeling shamed by her tenderness but most of all by the fact that she'd seen his sorry ass sprawled on her floor.

"Fine? That's why you're lying there flat on your backside all busted up?"

Her words had hit a nerve. He prided himself on being tough.

He'd stared at her through slitted lashes, pretending to ignore her 'cause Mia hated being ignored more than she hated anything. Even so, he saw the redheaded teenager place her hands on her hips as she hovered over him like a guardian angel. Tonight she'd worn skintight jeans, a T-shirt and red boots. When she'd sprinted back up the stairs, he'd noticed that she filled out her jeans and T-shirt with a woman's shape now.

She was too young to look so grown-up. Mia had exasperated and charmed him for years by chasing him anytime she got the chance. He would have felt easier with the bean-pole shape, freckle-faced kid that she used to be.

Mia had made a habit of disappearing from the Golden Spurs Ranch for long stretches and wandering about the county on horseback. Anytime she'd gotten hurt, she'd come crying to Shanghai. Anytime she'd made a good grade or had won a prize at school, she'd had to tell him first even if it meant riding over to Black Oaks.

Once when her daddy had told her he was going to shoot a torn-up mongrel sheepdog she'd found bleeding to death on the highway, she'd carted the pup to Shanghai in her red wagon.

He'd told her her daddy was right for once, and it would be a kindness to shoot him. But when she'd left the mutt and her wagon, the beast had given him a baleful stare. Shanghai had taken the dog to the vet and nursed it back to health. He still remembered how her eyes had shone, when she'd come back for her wagon a month later and had seen the black-and-white mutt napping on his front porch.

"Don't you dare tell anybody I saved him," he'd warned her. "They'd think I was plum crazy."

"Cross my heart." She'd hesitated. "What do you call him?"

"Dog."

She'd knelt and petted the animal. "Can I name him?"

"What's wrong with Dog?"

"I—I'd call him Spot."

"That's as bad as Dog."

"Not quite, is it, Spot?"

Spot had wagged his tail fit to be tied, and it was Spot from then on.

Shanghai put the memories of her childhood aside. She was a Kemble and all grown-up now.

No sooner had her door slammed upstairs tonight than Caesar had resumed tearing up the documents. Then he'd started pounding the table. Shanghai had found himself staring up at the underside of the table where the name, Mia, was scrawled dozens of times in bright red crayon alongside Lizzy's name, and he'd imagined Mia a cute kid with red pigtails under the table up to mischief with her sister.

Then Caesar had distracted him by raking the last of the ruined documents he'd brought onto the floor beside Shanghai and shouting they were garbage just like he was.

"Get out, you lowdown, lying thief. You aren't a damn bit better than your daddy. And we all know what he is—a lousy, no-good drunk. But at least he knows that he lives under my protection, which is more than I can say for you. You think you're somethin'! Well, you're nothin'! When I tell him what you tried to do tonight in *my* house, in front of my little girl…you'll be lucky if he ever lets you set foot in his place again. He owes me. And so do you. So does this whole damn community. You Knights don't have any friends around here unless I allow it. Don't you ever forget it. Without me— you're nothin', boy. Nothin'!"

Suddenly Caesar's red face had changed. "You've given me an idea, boy. A helluvan idea. A real winner. I know how I'll get rid of all you Knights, once and for all." He'd gone to a small cabinet, opened a drawer and pulled out a couple of fresh decks of cards. "I'll hunt up that daddy of yours, and we'll have us a friendly, little game of poker. That's what we'll do. We'll have a few drinks. Then I'll tell him what you did here tonight."

"No…."

Caesar had laughed at him.

Shanghai despised himself because in the next breath he'd begged and apologized.

"Please—I'm sorry. Please—leave him alone!"

Caesar had guffawed again. "Everybody in three counties

knows that cards and liquor are a fatal combination for your old man, boy. Kinky! Eli! Get him out of here!" Caesar turned back to Shanghai. "When I'm through with you, you'll have nothing and be nothin', boy! Mia will finally see you for the lowlife you are!"

"Don't you go near my daddy!"

When Shanghai had fought Eli and Kinky, Caesar had called for more cowboys. It had taken five of the bastards to fling Shanghai down the stairs into the rain.

When Shanghai had pulled himself to his feet, the last thing he'd seen was pretty Mia Kemble leaning out of her upstairs window. When he'd looked up, she'd thrown something down to him and then banged her window shut.

Pretending not to give a damn about her, he'd rammed his dripping Stetson with his lucky turkey feather on his head even harder than she'd slammed her window. Curious, he'd picked up the object she'd thrown. When he'd realized it was a red rose, he'd pitched it back into the mud.

Now that he was at his hunting cabin, Shanghai dreaded his daddy finding out that he'd gotten in a fight with Caesar. He might never let Shanghai go home again. His father didn't care if the Kembles had robbed the Knights of practically all their land. He just wanted to drink and gamble. Caesar kept offering to buy their last fifty thousand acres and his father kept refusing to sell, mainly because he and Cole begged him not to. The land was Shanghai's heritage, Cole's, too; part of their souls.

No use thinking about it. Shanghai knew he'd started something tonight that couldn't be stopped.

As he got out of his truck, he stood in the rain for a moment to inspect the mangled bottom step he'd just smashed. *Damn.*

He sprang to the second step, which was still sound, just as the sky flashed livid white fire and then went black again. Every timber of the tiny hunting cabin shook when thunder exploded again.

He threw open the front door, ripped off his wet, Western shirt and hung it on the back of a tattered leather chair where it dripped water onto the scarred oak floor. Then he went to the fridge and grabbed a couple of beers. He downed the first beer and paced restlessly.

He was twenty-four. What the hell was he going to do with the rest of his life? Cowboying and rodeoing were all he really liked to do. Not that he could stay here when there was no future at Black Oaks. At least not in the business of cows and calves and horses. Livestock prices had collapsed too many times, and Daddy had borrowed way too much money. There was only his kid brother, Cole, to consider.

Hell, Cole was twenty-one, which meant he was all grown-up…even if he was still in college. It was time for Cole to be on his own.

Shanghai didn't want to leave his home, but he hadn't liked feeling like nothing on Caesar's floor with Mia watching. If he stayed here, he'd be nothin' all his life.

He sank wearily into the leather chair near the open window. The only thing he'd ever done to make money besides working Black Oaks was rodeoing. He was good at bronc ridin' and bull riding. When he donned buckskin chaps with silver conchos, pointed cowboy boots with spurs and his Stetson, people cheered and screamed and then patted him on the back when he rode well. They went wild when he won. Pretty women threw themselves at him.

He was too tall and powerfully built for the sport, and he'd have to be damn good—the best ever—to make it really pay. Good or bad, you could get yourself stomped or gored to death in front of thousands. Champions died of injuries as small as a broken rib nicking an artery.

What choice did he have?

Hell, he'd been beaten up all his life, hadn't he? A man could become famous riding bulls, as famous as any Kemble, at least for a spell.

Nobody wrote country songs about lawyers or doctors, did they? He reckoned he could take about as much pain as any man.

His black brows slashed together as he watched the rain hammer the earth. Caesar had destroyed the sheaves of old journals and ancient bank documents he'd slung on the table—all the evidence he'd been gathering for nearly two years to prove that his family, the Knights, had as much right to the Golden Spurs Ranch and its staggering mineral riches as the Kembles did.

What should he do next?

A bolt of lightning crashed again. Shanghai's heart beat faster. He rubbed his sore jaw. After his quarrel with Caesar Kemble, the storm more than matched his mood. Since Caesar had refused to even talk about making a fair settlement, maybe he should think about finding a real lawyer. But he couldn't go to a lawyer until he reassembled at least some of the evidence Caesar had destroyed. Besides lawyers cost money.

Even though it was so obvious the Knights had been swindled, his father had told him not to fight the Kembles.

His father could go to hell. Most people probably saw his daddy as an easygoing, shiftless soul, who had a weakness for the bottle. But they didn't know. His old man could get really drunk, and when he did, he always went after Shanghai.

There was no talking to him then, no arguing with a drunk.

The lights in his kitchen flickered twice. Shanghai wouldn't have minded the thunderstorm if he'd been in a better frame of mind. Water was scarce in south Texas.

He was stretching his long legs out when he heard a car door slam and quick, light footsteps followed by a timid knock at his door.

Not wanting company, Shanghai hunkered lower and ignored the light taps.

Thunder crashed outside and was quickly followed by brilliant lightning. Then the world went dark again as the rain continued to pour down.

The door rattled as a girl's hand pulled it open. "Can I come in?"

Mia's soft whisper cut through the noise of the storm and sliced bits out of his bruised heart. Shanghai sprang to his feet as if she'd pelted him with buckshot. Then pain licked through him from the beating he'd taken from her daddy.

"Go away!" he growled. "You're the last person I want to see."

"Not till we talk."

"Damn your hide, girl. Git." His mouth hurt so badly he could barely speak. He rubbed it before he thought and orange stars flashed in front of his eyes. *Damn.*

When she didn't leave or say anything, he bit his lips in frustration. Then quick as a panther he flung his empty longneck so savagely into the trash can, it burst. Broken glass tinkled to the bottom of the can. His boots made hollow sounds that rang on the oak flooring as he stalked heavily to the front door, which he slammed open wider with enough force to show her she wasn't welcome.

Shanghai flipped on the outside light and saw her through the screen. She sure as hell looked different with her long red hair flowing like fiery amber about her pretty face and slim shoulders. Despite his injuries, he tensed when he saw that she sucked in a quick breath after looking at his bronzed shoulders and torso. Then she blushed.

She'd changed out of her jeans. Why the hell had she done that? She looked so soft and feminine and sweet. Her beauty caused a hard knot to lodge in the base of his throat. He'd never seen her in a damp, clingy white dress before; never guessed that a tomboy kid like her could have such a good figure. She was still wearing her bright red boots, though, and she was holding a mud-spattered rose.

What happened to the kid with red pigtails he'd felt so easy around?

He ran a hand through his black hair and inhaled a quick, raspy breath.

"Where'd you get that damn-fool dress?"

"Borrowed it from Lizzy."

"Figures. You should have borrowed some shoes, too."

"Her feet are longer than mine."

Since he was bare-chested and black and blue all over, she could probably see every mark her bullying father had inflicted.

He stood up straighter, maybe to intimidate her. "I wasn't expecting company. I'd better put on my shirt."

"No. It's probably soaking or something. You look... good." She blushed again and lowered her eyes.

"You shouldn't throw away the presents people give you," she said, pulling the screen door open.

When she twirled the rose under his nose, he grabbed it and threw it on the floor.

"Girl, don't you know better than to come looking for me—tonight...after..."

Shanghai notched his chin higher as he remembered regaining consciousness and finding Caesar Kemble standing over him, his hand still clenched into a fist and that awful grin on his face.

"I shouldn't have gone to your house tonight," Shanghai said. "And you shouldn't be here now."

"Don't you care that I hate what my daddy did to you?"

"No, I don't care."

"Why do you hate me?"

"Well, maybe 'cause your bunch has been stealing from my bunch for umpteen generations. Maybe tonight I want to be alone to sulk and drink and nurse my hatred for all things Kemble—including you."

"I saw you ride that bull last weekend at the Kingsville Rodeo. You were great."

He inhaled a couple of long, embarrassing breaths while she stared at his chest, and he tried not to stare at hers.

"You're very young," he muttered.

"What's that got to do with anything?"

"Plenty. Don't you know nothin'? You're not a kid anymore."

"I didn't think you'd ever notice."

"Go home."

"No."

"I'm twenty-four."

"So?"

"I've already got a girl."

"Wendy! I know."

"So go chase boys your own age."

Some of the sparkle went out of her eyes. Still, she was a vision in that white dress. He couldn't very well throw her off his porch into the rain. Not when he didn't trust himself to touch her.

Still, the last thing Shanghai needed tonight was a sassy virgin from the Kemble bunch to tempt him even further down the road that led to hell.

"Can I come in or not?" she whispered again.

"No!"

She laughed as she pulled the screen door open and sashayed past him.

"Are you out of your mind? How many times have I warned you to stay the hell away from me, girl?"

She pretended to count her fingers and then stopped. "Way too many." She went to his cooler, opened it and grabbed a beer. Then she popped the top off using the edge of his table. She would have taken a long swig of the stuff if he hadn't grabbed it from her and taken a healthy pull himself.

"You're not exactly the obedient type, are you?" He watched her as he took another long pull.

"Are you?"

That stopped him cold.

"I was worried sick about you," she said. "I had to come."

Her big, golden, long-lashed eyes met his. Again he noted the raindrops glistening like diamonds in her red hair. Most of all he fixated on that single sparkle that clung to the tip of her cute, upturned nose. She was wearing lipstick and eyeliner for a change.

"If you're looking to get yourself seduced, little girl, follow cowboys like me home and then throw yourself at them."

"You're not like that, and we both know it. You're nice."

"Nice? You don't have the gumption God gave a horsefly. Guys aren't nice. They're all out to get you."

"Where's Spot?"

"At the house."

Her teeth chattered, and she rubbed her arms to warm herself.

"If your daddy catches us together here, he'll get one of his bought-off judges to railroad me into some prison until I'm old and gray. Come back when you're eighteen."

"What if some other girl...like Wendy Harper gets you before then?"

He didn't answer.

"I'm all wet and cold. You could offer me a blanket or your shirt or something." She swallowed a quick breath, and he realized she was even more nervous than he was. Then she picked up the damp shirt that hung on the back of his chair and slipped her arms through the sleeves. When the long sleeves dangled many inches longer than her hands, she began to roll them up.

"Why can't you ever do what you're told?"

"Because then I don't get what I want." She paused, pulling his shirt close against her body. "Can I help it if I grew up spoiled instead of with a great big chip on my shoulder weighing me down?"

"What if I grabbed you and snapped you against my chest?

What if I gave you a kiss or two, would you leave me alone then and go chase somebody closer to your age?"

She straightened up to face him. Beaming brightly, she puckered her lips. "Cross my heart and swear to die."

"You're hopeless. Girls are supposed to let the guy do the chasin'," he said.

"That's stupid. You'd never chase me."

"You're too young."

"When I'm all grown up, eighteen, would you really want…"

"You're a Kemble."

"Kiss me," she whispered in a low, hypnotic tone. "If my daddy runs you off like he said he would, this might be my last chance. Then I'd have to live my whole life without knowing…what you're like."

Hardly knowing what he did, he strolled closer, leaned down and pecked her cheek lightly with his lips. The kiss accomplished, he intended to jump free. "There. Now go!"

"That's not the kind of kiss I meant, and you know it!"

Her gentle hands circled his wide shoulders, and she seemed to melt into him as she clung tightly. Even as he fought to loosen her grip, he heated where her warm breath brushed his cheek. He noticed that her damp body, although slim and petite, nestled against his huge frame, felt more like a woman's body than a child's. Damn her hide, she was a perfect fit.

His heart thudded painfully. He should burn in hell for this alone.

"On the lips," she pleaded. "Kiss me like you kissed Wendy at the rodeo."

"You little spy!"

"Just once—please."

He yanked himself loose. Still, he admired the way she went after what she wanted. Nothing had ever been handed to him, either.

She put her hand to her cheek. "My skin burns where you..."

It was the damnedest, most unaccountable thing, but his lips burned from the chaste kiss he'd given her.

One taste of her sweet, velvet skin had rocked him. She was innocent but willing and utterly, utterly adorable.

He wished he was ten years younger so he could crush her close and not feel like he was Satan's spawn.

He couldn't stand another second of this, so he stomped out of the house and stood on his porch and watched it rain.

She raced after him.

"Now you really have to go," he said roughly. "You promised."

She shook her head. "That was only if you kissed me on the mouth." Her voice fell so softly, he had to strain to hear it over the downpour.

Being protective of a Kemble was not a role he felt comfortable with. Not when she was so all-fired beautiful.

"Mia—"

When he turned and saw her backlighted by the porch lamp, he had to remind himself again she was jailbait. Standing there in her wet dress with her big eyes fastened on his mouth, she personified fresh, young sensuality and femininity.

"Go," he said.

"How come you still wear that turkey feather I gave you in the brim of your hat?"

"That doesn't mean anything, girl."

His heart thudded. Inside his jeans, he was hard and swollen. He wanted her. Even though it was wrong.

Before she could answer him, headlights flashed, and he heard a car down the road.

"Go to the kitchen. Don't make a sound. If anybody finds you here, I could end up in jail. Do you understand how serious this is?"

For once she obeyed, and he shut the door behind her. Scarcely had she hidden herself, than his own father stormed up to the porch.

As usual he was drunk. His thick florid face was set in a mask of hatred as he stumbled up the steps. "I—I lost the ranch tonight…or what's left of it…to Caesar Kemble. Because of you."

Shanghai sank to his knees and fisted his hands. If someone had slammed a shovel against his spine, he couldn't have felt more broken.

"It's your fault."

"Right," Shanghai whispered. "Blame somebody else like you always do."

His father weaved drunkenly. "You had to go over there and stir him up. He came looking for me just like you knew he would. And you just sat here and let him lure me into a game of cards. Entice me with the finest liquor. When it was over and he'd won Black Oaks, he told me you went to his house and strutted around like a bantam cock, like you thought you were somebody, like you thought you were as good as him."

"I am as good as him."

"You're a loser, born to a loser, who's sprung from a long line of losers."

"I'll drive you home and put you to bed, Daddy."

"Don't act so damned superior."

"It would've happened anyway!"

"The hell it would! You've got high-and-mighty airs, but you're no better than me. Caesar said it was time all of us Knights got what we deserved—nothing! But that's not the only reason I came over. Kinky called him and said Mia's run off again. Caesar said she was upset because he hit you, and they think she might've come over here. I don't reckon you know where—"

Shanghai shook his head just as a pot crashed in the kitchen inside the cabin.

"Who the hell's in there with you then?"

"Nobody."

"You lyin' son-of-a skunk! Caesar's on his way over here, you fool!"

His father rushed past him, whipped the screen door open and stormed through the house.

Mia screamed from his bedroom. When Shanghai ran inside, his father was dragging her out from under the bed by the hair.

"Let go of her," Shanghai yelled, shoving him in the back.

"It's not what you think, Mr. Knight," Mia began. "He didn't do anything. It was me. All my fault. He told me to go, but I—"

"I got eyes in my head. He's bare-chested and you're wearing his shirt. You were in his bed."

"*Under* his bed. I told you. I came over here on my own," she said.

"How long has this been going on?" his father yelled.

"Nothing's going on," Shanghai said.

"She's here, in your bedroom. It's the middle of the night. She's underage. You've got a wild reputation and you're madder than hell at her father. And you're trying to tell me that you didn't touch—"

"What do you care? You're the one who gambled the ranch away!"

His father lunged at him. "That was your fault and you know it! You set me up tonight! Laid a trap. I should've seen it coming. You've been a wild 'un since the day you was born."

"Wonder where I get it?"

"Not from me! 'Cause you're not mine, boy! The only reason your scheming mother married me was to get a daddy for her no-good bastard."

"You're lying!"

His father lunged. Together they crashed onto the floor.

When Mia leaned down to try to pull them apart, his father slugged her.

Unconscious, she slumped like a limp rag doll to the floor.

Instantly Shanghai forgot his father and dropped to his knees beside her. Smoothing her hair from her face, he touched her throat.

"I didn't mean to hit her," his father gasped, all the meanness going out of him at the realization he'd hit Caesar's daughter. "I meant to knock some sense into you. Not that that's possible."

"I think she's okay."

Shanghai picked her up in his arms and laid her on his bed. As he held her wrist and found her pulse, which was strong and steady, he saw headlights on the road outside.

Shanghai glanced up at his father and felt an utter coldness. "Somebody's coming. Go see who it is. I'll stay with her."

Her eyes flickered open, and she smiled at Shanghai. "This is where I've always wanted to be—in your arms."

"You're gonna be okay," he whispered, stroking her brow.

"It's Caesar Kemble." Through the doorway Shanghai could see his father was cowering drunkenly behind the front door. "He swore I could stay at Black Oaks till I died, but if he finds you and her here, he won't honor that. He'll have us both locked up for the rest of our natural born years—if he doesn't shoot us on the spot."

His father had gone so pale and looked so terrified Shanghai felt sorry for him.

"You never saw me tonight," Shanghai said. "I wasn't here. You don't know where or why I went—understand? You'll ask questions and act worried. You'll pretend that you're concerned about your missing son."

His father nodded, as if trying to understand, but his eyes were too glazed with booze.

Shanghai turned back to Mia.

"Your daddy's outside," he told her, reluctant to leave the brat until he was sure she was okay.

"Run," she whispered. "I'll catch up to you when I'm all grown-up."

In spite of himself he smiled. "When you're datin' age, you'll have every eligible bachelor in Texas chasin' you. You'll forget all about the likes of Shanghai Knight."

"No… I'll find you when I'm all grown-up. I swear. And I'll make you love me!"

He laughed.

"I will. Somehow I will."

"You do that then, little darlin'. But if I don't git—now— there won't be much left of me to find or love!"

Funny thing. His last act on the way out the door was to lean down and grab that dang-fool rose she'd pitched at him.

Then he hightailed it out the back door.

BOOK ONE

Smart Cowboy Saying:

You get used to hanging, if you hang long enough.

—L.D. Burke, Santa Fe

One

Fifteen years later
Big Bend National Park, Texas

Where was the damn plane?

"Where are you, you little shit? Why don't you be a good boy for a change and just come to Daddy?"

DEA Division Director John Hart squinted as he lowered his binoculars and shoved on his sunglasses. His pale blue eyes burned from eye strain from searching the skies so long for one tiny airplane.

So far the seizure was going off as planned. Except for one skinny, dark kid in ragged jeans, who'd run like lightning, eluding his best agents and their bullets, his men had rounded up Octavo Morales's ground crew. At this very moment the bastards were cuffed and cursing him as they sweated like pigs in a sweltering van parked out of sight in a sharply cut canyon beside the trickle of water that was the Rio Grande.

No way was Hart driving the traffickers to El Paso. Not when the pilot was rumored to be Morales's half brother. It was hard to be patient and wait, but Hart wanted this plane, its cargo, the pilot and the woman. He wanted them badly.

Ah, the woman.

Mia Kemble.

He still couldn't believe it.

Bringing Mia Kemble home to the Golden Spurs Ranch was going to be bigger than the seizure. Way bigger. Just thinking about who she was and what this could mean for him made his pulse speed up. His name would be all over the papers. He'd be a hero.

It was high time. Wasn't he capable and ambitious? Hadn't he worked hard for the agency for years? Hadn't he played it straight? Hell, for the past two years he'd worked his butt off on Operation Tex-Mex-Zero, which was an international Organized Crime Drug Enforcement Task Force investigation into the Morales-Garza (MGO) drug organization.

Since the U.S. Mexico border was the primary point of entry for drugs being smuggled into the United States, and he worked El Paso, he'd naturally been forced to play a big role. Operation Tex-Mex-Zero involved seventy separate criminal investigations conducted by dozens of federal, state and local law enforcement agencies, including Mexican and Colombian police officials.

Hart hated working on task forces. There were always too many egos and too much bureaucratic horseshit. When things went wrong, everybody got paranoid. Nobody cooperated. He'd been blamed for mistakes others had made. In the past year he'd gotten himself shot at twice by traffickers—once at point blank range. If he hadn't been wearing his vest, he'd be dead. He was damn sure he'd been set up, too.

Hell, he was nearly as sick of lawmen as he was criminals. Where had his hard work gotten him? He'd been passed over for all the big promotions for guys who knew how to kiss ass or blow their own horns.

Then the Sombra had contacted him, and things had started to change. He didn't know who this guy was or why he had it in for Morales, but if Hart could rescue Mia Kemble, get

Morales's half brother and make a major seizure to boot, all in one day, the name John Hart was going to be big on the Texas border. Maybe not as big as Morales, but big enough to suit John Hart. At least for a while. What he really wanted was to get Morales alone and chop him into little pieces.

The Chihuahua Desert was hot, rugged country even in early spring. Hart's armpits were ringed with sweat. Watchful for snakes, he grabbed his backpack off the ground and then squatted in the scant shade of a nearby boulder and kept his eyes trained on the sky. A dozen of his men were hidden behind other rocks, but he preferred his own company.

He shook out a cigarette. Lighting it, he inhaled deeply. Then he pulled out a crumpled photograph from his shirt pocket and studied the redheaded beauty on the magnificent, black horse. Next his gaze turned to the tall, sinister-looking man with her, who held the bridle.

Morales.

Hart inhaled again. Even now, having studied the images dozens of times, the picture still had the power to shock him.

What the hell was Mia Kemble doing with that drug-smuggling, murdering son of a bitch, Morales? The bastard had to be balling the panties off her. And she had to have more tricks up those panties of hers than a talented border whore, or why else would he risk keeping her alive?

Her plane had crashed fifteen months ago in the Gulf of Mexico in the dead of winter. Everybody in Texas believed she was dead. Hell, her own father and husband had had her declared legally dead—no doubt to get their hands on her money. Her husband had even remarried, her twin sister, of all people.

All John Hart knew about the mystery was that it was lucky as hell for him that the bitch was still alive.

Where the hell was the plane?

Impatient, he lifted his binoculars again.

Two

Chihuahua Desert
Northern Mexico

Be careful what you wish for.

The desert wind was blowing hard outside. Despite the close, suffocating heat, Mia shivered convulsively as little pebbles pinged against the fuselage of the Cessna 206 like buckshot. Her nerves were on fire. She wasn't sure how much longer she could stand being locked up in this tight, dark space.

What was wrong? Had she been set up? The plane, which sat on a dirt runway outside the tall walls of Tavio Morales's immense outlaw compound, should have been airborne for *el norte*, translation—the United States—hours ago.

Mia felt faint and slightly woozy as well as nauseated from the marijuana fumes, which reminded her, of all things, of the woodsy, slightly sweet stink of skunk urine back home on the Golden Spurs Ranch. Mopping at the sweat on her brow with her sleeve, she plucked her soaked blouse off her breasts. Then a gust rocked the plane so hard the towering bales shifted in the cargo hold, several of them falling on her.

When they struck her cheek, knocking her down, she screamed. Then she clamped a hand over her mouth. Being locked up was horrible, but being crushed was even worse.

Her heart thudding, she wriggled free of the heavy bales and sat up, straining to listen for the running footsteps of Tavio's thugs outside or a nervous spray of machine gun fire. When nobody stomped up with assault rifles or machetes, she fought to calm down, sucking in big gulps of air. All the deep breathing did was to make her grow even woozier from the marijuana.

In the total blackness, the thin walls of the sweltering Cessna felt like they were closing in on her. To calm herself, she tried to imagine that she was loping bareback on one of the Golden Spurs' endless green pastures instead of lying here trapped in this airless prison fearing imminent suffocation.

Ever since she'd gotten locked in the attic as a child at the Golden Spurs and that big, yellow-eyed rat had bitten her, causing her to have those awful rabies shots, she'd been afraid of two things—rats and being locked up. Then, after this year, her list of scary things had grown much longer.

Now here she was, a stowaway in a coffinlike cargo hold that was as hot as a furnace and getting hotter, and all because she was so desperate to get back to her little girl and her mother and her father and the Golden Spurs.

She wanted her life back.

Would she die here instead? Probably. Her throat tightened. Who would raise her little girl, Vanilla, then? Watch her grow up? Who was raising her now?

Her mother? Lizzy? Had Lizzy watched Vanilla's first step? Heard her say her first word? Lizzy. Always Lizzy.

Vanilla would be a feisty toddler now. Was she chubby or slim? Docile or as ornery as a terrible two could be? What Mia wouldn't give to know.

Everybody she loved believed she'd been dead for more

than a year, which gave her an eerie, unsettling sensation. It was as if the real her had ceased to exist. If something went wrong in the next few hours, Tavio would probably torture and kill her, and her friends and family would never know she'd been alive all these months, thinking of them, longing for them. Shanghai would never know how much she still loved him in spite of everything, either. Not that he would care.

"Oh, Shanghai…" As she sat in the dark, feeling lost and alone, she willed him to think of her, to remember her, at least sometimes.

The nightmarish seconds ticked by like hours. What was Tavio waiting for? Would Marco, his half brother, who was to be the pilot tonight, ever climb in and rev the engine? Would they ever take off? And what if they did? Would DEA agents really be there to save her as Julio had promised? Could she trust Julio?

It got so hot her skin prickled and burned as if she had a heat rash. She had to get out of here, to feel fresh air on her face and soon, or go mad.

No. Ever since Julio had risked his life to hide her, assuring her the plane was flying into a trap, she'd known this was her best shot at freedom. Clenching her nails into her palm, she fought to hold on to her sanity and courage.

Somebody *up there* had a twisted sense of humor. Mia wasn't naming names because she didn't want to tempt fate.

"I don't want to sound whiney… Yes, I know I have abandonment issues because Daddy didn't want me and neither did Shanghai, not even when I told him I was pregnant with our baby after that night in Vegas. Yes, I know I prayed for the next man I met to be struck by a thunderbolt and love me so much, he'd never want to let me go.

"But Tavio Morales and his sick obsession? A drug lord?"

Mia knew it wasn't a good sign about her sanity that she talked to herself so much. But could a woman, who'd gone through even half of what she had with Tavio and his criminal army for more than a year, remain entirely sane? She knew she was only holding on by a thread.

Fifteen months ago she'd been married to Cole Knight, having married him because he was Shanghai's brother and for a host of other wrong-minded reasons, which was ironic because everyone in Spur County had thought Cole had married her to get her stock in the ranch.

When things had settled down, she'd had a new baby daughter, Vanilla, to raise and had been working with the horse program at the ranch. If her life hadn't been totally what she'd wished for, at least it had seemed all planned out and stable.

On a whim, because Daddy had said he was flying, too, she'd chosen to fly with Cole the day he'd crashed their plane into the Gulf of Mexico. Cole was probably dead, and there had been times, hellish times, that she wished she were dead, too, like when she'd heard screams coming from that forbidden zone at the compound. Listening to those pitiful cries, she'd suspected that Tavio's men were torturing their prisoners before they murdered them. From her bedroom window, she'd seen blindfolded, handcuffed people brought to those buildings against the north wall of the hacienda, and she'd never seen any of them leave.

The irony was she would have drowned if Tavio Morales, who'd just stolen a yacht, no doubt, after murdering its owners, hadn't been so high on his crack-laced cigarettes he'd seen diving into those stormy, icy forty-foot seas and plucking her to safety as an adventure.

She knew he'd removed her wet clothes that first night, that he'd wrapped her in blankets and warmed her with his own body. Not that she liked to think about that. Since that night, he'd never held her or stroked her or even kissed her because he was waiting for her to want him, too.

She loathed his attentiveness and deadly patience. Ob-

sessed with her, he'd nursed her back to health and brought
her to his rancho in the Chihuahua Desert. He'd treated her
as kindly as a man of his sort keeping a woman prisoner
knew how, she supposed.

When he'd found out she liked horses, he'd let her groom
and ride his fine, Polish-Arabian stallion, Shabol. Except for
those horrible, forbidden zones, she'd been free to roam and
ride Shabol as long as she stayed within the confines of the
high walls surrounding his adobe mansion.

When she'd wanted something to read, he'd brought her
newspapers. Sometimes he ranted about the stories written
about himself and his operation by a certain Terence Collins,
who was a liberal reporter for the *Border Observer* in El
Paso.

Even though there was no free press in Mexico, these articles were translated and reprinted in all the Mexican papers
owned by Federico Valdez, whom Tavio seemed to hate with
a special vengeance. The coverage incensed Tavio mostly
because his business ran more smoothly if he kept his affairs
quiet. But also she sensed some deep personal vendetta between him and Valdez.

Tavio had threatened the reporter, and Collins had printed
every threat, which added to his fame.

Tavio would turn red as soon as he saw his name in a
headline or a sidebar. "I will kill him!" he would say as he
wadded up the paper. "I will kill them both."

"No," Mia would plead.

"Soon! You will see, Angelita."

Publicity made the officials Tavio bribed look like fools
who couldn't do their jobs. If Tavio got too much press, he
explained, the federal police *comandantes* would be forced
to demand expensive drug busts to make themselves look
good. The United States would put pressure on the politicians
in Mexico City, who might demand his imprisonment or
death. After all, individual drug lords were replaceable.

Tavio was camera shy and banned all cameras from the compound because he didn't want recent pictures of himself in the newspapers.

But despite his problems he thought of her happiness. When he realized how lonely she was in her room with nothing except week-old, Mexican newspapers to pore over, he'd sent his brother-in-law's girlfriend, Delia, to be her maid. Delia was sweet if down-trodden, but dear Delia couldn't be with her all the time, either, so he'd rescued a kitten his men had been about to use as target practice and had given it to her. She'd named the poor little black cat Negra.

When Delia had confided to her about her troubles with Chito, Mia had observed Chito more closely. He was Tavio's second-in-command, and the worst of a bad bunch. A man of dark temperament, he was as sullen as Tavio was outgoing. Chito always wore a grisly necklace made of real human bones. When he gazed at Mia, he formed the habit of stroking his neck, as if to call attention to the gruesome ornament.

Tavio spent time with her himself, of course. He liked to drive around in the desert in his truck shooting at whatever poor creature darted in his path. When he could, he took her with him on these outings. They were always trailed by jeeps full of armed bodyguards.

Strangely she did not find him totally unattractive. If he hadn't had that scar across his right cheek where a bullet had creased him, he would have been as handsome as a movie star. A born leader, he was ruggedly virile and charismatic. Unlike his men, who were mostly short, dark and stockily built, Tavio was tall with light skin, thin fine features, an ink-black mustache and bright jet eyes that flashed with intelligence and intuition.

He liked people. He paid attention to them. He understood them. When he turned those eyes on her, she was terrified he could read her thoughts. Once he'd told her that when he knew a person's weaknesses and strengths, he knew how to use him.

"People are my tools," he'd said in Spanish, which was the language they usually spoke for she was more fluent in his tongue than he was in hers. "I have to know who can do what for me, no?"

And me? Why has he toyed with me so long?

His mother was the most feared *curandera*, or witch, in Ciudad Juarez. His men believed he had special powers and that was why he could manipulate people so easily.

He was as fierce and brave as any warrior or pirate king. He was a good father and son. His mother had had some sort of breakdown, and he called Ciudad Juarez constantly to make sure she was being properly cared for.

He was smart, a criminal genius probably. He ran a huge empire that reached to the highest levels in the government from this remote rancho. Army *comandantes* came to visit him on a regular basis. They strutted around his mansion and barns and he let them take whatever they wanted. Always, they left laughing with thick wads of pesos stuffed in the bulging pockets of their uniforms. Politicians from Mexico City came, as well. When they drove away in the stolen trucks he'd given them, he cursed them for being so greedy. Then he bragged to her, usually in front of an audience, that he had protection at the highest levels in Mexico.

Tavio was responsible. He took international phone calls on his various phones. He worked hard, sometimes day and night, as he had for the last three days and nights, taking pills and chain-smoking those crack-laced cigarettes she hated because they made him edgier and less predictable. He was a highly sexual man, and she was increasingly unnerved by the way his eyes followed her.

He bought her beautiful clothes, including French lingerie, but she refused to wear them. She never smiled at him, either, for fear of charming him.

He wore a gold-plated semiautomatic in a shoulder holster and had a habit of shooting at targets that took his fancy.

Despite his kindnesses and obsession to have her, Mia never forgot that he was a vicious, notorious drug lord, who claimed to be the most powerful man in all of northern Mexico. He said he was linked with another powerful cartel headed by Juan Garza in Colombia, and she believed him.

Terrible things happened here. Hostages were brought here, some of them girlfriends of Tavio's men, girls whom the men said had cheated on them. Sometimes she heard screams and then gunshots. She had watched men carrying heavy sacks out into the desert and feared the worst. Tavio had touched her red hair once and told her she would be smart to love him because there were many graves in his desert.

"Women you have loved before?" she had whispered

He had laughed with such conceit she'd known there had been countless women before her. She'd sensed how his awesome power had corrupted him.

"Are you threatening me?" she'd asked.

"No, my love. But I am not a patient man." His soft voice had been deadly.

"You are married to Estela."

"This is different—you and me. For you—I send my wife away. This make Chito, her brother, very mad, and that is a dangerous thing to do. I am not like other men. I bore easily. I live for danger. Still, I cannot divorce my wife, the mother of my sons. Not even for you. I am Mexican. Catholic."

Mia had been amazed that he, a notorious drug lord and addict, saw himself as a religious person. Estela had had such jealous fits of rage when he'd brought Mia home, throwing pots and pans at Tavio, that Tavio, to preserve the peace, had personally driven her and their two sons in an armed convoy of jeeps to another walled and heavily guarded mansion he owned in Piedras Negras.

If only Shanghai could ever have been half so fascinated by her as Tavio, none of this would ever have happened. When she'd gotten pregnant and had tried to tell him, he would have listened and believed her. She wouldn't have thought she had to marry Cole. She wouldn't have been in that plane crash.

Suddenly her eyes stung. What was wrong with her that the men she'd wanted, first her father and then Shanghai, hadn't loved her, and a criminal like Tavio did?

The wind was picking up. Rocks hit the fuselage like bullets now. Gusts made the plane shudder. Where was Marco?

Wrapping her arms around herself and bending over, Mia swallowed.

She had to get out of here!

Suddenly she heard shouts outside. The cockpit door was slammed open. Then Chito yelled, "Angelita, come out! We know you're in there."

Tavio didn't know her real name because she'd been afraid to tell him. When she'd pretended she suffered from amnesia, he'd nicknamed her Angelita.

"Tavio, he send me. The peasant, Ramiro, he tell him hours ago where you are. Tavio pay Ramiro. Then he break many things with his gun. He say to surround the plane until you get so hot you come out. But you don't come out, and he's scared you're dead. And we have to fly."

When she didn't answer, Chito yelled at his men to unload the plane and drag her out. It took them less than ten minutes to unload enough of the heavy bales to reach her. They shouted to Chito when they found her, and he then climbed inside. As always he had a gun in his belt and a knife, which she'd seen him throw with deadly accuracy, in his cowboy boot.

With a low growl, he crawled toward her, grabbed her wrist and yanked her from the plane. She fell to the ground so hard, she lay there stunned for a minute.

"Get the hell out of here," he told his men, who at his gruff tone, sprinted toward the high adobe walls of Tavio's desert fortress.

When she would have run from Chito, he grabbed her hand and tugged her unwillingly behind him until they reached the compound. She thought he would take her to Tavio's mansion in the middle of the compound. Instead he headed for the forbidden buildings that lined the north wall. Opening a door of one of the low dwellings, he threw her across the threshold. The tiny room was dark and dank and reeked of urine and feces and vomit.

He screwed a low wattage bulb into a socket. In its dim light she saw chairs, ropes, a cot, slop buckets, whips, handcuffs and electric cattle prods.

When she gasped, he grinned.

Did he intend to torture her, rape her? Had Tavio given her to Chito? With a cry, she turned to run.

Laughing, Chito slammed the door and barred her way.

"You run from Tavio," Chito said, his thin smile chilling her, as he fingered the irregularly shaped bone fragments strung on a gold chain that Delia said came from Pablito's skeleton, a fellow drug dealer Chito had shot for double-dealing and dragged behind his jeep in the desert for hours while he drank tequila. "Maybe you want me instead?" He leered at her.

"Go to hell!"

He laughed, but his black eyes were as cold as ice chips as he leaned down and placed a wedge of wood beneath the door. "Who are you, bitch? Who hid you in that airplane?"

When he lunged for her, she kicked him in the shin and then kneed him in the crotch.

He doubled over, grunting in pain. He tugged the knife loose from his boot. "Now Tavio will realize how dangerous you are."

Adrenaline pumped through her as she raced for the door. He picked up a pair of handcuffs, shook them so they clinked and laughed at her when she pulled at the door and it didn't budge.

"He has killed many for less, *gringa*. But you very sexy. I see why Tavio like you. If you are nice to me, maybe I put in a good word for you, so he don't kill you. Now—who helped you?"

She hesitated and watched him warily, her gaze flicking to the white chunks of bone at his throat. He was small, only an inch taller than she was, but he was strong and muscular. He could kill her in an instant if he wanted to.

He had black hair and dark skin and a sullen mouth. He had a hair-trigger temper and suffered from paranoia. He didn't get along easily with anybody. Not even Tavio. Delia frequently sported black eyes and bruises. Once Mia had asked her why she stayed with him.

Delia's big brown eyes, which were always so sad and hungry had widened with a strange yearning. Then all the light had gone out of her thin, young face.

"You rich in America. Everybody rich. I see TV. Even the women. You don't understand how it is down here. For women like me. Chito, he protect me. He don't share me with nobody."

"And that's enough? Do you like him? Love him?"

"My father, he was worse. My older sister…she run away…to Ciudad Juarez." She strangled on a sob as if there were some horrible end to that tale. "Chito, he help me. He give my family food and money. You lucky. Tavio, he protect you. You should be nice to Tavio."

Suddenly Chito lunged for Mia, the lust in his eyes, his strength and the stench of his garlic breath bringing her cruelly back to the present. Catching her again even as she pummeled his thick chest, he dragged her screaming to the cot, where he threw her down. When she fell, her head struck a wooden bar on the cot, and she could only stare up at him in dazed confusion.

"Be still, or I will hurt you worse." He smiled at her as he took his time unbuttoning his trousers.

She was struggling to sit up when the thick wooden door behind them crashed against the adobe wall. Suddenly Tavio was a black giant in the doorway, his legs widely spread apart. He twirled his golden gun idly.

Instantly the air grew even more charged with electric, hostile danger.

Sweat popping across his brow, Chito jumped back from the cot, his knife falling with a soft thud to the dirt floor.

Feeling like a trapped animal, Mia got up and hurled herself into Tavio's arms and clung to him, shaking, even though he smelled of those awful crack-laced cigarettes.

"Why is your heart beating like a rabbit's?" Tavio whispered against her ear, pressing her closer for a second. He turned toward Chito. "I told you to bring her to me. What are you two doing here?"

"Teaching her a lesson since you won't."

She scarcely dared draw a breath as the two men exchanged dark, dangerous looks.

"I will deal with you later for the trouble you cost me, Angelita. Go to your room," Tavio said, releasing her in an instant. When she hesitated, his whisper grew vicious. "Go! *Ahora!*"

"Don't kill him."

"Don't tell me what to do, *woman!*" Although his voice was soft, every word bit her, especially the last one.

And then to Chito he said, still in that soft, deadly tone as he knelt and retrieved the knife. "What were you doing with my woman alone—here? Why was she on that cot?" He began to curse and make crude sexual accusations that terrified her.

As she walked toward the door, she heard Chito's shrill, raised yelps. Then Chito's knife whizzed past her and hit the exact center of the door.

She gasped. Just like that—she could have had a blade in the back of her neck and been dead.

A slop bucket hit the wall, splashing its foul contents. Chito screamed that he wanted her punished.

"It is not for you to punish my woman." Another bucket was knocked over, increasing the sewerlike stench. "I will punish her myself."

Mia flinched.

"She knows too much. It's dangerous. She tried to escape in Marco's plane. We can't trust her."

"I never trust her before," Tavio said. "So—she try to escape? So what? She is a *gringa*. A nobody."

"Don't be so sure. A traitor helped her. She will betray us. I can feel it. In my gut."

"Let me do the thinking. With my brain."

"You are married to my sister. This woman…"

"She has nothing to do with my marriage. Your sister is still my wife."

"The men snicker behind your back. They say it is sick the way you follow her around like a lovesick dog. Like you have no balls, *mano*."

"I will prove to you and to her that I have balls—tonight. I will take her. You can stand outside in the hall and listen to her screams. But first, I will teach you a lesson."

She heard fists, blows, a life-and-death scuffle. Chairs were overturned. A body hit the ground. When gunshots exploded, and metal pinged, Mia pulled the knife out of the door and then ran all the way to her second-story bedroom. She went to her bathroom.

Setting the knife down, she stared at the wild woman in the mirror. Her face was still flushed from having gotten so overheated in the airplane and from her struggles with Chito. Her own sweat had plastered her hair to her skull. Not that she cared.

She was too afraid. If Chito came instead of Tavio, she would either stab him or herself. She couldn't bear for him to touch her ever again.

Too upset to shower, she ran a shaky hand through her hair. The wet tangles just fell back in her eyes. Squeezing her eyes shut, she fought against her rising fear.

For a long time she stood there, paralyzed. Finally Negra came up and rubbed her leg. Then the cat began to purr. Picking the animal up she returned to her bedroom and sat down on the bed where she began to stroke the cat's soft fur. Doing so restored her a little. If only she knew where Julio lived, she would try to find him and warn him and tell him that he must flee.

For a while Negra endured her affection. Then as if sensing her nervousness, the independent creature sprang to the floor and curled up to sleep on a little rug under a chair. A door slammed downstairs and she heard Tavio shout to his men.

Feeling only slightly relieved, she placed the knife under her pillow and waited. As the awful seconds ticked by, Mia began to feel dull and hopeless. She could do nothing but sit here and wait.

Hours later, when Tavio still hadn't come upstairs, she finally drove herself to get up from the bed and shower. As she toweled off, she was surprised that such a little thing had made her feel better. After she dressed, she paced back and forth at the end of her bed, her heart racing every time she heard Tavio or one of his men shout angrily below.

She should go to bed and yet she was afraid of the bed and what it might mean tonight. As she stared at the melon-colored adobe walls that imprisoned her, they seemed to close in on her more than ever. She wanted to run, but she knew that behind those high, thick, adobe walls, Tavio Morales's immense, adobe mansion was a veritable fortress. An army of gunmen patrolled the rancho and airstrips in trucks and SUVs.

A natural spring with cold, icy water bubbled up from the ground not far from the stables, so there was a sure source of water. Tall cottonwood trees grew around the sparkling pool.

Beyond Tavio's private army, every Mexican peasant, poor men like Ramiro, in the desert belonged to Tavio, as well. If one of their children was sick, Tavio paid for the doctor, buying their undying loyalty.

"They are my ears and eyes," he'd told her. "I love them. And they love me. I protect them, and they protect me. I very important man here. I am *much* loved." He'd smiled as if that thought pleased him. "If you try to escape, my little friends will tell me. If anyone try to help you, they will tell me, and I kill him."

Remembering Ramiro watching her again, she bit her lips. Worrying about Julio, she went to the barred window. She had to get away or go mad. She had to.

Since the ranch house was located on a slight rise above the desert floor, Mia's plush room with its heavy furniture and red-velvet spread and draperies had a view of the Chihuahua Desert and Tavio's airstrip. She'd spent long hours watching the dusty two-lane road that led across the parched earth to the airstrips. Sometimes she'd watched huge dirt devils race across the barren, beige moonscape, and always she had wished she were free to whirl away.

She'd watched the birds, the vultures, hawks and the eagles with special envy because they could fly. In her other life, she had taken freedom for granted.

If I'm ever free again, I will treasure every single moment. *She had to get out of here.*

"Oh, Shanghai…" She called to him, willing him to think of her, willing him to care, willing him to come.

Had she gone mad? Maybe she had if she believed Shanghai could hear her thoughts or that he would be moved by them.

She picked up her brush and sat down on her bed to work with her hair. Despite the thick adobe walls and floors, she heard telephones ring and more doors slam downstairs. She heard men come and go. When heavy boots stomped up the stairs, she cringed.

Tavio's door opened and slammed.

The noise downstairs continued. Much was going on tonight. Trucks roared up to the compound. Planes took off and landed.

After a long time, most of the activity stopped, but still she listened to the silence, almost fearing it more, because soon Tavio would finish whatever he was doing in his own bedroom and come.

Finally she grew so weary, she lay down. At some point she must've fallen asleep because footsteps in the hall awakened her. When her door opened, her hand went to her throat. She sprang up, her heart pounding.

"Are you all right?" Delia whispered across the darkness.

"Delia! It's only you. Come in! I'm so glad to see you! Turn on the light!"

"I know you are in that plane all day. I worry about you."

Delia lit the lamp, and Mia forgot her own fears when she saw that Delia was limping. The poor girl had a cut lip and two black eyes that were swollen nearly shut. Her hands shook.

"Did Chito beat you again?"

Delia hung her head. "Tavio, he very scared and angry. The Cessna you hide in—it not return. He is afraid, it no going to. He is afraid for Marco. He ask everybody who hide you. Even me."

Delia sat down beside her, and Mia clutched her hand, finding strength in her kindness.

"Everybody scared. Many rumors. Tavio, he think one of us betray him. He walk back and forth on the balcony outside his bedroom like a big wild cat. He listen for Marco's airplane motor. He smoke too much. The crack make him mean tonight. Meaner than Chito even. He accuse everybody of giving information to the gringos. I ask him if he want more tequila, and he jump at me, his eyes burning me. He so crazy he scare me just by looking at me. I don't go near him. Be careful when he come."

Mia shuddered. "What about Chito?"

Delia shrugged. "So—they fight each other. Over you, no? It is not the first time they fight over a woman. Then Chito, he hit me. Now he feel better."

Mia went to her and hugged her. Then she led her to the bathroom and gently washed her face with soap and water.

There were shouts from below. Her eyes large and fearful, Delia pulled away and rushed to the door.

"Stay with me a little while," Mia pleaded, not wanting Delia to suffer more abuse.

"I have much work. The men, they are hungry.... You hear them...."

"I will teach you to read. Like before."

Delia's eyes lit up for the briefest moment, and then her face became dull again. She was very intelligent, but her family hadn't been able to send her to school for more than a single year. As long as she was with Chito, she would have a life of dreary servitude and abuse.

"All right. For a little while," Delia said.

When Delia handed Mia the cartoon page from the last newspaper Tavio had given her, Mia forced a tight smile. They sat down on the bed. Pulling the sheets over themselves, Delia began to read.

The gloomy atmosphere from down below seeped into the bedroom. Mia was glad that they had some occupation to distract them.

In between Delia's nervous, halting words in Spanish and Mia's gentle corrections, Mia heard the rising wind outside but no plane engine. In the passing of the next half hour, she began to feel Delia's severely repressed uneasiness. The girl stumbled over words she'd read easily only yesterday. The men had grown silent downstairs, and again Mia's own fears escalated at the thought of Tavio coming. But still they continued to read the cartoons until Tavio's bedroom door banged again. When they heard his heavy-booted footsteps in the hall, Delia stopped.

Then Tavio burst into her bedroom, flipped his cell phone shut and stared at them with wild, unseeing eyes.

"Marco's dead," he said.

Delia gave a cry. Newspapers slipped to the floor, and she ran from the room.

"Why did Marco have to get out of the plane?" Tavio whispered, more to himself than to her. "He is the pilot. He never gets out. He should have taken off again. When the DEA agents pointed their guns at him, he panicked and backed into the propeller. He…"

"Oh, no…."

At the sound of her voice, his bloodshot black eyes focused on her face as if he realized she was there for the first time. His dark scowl was terrifying.

He'd been smoking, she knew. As a result his tense, vicious, grief-stricken mood was worse.

"I want you," he whispered.

She sat up in bed shivering. "Please…no… Not like this!"

"Like how then?" he yelled as he strode toward her. "I want. I take. I'm a beast. A big rat!" He pounded his chest. "A criminal! That's what you think! That is why you hide all day in that plane. I know you are burning up in there, but you won't come out. I get scared you'd rather die than be my woman, so I send Chito. He nearly rape you. I save you, and still you say no to me."

She didn't look at him. Even so, his burning lust and her fear lit the air between them like a fuse. She could almost feel sparks rushing toward dynamite.

Wrapping the sheet around her, she got out of bed. She was shaking so hard she could barely breathe. "Rape me then. Be like Chito. Go ahead. Take me like an animal. What are you waiting for? I've heard those other women scream."

"Would it be rape?" In two more strides, he was beside her, towering over her like an angry giant.

Not that she cowered.

His rough hand slipped under her hair. "Let go of the sheet. I want to see one of those nightgowns I ordered for you."

"I'm wearing jeans."

"Pull the sheet down!"

She flinched and released the sheet. Even when she felt his eyes and her body heat with shame, she did not scream or struggle.

He lowered his dark head to kiss her, his mouth coming so close to hers, she felt his hot, tobacco flavored breath fanning her lips.

She shut her eyes tightly like a child forced to take medicine she feared would taste worse than poison.

Seconds ticked by as she waited for him to kiss her.

Instead of doing so he pushed her roughly away.

"I am not a snake," he yelled, with the pain of one mortally wounded. "Who do you think you are? Who are you, Angelita? This woman who control me? Me, Tavio Morales? A princess?"

"I am Angelita."

"Who helped you today?"

The silence was so vast between them she could almost hear the desert wind through the walls again.

He circled her throat with his hands. His touch was gentle. Even so, she sensed his deadly strength.

"Nobody...nobody.... I swear it!"

His fingers tightened. "You lie. I will find out with or without your help. If you set up my brother, I will kill you myself."

Letting her go, he picked up a chair and hurled it. Then he stomped across the broken bits of the chair and left her room.

When his door banged, she sank back onto her bed and lay under her sheets, feeling limp and helpless, and cold, so cold, even though it was a hot night.

Too wired up to even close her eyes, she lay there, staring at the ceiling for hours.

She had to get out of here.

Finally she slipped into a fretful sleep. At first she dreamed of a little girl with brilliant blue eyes and down-soft black hair. The child was holding a rusty spade and digging in the soft, tilled flower bed in the shade near the big house.

Mia tossed her head back and forth and cried out for Shanghai. Suddenly he lay beside her. They were in Vegas. She neither touched nor kissed him even though she ached because she was waiting to see if even once, he'd make the first move. Finally he bent his dark head, and his lips caught hers at just the right angle.

The heat of his mouth made her sigh in surrender and say his name aloud again.

"You shouldn't have come here. We can't be together— not ever," he said. But he kissed her again, and that one kiss turned his words into lies and was everything she'd ever wanted from him and way more.

In her dream she relived how he'd made love to her all night, so tenderly, so sweetly, and so passionately. How he'd given her countless climaxes, and still she'd begged for more.

He'd been tough loving, tender—and sexy. Oh, so sexy.

But he'd rejected her the next morning as if their night together had been nothing.

Next she was on Tavio's yacht shivering, and Tavio was wrapping her freezing body in blankets and telling her in Spanish that she would be all right.

Her dream changed. She was sleepwalking on Tavio's yacht. Only was it Tavio's? She'd found pictures of a blond family buried in a drawer in the stateroom Tavio had locked her in.

In her dream her stateroom door was unlocked, and she wandered out onto the deck and made her way shakily to the stern where she saw a thick chain attached to a huge cleat. An object bobbed that was being dragged in the white frothy wake behind the boat.

The moon was full and the transom light bright. As she leaned over the railing and stared at the thing dancing on the thick chain in the heavy seas behind the boat, trying to make sense of it, she suddenly realized it was the skeleton of a human being, and there was still some flesh on the torso.

Suddenly the skeleton turned into a giant rat and hopped onto the boat. She began to scream and scream for Shanghai to save her.

But Shanghai didn't come. When she turned, the monster chased her straight into Octavio's arms.

As always when she had this nightmare, she woke up screaming. And as too often was the case, Tavio was there, holding her.

"It's all right. There's nothing to be afraid of," he said gently, pressing her against him as he sat beside her on her bed.

He was so hot, he felt like he had a fever. Even though she was still shaking, she quickly pushed away from him. Gathering the sheets to her neck, she shrank against the immense headboard.

"I'm all right. Please, just go."

He hesitated longer than he usually did, and she knew he was remembering the lustful rage he'd been in earlier. "I still want you. No matter what you've done."

"And all I want is for you to let me go."

"Who is this Shanghai?" he growled. "Did he love you even half as much as I do?"

His question made her eyes burn.

His white smile flashed across the darkness. "No?"

Sensing she had to tell him something, she said, "He's dead."

"If you lie and I ever meet him, I kill him, Angelita. Maybe I kill you, too, if you don't choose me."

"Please, just let me go to my country. This isn't going to work. I don't understand your life. You could never understand mine, either. You can't make people love you. Believe me, I know!"

"I throw my wife away for you. Already my men are laughing at me because of you. You try to run away. Some traitor help you. Maybe an informant. They say I am weak because of a woman. Me? Tavio! I have to be strong, or they will cut me to pieces and throw me to the dogs. Every day this Terence Collins, he write more bad things about me, and Federico, he publish these lies because he hate me. The DEA wants me. They put pressure on the authorities here. Do you understand? *Intiende?* They demand drug busts like tonight. I think Collins and Federico cause Marco to die. And maybe you know who tell them these things about me. Maybe they hate me so much they help you."

"No. I…"

"In the desert, the weak die. I never, not in all my life, have feelings for anyone like I have for you. My wife, she do nice things for me. She nice woman. But I do not love her. Is different with you. Is fate. You are strong woman. I am strong man. I would make you my queen."

"You're a drug lord."

"If I wasn't, maybe then…you could like me a little?"

"But you are. You torture people."

"So do the police."

"Collins says you kill people. Many people."

"Bad people. Children look up to me. I am a hero."

"Maybe that's what I hate the most." She stared at the shadowy walls. "I hate this life and everything it means. Poor people are forced into this business." She was thinking of Julio. "I hate the power you have over me…to keep me here. Of course, I try to run away."

"I do not rape you."

"Yet."

He laughed.

"When you do, you will kill the thing inside me you like."

"Maybe that would be for the best," he lashed violently. "Maybe then I kill this thing inside me and I will be free."

Feeling weary and hopeless, she shut her eyes and willed him to go. Finally she prayed, and after a while, a sense of peace washed her even in this awful place where she felt so lost and weak and helpless.

For a long time, Tavio stayed beside her. She could feel his predatory eyes on her face and body and smell the tobacco on his breath as she prayed for help, for strength, for a miracle. She didn't dare get up and run because she feared any movement might entice him, that he was that close to the edge.

Seconds passed.

Finally the bed groaned. When she opened her eyes again, he was gone, and she was alone and shivering in the darkness.

Then Shanghai's deep voice said, "You are not alone."

She felt his strength envelop her. For several seconds it was almost as if he held her in his arms. Her body grew warm.

Knowing he couldn't be here even though she felt his presence so keenly, she jumped out of bed, her eyes searching the darkness.

"Shanghai?"

The only sound was Negra purring from her carpet under the chair.

Mia sank wearily back onto the bed alone and felt more crushed by her loneliness than ever.

Shanghai wasn't here. He'd never been there for her.

The night when she'd pledged her heart and soul and body to him forever had been nothing more than a one-night stand to him. He'd left her for another rodeo the next day.

As always, she had only imagined that Shanghai cared.

She gripped the sheets. She was all by herself in this awful place, and if she didn't find a way to make something happen, she'd never be free.

Julio. What would they do to that poor boy?

Three

Marco.

Tavio seethed. Instead of the bubbling springs that glimmered like black satin in the moonlight, he saw a dozen DEA agents, their guns trained on Marco's belly as the kid helplessly backed into that whirling propeller. The image repeated itself in Tavio's brain and was always punctuated by Marco's final scream of agony.

His younger half brother had been a mere twenty-five. He'd been smart and loyal. Tavio had had him educated and had taught him to fly. The kid would fly in any kind of weather with any kind of load, land anywhere, day or night. He'd trusted Tavio to take care of him.

Tavio shut his eyes. He'd had such high hopes for Marco. He'd hoped that someday he'd take Chito's place.

Tavio kept seeing Marco and that propeller and blood. So much blood.

His head began to pound. It was the crack and the tequila. He'd smoked too much and drunk too much over too many days and nights. It was making him crazy.

Collins and Federico had stirred up a storm that had led to this. Some snitch within these walls had tipped them and the

DEA off. Maybe the same person had hidden Mia in Marco's plane. Why? Did she have something to do with Marco's murder?

Tavio felt anger coil in his gut. Slowly he set his golden gun down on a rock, and when he did, it shot blinding silver fire just as the ripples of the pool did. He blinked. His pupils were dilated. He'd been so busy organizing the runs, he hadn't slept for three days or nights.

He squinted. The light hurt his eyes. Things were too bright and too dark. That, too, was partly because of the crack.

When Angelita was upset, she came here and stared at the reflections of the pool for hours sometimes. Was she looking at herself or the clouds when she did that? He clenched both fists. He wanted to know, damn it. He wanted to know everything about her.

Staring into the black glitter of the water failed to calm him as it did her. In fact it made him feel even more strung-out. But then he was not like her. That was their problem.

Tonight he needed more than sex from her. That was the only reason he hadn't raped her. He needed the comfort of Angelita's arms around him. But she didn't want him. She couldn't love him, and the torment of that was driving him mad.

Estela would have held him close, but he'd sent her away for Angelita. He hadn't touched another woman because of Angelita. He'd waited for this white woman longer than he'd ever waited for a woman, even for Estela, who'd been a teenage virgin.

He could have taken Angelita anytime. Did his restraint mean nothing to her?

He still didn't know how he'd walked out of her bedroom two times tonight. Twice!

Any other woman he would have taken repeatedly until she learned to submit to his every demand.

She wasn't *that* beautiful. But she was to him. He adored

her trim body, her breasts that were in perfect proportion to her body and long legs. Her red hair had natural highlights and her skin was smooth and pale like porcelain. She was as beautiful to him as a goddess. Her full, lush lips haunted his dreams. He longed to taste every inch of her. He wanted her kisses all over his skin until every cell in his body caught fire. But afterward he wanted her to hold him in the darkness and be his tender friend. He had never wanted such things from a woman.

But she was strong and mysterious. She was egotistical in the way a man was egotistical. She knew what she wanted and what she didn't want. He wanted to know her mind, to be her friend. He wanted her to care, but she hated his rotten business too much to see him as man, who was just like any other man. Why couldn't she see that he was trapped just like she was in this nasty life he'd created and now hated because white men like Collins and Valdez believed he was an animal?

Valdez! How he hated Valdez!

Didn't she know he would have preferred to be a legitimate businessman as his father had been? But he'd been born a despised bastard. In fact Federico Valdez was his half brother, his father's most honored son, who now ran the family business. Valdez was his rich, white half brother who thought Tavio was dirt.

His brilliant father, also named Federico Valdez, could trace his ancestors to the Spanish *conquistadores*. He had been powerful in Ciudad Juarez. He'd belonged to an old and much-respected border family that had accumulated wealth over several generations. Tavio's Indian mother had been a maid in his house. They had fallen in love briefly. Tavio was the result.

Since his legitimate children were years older, his white father had made Tavio a pet when he'd been young, carrying him with him everywhere—to his factories, farms and offices. This had incensed his blond, American-born wife and her

white sons, especially the eldest, Federico. But their father
had never claimed Tavio as his son. After all, his wife and he
had six legitimate, white children.

His father had sent Tavio to a good private school, and
school had been easy. Just like making money was easy if you
got into the right business. Tavio had wanted to be rich like
his father. When he'd graduated from college, he'd begged his
father for a job in one of his companies, even a lowly one.
Federico, who'd been running the business, hadn't wanted
him. Tavio had been hurt and furious but determined to become even richer than his father and brother. Drug running
had seemed the quickest way toward realizing his dreams of
being as rich and successful as the family that had spurned
him.

In the beginning, like all young fools, the drug business
had seemed exciting more than dangerous. He'd hired des-
perately poor people as his runners. They'd taken all the risks.
When they'd been busted, he'd lost his shipment, but they'd
gone to prison.

Poor women, too many of them to count who would do
anything to feed their children, were sentenced to thirty years,
which meant their children were orphans. That had meant
nothing to him then. But sometimes, late at night or when
peasants came to him begging him for favors, these things
haunted him now.

His business had grown, *sí*, and soon he'd had to fight off
competitors. To expand he'd entered into an ever-changing,
complex relationship trafficking cocaine for the Colombi-
ans. In time he'd been forced to kill many people to maintain
control of what was his. He did not enjoy killing, but it was
part of doing business.

Too late, he'd learned what a vicious, deadly game he was
in. When he killed, he made more enemies, and he'd had to
become tougher to survive. His best men, like Chito, were
those he could trust the least because they wanted to take over.

The rules of his business were as simple as those the desert animals lived by. Win—or lose. Live—or die. Kill—or be killed. When you lived like that long enough, it changed you.

When he'd been young, he'd thought he'd retire with a big ranch in northern Mexico. He was now rich enough to retire, richer than he'd ever dreamed of being. But if he ever quit he would have to leave Mexico. Then many of the people he protected would die.

So what? The little people always suffered in Mexico. But as long as he was alive, certain people in the business would be nervous. Hit men would try to track him down and kill him. So, he stayed, and to stay, he had to be strong.

He hadn't thought of leaving the business for a long time. Not until Angelita. She made him think of Paris or London or maybe a Caribbean island or South America. Never her country, America, because he was a wanted man there.

He still desired her, more than ever, even after tonight when she'd turned him away when he'd been crazed with anger and fear and desire. Even during saner periods, when he was alone, his blood would pulse as he thought of her in one of those thin nightgowns he'd bought her that had cost enough to feed a family of peasants for a year.

How much longer could he play this waiting game when his men were taking bets on how many nights it would take him?

Angelita was afraid of him. Always before he'd liked the edge fear lent to sex. It was like a spice to make a dish hotter. But not with her. He did not want her afraid. She was an intelligent creature of light and love, and he wanted her to stay that way.

He remembered going into his white father's mansion as a small, impressionable boy. His father's white wife had seemed like a queen.

Tavio wanted to know Angelita and for her to know the real him. He wanted her acceptance and her trust, and he had no idea why these things mattered or why she mattered. They just did. He did not want to believe she'd had anything to do with Marco's death.

Disgusted with these thoughts, he ripped off an ostrich-skin boot and flung it on the ground. Then he yanked off his other boot. Next he whipped his leather belt out of the loops. Last of all he took off his thick gold Rolex. Without bothering to remove his jeans or shirt, he dove into the icy water and swam to the bottom to where the caves began, willing to brave the freezing spring in an attempt to kill the molten desire that was devouring him.

His head broke the surface again, and he stared at her window, which was dark now. He had never loved anybody before. He knew that now. Not enough to sacrifice everything for them. He'd admired his father. He'd longed to love him and be loved by him like little Federico had been loved, but it hadn't happened. No matter how hard Tavio had tried, in the end his father had refused to claim him as his son. When his father had disowned him in favor of Federico, who was weak and spineless, walls had grown around his heart. He'd never intended to let anyone make him feel that needy again.

He stared at his mansion. He had so much. How could not having this one woman care about him matter?

He loved his golden gun that had been a gift from a former president and his machine guns. He loved his prized Polish-Arabians. He loved his rancho and his trucks. He loved his planes. He loved the power he had over other men. He loved the way their eyes glazed over with fear when he got a certain edge in his voice. He had loved his little brother, too.

So many things made him feel big and powerful as he had not felt when he'd been the bastard son of a rich man. He loved the pale-brown desert and the barren red mountains.

He liked animals, even Angelita's good-for-nothing, scrawny black cat. But other than Marco and his own sons, he had never loved people much.

Who was she, this woman who so possessed him? She kept her secrets. Never before had he felt such a visceral link with another human being. He thought that lack was what made him strong. Now he thought he'd been a dead man all his life.

Until Angelita he had been going through the motions of living. When he had pulled her out of the gulf and she'd been so white and cold in his bed, whimpering and shivering as she'd slept for long hours in his arms, a tenderness he'd never known before had taken possession of his heart. Even when she'd been weak and defenseless, he'd sensed her strength and fierce independence. When she'd opened her eyes and looked into his, she said, "Shanghai," and had smiled with an infinite yearning that had melted his heart. Then she'd snuggled closer and clung to him, repeating that name again and again.

He had wanted to be that man. He wanted her to say his name and look at him that tenderly.

Estela, his wife, was an easy woman, who got what she wanted through sexual manipulation and feminine wiles. She did as she was told. It had been pleasant living with her until he'd brought Angelita home. Estela had never minded his other girlfriends. She'd understood he was simply a man. But from the first when she'd seen how he was with Angelita, she'd gone crazy with jealousy. Even now she screamed at him on the telephone if he called his sons. He felt bad to cause her so much pain, but he couldn't help himself.

Angelita was fate.

The sound of boots stomping across the hardpacked dirt broke into his thoughts. When he saw it was Chito, he swam for his gun. They hadn't seen or spoken to each other since their fight and the bust, and he didn't trust him.

"I'm sorry about Marco and the plane and the cargo," Chito said. Then he threw a bunch of newspapers and a videotape onto the ground.

"What are those?"

"More articles written by that *pendejo*, Terence Collins.

And a videotape." Chito lit a cigarette. "She throw you out, no? She's the reason you're swimming in a cold pool at night, eh?"

"Shut up. What's Collins up to?"

"Take her. Force her. Get it over with. Break her, like you would a horse. Find out what she knows. If she had a hand in Marco's death, you must kill her, so the men will respect you again."

"She had nothing to do with Marco!" Tavio wished he knew that for sure. "I have heard there are new ways of breaking horses. Gentler ways."

"You scare me. Don't go soft. If we get soft, we die. Don't let her change you."

Live—or die. Kill—or be killed.

"I came looking for you for another reason," Chito said. "There's been a second drug bust on a ranch north of El Paso. We lost Paulo's plane, too—the crew, the pilot and the load."

Tavio let out a stream of obscenities.

"Juan just flew in with these latest newspapers from Ciudad Juarez. Collins wrote an exposé on you and some of the politicos we pay for protection. He aired this videotape on a local news show in El Paso. There's some footage of you with Garza in Colombia. And some of you and me paying off Lopez in Chihuahua City. Your brother ran it in Ciudad Juarez on his television station."

"Collins got all *that* on film?"

Chito nodded grimly. "Something big is going on. Lopez is under house arrest. I called Comandante Gonzales to see what he knows, and he wouldn't take my calls. Somebody's feeding the DEA and Collins a hell of a lot of information."

Tavio frowned. Federico had always been jealous of him. Was he in the middle of this? "But who is selling me out?"

"Any one of the bastards. If the price is right…. We must find this traitor and kill him. If you have to kill ten men to get the rotten *manzanas*, you must do it."

Kill—or be killed.

Tavio was silent for a long time.

"Maybe we don't have to kill so many. Maybe just one or two—to set an example."

"But—"

"You're right."

"Who do we go after first?"

"Angelita knows who helped her. Rape her. Threaten to cut her. Make her tell you!"

"*Bastardo,* did you hide her in that plane?" Tavio demanded, knowing the answer.

Enough pesos would buy almost anything. In the end he had not had to rape Angelita to find out who'd hidden her. He'd simply put up a reward for the information. Three peasants had come forward with different versions of the same story.

Julio's thin form shook with fear as he stumbled ahead of Tavio through the brush-studded sand hills at the foot of the red mountains.

"Tell me, and I'll spare your life."

The boy said nothing.

"Did she let you fuck her?"

The boy ran faster. "No! I never have nothing to do with her."

"Who pays you? How does he contact you?"

The boy fell on his knees, mumbling incoherently.

"Get up!"

When they were far enough from the compound so no one could see what he was about, Tavio stopped and raised his golden gun, taking careful aim at the middle of Julio's thin back.

Not wanting the details of the boy's death to get back to his father, Tavio slowly lowered his gun. The kid was too young. His father was a hardworking peasant and devoted to

Tavio. The boy hadn't wanted to work for Tavio, but his father, whose face and body were wrinkled and worn beyond his years, had forced him because the money was good and there were so many mouths to feed. Tavio hated himself for not having the balls to shoot the kid in the back.

"What the hell's wrong with you?" Chito screamed. "He's *chota*—a cop—he's been ripping us off. Because of him we lost a load in Del Rio. We lost Paulo. And maybe Marco. He talked to the DEA and to that bastard reporter. Remember the videotape."

"Shooting him is too good for him. Let's put him in the cave. We'll let him die slowly with the snakes."

"Snakes!" the boy moaned, whirling around. "I didn't do anything! I swear!"

Chito's savage, gloating smile was a blur of white and gold that matched his necklace. Tavio wished he was enjoying this half as much as Chito, but he felt sorry for the boy. And even sorrier for his father.

He thought of Marco. Then he reminded himself that this was business. Killing Julio was but the tiniest piece in their game plan for revenge.

Four

Ciudad Juarez, Mexico

Terence Collins pitched his cigarette into a dank gutter. The squalid backstreet that stank of cheap whores, garbage and sewage wasn't far from Ciudad Juarez's Avenida Juarez.

So far and yet so near.

Collins's gaze turned heavenward. Ominous black clouds hung low over El Paso.

Rain? Not likely. But rain was always welcome in Juarez.

He pulled out his pack of cigarettes and shook out another cigarette. When a white, bulletproof limousine followed by two armored black SUVs crammed with armed bodyguards whipped past him, he put the cigarette back in his shirt pocket.

The convoy made a sharp u-turn, and the limo pulled up in a swirl of dust.

Tinted windows rolled down, and Collins stiffened as a dozen bodyguards inspected him coldly.

Valdez was on time—as usual. The bastard!

A burly man in a brown uniform carrying an assault weapon leapt out of the passenger side of the limo to open the door for him.

When there are no rules at the playground, the bullies rule.

"Do you mind if I smoke?" Terence asked in a mild tone as he pulled his cigarette out again and climbed inside, knowing the answer full well.

"I'm allergic," Federico Valdez snapped, his lip curling as he stared at a yellow stain on the cuff of Terence's shirt. Federico fastened his seatbelt.

"Thanks for continuing to allow your newspapers over here to translate and publish my pieces on Morales."

"My pleasure. After all, you did get yourself nominated for a Pulitzer once."

"Ever since Pete Cantú got gunned down last year, my boss, Juan Ramos… You may know him—"

"I've heard of him, yes. Good things."

"Well, he's got less backbone than a squid. A few months back he told us to censor everything we write about the drug cartels."

"Pete Cantú?" Valdez looked puzzled. "Oh, right," he murmured. "That journalist in El Paso, who wrote about the Morales-Garza cartel and then got shot in his driveway when he was playing with his kids."

"Ramos says we've lost the war, so why should we risk our necks—"

"Smart guy. But you're too stubborn to stop—like always."

"My mother said I was born with a death wish. And you? You're not one for causes. I'm surprised you give a damn about Morales."

Valdez looked bored. "People are full of contradictions. That's what makes them interesting."

"With your factories, you're exposed. Why risk such an enemy?"

On the surface Valdez appeared unruffled, and yet there was something hard in his eyes. "It's personal."

Without bothering to fasten his seat belt, Terence sank

wearily into the plush leather and stared out the tinted window at the decaying buildings. He fought to ignore the bodyguard leering at the girls, whose smiles were glossy as they waved to him, halving their prices. The baby-faced hookers in their boots and miniskirts were hard up to sell themselves at this hour since the American teenagers, who paid for their services on Friday and Saturday nights, were soundly asleep in their suburban homes in El Paso.

The seat felt too good. Terence was glad the windows were tinted. Once this city had inspired him to write prize-winning journalistic pieces. Today he needed blinders against the daily brutalities of Ciudad Juarez. If he closed his eyes, Terence would be asleep and snoring in seconds. With a tight smile, he placed the forbidden cigarette between his lips.

When Federico frowned at his idiotic show of defiance, Terence scowled back just for good measure. Normally he didn't give a damn how tired or shaggy he looked. Nor did he worry about making a good impression on assholes like Federico, who were part of a big problem that had millions fleeing from this country to *el norte* in search of decent jobs.

For some strange reason Terence felt at a disadvantage today. He yanked the cigarette out of his mouth and stuffed it into his shirt pocket. Maybe he was getting old. Or maybe he felt off balance because Valdez, who'd once been his brother-in-law, had set up this little family reunion.

Valdez was using him to piss off Morales. Why?

That Valdez had tracked him down was no easy feat, but then he probably had spies everywhere. For various reasons, Collins moved around a lot. One was money. Another was that he'd made a lot of enemies and didn't want to be easy to find when his eyes were shut. Right now he was bunking in with three newly divorced guys, who were such slobs they disgusted even him.

Behind his scowl Collins hoped like hell he didn't appear as tense and unsure as he really was as they were whisked through the garbage-strewn streets while being tailgated by the black SUVs.

Rich bastards like Federico, who stank of money, ran the developing world, or at least this dusty stretch of it, and there wasn't much one loud-mouthed journalist, who was growing old before his time, could do to make things right.

Leaning back against the leather, Valdez stretched his long legs. Valdez's short hair was as black as outer space. The bastard probably dyed it. But even without his talented barber and the accoutrements of wealth, he would still have been handsome in that unfair way.

Terence studied his carved profile and realized he reminded him of somebody he'd seen in a photo recently. Who?

Valdez was as tall and aristocratic in his gray Armani suit as Collins was rough and unkempt in his wrinkled shirt and khakis that he'd lived and slept in for the past two days on the road in his ancient van with his camera crews, boom mikes and photographers.

Partly because he hadn't been able to find his comb or his razor in the debris of his beer-can strewn apartment, Collins hadn't bothered to shave his craggy jaw or comb his too-long, salt-and-pepper mop, either.

What the hell? Other than some junk food he'd grabbed at gas stations he hadn't even been bothering to eat lately. He'd been too busy rushing around with his motley crew filming a low-budget documentary about the contaminants in the Rio Grande.

At fifty Valdez looked as vibrant and arrogantly full of himself as he had at thirty. Collins was a battle-worn forty-nine. He had lines beneath his eyes and grooves on either side of his mouth. His skin was as dark and leathery as a shrunken head's. Dora had divorced him long before she'd died, but once, long ago, she'd been the beautiful, younger sister of Valdez's American-born wife, Anita. Valdez men always went for fair-skinned Americans.

The border was a hellish place. Smugglers were taking over the border towns at a rapid clip. They bought off the authorities or killed the ones who couldn't be bribed. Then they trafficked in drugs and people at their will. Corporate bandits like Valdez worked the poor like slaves and polluted without restraint. Thousands of people ate garbage, literally, from the dumps in northern Mexico. Nobody cared that millions of kids got almost no schooling because their parents couldn't afford books and had to put them to work. Thus, generation after generation grew up to be unskilled and were sentenced to lifetimes of manual labor. There were lots of kidnappings both for money and to make people disappear. Ordinary women were their husbands' chattel. Most people didn't think much about these atrocities. They were simply a way of life.

Still, such a hell attracted its share of saints, who naively set up clinics and soup kitchens and schools and churches on both sides of the border without bothering to buy the proper authorities. When these trusting souls got into trouble—recently there had been a lot of kidnappings for ransom—they would turn to the media and tell their desperate stories about the plight of the poor and the exploitation of those who fought to help them. It made for interesting reading, but nobody did anything.

Terence had been as young and idealistic as the most naïve of them when he'd arrived here in his twenties. Dora, his wife, had been just as inspired as he'd been, but after she'd lost the babies and they'd adopted the twins, she'd wanted more than poverty and chaos and struggle. She'd wanted him to make money. Then they'd lost Becky, too, and been left with only Abigail. Dora had blamed him for Becky and had demanded that they leave the border.

"It isn't fun anymore," she'd said. "It's become dangerous."

The day he'd been nominated for a Pulitzer for doing what he believed in, Dora had sucked up to Daddy and gone back east to resume the upper-class lifestyle to which they'd both been born and had grown up hating. He'd stayed on, growing wearier with the same old battles and lonelier as the years had passed.

When Dora had died Abby had returned to Texas. She was grown now, and he rarely found time to see her. Strangely she loved him, and was proud of his work.

Thus, he'd never had a life of his own. Like a lot of people in their fifties, he gave his life a grade. Lately he'd begun to wonder what difference anything he'd ever done had made. The border was a worse pit than ever, and it was still ruled by slick creeps like Valdez. And by drug lords far more vicious than Valdez. He had a neglected daughter, who barely knew him.

He stared at Valdez's aquiline nose. *Who the hell did the arrogant jerk remind him of? Who?*

The limo and its convoy slipped through the dirty streets like stealthy sharks slicing through dark waters.

"So, why did you call and invite me to Mexico to interview you?" Collins said at last, his voice cold.

"For once you and I are on the same side."

"Will miracles never cease?"

Valdez pressed his mouth together.

This was a setup. Collins could smell an agenda a mile away. Still, being able to talk face-to-face with Valdez, the CEO of Dalton-Ross Chemicals, a major polluter in the area was a rare opportunity he could ill afford to miss.

When the limo approached a clump of people standing in front of a stunted tree in someone's front yard, Terence leaned forward and told Valdez's chauffeur to slow down. Terence rolled down his window and smiled faintly at the crowd of people, who were kneeling and crossing themselves and placing cards and photos in front of the leafless tree.

"They're transforming that pitiful trunk into a shrine because the lady who lives there found the image of the Virgin de Guadalupe in its bark," Collins said, breathing in the stifling dust and heat that smelled faintly of sewage.

"I know. I read your story on the miracle yesterday." Valdez stifled a yawn. "At least it gives the poor something to read about besides the constant murders on our streets."

"So why did you call me?"

"To discuss our dangerous enemy, old friend."

Terence started at the real concern in Valdez's voice. Despite the air-conditioning that was all but blasting ice from every vent, Terence began to sweat a little under his rank collar.

Valdez's black gaze sharpened. "Octavio Morales has a price on your head. That's nothing new. But he'll pay ten times more if he gets you—alive. The sicko wants to play with you before you die. His men are already in your city."

"So? I lived through Mexico's thuggish Interior Ministry investigating me."

"This is different."

"Why do you give a damn?" Terence said, making his voice blander than he felt.

"Let's just say Morales is a hobby of mine."

"Why?"

Valdez's eyes turned hard and cold. A nerve ticked along his jawline. "If I reveal a family secret, will you promise never to write about it?"

Collins hesitated. Suddenly he knew who Valdez's carved features resembled. "All right."

Lowering his voice, Valdez leaned toward him. "Octavio Morales is the son of a *puta* who once slept with my father."

"He's your brother?"

"No!" The denial held ferocious hatred. "I have five brothers. He is my father's bastard. Several years back Tavio sucked a favorite cousin of mine into the drug trade. The DEA busted him, and he was forced to sell Morales his beautiful rancho at a very cheap price in the Chihuahua Desert…to make up for the drugs and the money he owed Morales. Then Morales accused him of sleeping with one of his girlfriends. My cousin never made it to prison. Morales shot him and dragged his body all the way from this city to his rancho."

"I see."

"The rancho had been in our family for six generations. Morales wants what I have. He wants to be me. My father made the mistake of educating him beyond his station. When my father wanted me to let him enter the family business, I said no. Tavio decided to destroy me. One of my executives was stabbed in what looked like a robbery last week.

"The more powerful he becomes, the worse it will be for me. The reason I publish your articles is because he's phobic about making the papers, especially when there are photographs of him. A lot of peasants see him as a folk hero. He eats that up. But he knows that when the real truth about all his sordid atrocities is made known, there will be a public outcry to stop him.

"So, I have come to you with a big story that could get him the kind of international notoriety he most hates. This story has all the right elements. It's a mystery…about a beautiful American woman who disappears into Mexico. It's also a beauty and the beast tale."

Fascinated, Terence stared at Valdez.

"Tavio's prisoner is a celebrity. If he'd known who she really is, he would have let her go or shot her and dumped her body months ago."

"And you know who she is?"

Valdez smiled. "I have a picture of her on a magnificent Arabian Tavio lets her ride. He's holding the bridle. She's a famous Texas heiress. If you were to print the picture—"

The hair on the back of Collins's neck stood on end.

"Give this to somebody else. I don't do disappeared people."

"I remember what happened to your daughter…Rebecca. I'm sorry." He hesitated. "But with your personal knowledge about such a situation coupled with your immense talent—why, you're the only person who can write this story. You would tell it with compassion."

Terence rubbed his eyes. Valdez had still been his brother-in-law when Rebecca had vanished into Mexico. He tried never to think about her, but he couldn't stop himself. He still wondered…on a daily basis if she was alive.

"If I wrote such a story, he might kill her."

"Or feel pressured to let her go. Remember, he wants the poor to see him as a folk hero. You could make people identify with the kidnap victim and sympathize with her family…instead of him. If her family brought the right kind of pressure, he would have to release her."

"Sorry."

"You owe me."

When Collins looked up in surprise, Valdez's smile was sly. "Who do you think has been feeding you information about him all these months?"

Suddenly Collins could barely contain himself. For months he'd wondered who the Sombra was.

"I sent you that videotape of Octavio and the *federales*."

"But how did you penetrate his organization…?"

Valdez's smile grew hard. His eyes were equally cold. "Like all shadows, the Sombra has secrets he must keep."

"Okay, I'm curious. Who the hell is this 'disappeared' heiress?"

"Mia Kemble."

Terence whistled. "Of the Golden Spurs Ranch?"

Valdez handed him a photograph of a redheaded woman on a magnificent, black Arabian stallion. She was pale, and her eyes looked haunted. Tavio was holding the bridle as he stared up at her. Everything was just as Valdez had described. The murdering son of a bitch was besotted.

Terence's blood congealed even as his heart began to thump at a maniacal pace.

"How do I know the picture isn't fake?"

"Has the Sombra ever lied to you before?"

Terence shook his head. He couldn't help but think of Abby. For her sake, the Kembles of the Golden Spurs Ranch were the last people on earth he should mess with.

If he refused, the Sombra would simply tip off some other reporter.

Hell. Once a bastard, always a bastard. When had he ever let his personal life get in the way of a good story?

"Can I keep the picture?"

Valdez smiled.

Five

"Tonight's *the* night."

Shanghai gritted his teeth. The jeering note in Wolf's deep voice on the other end of the line set Shanghai on edge so much he wanted to punch him.

"You're doing it, *hombre.* You're asking her *the* question. Tonight! Before you leave for the big rodeo in Vegas."

"Don't remind me, brother." Shanghai's stomach tightened as he clutched the cell phone a little closer to his ear. To settle his nerves, he took another long pull from his Lone Star.

What was he waiting for?

"You still there, brother?"

"Where the hell do you think I am?" Shanghai shot back in the space of a heart beat.

"So, what's the big deal? You know she'll say yes."

"Hell, maybe *that's* the big deal. You ever been married?"

"Twice. When I was still in the military."

Wolf had flown helicopters in the Middle East. Recently he'd been honorably discharged from the National Guard.

There was a short silence. "Divorced twice, too," Wolf admitted.

"Then you're a two-time loser."

"I was gone a lot. Top-secret shit. They couldn't take the stress."

"Why the hell am I asking you for advice?"

Ever since Shanghai's daddy had run his mother off, he'd been afraid he'd do the same.

"Just ask her, okay. Just get it over with, you wuss."

"I ain't no wuss."

"Not when we train. You can take any kind of pain then. But you're a wuss."

Wolf was his physical trainer. Modify that—his psycho trainer. Wolf was six foot six and built like a lethal African-American god. He had a black belt in karate and had been in Special Forces. He'd even done a bit of bull riding. The man worked him until every muscle in his body ached.

At thirty-nine Shanghai was hardly the newest kid on the block. Not that he ever liked thinking about his age.

Bull riding was an extreme sport. He put up with Wolf's abuse to stay in shape to ride bulls.

Why the hell did he still want to ride bulls?—that was the million-dollar question. He'd proved himself—hadn't he?

Unlike most in his profession, he'd made a lot of money and had invested it well. His land, which was just south of the Austin airport, was worth more every year. Why did he keep putting off moving here and ranching full-time? He couldn't tell himself he rode just for the money anymore.

"When it comes to women, you're a wuss. You see a pretty little filly you've bedded a few times and you like a lot in your rearview mirror, and you stomp on the accelerator. When things start getting serious, you do it every time, brother. Every time." Wolf laughed. "Zoom."

"If you were here, I'd punch your lights out."

Wolf roared. "No, you wouldn't. Even you've got enough sense not to start something you can't finish."

He was so right. Although some of his bull riding friends might disagree, Shanghai didn't have a total death wish.

"Gotta go," Wolf said. "A mama just walked in with her fat kiddo, who probably wants to take karate lessons. No can do. The kid's gotta lose some major weight first. Do some jogging. Eat broccoli instead of fries."

"Go easy on 'em, huh? Eating broccoli may be a radical thought."

Eager for their blood no doubt, Wolf roared with laughter again as he hung up.

The fat kid and his mama would be in tears long before Wolf got through talking to them. Wolf either toughened you up or he made mincemeat out of you.

Shanghai inhaled the aroma of pine and smoke. There was nothing better than the smell of two fat grass-fed sirloins sizzling on a grill out in the country, unless it was knowing you were going to sit across the table and eat them with a loving woman, who just happened to be a gorgeous blonde and a rancher, and then share her bed. Or rather his bed.

He would ask her. He wasn't a wuss.

He lifted his beer to his mouth again. Abigail Collins was better than a bar full of adoring buckle bunnies, and he'd had his share in his years on the road. Despite the ace bandage on his right arm, and maybe because of the Bufferin he'd been gulping like malted milk balls along with the beers, he was feeling pretty good.

It was time he settled down. Way past time. For fifteen years his family had mainly been his rodeo pals. A lot of his friends his age were already retired and married with kids. What the hell had been stopping him?

He knew what—Mia Kemble. For years he'd told himself she didn't matter. Then two years ago she'd seduced him in Vegas and run off before he'd figured out how much he'd wanted her to stick around. He'd thought he hated her for what she'd pulled—coming on to him all hot and heavy when he'd been injured and then confusing the hell out of him the next day after they'd had sex. She'd picked a stupid fight, demanding to know how he felt and what he'd thought about her and what had happened. As if he'd known or could have put it into words.

He'd said a bunch of idiotic stuff and had driven off furious, and so had she. Hell, he couldn't remember what he'd said.

Then a month later she'd called and wanted to toy with him some more. Since he'd been thinking about her for a solid month and longing for her, he'd felt off balance and tongue-tied. They'd immediately gotten off to a bad start again. His feelings had put him under some weird pressure. Maybe hers had affected her the same way.

How come you didn't call me, cowboy?

How come you ran off, darlin'?

I didn't think you wanted me to stay.

You didn't think period. Neither the hell did I. So we wound up in bed when we shouldn't have.

Is that what you think? What if I'd gotten pregnant that night, huh? Would you even care?

Anybody who'd known him as long as she had had to know he thought the world had too many stray kids. Hell, he might be one himself for all he knew. Maybe he was the reason his sorry old man had gone so wrong.

What kind of lowdown cheap shot was that from a girl? How many times had he turned her question over and over in his mind when he thought about her and Cole and *their* kid?

His rational mind did hate her.

He'd left his home and kin to get clear of the Kembles, stayed away, too. Only she'd tracked him down just like she'd promised.

As if going to bed with him was nothing, she'd married his

brother and had a baby. When she'd gone and gotten herself killed, conflicting feelings he hadn't known he'd stored a mere one layer under his thick skin had burst inside him. The pain had been like claws shredding his heart. He'd thought he'd bounce back, but apparently without her on this earth, his world had permanently darkened.

He would have retired from bull riding but for her accident. Hell, he'd needed to do something to forget.

Ever since her plane had gone down, he'd ridden bulls with a death-defying vengeance. He was looking forward to riding in Vegas way more than he was to proposing to Abigail.

Damn her hide. Mia was a Kemble through and through. She'd hopped in his bed and stolen his heart—without him even knowing it until it was too late. Before he'd figured out what was eating him she'd had the bad taste to call him and taunt him that she could have gotten pregnant.

Just about the time he'd faced his feelings and had decided to go lookin' for her, she'd up and gotten herself hitched to his brother.

Hell. Somehow she'd made him care.

He wasn't supposed to love her. They'd never really dated. For most of their lives, she'd been too damned young for him. Then there was the not insignificant fact she was a Kemble.

She'd been a fixture in his young life. He wasn't sure when annoyance and affection had changed to love.

She was dead.

Love or not, he had to move on.

"Then why doesn't she feel dead?" he whispered, clenching his longneck a little tighter and hoping she wouldn't choose to haunt him tonight while Abby was here.

Sometimes he woke up at night with the strangest feeling that she was screaming his name and begging for him to come. He'd pace for hours whenever that happened.

The fact that she didn't feel dead was another thing that

didn't bear dwelling on because it made him worry he was crazy for real.

When Shanghai heard what he thought was Abigail's gentle footfall behind him, he deftly moved the steaks to one side and shut the lid. Then he turned around, hoping to take Abigail into his arms and steal a kiss. Not that her kisses needed stealing any more than Mia's had.

Abigail had a big job in Austin. She sold creativity, whatever that was. People came to her with ideas and she would invent concepts for them and name things so they could market their ideas. She was so successful that she had an apartment in Austin as well as the small ranch next to his.

Lucky for him she had a weakness for cowboys.

Abby had ridden over on her golden palomino, Coco, and had thrown herself at him right after he'd bought this place. She'd brought him a chicken casserole. Hell, hadn't he been running from females for just about as long as he could remember?

Shanghai... Mia's voice seemed to whisper from the trees.

When he turned, no one was there. Unless you counted the flying squirrel that leapt from his deck to the ground, he was the only mammal within shooting range.

He picked up his beer and took another long swig as the wind sighed in the pine trees. Then he grabbed a handful of the peanuts Abigail had set out and munched a few.

Mia was dead. Abigail and he were alive.

For a month, hell, ever since he'd bought the ring, he'd been trying to work up his nerve to ask Abby this one little question. His bull riding buddies thought this was as big a hoot as Wolf did.

"Damnation, Shanghai, you ain't scared of gettin' in a coffinlike chute with the rankest bulls professional rodeo can throw at you, but you're scared to ask a shy, blue-eyed, little girl to marry you," Matt had taunted him last night at the Stampede Bar while all their bull rider buddies had laughed.

"Consider her asked," Shanghai had said. "And her eyes are hazel. Not blue."

"Consider yourself hitched then. Your skinny ass is *hers*."

He'd thought of Mia, and his chest had tightened with aching regret.

The last light of the evening flared above the fringe of cedar, pine and oak along the fence line of Shanghai's Buckaroo Ranch, painting the sky until it was as bright as the flared match he'd used to light the gas grill. The air smelled sweetly of pine, which was a change for Shanghai.

Born and bred on the vast, hot, humid, mesquite-covered plains of south Texas near the Golden Spurs Ranch, it had taken a spell for this place he'd bought acre by acre with his rodeo winnings to feel like home, set as it was twenty miles south of Austin among Bastrop's lost pines. Not that he ever wanted to go back to south Texas. He'd given up his foolish plans for revenge a long time ago.

Other than his ranch, his rodeo buddies, Wolf and Abigail, he had no family. None at all. Family could cut you like nobody else in the whole damned world. When a boy was raised by a drunk who didn't even claim him, and he had a mother who'd run off, should it come as a surprise if the grown man didn't feel connected to his blood kin?

Not even to his brother? He hadn't kept up with Cole. He hadn't kept up with anybody.

Sometimes he felt a little guilty about Cole—mainly because he blamed himself more than he should have for the loss of Black Oaks. Still, Shanghai had decided long ago, he wanted nothing to do with his past and that included Mia.

He set his beer down. Where the hell was Abigail? Usually she was all over him by now.

Just like Mia used to be.

Don't think about her.

Impatient suddenly, maybe because he was so damn nervous at the thought of marriage—not that Abigail wasn't perfect—he stomped into his ranch house to find her. Finding the kitchen empty, he strode through his high-ceilinged den, past the glitter of twelve championship gold buckles. When he shouted her name, he was a little surprised that she didn't come running.

Curious now, but determined, because there's nothing like a chase to whet a man's appetite, he headed for the back of the house, thinking maybe she'd gone to the bathroom.

He frowned when he found the bathroom empty but saw a strip of gold glowing along the oak floor beneath his closed bedroom door. Curious, he pushed the door open. With a startled cry, she jumped from where she'd been kneeling beside his bedside table. The little velvet box with the engagement ring he'd bought for her spilled to the floor and glittered.

"Abigail?"

Her butterscotch-colored hair glistened in the lamplight. Her large, hazel eyes flashed with guilt. Flushing, she hurriedly crawled away from him on her knees toward his bed. Her shrink-wrapped white halter top and tight white jeans were way sexier than her usual clothes.

Not that he was in the mood to notice the way her breasts bulged so enticingly. He was focused on his ring that had rolled to a stop right in front of the pointed black toe of his alligator cowboy boot.

Slowly he leaned down and picked up the ring and velvet box. With a gasp, her frightened eyes lifted to his.

"Shanghai—I—I didn't mean… I—I was looking for a fingernail file." Her cheeks flamed.

"Sure." Even though he hated liars more than he hated snakes, he kept his voice soft. He slid the ring inside and snapped the lid shut.

"In the bathroom," he said tightly. "Second drawer to your left."

"What?"

"The fingernail file you were looking for."

"Oh…right."

Tossing the box into the drawer, he slammed it shut. "The steaks are going to burn if I don't go see about them." Feeling the need for air, he turned to go.

"You can't just walk out," she cried when he was nearly to the den.

"I'm hungry," he muttered, furious at her and at himself.

"Is that all you're going to say?"

"What the hell do you want me to say?"

"Don't you want to ask me…something?"

"No," he admitted in a glum, dark tone. "Not anymore. At least not tonight, anyway."

"Then when?"

"Don't chase me, girl."

"I—I'm sorry I—I searched your bedroom, Shanghai. I had no right… But, look, Matt told me weeks ago you bought the ring."

"He wasn't supposed to say anything!"

"I—I was just so curious and excited after he did. Then when you didn't ask me, I kept wondering if you had another girl maybe in some other city. I started getting scared that maybe you'd given it to her."

"I don't have another girl," he growled, stung. "You're my only girl. Hell, if you don't know that by now, we're in big trouble."

"Wolf said…"

"Who are you dating—me or Wolf?"

"He talks to me more than you do."

"Then maybe you should marry him. I hear he's between wives."

Her eyes glistened. Her mouth was trembling. She was near tears and it was all his fault. She hadn't done all that much. He was just ticked. He should take her in his arms and say he was sorry, but his chest felt constricted.

"I'd better check the steaks," he said.

"Don't you walk out of this room before we're done."

Sometimes Abigail had way too much spirit as far as he was concerned. She had lots of famous clients. He'd thought she was wild at first, but she had a serious, responsible side. Maybe that was why she made demands the girls he met on the road didn't.

"I don't know about you, but I'm done," he said, stomping down the hall.

"Then maybe so am I. Who do you think you are? Oh, I know you're a rich famous rodeo star, you can have your pick of women. But I'm the kind of woman who wants a guy, who wants *only* her. Maybe that sounds crazy to you."

"I don't think it's crazy," he muttered, but he kept on walking.

"You travel all over the country in your friends' private planes or your souped-up truck," she said, running after him. "You think you are hot stuff. Everybody's always clamoring for your autograph."

"Kids." He turned. "I can't say no to the kids." Not when they came up to him with stars in their eyes and were almost too tongue-tied with awe of him to speak. "Big deal. I sign autographs."

"Girls chase you, too. You don't call much or write much when you're gone."

It was a fault of his, staying too busy to keep in touch.

"I don't have to. You always call me," he said.

"Yes. I do…because I thought you loved me."

He'd thought so, too. "Hell."

She raced in front of him, blocking the glass door.

"I've got a career, too. My daddy says I should marry a lawyer or a doctor…instead of some rodeo character."

"Then why don't you?"

"Maybe I will. Two handsome guys bought the ranch on the other side of mine. Connor and Leo Storm. Connor's a cowboy. Leo's a corporate type. Runs a big ranch in south Texas."

"Go for Connor. He seems more like *your* type."

Her eyes that were usually so adoring flashed with resentment. "I don't want either of them.

"Did you take them a casserole, too?"

She flushed.

"I just wish you'd call me sometimes. Like tonight. Who called who first to set the time for dinner?"

"Who the hell notices stuff like that?"

"I do, Shanghai. My father was too busy saving the world to ever call me. In fact, he never paid any attention to me at all. I—I don't have a brother…or a sister…." Her voice quivered. "When I marry, I want a strong, loving family…for a change. And a big part of the equation is going to be a strong, loving husband."

"Hell."

"Is that all you can say?"

He was getting into trouble with Abigail faster than when he'd caught his boot in the chute three nights ago, and the gate had opened on him before he'd been ready, and that monster, Tilly, had crushed his arm brace.

Love. Sometimes he thought the closest thing he'd ever felt to love was the applause he got after a winning ride. He'd take off his helmet and hurl it toward the sky. Then he'd throw his hands up in the air. There was nothing like the roar of his fans to make him feel big and important.

"Abigail…can't we just eat…."

Shanghai—

There it was again!

Mia's voice stopped him cold. He pivoted wildly, his eyes scanning the darkened hall for her ghost.

Her voice kept calling to him, like she was in trouble.

Shanghai!

"Do you hear anything?" he whispered.

She got a funny look on her face. "No."

"Listen then."

His gaze focused on the pine paneling. Crazy fool that he was, he felt so powerfully connected to her, he halfway expected to see Mia materialize out of nothing.

But, of course, she didn't. His stupid, mixed-up brain and heart were playing tricks on him again.

"What's wrong now, Shanghai?"

"Nothin'."

This wasn't the first time he'd felt Mia calling to him. When she was a little girl in trouble, she'd always come running to him. The instant she'd headed his way, he'd known she was coming.

She was dead. He had to get over her.

"Go away," he whispered, not realizing he'd spoken aloud. "Get the hell out of my life!"

"Go away?" Abigail wailed, sounding truly hurt.

"Not you, honey," he muttered in utter exasperation as he gazed forlornly down the empty dark hall.

He felt Abby's arm on his sleeve, shaking him. "Shanghai, are you all right? You're as white as your shirt. If you weren't talking to me—then who were you talkin' to?"

He stared down into Abigail's inquisitive eyes, hoping they'd ground him.

"I asked you who you thought you were talking to?" she repeated.

"Nobody. Look, Abigail, forget it. I'm sorry I got all bent out of shape. The pace has been a bit much lately. Too many rodeos. Too many motel rooms bunkin' with Wolf or the guys. Too many Bufferin along with the beers. My arm's killin' me. Let's just forget the ring and this silly quarrel for now. Why don't we just eat?"

"Who were you thinking of just then when you got that faraway look in your eyes? You do have another girlfriend, don't you?"

"I was thinking about those damn steaks," he muttered. "If we don't get our asses out on that deck, they're gonna be burnt to crisps."

She leaned into him and pushed at his chest with both hands, shoving him toward the deck. "Go ahead then. I don't care about your stupid old steaks! I don't care about anything, not even you, you big lying lug! And you can flush that engagement ring down the toilet for all I care!"

"What I'd do? You were the one snoopin'."

"If you loved me, you would have asked me already," she said. "I wouldn't have had to snoop."

"I was going to ask you tonight," he admitted.

"Then why don't you?"

"'Cause I'm not in the mood anymore."

Her face went as white as his. "Well, neither am I."

"You satisfied now?" he growled.

"Perfectly." She crossed her arms over her breasts and ran down the hall.

Her quick, strangled sobs cut him to the quick because Abby wasn't one to cry. He almost ran after her. Then his front door opened and slammed so hard his whole house shook.

He was halfway to the door when he stopped midstride. When her car didn't start, he knew she was giving him time to chase after her. For some reason that he didn't understand, his broad shoulders sagged, and he stayed put.

Suddenly Shanghai wished he was in a chute in a rodeo arena, his gloved palm tightly wrapped in a yellow rope, about to nod at the chute boss. He craved the excitement of the arena and the adrenaline-jingling moment when the gate swung open. He craved the fans' shouts, the clanging bell, and the bull's plunging jumps and wild snorts. He knew what to do when he was in a life-and-death battle to stay on a bull.

Bull riding was easy compared to women.

When Shanghai rode well, sometimes the bull and he became one. On nights he got it right, nothing else mattered, nothing at all.

After Mia had seduced him and then left him for Cole and then had the baby, Shanghai had told himself he'd gotten lucky again, that he was free, that he had his bull riding, his ranch, his horses and his rough stock. There had been plenty of women on the road to make him forget. Only the more women he'd used to forget her, the emptier he'd felt. Even after he'd met Abby, late at night he'd still feel lonely.

He'd ignored his loneliness and had told himself that when he retired he would marry Abby and be a rough stock contractor. He'd settle down and raise the best rank bulls in the business, the best saddle broncs, too. They'd have lots of kids, too. They'd be happy.

Shanghai… Again he felt powerfully connected to Mia's ghost.

"Leave me the hell alone!" he yelled.

Mia's voice cut him like a knife.

For a couple of seconds the house was quiet. Then his cell phone rang.

He picked it up and read Abigail in bright blue letters. It rang two more times. She was out in the car, calling him already. Inhaling a deep breath, he flipped it open.

"Hi, darlin'," he said softly, feeling sorry for her somehow.

"I'm sorry," she said.

"You're forgiven," he whispered but in a tight, unconvincing voice. The fight wasn't really her fault and he knew it. She always called and apologized.

"Are the steaks all burned up?" she murmured.

"If they are, I'll take you out."

"I have a better idea," she said, her voice honey-soft.

He smiled in spite of himself. He knew exactly what she meant. She thought that if she got him in bed, she'd get him to pop the question.

She deserved better. He didn't know what to say. Feeling doomed, he opened his front door and stood in the doorway. She came flying out of her car and into his arms.

But as his mouth closed over hers, he heard his name whispering in the pines.

Mia's voice sounded as small and scared as a frightened little girl's, and it tugged at him on some soul-deep level. She'd used that same voice when she'd pleaded for him to save Spot.

Abigail kissed him. "I want you to love me, just me, Shanghai. If you can't do that, tell me now."

Shanghai—

It was Mia again, and when he shuddered in panic he knew he had to be close to some edge.

"Do you believe in ghosts?" he rasped in agony.

"Of course not."

"Lucky you, darlin'. I've got a lot of ghosts."

"It's called baggage. Don't tell me. Just kiss me. I promise I'll send all your ghosts away."

But when she kissed him, he wanted Mia so badly he had to push her away.

For a long time they just stared at each other.

"Make up your mind, Shanghai. Even an idiot like me isn't going to wait forever."

When he let her go, she turned and ran.

El Paso, Texas

It was late, nearly 2:00 a.m. Outside Terence's ground-floor apartment, the wind was still howling, which meant the air would be so thick with dust a man could barely breathe.

"Answer, damn it," he muttered wearily just as an operator's voice came on and apologized that all circuits were busy.

Attacked by guilt about Rebecca, Terence slammed the phone down and stared at his computer. He still couldn't quite believe his bad luck—that he, of all people, should be the one to break a story about the Kembles. They were the one family in Texas that was off-limits as far as he was concerned. It was ironic that tomorrow, because of him, folks all over Texas would know that Mia Kemble was alive.

Maybe because of his story, she would die. Still, more often villains operated because truths weren't told or faced.

Terence had been trying to call The Golden Spurs Ranch to notify Mia's family about the impending story, but high winds had the phone lines down near the ranch. So far, he hadn't been able to get through. Personally he didn't want to talk to them, but he knew what it was to lose a daughter.

Terence rubbed his forehead. The weather was bad all over Texas. There were thunderstorms, high winds, even hail and tornadoes. Not that Terence ever gave much of a damn about the weather—except when he couldn't get important phone calls through. He'd e-mailed the ranch but hadn't heard back. There was nothing for it but to call the authorities in El Paso and ask them to notify the authorities in Spur County.

Terence made the call. Then he poured himself another cup of black coffee and swallowed still another antacid tablet.

Time to concentrate on his film. He inserted a DVD into his computer, leaned back and sipped cold coffee while he booted it up.

For a week he'd been working too hard and doing without sleep. He was exhausted, but he was too wired to go to bed. He had a deadline and the headache from hell and he'd maxed out on aspirin. Four cups of coffee on an empty stomach while he chain-smoked had him feeling reptilian.

It had been twenty-four hours since Collins had interviewed Valdez in the limo. In between working on the film, he'd written the article on Mia and Tavio and e-mailed it to the *Border Observer*.

When the music started playing as the titles ran, the wind began to blow so hard, bits of dirt bounced off the dark windowpanes of the apartment. Not that Terence looked up from his computer screen where men wearing Dalton-Ross uniforms dug holes right by the Rio Grande and then dumped in truckloads of milky-white chemical waste. More grainy footage showed the same men bulldozing over the holes.

As long as they got their paychecks the bastards didn't care if they contaminated the water supply for everybody who lived in the area as well as for those downstream.

There was some footage of human excrement floating in the Rio Grande. But that was nothing compared to his sequence that dealt with anencephalic births—babies born with partial or missing brains. Next he watched a sequence of young people with facial deformities and mental retardation, whose mothers had worked with solvents and PCBs in the seventies.

It was pretty grim stuff until he got to the shot of the chicken that wobbled up to the river, took a sip and keeled over dead.

Terence laughed out loud. "I'm a sick bastard," he said to no one in particular.

Sick and getting sicker. Still, if a man didn't laugh, all he could do was cry. Terence hadn't cried in years, and he had a lot to cry about. His idealism was as tarnished as the rest of him. He was beginning to believe that men like Valdez had a sharper view of the future, that America was really just a corporate democracy, that America was every bit as cynical as Mexico, that it didn't give a damn about people or injustice.

Leaning back in his borrowed folding chair, his gaze drifted to his journalism degree framed on the wall. Beneath it was a recent picture of Abigail on her golden horse. The surface of his card table, which served as his makeshift desk overflowed with stacks of books and newspapers. He eyed the blotter that he used to jot notes when he did phone interviews. On top of it lay a picture of the twins together when they'd been kids. He didn't want to go there. Still he picked it up. In it they wore jeans and identical white blouses. Their hair hung in braids. The photograph had been taken right before Becky had been kidnapped.

He picked it up and stared at Becky's face for a long time before slamming it down so hard the table wobbled.

Was she dead? Murdered? What was it like to know you were about to die? What had she felt?

If Mia Kemble "disappeared" for good, he'd have another notch on his belt.

He shut his eyes for a long time. Then he yawned and replayed the chicken shot again. He laughed so hard tears sprang behind his eyelids.

His guilt about Becky receded a little.

Was the chicken shot over the top? Was he hysterical? Did the film work as a whole? Was he telling the truth? Who cared about truth in today's world when it was easier just to go for spin and public relations hype?

He leaned forward to grab his cup of coffee again. No sooner did he guzzle the final bitter dregs than he heard the crunch of a beer can behind him. Thinking it was Sam, his roommate who'd been in the back bedroom snoring earlier, he didn't bother to turn around.

Collins replayed the chicken scene, hoping Sam would notice. When the chicken sipped and fell over dead, a man's harsh laugher rang from behind his left shoulder.

It wasn't Sam.

Terence's blood turned to ice.

He whirled and saw the glint of gold and the little bones strung together at the stranger's throat. The man held a gun.

"What the fu—"

Adrenaline surged through his body, but he wasn't nearly fast enough. Before he could lunge, he was struck from behind.

"Gotcha, *gringo*," an amused, heavily accented voice rasped.

The computer screen spun sickeningly as Terence went down facefirst into beer cans and fast-food wrappers, his fall as ignoble as the chicken's in his film.

Six

Mia was alive! After fifteen months, she was alive!

After more than a year of grief and then acceptance, Joanne Kemble was back on a wild roller coaster ride. One moment she was ecstatic and filled with hope; in the next, she was trembling with fear that Collins's article, which was all over the Internet, might somehow trigger Morales to act vengefully toward Mia.

When Joanne Kemble had first heard Mia's plane was missing, she'd prayed for a miracle. Then Cole had been found. After that she'd gone on hoping and praying that maybe, somehow, Mia might be alive somewhere, too. But as the months had passed and there had been no word, her friends had told her to give up. Even after Caesar had had Mia declared dead, deep down, Joanne had never found closure. She'd had constant nightmares about her daughter, and there were still times when the phone would ring, and her heart would leap at the thought it might have to do with Mia.

Early this morning Gigi, her best friend, had called and screamed, "Mia is alive! It's all over the Internet!"

After she'd hung up the phone had started ringing off the wall. Now that Mia's whereabouts were known, if the ranch were on fire, there couldn't have been more hysterical excitement. Distant family members and friends wouldn't stop calling. Nor would the press. Everybody wanted to know how Mia had survived the crash and how she'd been kidnapped and what was going to be done to get her back. The incessant chorus of the phones alone had become more hubbub than Joanne could handle.

Her brain felt like it was buzzing. She wanted to know more about her daughter, too, but Terence Collins wouldn't answer his phone. She was sure Mia was still in terrible danger.

Cole and Lizzy had been fielding all the calls from friends, family, the ranch's corporate headquarters and the press as best they could. But even they were overwrought.

Near panic, Joanne raced toward the library clutching her cell phone against her breast. When she opened the tall doors, the vast room was hushed. Her heart, however, was beating so loudly, thundering in her ears, she thought she might be having a heart attack.

Joanne had to sit down. Touching the newsprint likeness of her daughter one more time, she scurried past the tall cherry bookcases in the library toward the deep leather couches.

Switching on a table lamp, she sank onto the couch nearest the massive fireplace. She was so agitated she could barely hold a coherent thought in her head. Frowning, she placed her mobile phone, which had an unlisted number, on the table beneath the lamp. Then she leaned back against the leather.

Why wouldn't Mr. Collins call her back on her cell? She'd read his stuff in the past and found him so brilliant she'd been sad when he'd been passed over for the Pulitzer. Now she was angry and disappointed in him because he'd irresponsibly broken this story that could get her child killed without even notifying her or the ranch first. Worse, having written the piece, he'd gone underground, refusing to answer his phone or return her messages.

Exasperated she'd finally demanded to speak to his boss at the *Border Observer* but had been given his voice mail, as well. She'd called back a second time, demanding to speak to a real person. Ramos's secretary had sounded tense and frightened when she'd told her Juan Ramos was in a meeting. A hellish half hour had passed since then.

Joanne thrummed her nails on the table. The windows were open because of the mild, spring temperatures. How she loved the sight of open vistas and the smell of wet grass as well as the murmurings of the rain still pouring off the roof and misting along the verandah railings.

She took a deep breath and put her hand over her racing heart. She'd prayed for so many miracles in her forty-eight years. But the answer to this one was pure torture.

Mia was alive, but for how long—thanks to Terence Collins?

When she'd been young and pregnant and in love, she'd prayed for Jack, her fiancé to be found alive when he'd ridden off and had failed to return. But he'd been bucked off a half-wild horse he never should have tried to ride in the first place and had died of a broken neck.

When Caesar, Jack's brother, the husband who'd never really loved her, had had his stroke last year, she'd prayed for him, too. Before his murder, she'd learned he'd cheated on her with Electra and that he'd had two secret daughters, twins, in addition to Lizzy, and that they were *out there* in the world somewhere. Lizzy had asked Leo Storm, the ranch's CEO to hire a detective to find them, but so far they'd discovered nothing.

Joanne had prayed for Cole to get his memory back, and lately he'd started getting better, but that had caused a few problems between him and Lizzy. They had old issues, the worst of which was that he'd married Mia first instead of her.

So, Mia's return could fan old sparks of resentment back to life.

Oh, it was all too much.

When her housekeeper's hushed steps sounded in the doorway, Joanne looked up and tried to smile, but her face felt too stiff to answer to her command.

Like many of the people who worked at the Golden Spurs, Sy'rai had been with her so long, she was more like her sister than an employee.

"Can I get you anything from the kitchen?" Sy'rai asked in a kindly tone.

"Maybe a cup of tea."

Sy'rai nodded. "Oh, goodness, this is happy day!" Her olive, fiftysomething face lit with an encouraging smile.

To still the tremors in her hands, Joanne clasped them in her lap. "If we get her back after what that horrible man wrote…just to increase his fame."

"She'll be home in no time. Cole and Mr. Storm will think of something. You'll see."

Leo had called Cole repeatedly from the Golden Spurs' corporate offices in San Antonio this morning. Leo had been contacting hostage negotiators in Mexico as well as high-placed U.S. officials, anybody who might be persuaded to bring pressure on the government authorities in Mexico, who in turn could turn the screws on Morales.

"I'm going to go downstairs and make you some tea," Sy'rai said.

"That would be lovely."

Joanne didn't want tea. Why did everybody think one always needed to eat or drink in times of crisis?

When Sy'rai had gone, Joanne picked up her cell phone, and then set it down. Why didn't Ramos call? Why didn't Leo and Cole do something besides talk on the phone?

If only Caesar were alive! He would have stormed hell itself, to bring a daughter, even Mia, home.

When her cell phone suddenly rang, she answered it instantly.

"Juan Ramos. I'd like to speak to Mrs. Kemble."

Before he could say anything, she launched an attack. "Speaking," she said coldly. "How could you publish an article about my daughter without even notifying the Golden Spurs? And now Collins won't even do me the courtesy of phoning me back."

"I'm very sorry about your daughter, but as for Collins…" The sorrow in his low tone sent a chill through her. "I'm afraid he's 'disappeared.'" He drew a long breath. "I was being interviewed by the police about the matter when you called."

Her pounding heartbeats quickened, roaring in her ears now.

"The police have reason to suspect Octavio Morales is involved. There are no witnesses nor many clues, but they have informants. Collins's roommate was struck over the head and Collins's computer was smashed. There were signs of a struggle. But the police think they took him alive."

"Oh, my God." What would Morales do to Mia now?

"I warned Collins repeatedly not to take so many unnecessary risks. But he was headstrong and fearless. He's had close calls before. He moved constantly, so at least he wouldn't be a sitting duck." Ramos paused. "A lot of mummified bodies turn up in our desert and garbage dumps. Mostly they remain unidentified. Life is precarious down here, Mrs. Kemble, and not just for poor people. I won't be surprised if we find Collins's body in the desert."

"What about my daughter?"

"We can only speculate." He sounded weary. "Morales is highly unpredictable. It's part of his genius. He's kept her alive all this time. Who knows what he'll do? I wish I could be more hopeful, but I'm afraid we don't find too many of Morales's kidnap victims alive, Mrs. Kemble. In fact I can't remember a single time… We'll probably never know what happened to Collins. He'll be missed."

When they finally hung up, she felt worse than ever. Joanne's mind felt as shaky as her body. She could barely hold a coherent thought as she scanned the photograph of Mia on the black Arabian again.

Mia looked thinner, especially in the face. Her eyes were enormous but sunk deep in their hollow sockets. She wasn't smiling. Everything about her was more subdued somehow. And yet the strong-featured Octavio Morales with the scar across his cheek looked smitten.

Were they lovers? That was what everybody would think from this picture. The man definitely eyed Mia as if he considered her his property.

"I don't care what you have to do," Joanne whispered. "Just stay alive."

The tears that coursed down Joanne's cheeks went unheeded until Jay, the sheriff's deputy, came inside with a stack of newspapers.

"I was just going over a few things with Cole, but I wanted to say hi. I had my men pick these up in case you wanted more copies."

She dried her eyes. "Thank you, Jay," she said, turning to face him.

"If there's anything I can do—"

She shook her head. Not long after she'd showed him to the front door and returned to her couch in the library, Sy'rai reappeared, quickly setting three cups of tea and a plate of chocolate chip cookies on the table. Joanne, who'd begun to have to watch her weight a few years back, was about to say she didn't want cookies or tea when Cole and a distraught Lizzy entered.

"Leo's on the phone again," Cole said, handing her his cell as he sat down beside her.

"Joanne!" Leo's deep voice was abrupt and gruff. "I've got

a top hostage negotiator, Pablo Cisneros from Mexico City, flying into Ciudad Juarez, as I speak. I've talked to a lot of important people in Texas and Washington, anybody who can pull the right strings. They're all talking to influential people, too. I don't want to get your hopes up, but Collins being kidnapped was a major break for us. Not only is he famous and apparently a darling of the press, but he comes from a powerful, well-placed family with all the right connections. His father is a longtime friend of the president's father. Maybe it won't be too long before we get some major results."

When Leo went on enumerating the complexities of the various politics involved in dealing with two countries, her mind wandered. It was increasingly hard for her to focus.

"I have to warn you, though. Working all this out won't be easy," Leo said. "Nothing about Mia's 'disappearing' or kidnapping by Morales is normal."

Leo went on to warn her that Morales and Gonzales, his Colombian connection, were believed to be behind many "disappearings" in Mexico, and never once had any of these "disappeared" people turned up alive.

"Usually Mexican kidnappers are quick to demand ransom," he said. "Morales is a major trafficker with high-placed connections of his own. But he's not in the business of kidnapping Americans to ransom them. So what does he want with her?"

"I—I can barely think right now, Leo."

"If we do get her back," he persisted.

"Please...don't say if."

"When...there will be major problems for the ranch," he continued. "But first things first. For now keep the phone lines open. Whatever you do, don't talk to the press. If Morales calls demanding a ransom, act scared and let him do the talking. Cisneros's top man is on his way to the ranch to give you the right prompts if Morales calls. *But no press.* They'll pressure you, but there's too much at stake."

She sucked in a breath. "It won't be hard to sound terrified."

"Let me repeat. Collins is a hero of the press, and Mia is well known. This is a big story. As for the rest—big name reporters are already bugging me about the details concerning Lizzy's and Mia's marriages to Cole.

"Out-of-state newsmen, who don't understand South Texas can't comprehend how Caesar and Cole could declare Mia legally dead so fast without her body. Most of all they want to know who he's really married to. I can see the headlines now—*Cole Knight Married To Both Kemble Sisters.*"

"That doesn't matter right now. We've just got to get her back."

"Right. But I like to stay one step ahead of the jackals. I've consulted our legal team, and they've done some research. Since Caesar had your local J.P. declare Mia legally dead without a body..."

"I don't want to hear about any of that."

"But every other Texan will."

Always, always, the Golden Spurs' reputation had to come first.

"I know how hard this is," he said.

She wanted to scream, *No, you don't!*

"After all the negative publicity concerning Cherry Lane's murder as well as Caesar being killed by his favorite nephew, I'd like to have some control of this situation when we *do* get her back."

Last year her husband, Caesar, had had a notorious affair with Cherry Lane, a Houston stripper. They'd even become engaged and then Caesar had suffered a stroke in Cherry's bed. Leo had been frantic because the scandal had been horrendous for the ranch from a business perspective. But when had he or the board ever worried about her?

"I just want Mia back in one piece!" she said, her nerves shredded.

Leo kept on. "Under Texas law, since Mia was legally dead, Cole's marriage to Lizzy will be the one to stand. Mia is single again."

"All right. All right. Just get her back."

When Joanne hung up, she couldn't look at Cole or Lizzy together. Even so, she was aware of how still and silent they were.

Lizzy loved her sister and Vanilla, but the two girls had always been rivals. Whatever one had, the other had always wanted—apparently, including Cole.

What if Mia was still in love with Cole?

"I hope I wasn't rude to Leo, but nothing matters except bringing Mia home," Joanne said aloud.

Cole lifted Lizzy's hand to his lips. "You're right, Joanne. We have to get her back."

"But how?" Lizzy threw herself into his arms and buried her face against his shoulder.

"I don't know yet." Loosening Lizzy's arms, Cole stood up. "For now, the phones are ringing, and I'd better get back to my desk."

When Cole excused himself, and Lizzy trailed after him like a lost puppy, Joanne felt desperate and lonely in the immense library.

Joanne was numb as she got up and went to the window and watched the tall green grasses that stretched to the horizon sway in the damp wind. When she'd first looked at Mia's picture and learned Mia was alive, she'd been exhilarated.

Now she felt nothing, nothing at all, not even fear.

She was simply numb and too drained to think. Then slowly as she watched the grass, memories of Mia's birth, of Mia's first ride on a pony, of other firsts flooded her tired mind. Mia had been such an energetic, eager child, so anxious to please Caesar, who had never bothered to notice.

Joanne closed her eyes, and as her lips began to move, she felt as if every defense, her wealth, her position, her rigid nature had been stripped away. She was naked to the bone as she sank to her knees and begged God to spare her daughter's life.

"Let me hold her again—please!"

Comandante Guillermo Florentino Gonzales was a big fan of the American gangster movies. Particular favorites were *Scarface* and *por supuesto,* all the *Godfather* movies, but especially the first one.

Guillermo was known for his jolly temperament, especially with pretty, young *señoritas.* Still, like a lot of men in stressful, violent professions, there were times when he had darker urges. He liked to tie women up as his stepfather had once tied him up. He liked to see their big dark eyes grow huge with fear when he unzipped himself and began to stroke his big pink pipe fondly before forcing them to do it for him.

He liked to hit them, to strip them, to plunge into them when they were dry and didn't want him. At such times he felt as big as a bull. He liked to flip them on their backs and take them in perverted, animalistic ways. Sometimes their screams were enough to satisfy him. And always the last thing he did was extinguish his cigar in their left butt cheek, so that other men would see his mark and know he'd been there first. Because he was the *comandante,* there were plenty of opportunities to enjoy his pretty prisoners when such urges struck him.

Still most of the time he was jolly. Although he was short, he was big where it counted. Like Sonny Corleone from *The Godfather* Guillermo found inordinate pride in his endowments. In any case, he was always ready to show off these gifts to willing lovers or to unwilling ones.

He had girlfriends all over Ciudad Juarez. He had a few in El Paso, too. In fact, he'd been planning to quit early to take his latest to a new gangster flick when Enrique dashed in, damn his hide, and slapped an official looking envelope on his desk.

"This has been sent to every Customs enforcement office along the U.S. Side of the border, *Comandante*. Ancera is on the phone, too."

Ancera was his superior in Mexico City.

As Guillermo pulled out a single sheet of vellum and saw that the letterhead was indeed U.S. Customs, a ripple of unease traced through him even before he took Ancera's call. Once he read it, his bushy black brows drew together in a lengthy, pronounced frown. He reread the official memorandum a second time before wadding it up and pitching it at a trash can.

The Americans! *Siempre los norteamericanos!* Piss on the Americans! Who gave them the right to run the world?

Finally he took Ancera's call, which began with Ancera screaming about Terence Collins's most recent article and kidnapping, reciting the Americans' outrageous demands for his return and the return of a woman named Mia Kemble.

"*Idiota! Estúpido!* You think you are this trafficker's friend. You mishandled everything! You let him get out of control!"

When their conversation ended, Guillermo was white and shaking.

He made a fist. Then he pressed the buzzer that summoned Enrique. The little sneak must have been waiting by the door because he appeared instantly.

With a frown Guillermo scribbled pretty Marisol's phone number. "Call her and tell her something's…er…come up…police business, and we'll have to put off our meeting for today."

When Enrique dashed back to his phone, Guillermo sighed. He should have known the city had been too quiet, his life too easy. He should have expected trouble.

Well, here it was—like a venomous snake, only hand-delivered. The Americans were threatening to close the border from San Diego to Brownsville if Terence Collins and Mia Kemble-Knight weren't delivered to them within forty-eight hours. Ancera was going to have his ass if he didn't take care of this problem.

Gonzales hated Terence Collins. The man had written numerous stories about the murdered girls of Ciudad Juarez. Always the *pendejo* reported that the Mexican police were incompetent, corrupt, cowardly thugs. He'd even named Gonzales by name more than once. There had been hits out on the reporter in the past even before he'd gone after Morales.

What kind of fool launched vicious attacks on Morales in the newspapers? Sooner or later Collins would turn up dead, just another corpse in the Chihuahua Desert. Guillermo, for one, wouldn't shed a tear.

On the other hand, Octavio Morales's payments were prompt and enormous. Guillermo liked drinking and shooting and whoring with Morales, too. Tavio shared the same taste for the occasional bout of rough sex. Fondly Guillermo remembered a night when they'd savaged two pretty whores who'd tried to overcharge them. After hours of rough sex, they'd handcuffed them naked to a fence post in the desert, and told their men where they were in case they wanted a free ride.

Morales had given him his favorite Arabian when he'd admired it, not to mention numerous automobiles and gold watches. Gonzales felt big and tough when he was with Morales, almost as tough as a movie star gangster.

In short, Morales was almost a friend of his. He turned over the *independientes,* the independent drug runners, who did not pay as they should, too. In his way Morales was a good man.

Guillermo got up and went to his private bathroom. When he shut the door and unzipped his pants, he caught a glimpse of his oval, olive face framed by his thick, wavy black hair. He smiled at his reflection and admired his straight, white teeth. His new whitener was working rather well. Rubbing his teeth with a fingertip, he smiled and glanced at himself from several angles. Then he tweaked his inky mustache until it was perfectly balanced. Only then did he take a leak.

Should he call Morales and tip him off? Or organize a squad to attack him by surprise tonight?

Morales would never surrender the hostages. Guillermo's only chance lay in a swift surprise attack.

Damn Morales! *Idiota!* He should have stuck to pretty young whores like Marisol. Why the hell had Morales gone and kidnapped two famous Americans with powerful friends?

Sí, Morales paid him big money.

But an open border paid more.

The *comandante* knew how long he'd last if the border was closed, and he was blamed for an international incident of that magnitude. He would be called worse than incompetent and corrupt. A wavy black head with very straight, white teeth would roll.

What if there was a trumped-up investigation and he was found guilty? He, not Ancera, would go to prison.

When he got back to his desk, Guillermo picked up his phone and reluctantly made the necessary call.

Seven

The door shut softly behind Delia. Staring at her supper tray, which was a plate of beans and tamales, Mia listened for the click of the key turning in the lock. When there was only the sound of Delia's soft, receding footsteps on the stairs, Mia ran to the door and touched the doorknob. When it turned easily, her heart beat faster.

Cracking the door a mere inch, she stared out into the hallway. All was quiet, so she tiptoed outside.

On Tavio's orders she had been locked in her room all day. Why?

Something was wrong. Something that concerned her.

Even now the house was as still as a tomb. It had been unusually silent during the morning and afternoon and even tonight when the men had dined. She'd caught glimpses of Tavio in the courtyard. He'd dressed carefully in a black silk shirt, black jeans and his ostrich cowboy boots, but he hadn't come to her once.

He was trying to impress someone. That was odd, frightening even. His infatuation was all that had kept her alive.

Trembling as she made her way through the hall downstairs, Mia sensed some new danger to herself.

Tavio had a new prisoner. Never before had he avoided her

like this because of a prisoner. Was it a woman? She'd seen a truck pull up to the buildings last night. Then Chito had thrown a tall person, whose head had been concealed beneath a black hood to the ground. Two men had dragged this individual inside by the feet, careless of his or her head being bumped along the ground. All day from her window, Mia had watched Tavio looking grim and fierce as he came from and went to that forbidden building.

What was going on? Who was in there? With vivid horror she remembered the handcuffs and electric cattle prods in that awful cell. She never wanted to go near that building again. Still, she was sure this new development had something to do with her recent escape attempt.

The desert air was warm and dry as Mia sprang out a back door and crouched behind a low bush. A guard on the wall struck a match. His cigarette flared, illuminating his hard jawline. Clumps of guards near the house were laughing and talking and smoking. Their voices carried as they spoke of women they'd had and drug runs that had gone bad.

Then Negra meowed at her, and Mia jumped, stifling a scream. How could she have forgotten about Negra when she'd slipped out? If anybody saw her cat, he might go check on her to make sure she was securely locked up.

Her hand covering her mouth, Mia stayed where she was and waited for a long time to see if any of them had noticed her or the cat. Finally, keeping to the shadows, she snuck around the corner of the house and froze. Breathing hard, she stared at the lighted window of the forbidden building and fought for the courage not to run back to her room.

When the men turned their backs, Mia stole from the main house and dashed across the courtyard. After that it was easy enough to creep along the adobe wall until she reached the torture chamber. Once there, she huddled beneath the barred window and was still when she heard threatening voices from within.

Struggling to comprehend the soft, rapidly spoken Spanish, she stood up a little. Her heart raced wildly, but the guards took no notice of her and continued with their crude, sexist jokes as they smoked.

She wore dark jeans and a black shirt, and she'd covered her hair with a black shawl.

"Who's your source?" Chito demanded, his voice louder than before.

Mia climbed onto a tree stump and raised her head above the windowsill. The same single, low-wattage, bare bulb hanging from a cord lit the adobe room. Cigarette butts, rumpled newspapers, handcuffs, cattle prods and broken beer bottles littered the floor. Five of Tavio's meanest men with guns leaned against a back wall, watching Chito hold a tall, skinny man's head in a bucket of foul, dark liquid. The prisoner was stripped to the waist and wore only his boxer shorts. His long legs thrashed violently, raising little puffs of dust as he fought to free himself.

When Chito pushed his head deeper, the men laughed. She nearly cried out when the prisoner's thin body went limp and his long legs stopped moving.

She had to do something fast, before they drowned him the way they had Negra's kittens last winter.

Just when she was about to scream and run inside and beg for his life, Chito yanked the man's head up.

When the prisoner hung limply, Chito ripped the wet black hood off. The man's eyes were closed, his narrow face gray and lifeless.

Chito threw him on the ground and rolled him over with his boot. Then he pounded him on the back until he gagged and puked dank water all over the newspapers and broken glass. Mia was moaning and hugging herself as if she herself were being tortured. When Chito finally stopped hitting him, he kicked him in the ribs for good measure. The prisoner grunted and grabbed his stomach, choking and struggling for every breath. The men against the wall laughed.

"Eh, Chito, why don't you burn his balls with the cattle prod again?"

At that the prisoner sat up, and when he did, his agonized gaze locked on hers.

It was Terence Collins. Not that the thin, gray face looked much like the smiling photograph she'd seen above his byline.

"Who's been talking to you?" Chito yelled again. "If you tell us, you can go home. Who gave you that photograph?"

Terence's gaze left the window. When he looked straight at Chito, he puked more water.

"Who are your sources? How did you find out about this Kemble woman?"

Oh, my God. Tavio knew who she really was. Chito would torture Terence until he talked. Then he'd kill him.

She sank to her knees and gripped them to her chin. Her heart beat frantically even as her mind raced.

What could she do? What could she possibly do? She had no plan, no weapon, nothing. Tavio's gang had AK-47 assault rifles, grenade launchers and bazookas. Once Tavio had shown her a warehouse full of such stuff.

She stared wildly at the big house, the spring beneath the cottonwood tree, the trucks, the trees and bushes. The lethargy that had enveloped her since she'd tried to escape the last time was gone. She had to save this man and save herself.

Suddenly dust tickled her nostrils. Before she could clamp her hand over her nose, she sneezed.

Chito shouted. The men against the wall stormed out the door.

Negra jumped down from a ledge and ran past them.

"It was only the woman's cat," the men cried. One of them picked up a rock and threw it after Negra.

Chito came to the door and stared out into the darkness, frowning at the cat, which sat preening out of range.

Everybody knew the cat followed her everywhere. Sure

he'd think about that and find her, Mia held her breath, waiting.

Then one of the men broke the silence and suggested they get back to torturing the prisoner.

Chito laughed.

One minute the Kemble woman was there. Then she was gone. Terence was in so much pain, he soon wondered if he'd only imagined her.

"I'm going to break every bone in your body—slowly. You will beg me to burn you then," Chito said softly.

Terence lay on the ground, struggling for every breath. Morales's two-bit thugs *were* going to kill him—after they got him to reveal his sources. Because of him, they'd probably kill the girl, too.

All through the night, the bastards had jabbed him with a cattle prod, sending searing jolts of electricity through him while they'd laughed until he'd gone so mad he'd laughed, too, in between tears of agony.

Octavio himself had appeared this morning dressed like a rich *hacendado* of old, carrying an ornate silver breakfast tray. The villain had told him he had *huevos* and that even though he was a *gringo,* who'd written lies about him, he deserved a good meal before he died.

Terence had hated the slick, handsome, smiling bastard way more than his cheap thugs. Still, he'd eaten breakfast with the man and had dragged it out, a brief respite from torture.

Morales had wanted to talk about Mia Kemble. Mostly he'd wanted to know about her family and the ranch and how much money they had. But he'd also wanted to know about the men in her life.

When Terence had refused to answer any of his questions, Tavio had stomped away in a fury.

"Why don't you let her go?" Terence had yelled after him.

Tavio had turned. "Because she is mine, *gringo.* Because nobody tell me, Octavio Morales, what to do ever again."

Since then Terence had suffered ceaseless torture and had felt utterly bleak and without hope until he'd seen Mia's pale face framed in the bars of the window. Curiously, this sighting, the idea that she was out there, that a friend was near, filled him with new strength.

Holding the cattle prod, Chito grabbed his wet hair. "What did you see? At the window?"

"Nada." Terence spat the word.

"You lie!" Chito kicked him in the abdomen and Terence doubled over again, grabbed his waist and lay writhing. "When we're done, I'm going to gut you with my hunting knife and feed you to my dogs."

Five men sprang toward him. Chito waved the cattle prod and yelled, "Strap him to the bench again!"

"Smoke!" one of the men yelled, dropping the rope he held.

Wild shouts were heard from outside the doorway. "Fire! Near the trucks!"

Outside, against a black velvet sky, tongues of flame raced up the canvas covering of a truck bed. Suddenly the truck exploded.

Except for Chito, the men grabbed their guns and ran. Chito turned around, raised his pistol and took aim right between Terence's eyes. "For this you die."

Just as Chito began to laugh, a slim shadow danced into the cell, leaping and twisting across the wall behind him.

Chito's trigger finger inched the trigger backward. Mia, a hooded figure in black, scooped up a slop bucket and slammed it down hard on the back of Chito's skull, causing him to topple lifelessly into the filthy sewage.

"Hit him again!" she said, her voice steady. "Make sure he's out cold! Get his gun and follow me!"

Terence grabbed the gun and bashed Chito. Then he picked

up his slacks and shoes. Limping after her, he found himself outside in a courtyard that burned brighter and hotter than hell itself.

She ran ahead of him, darting back and forth, and he fought to keep up, but in his weakened state, he lagged behind. By some miracle they made it to a truck. She jumped behind the wheel, and he threw himself in beside her. Out of nowhere a slim, dark woman appeared.

"Don't leave me!"

"Get in then, Delia!" Mia screamed. *"Rápido!"*

Starting the engine, Mia shifted, grinding the gears. Her seat was too far back, and she could barely reach the pedals. As she fastened her seat belt, they careened toward the big gates in fits and starts. When she shifted again, into third instead of second, the truck jerked.

Then a tall, dark man sprinted toward them at an angle.

Tavio shouted at her before jumping in front of the truck and yelling at his men to hold their fire.

"Angelita!" Morales yelled. "Don't leave me!"

The brazen bastard held up both his hands.

"Flatten him," Terence growled.

Tavio spread his legs wide, crossed his arms over his chest, and raised his chin higher, his white grin daring her to murder him. When Mia stomped harder on the accelerator, the girl in the back seat leaned over and tried to grab the wheel.

But it was Mia, who swerved so hard to the left at the last second, the two right tires flew off the ground. Skidding in the dirt on their side, they nearly rolled.

"Damn. You should have killed him," Terence hissed.

Mia pressed her lips together. "Get down or fasten your seat belt. Cover your eyes, too!"

The heavy locked gates of the compound loomed in front of them like a solid wall. She stomped harder on the gas pedal, causing the truck to ram the gates full speed.

The impact jarred the truck, but thick beams splintered.

Wooden boards flew toward them like fence palings, battering the hood. A two-by-four pierced the windshield, showering glass into Terence's lap.

Then they were outside—free, the gaping hole in the adobe walls growing smaller in their rearview mirror. The warm air blasting through the windshield smelled of sage and dust.

Mia gripped the steering wheel as they bounced over rocks. "You don't know how I've dreamed of this moment," she said.

"Are you suicidal, or what?" Terence said as he used the gun to shove bits of glass off his bare legs onto the floor.

"Typical," she whispered.

"What?"

"A girl risks her ass for a man, and he complains."

The girl in the back seat had turned around and was staring at Tavio's rapidly receding compound.

"You're crazy," Terence said as they bumped over the deep ruts in the rocky road.

"Living with Tavio Morales doesn't make for sanity."

"I've never heard of Morales not killing a hostage. You probably have quite a story."

"You wouldn't believe me." She stared straight ahead at the meandering dirt road.

"A reliable source told me Morales had you here. I wrote my last story about you."

"So my family knows?"

"I'm sure they must. I tried to call them, but Chito got me before I could get through to them."

"What did you write?"

"That you were his prisoner."

"Oh, my God."

"So, why didn't he kill you?"

"How should I know? Lucky, I guess."

"Why'd you swerve for the bastard then?"

"You want to know why? I don't know why." She flashed Terence a wan smile. "I'll kill him next time, okay?"

Terence laughed so hard his rawly burned shins ached. Then he saw the headlights in the rearview mirror.

He whirled around.

"Step on it. We've picked up a tail. Probably your friend, Morales."

The girl in the back began to sob.

The road curved around a hill. Except for the lights, darkness blanketed the desert as Mia sped along the bumpy road. When Terence turned around again to see if Morales was catching up, she suddenly slammed on the brakes.

"We're surrounded!" she cried. "Look! Ahead!"

A dozen jeeps and armored trucks that had been heading around the curve toward Tavio's compound without their headlights flashed their high beams at them. When Mia didn't come to a full stop, an explosion of bullets bit the dirt on all sides of her.

"We're done for!" Mia hit the brakes again, this time skidding to a stop in the deep sand just as Tavio roared up from behind in his armored SUV.

The bastard jumped out and ran straight at her with his pistol held high. When Terence raised his gun, Mia was in the way.

Yanking her door open, Tavio grabbed her and hauled her into his arms. His gun at the ready, Terence watched their exchange.

She hit Morales as hard as she could.

"Let me go!" she screamed. "I want to go home!"

The trafficker winced, grabbed her wrists and pinioned them behind her back. While she yelled at him, he simply stared down at her, waiting for her to give up.

"Your home is with me," he whispered, his narrowed eyes glittering. "I'm almost glad of this. You leave me no choice. Tonight you're mine, Mia Kemble."

Ignoring, the armed men, who'd sprayed them with bullets, he lowered his mouth to hers.

"Not so fast, Morales." A short, cocky fellow strutted up behind them.

"Is that you there in the dark, Guillermo?" Morales's voice held friendship and affection. "This is one woman I won't share—even with you."

"We've got you surrounded, Tavio. You don't have a chance," Guillermo said in a small, shaking voice.

"What?" Finally comprehending that Guillermo and his men had come on a raid, Tavio let go of her slowly. Then yelling expletives in Spanish, he lunged for Guillermo's throat.

"Seize him!" Guillermo screamed as the bigger man hurled him to the ground. "Get his gun!"

Four young policemen ran forward, grabbed Tavio's gun, and then tried to pull him off their *comandante*. Morales wouldn't let go of the man's throat. Fighting them like a dozen cougars, Morales kicked, punched, bit and choked the men. It finally took ten of them to push him facedown into the dirt and cuff him while Guillermo lay beside him choking and retching.

"You will die for this, *gringa*," Tavio muttered as the little *comandante*, who'd finally gotten his breath, struggled to his feet and dusted off his uniform. Then he began to tweak his mustache. "And you, too, Comandante Gonzales."

Guillermo strode over and kicked him in the stomach, causing Tavio to grunt like an injured dog.

"It is not for you to say who will die anymore!" To his men he shouted, "Throw him in my truck! His woman, too! We're hauling them to prison!"

Three men grabbed her and cuffed her and threw her down in the dirt beside Tavio.

"*Cállate, puta!*" When the *comandante* kicked her, Terence threw his gun down and climbed out of the truck to make sure she was all right.

Forgetting Mia, the *comandante* turned to the girl cowering in the front seat. "For a long time I've wanted to know why Chito thinks you're so special. Put her in my personal truck. Delia is my reward."

"No!" Delia tried to run, but his men caught her and dragged her back, screaming.

"Let her go," Mia pleaded as Delia struggled.

The *comandante* laughed. "*No te preocupas.* Tonight she will fall in love with me. All the women fall in love with me, *gringa.* She will forget she ever knew Chito."

"And you, *gringo,* eh?" The *comandante* whirled on Terence, who was kneeling beside Mia.

His men raised their guns and strutted toward him.

"You write bad things about me, no? About my men? What the hell am I going to do with you?"

BOOK TWO

Smart Cowboy Saying:

The meanest bronc can be broke, a bit at a time.

—L.D. Burke
Santa Fe

Eight

No matter where he was or what he was doing Shanghai hadn't been able to stop thinking about Mia. As he stepped out of his hotel room into what looked like the longest hall in the universe, he was filled with relief that she was alive and with anger, too—anger because he still gave a damn.

The phone rang before the door shut. Thinking it was Abby again, he loped back inside, flung his hat onto the bed and picked up the receiver. He might as well take the hell she was bent on dishing out now rather than later.

"Shanghai, it's me—Cole."

At the sound of Cole's deep, familiar voice on the other end of the line, all the old bitternesses that had to do with Cole marrying Mia curdled Shanghai's stomach.

He had a rodeo to win and a fat paycheck to collect. He needed to focus on the rodeo, not on the brother who'd married the woman he'd loved.

Loved? He wished he could reject that as merely an inane thought.

"*Damn,*" he said, and loud enough to tick Cole off.

Ever since Mia and Octavio had started making the newspapers, his love for her was like a virus getting a death grip. He was half sick to death over her. Now Cole was calling him, too. Shanghai didn't like it. Not one bit. He wanted to be free of Mia Kemble.

"Catch you at a bad time?" Cole asked. Not that he sounded like he much cared.

One helluva bad time.

Shanghai had taken a bad fall off a bull in front of thousands of fans not an hour ago, and his hands still stung like ants had bitten them.

"I thought you were Abby, my girlfriend," Shanghai said.

"Sorry," Cole said.

No sooner had Shanghai made it to his room at The Golden Nugget than Abby had called from her dad's in El Paso. She should have known better than to bring up Mia again.

"Dad says that Mia Kemble was really something. Tavio's men were buzzing him with cattle prods and drowning him," Abby had said. "She set a truck on fire and saved his life."

"If she's so great why the hell's she in jail?" Shanghai had demanded.

"Dad says somebody ought to do something—"

Shanghai had lost all patience with her. "Look, I can't be thinking about *her.* My hands feel funny, and I'm only ahead by a thousand dollars. Trevino's ridin' like a bat out of hell. I've got to focus on bulls, not Mia Kemble."

He'd hung up on Abby because he was bent out of shape about Mia, and now he needed to eat and get to bed early. He didn't have time for distractions. Especially not his brother!

"Cole, can we put this on hold? I've got a lot on my mind...friends waiting for me in the bar." He shook out his right hand because it was going numb on him again.

"Mind if I join you?" Cole said.

A vein in Shanghai's head throbbed.

Yeah, he minded. "What the hell? You're in town?"

"I've got to see you," Cole said.

"You should have called before you wasted plane fare. My calendar is jammed."

"Unjam it. This is urgent."

"I don't hear squat from you for what is it—fifteen years—now you want to see me in thirty damn minutes?"

"You're the one that left Dodge without ever even sending your brother one lousy postcard."

"My handwriting's so bad you probably couldn't have read it anyway."

"Mia's alive."

"Tell me something I don't know. My girlfriend's dad wrote the breaking story about her. Then Morales kidnapped and tortured him. Maybe she masterminded that crime, too."

"That's bullshit."

"Mia's got nothin' to do with me now."

"She's rotting in a Mexican prison, and Morales has ordered a hit on her. We've got Mexican attorneys and hostage negotiators, but we're getting nowhere fast. The police have charged her with trafficking."

"Any woman who's been living with and working for Morales and lettin' her family think she was dead deserves what she gets."

"Those charges are trumped-up horseshit! She was his prisoner."

"She was kissing Morales when the cops caught them. Morales says she was working for him before that plane crash."

"He's lying because he doesn't want her to get out of Mexico alive. She hates drugs. She wasn't a trafficker. She was raising horses and taking care of Vanilla. She went down with me in my plane. It's a miracle either one of us is alive. I don't know how she got tangled up with Morales, but I'm not going to sit in judgment of her until I get the facts."

"She could have run Morales down when she got Abby's father out, but she didn't."

"So—she's not a killer."

"Collins says Morales was besotted with her."

"You're mighty pissed at her for a man who doesn't give a damn."

"Hell, she left me for you! She's been living with that outlaw and probably screwing his brains out. A woman like that doesn't deserve the time of day."

"Shut up and listen. I want you to go down there with me and help me get her out before Morales kills her."

"You've got some nerve. You married her. She's your problem."

"You ever wonder why she married me?"

"Yeah!" Shanghai slammed the receiver down. "To piss me off royally! Which she did! And so did you!"

He grabbed his Stetson with his lucky turkey feather off the bed and slapped it on his head.

When the phone rang again, he stalked out of the room, kicking the door shut behind him.

Mia was sleeping when suddenly her blanket was jerked off her and thrown onto the filthy concrete floor.

"Tavio Morales is going to *keel* you," shrieked a stick of a woman with a mashed-in-nose, missing front teeth and tangled black hair. "Everybody in El Castillo knows it."

"Raquel?"

Raquel was the lunatic from two cells down, who restlessly wandered about the prison, stealing anything that wasn't tied down. She liked matches and set fire to other inmates' hair and punched them when they weren't looking.

"You won't need a blanket after they cut you up," Raquel whispered.

Blinking as well as yawning, Mia grabbed her blanket back and pushed Raquel away with the flat of her hand. The woman howled as if she'd been mortally injured and pulled even harder at her corner of the blanket.

"Leave me alone, you insane witch! Go back to your own cell!"

"Nobody snitches on Morales and lives. He's already got somebody inside. They sneak *heem* in through the…"

"Shut up!" Roselia said.

"He's short and dark and wears a dead man's bones around his neck!"

"You're lying!" Mia whispered.

"With the right connections and enough pesos, anybody can buy their way in here, especially now!" Raquel started cackling.

A chill raced through Mia. "It wasn't my fault Morales was captured. Go away and tell that to your friends."

"He was good to the poor. You deserve to die for what you did—*gringa!*"

Mia yanked her blanket free of the woman. Wrapping herself with it, she lay back down and closed her eyes so she wouldn't have to look at Raquel or the bugs on the dirty walls or the bars.

Would her family ever come? Did they believe the Mexican police? Foolishly Mia had hoped the cops were the good guys and that they would release her after she'd told them who she was. But that wasn't the case. Comandante Guillermo Gonzales had ogled her when he'd questioned her and smiled when she'd blushed.

When he'd finished interrogating her, he'd said, "I cannot let you go." Then he'd handed her Tavio's signed confession in which Tavio had written that she'd been living with him for over a year and had been working in his smuggling operation in Texas before that.

At first she'd thought her arrest was a mistake or a joke. Then panic had set in when the cops had kept her in handcuffs and had stared through her like she was garbage.

"I want a lawyer. Morales is lying. And…and…I saw you at his house, *comandante*. Which means—"

"Be careful who you accuse, *señorita*. In Mexico prisoners, even *gringas*, are believed guilty until they prove their innocence."

"What did you do to Delia?"

"Take her away," he'd said to his guards.

"Where is Delia?"

"Why you worry about her? You have bigger problems than she has."

That night they'd brought her to El Castillo on the edge of Ciudad Juarez. She'd been strip-searched while the *comandante* leered. Then she'd been given a blank confession to sign. When she'd refused to sign it, two guards had said they'd be back to interrogate her. Then they'd thrown her in a cell.

The guards' threats seemed to have been made days ago, but she wasn't sure of anything anymore. The window high above her cell had been boarded up. Without daylight or darkness to guide her, she'd lost all sense of time.

That first night the prison had seemed a madhouse. Women had screamed or wept all night. Babies had cried. She'd lain on her cot, longing for Vanilla, a constant choking fear as well as a fierce longing gripping her. She'd thought surely she'd lose her mind. But slowly she'd gotten used to the other women, and they'd grown accustomed to her and had even confided to her their dismal stories.

Muttering to herself, Raquel drifted out of her cell, and Mia closed her eyes, trying to shut the nightmare out. When she woke up again hours later, this time from a pleasant dream, a guard was shaking her, jolting her back to harsh reality.

Were they going to interrogate her—translation: *torture* her—until she signed their blank confession?

"You have a visitor." The guard's black eyes radiated loathing.

"Who?"

"Get up. Hurry."

She was led down a long straight corridor, past many cells. Then they left the building and went into a courtyard out into the sunshine. Mia looked up at the blue sky and the clouds drifting above her and felt a sense of freedom. She ran her hands through her tangled hair and tried to neaten it. She hadn't showered or changed clothes since coming here. She stank, too.

"*Venga.*"

The guard grabbed her arm roughly and then pushed her towards an administration building and then into a small, poorly lit visiting room where a tall woman stood waiting in a dark corner. The low-wattage lightbulb was behind her, and her face was in shadow.

Mia would have known her anywhere.

"Mother!" she cried. "You came!"

"Darling!" There were tears in her mother's soft voice.

Neither could stop staring at the other. Her mother looked younger, more glamorous somehow. Her hair was redder and streaked, and yet her eyes were luminous with pain.

"I couldn't bring Vanilla, but I brought pictures of her." Joanne spoke in a low, halting tone. "You won't believe how she's…"

Mia moistened her lips with her tongue and then nodded. She pushed her hair out of her eyes, but, of course, a thick, lank clump fell back.

"I must look—"

"Don't—" Her mother began sifting through the pictures. "Cole built this play set for her behind the house with swings and tunnels and stairs. She plays on it every day."

Lines of sorrow were etched in her mother's face.

Suddenly the faraway world that had once been her real life seemed very near. They moved closer. Mia had never felt such love as she experienced now for her mother even though she felt reticent, too. She felt intensely anxious, almost overwhelmed, at the prospect of seeing pictures of her little girl.

"I—I wasn't sure I'd ever see you…or her again. Oh, Mother…"

"Are you all right?"

"I'm fine." Mia took a deep breath and looked up at the ceiling. "I hope you don't believe what they're…"

Shaking her head, her mother's fingertips touched her lips to hush her daughter. Next her hands clasped her to her, and Mia clung tightly as if she'd never be able to bear to let her go. Mia shut her eyes and felt calmed by her mother's embrace.

She caught her breath, afraid she'd open her eyes and her mother's dear presence would be a dream. A drug lord had imprisoned her and terrorized her. He'd told the authorities she'd been his partner in crime. Now Mia was in a Mexican prison, and if the Mexican authorities had their way, she'd be here until she was an old woman. Worse than anything was the loss of her family. A wave of homesickness crushed her. She wanted to be home; she wanted her life back.

"I—I don't know how this happened to me. I—I don't know…"

"We're going to get you out. We've hired attorneys." Joanne looked around, her eyes glancing worriedly at the video camera in one corner. "One way or the other Cole's going to get you out." Her mother leaned closer, her voice low, her expression guarded. "Be watchful…ready for anything."

When the guard shifted from one foot to the other, her mother let go of her hands and placed three pictures on the table beside them.

The first one was of Vanilla sliding down a big red slide.

Her hand shaking, Mia lifted the picture. "Oh, she's beautiful! Her hair…"

"She has natural curls…just like you did."

In the next picture Vanilla was climbing a plastic mountain with handholds. By the time Mia flipped to the last picture, her cheeks felt hot and damp and her chest was so tight she could barely breathe. Her little baby had grown up without her.

In the final shot a smiling cherub splashed in a swimming pool with a float around her plump tummy.

"She looks so happy and trusting, so carefree and positive," Mia said. "Like she thinks the world is a wonderful, safe place."

"She's going to love you so much."

"Mother, I'm sorry to cause—"

"You haven't done anything. It's just so wonderful to be with you now."

The guard looked at her watch. Then she got up and clamped a heavy hand on Mia's shoulder, signaling them that the visit was over.

As her mother turned to go, Mia's eyes burned. It took all her willpower not to scream or to chase after her. When the guard opened the door, Mia had never felt so alone or so weak.

The door closed without Joanne ever looking back. The last thing Mia saw was her mother's ramrod straight spine.

When the guard grinned at Mia, she notched her head higher before walking out the door to make her way back to her cell. In the courtyard, once again, she paused to stare up at the blue sky. Three black grackles flew by squawking.

In her cell, she sank onto her cot and gazed up at the boarded window.

She could give up.

Or she could go on.

She had come this far. Somehow she would get through this awful time.

Somehow she had to hang on.

She remembered the *comandante* kissing Delia and bit her lips. She couldn't think about Delia. She simply couldn't.

Her mother had told her to be ready for anything.

* * *

The *comandante's* waiting room was dingy and old, the puke-green walls yellowed from smoke. Its atmosphere was oppressive.

Joanne had been sitting in the unvarnished wooden chair so long, she felt stiff. Most of the other women waiting to see the *comandante* were peasant women dressed in black with dark shawls. They bounced wriggling children in their laps. A few men in ragged pants and stained shirts and *huaraches* hunkered low against the back wall, smoking and muttering amongst themselves without the slightest animation lighting their faces or eyes. Watching them, Joanne thought they had the look of men who'd been downtrodden their entire lives.

Footsteps clicked on the dirty tile floor and came to a stop near Joanne's chair. When Joanne lifted her chin, she found herself staring into the narrow, guarded eyes of the *comandante's* assistant.

"*Nombre?* Name?" the man said.

"You know perfectly well who I am. I had an appointment this *morning* with Comandante Guillermo Gonzales. And now it's…" Joanne glanced at her watch.

The chattering in the waiting room ceased. Even the babies stopped squirming when their mothers leaned forward in their chairs. Dozens of pairs of avid black eyes focused on her face. The men's cigarettes hung suspended in their frozen brown fingers, thick smoke curling upward toward the window on the back wall.

Joanne drew a deep breath. She fought to contain her anger at this little man who savored his power with such relish.

Mia had looked terrified yesterday. She'd been filthy. Tavio Morales had a hit out on Mia's life, and the *comandante* didn't want to see her.

"It's nearly 5:00 p.m.," she said.

He shrugged. "The *comandante ees muy importante* and very busy, *señora*. Ciudad Juarez *ees* very dangerous city."

Joanne had seen people enter and leave the comandante's office all day. She'd heard a lot of jolly laughter.

There was another moment of awkward silence.

"When is he going to see me?"

"*Mañana.*"

"That's what you said yesterday."

"*Lo siento.*" Rather than looking apologetic, he grinned.

"My daughter is innocent."

He smiled. "You will have to discuss that with the *comandante.*"

"How can I if he won't see me?"

The man shrugged. "*Mañana.*"

Nine

Under a steel-beamed ceiling the rodeo crowd was roaring like ancient Romans screaming for their gladiators. Ignoring them, Shanghai methodically donned a left-handed, deerskin, riding glove, tied it on and then coiled his rope into a large loop.

Shanghai—

Mia's soft voice seemed to call to him again.

Help me!

Shanghai gripped his sticky rope tighter and fought to pretend he didn't hear her or feel her in his bones. But he did. Ice trickled down his spine, and his fingers started tingling again. He shook his hands hard. Setting his rope down, he scraped his glove over rosin to make it even stickier. Then he bound his arms.

He had to focus on the ride ahead of him. Bad Boy was a supremely rank bull. The scores were tight, but if he could stay on this beast, he'd win the rodeo.

If…

As he slipped into his black, protective vest and arm brace, he heard Bad Boy snorting and kicking inside the chute. Slowly Shanghai put on his helmet. Then he picked up his rope and re-coiled it before he headed toward Big Boy.

Cowboys parted for him, slapping him on the back or nodding as he passed. Then right before he climbed into the chute, he looked up at the stands and shot his fans a final grin.

When he saw Cole in the first row to the right of the chutes, the air went out of his chest.

"Damn."

Cole's blue gaze locked on his face. Seconds ticked by, and Shanghai couldn't look away. When he finally did, his jaw was tight. Then he was all business as he strode toward the big black Brangus bull and swung himself up and over the railings into the coffin-shape chute. Next he slowly lowered a booted foot onto Bad Boy's back so the bull would know he was there.

Then it was just Shanghai and Bad Boy and the yellow rope that Wolf was pulling tight over Shanghai's gloved hand. The bull stood still in his cage, his hooves in the dirt as he stared at the gate. When Shanghai was ready, he nodded at the chute boss and the gate swung open.

Like an erupting volcano, Bad Boy blew out of the chute, bell clanging—bucking up and away from Shanghai's hand. The bull jumped and began to spin even before he hit the ground again, centrifuging Shanghai into losing his seat. Writhing, twisting, shuddering, the bull rose and swooped, soaring into the air and then thudding violently to earth, his hooves causing dusty swirls to explode around them.

Somehow Shanghai hung on, but flailing.

The bull sensed the slip and spun in the opposite direction to finish him off. Shanghai flailed again, his free arm waving frantically to regain his balance.

"C'mon Shanghai," the announcer taunted. "C'mon!"

The crowd howled. All Shanghai could see was the bull's thick bobbing neck and the occasional flash of silver conchos on his buckskin chaps. All he felt was the powerful surge of the beast beneath his legs.

Bad Boy was good and mad now. He bucked higher and harder, kicking up and out with his back hooves. In a rage, he threw his neck up so fast he hit Shanghai's helmet, causing metal to graze his chin.

Shanghai responded to the bull's every trick, trying harder than he'd ever tried. Incredibly he lurched two seconds past the horn even, hanging on for longer, partly because he was stubborn but mostly because all of a sudden he was having such a helluva good time. The fans were on their feet, stomping and screaming.

Then it all went wrong.

Nostrils flaring and steaming, Bad Boy jerked to the left, and suddenly Shanghai was thrown—all of him except his hand, which had twisted and jammed in the rope's handle. Maddened that the man still hung on him, Bad Boy raced toward a bullfighter, spitting and snorting, dragging Shanghai in the dust along with him.

Bad Boy jumped and spun, trying to rid himself of Shanghai so he could stomp him to death, no doubt, but Shanghai's hand remained hung up even as he fought to untangle himself. It was all he could do to keep jogging alongside Bad Boy. As a maddened Bad Boy raced around the arena, Shanghai was tiring fast. He gasped for every breath. His leg muscles felt as limp as spaghetti noodles.

A dozen off-duty bullfighters jumped out of the stands to help. Even Wolf ran up and struck Bad Boy in the nose with a fist and a riding crop, only to be rammed in the arm with a horn and sent ricocheting like a bowling pin against the rails.

Then Cole was there, running alongside Shanghai, calling to him to hang on, lunging at the rope, trying to pull Shanghai loose. The crowd was on their feet, stomping and screaming like madmen gone wild, hating the dance with death, but loving it, too.

Bullfighters yelled and ran at the bull. A full minute passed before Cole could get a hand in and free Shanghai. Then they fell to their knees in a tangled heap. Crawling, scrambling to his feet, Cole dragged Shanghai to the right just as Bad Boy charged past them, snorting like a runaway locomotive on thundering hooves.

When Shanghai got to his feet, he was so weak he stumbled and collapsed headfirst onto the ground again. His shoulder muscles were cramping. He was so damn tired he didn't think he could get up until Cole lifted him to his feet and dragged him toward a gate. Finally Shanghai managed to stand straighter, but he was still panting so hard, he wasn't sure he could have walked without Cole's help. When the announcer told everybody that Shanghai's brother had freed his hand and was walking him out of the arena, the crowd got to its feet again, clapping and cheering.

Shanghai stopped and threw his hands up and smiled at the adoring fans. Wolf raced up to them with the onsite doctor, who offered to check Shanghai out as they strode out of the arena.

"I'm fine," Shanghai said.

"Don't be so damned bullheaded," Cole said.

"Don't be so damned bossy." Turning his back on Cole, Shanghai ripped off his helmet and coiled his rope. Putting on his Stetson, he turned to stare at the scoreboard.

He was fine—thanks in large part to Cole. Except for his tingling hands and the cut on his chin and some bruises—he was fine.

His score flashed on the scoreboard, and the announcer began to babble excitedly.

"Looks like you won," Cole said. "Let's just hope your luck hasn't run out. You'll need it for Mexico."

"No way in hell am I going to Mexico."

Cole's quick grin and easy confidence made Shanghai slightly uneasy. His brother had the sly look of a man who had an ace or two up his sleeve. Just as he was about to thank

Cole for saving his ass in the arena, a shy-looking kid in a cowboy hat two sizes too big for him walked up and smiled up at Shanghai with huge, awestruck eyes.

"Can I have your autograph, please?" the kid asked.

Shanghai felt his frown melting into a smile as he gazed at the boy. Slowly he knelt and placed the kid's program on his knee.

"What's your name, big guy?" He lifted the kid's pen.

"Robert Black."

"Well, sir, Mr. Black, I hope you're not going to ride bulls when you grow up."

"I am! I want to grow up and be just like you!"

"Oh, no, you don't," Cole said. "I could tell you a story or two that would change your mind in a heartbeat."

But the kid gazed past Cole at Shanghai adoringly.

"Save your breath, little brother," Shanghai muttered as he scribbled his name.

When he stood up, the kid raced back to his friends.

"Fame and glory," Cole said. "Is this why—"

Shanghai stared at his brother for a long, awkward moment. "Hell, why does anybody do the crazy things they do?"

When Cole didn't say anything, Shanghai felt the need to add more. Even so he hesitated for a few seconds. "Thanks—for pulling me loose."

"My pleasure. You kept Daddy off me."

"The only reason I ever felt bad about leavin' was 'cause of you...'cause of leavin' you with him, I mean."

"He never had it in for me like he did for you."

Shanghai felt his muscles tighten.

"So—since I saved your life—you ready to talk about Mia?"

"Shut up about her. Just shut up."

"Okay. For now."

Rock music pulsed in the bar. Sheila, a beautiful, young stripper with long blond hair, was rubbing her body wantonly against a pole right above Shanghai while her cowboy audience threw their Stetsons in the air, yelling and stomping for more. Smiling down at Shanghai, she wrapped her legs around her pole and then did a very talented back bend as she slid down the pole and began to move up and down.

Not that Shanghai was paying much attention to her heavy breasts or the waves of blond hair spilling over his shoulders as he took a long pull from his beer bottle and stared at Cole. He was too damned tired and too damned sore. He couldn't even feel his right hand.

"You're wasting your time. I'm not risking my hide for Mia Kemble."

"If you gave a damn about your hide, you wouldn't ride bulls." Cole lifted his own bottle to his lips.

"Why don't you hire a professional, somebody with connections down there?"

"Leo's talked to lots of people. He hasn't found anybody he thinks we should trust. Terence Collins says he knows somebody who might help us, though…if we did our own thing."

Even though Collins was Abby's father, Shanghai didn't trust his motives. According to Abby she'd never seen much of the glory-seeking bastard.

Wolf, who was the nearest thing Shanghai had had to a brother since he'd left home, smiled fiendishly at the two brothers as he listened to them.

It galled Shanghai that he appeared to love every minute of this little brotherly reunion. Shanghai scowled at him for good measure.

What the hell was he smiling about?

The wolf didn't smile much usually. Maybe because smiling projected the wrong kind of attitude for a tough guy in his business. And he was tough.

Wolf was made of solid muscle. His neck was a hunk that ran from his ears to his wide shoulders. His chest was as big as a barrel. He didn't slim down any at the waist, either. If ever a human being was built to be a battering ram, Wolf was such a man.

Shanghai decided not to let Wolf's amusement get to him. Turning his back on Wolf, Shanghai shot his brother a dark look.

"Like I said, she's your wife, Cole. So she's your problem. I got my ass kicked out of south Texas by the Kembles a long time ago partly 'cause of her."

"Maybe. But that wasn't the end of you and Mia."

Shanghai took a long pull. "It should have been."

"But she tracked you down at a rodeo. And you weren't exactly...unfriendly."

Shanghai's frown deepened. Had the two of them gossiped about him in their marriage bed?

"Vegas in the spring time?" Cole pressed. "Am I right?"

"What difference does it make? I've got a fiancée now."

Wolf lifted his eyebrows and shot him an ironic smile. "Congratulations, wuss." Before Shanghai could snap out a retort, Wolf turned his back on them and yelled through the stripper's legs at the bartender for another round of beers.

"The only reason Mia asked me to marry her was to give *your* baby *your* last name."

Shanghai choked on his mouthful of beer. The loud music seemed to fade even though his ears kept ringing. Cole's dark face spun in a smoky haze as he spit beer and fought to swallow.

"Vanilla's your daughter! Not mine!"

The strangling got so bad, Wolf pounded him on his back with a meaty fist.

"Stop it! I'm fine!" Shanghai leaned across the table. "What the hell did you say?"

"You heard me." Cole slapped a few bills on the bar and handed Shanghai a business card. "I was nothing but your stand-in. We didn't have what you'd call a real marriage." He stood up to go.

"Hey? You married her—without bothering to tell me she was pregnant. What kind of brother would do a damn-fool thing—?"

"She told you. Said you called her a liar. You and I weren't exactly close back then, remember?"

"Maybe you just saw a way to get a piece of the Spurs."

"What if I did? That's what a lot of people think. Since the plane crash, my memory's been fuzzy. It's coming back in fits and starts, but it's not perfect. I got hit on the head pretty hard. I think there's some damage. Bottom line, Mia and you have a humdinger of a daughter. I can't ever look at her without thinking about you. It'd be a shame if you never got to know her." Cole wiped the table off with his napkin. Then he yanked a stack of photographs out of his shirt pocket and slapped them in front of Shanghai.

Another blond stripper stepped onto the bar. Not that Shanghai looked up even when the two women began undulating to the wild, frenzied rock tempo as other cowboys moved closer to the bar to watch them.

The top picture was of a dark-haired little girl on a big red slide. One glance at it made scenes from Shanghai's past reshuffle themselves, and take on a disturbing new significance.

He saw Mia galloping behind his truck in his rearview mirror. He saw her at the Christmas Fling when she'd been a pretty thirteen. He saw her radiant face on his pillow, her red hair fanned out after they'd made love the first time in Vegas. He'd still been inside her when he realized that the course of his life had shifted because she'd made love to him. He hadn't forgotten how she'd felt or how she'd tasted, no matter how hard he'd tried, and he knew he never would.

Above him the women's graceful young bodies twirled close enough so that Wolf could slip wads of bills into their G-strings and grin his appreciation.

"I can't believe you want your kid to grow up motherless— the way we did," Cole said.

"Go to hell."

"Do you want your blood kin to grow up all Kemble? Is that what you want?"

"Damn it, Cole." Shanghai rubbed forehead and shut his eyes. "You just sprung this on me. A kid?"

Against his will Shanghai thumbed through the pictures. In another one the little girl was climbing a plastic mountain with handholds. In the third one she was a plump toddler splashing in a pool. In another she was naked playing in a muddy hole.

Damn it if the kid's eyes weren't the exact same shade as his and Cole's. And she had the cutest smile—Mia's smile. But his, too. Her hair curled just like Mia's used to. The rest of her was all Knight.

A wellspring of longing swept Shanghai.

Feelings that he didn't want to have for Mia rose up to swamp him.

They had a kid. The cutest kid in the whole damn world.

His throat caught as he slowly and very carefully set the pictures down.

He remembered his daddy beating and berating him. He wanted to be a *very* different kind of father.

He glanced through the pictures again. Then slowly he looked up at Cole.

"It's my fault she's down there. I was flying the plane. If you don't go I still have to. 'Cause I couldn't live with myself otherwise."

"Did I ever tell you how much I hate Mexico?" Shanghai's voice was deadly soft. "I hate it more than most anything."

"Then I take it you won't object if we make it a fast trip?" Cole said.

Wolf snorted as he raced down the long hotel hall after Cole and Shanghai.

"Are you two crazy? You hate Mexico and you're going

down there to break a woman you've been running from out of prison? She married your brother!"

"Who's the wuss now?" Shanghai jammed the piece of plastic that served as his room key into a slot in the door.

When the door opened, Shanghai kicked it wider. He went to the bathroom and scooped up his toilet articles. Then he stomped back into the bedroom and threw them into an oversize backpack.

"There, I'm done," he said, yanking the zipper closed. Slinging the backpack over his broad shoulder and grabbing his rigging bag, he headed for the door.

Cole chased after him.

The two brothers looked a lot alike except Shanghai was a bit broader, especially through the shoulders. He was bigger-boned, too, and a little swarthier.

"If the Mexicans find so much as one lousy bullet in your car, they can put you in prison for years and years," Wolf said, following them. "If they catch you trying to break Mia out of prison, you could get shot or arrested and tortured. Then there'll be three of you rotting down there instead of just one."

"Four," Shanghai slammed to a stop so fast, Wolf nearly ran into him. "We're not driving into Ciudad Juarez. We're flying straight in to the prison. Cole says we're going to need a helicopter, Wolf."

"That's the damnedest idea—"

"Remember that story you told me about when you flew into that hellhole in Kuwait and got your buddy out?"

"Hey—have you been listening to me at all?"

"Yeah. To every damn word. But it doesn't change anything. We've gotta get her out."

"What's this *we* shit?"

"If you're a wuss, Wolf, find me somebody with more try."

Wolf stared at him. "This isn't about try. This is suicide."

"You saw her pictures. That's my little girl, Wolf. Mia and

me, we're a mess. She lied to me. She did me wrong. But, hey, that little girl's pure angel. And she doesn't even know me." His voice softened. "Someday when she does, I want her to look up to her daddy. I don't want her to think I left her mommy to die in Mexico. Do you get that?"

"But…"

"Okay, Wolf. So, you can't do this. So, put me in touch with one of your craziest pilot friends—somebody who's got what it takes. Somebody with try."

Federico's eyes narrowed on Collins's gaunt face. Then he eyed the door of the posh Ciudad Juarez restaurant and bought more time by toying with his steak milanesa.

"You ask too much," he murmured when he met Collins's gaze again.

"Valdez, you and I both know that if a man has the right protection, he can do anything in Mexico. You own everybody who's anybody in this city. Why can't you get the *federales* to drop their charges against Mia Kemble?"

"I've tried."

"Try harder. If you don't, they want to go the other route. If they're forced to do that, can you buy them the protection they'll need?"

"To land a helicopter in El Castillo itself?"

"Yes."

"Even if this was something I wanted to do, your plan is *loco*. I won't help you and Mia's crazy husband bust her out of El Castillo."

"I broke your story, and now Morales is in prison. I nearly died doing it. I would have—but for Mia. I've got to do what I can for her. You got what you wanted. You owe me."

"I can't do it."

"If you don't, she'll die."

"So…lots of pretty young women die in this city. Write a story about her."

Federico sliced off a hunk of his steak and chewed silently. The meat was tough, and he had to work on it for a long time before he swallowed. Or maybe he was just stalling. Finally he met Terence's eyes again. "What you ask is very difficult."

"We were brothers once," Terence said.

"That was a long time ago."

"Those bastards were burning me with a cattle prod!"

"Okay. Okay. But you don't have much time." Federico tossed his fork onto his plate and bolted a shot of tequila. "This is complicated. There was going to be a break at El Castillo today. Some people on the outside bought land two hundred meters from the prison. They built a shack and then dug down through the rock until they hit some sewage tunnels. They used rag-covered tools so nobody would hear them. If you don't get Mia Kemble out before the prison break, it'll be too late. Another thing, Morales wants her dead. They're postponing the break, so he can send somebody through the tunnel into El Castillo tonight to kill her. After the break the authorities will seal the prison so tight that not even I will be able to help you. Can your people move that fast?"

"What choice do they have?"

When Cole, Wolf and Shanghai flew along the border, the bridge on the Mexico side and the El Paso side was backed up for three miles in both countries.

"It's worse than I thought," Wolf said, tensing as he stared down at the glistening vehicles. "Remember how I told you the U.S. government is fingerprinting anybody who looks the least bit suspicious before they let them enter the States—"

Wolf veered away from the river.

"Good thing we decided not to drive," Shanghai said.

Closing his eyes, he tried not to think about Mexico or Mia and all that lay ahead. He wasn't kidding himself. Bribe or no bribe, lots of things could go wrong and probably would. He could die. He could get her killed.

"Aw, hell." He'd given up the idea of dying old when he'd made bull riding his profession.

And Mia… Rotting in a Mexican prison had to be worse than a quick death.

He'd get her the hell out of Mexico or die trying.

So what if he didn't end up a skinny, old man in his nineties sitting out on his front porch in a rocking chair?

Ten

Some mistakes are too much fun to only make once. Dressing in drag wasn't one of them.

As Shanghai headed toward the pair of huge steel doors set centrally in front of a high stone wall, a man driving by in a rusty, red pickup swerved closer to the curb. Pounding the side of his pickup, the man let out a shrill wolf whistle.

Feeling like punching the macho bastard in the jaw, Shanghai cringed in what he hoped would be a feminine, coy come-on. Clutching his hot-pink purse against his fake breasts and tossing his curls, he walked faster, swinging his ass.

"Ey, gringa!"

Either the ass work was passable, or the poor, thickheaded fool was half blind. Shanghai knew he was too tall and too masculine to be very sexy in drag. The pointed tips of the cheap red high heels pinched his toes so badly they'd gone numb on him. He'd chosen the loose-fitting black dress and shawl to conceal rather than reveal. Still, this *hombre* dug him, which just went to show that a lot of guys went for *something strange*.

The lipstick, foundation and rouge made Shanghai's face and lips feel hot and greasy. The tight panty hose were so short they tugged at his balls with each mincing step. When he finally reached the doors, he rang the bell with one fingertip and waited with his other hand on a hip, just as Joanne had told him to do.

When he got through security, he signed in as Joanne. As the final guard looked him over, Shanghai held his breath. Hopefully Collins's friend had paid off the right people and he wouldn't be strip-searched.

"You're going to die tonight!" Raquel was screaming at Mia through the bars, her black eyes burning with hate as Mia finger-combed her wet hair.

Mia shuddered. She was a little chilled from having just bathed herself and washed her hair under a lukewarm faucet in the kitchen.

Suddenly a guard pushed past the crazy woman, unlocked the cell door and bawled out Mia's name.

"Kemble, you have a visitor."

Ignoring Raquel, Mia scurried after the wide-shouldered woman. "Who?"

"A woman."

Her mother, no doubt.

Happiness and an intense nostalgia for the ranch and her child flooded her as Mia rushed after the woman through the dusty courtyard. Five minutes later she was still smiling when she stepped into a tiny, gray-walled visitor's room with a single video monitor hanging on the wall. Then she raced eagerly toward the figure seated at the table. Only to freeze when the woman looked up and she met *his* steel-blue gaze. Mia's breath caught in her throat. Her heart knocked wildly.

Not Shanghai Knight.

Sensing her extreme reluctance toward her visitor, the guard chuckled sadistically and shoved her farther into the room. When the door slammed and Mia was locked inside with him, she backed toward the far wall. Hovering there, she twisted a strand of wet hair around her finger and then nervously tucked it behind her ear.

He stared at her, his mouth curling so insolently, she knew she must look terrible.

"Come here and sit down," he commanded coldly. "And smile. Show your dimples. Act like you're glad to see me. I signed in as your mother."

"Oh, my God." Her voice shook.

"Get a grip." His eyes flicked to the monitors. "They may be watching."

"I think they're broken," she whispered as she slowly made her way to the table.

With stiff fingers, she pulled out a metal chair and then fell heavily into the seat opposite him. For another long moment they stared at each other. His square-jawed face was leaner and harder than she remembered. His eyebrows were still as dark and rich as Texas soil. Despite his feminine attire, he seemed as ruggedly virile as ever. His skin was brown. His blue eyes were the color of cold steel. As always he seemed even bigger than he was.

"As soon as the sun goes down, be in the courtyard," he whispered.

"But they do a count and lock us…"

"They won't tonight. Your door will be unlocked." His mouth curled again, this time with a mixture of cruelty and contempt.

"What are you doing here when you clearly—"

"My personal feelings about you aren't relevant," he said.

"You don't even want to help me."

"This isn't about you or me or what you've done." His deep voice held world-weary cynicism.

"I've done nothing."

"Save that line for your mother. She believes your bullshit story."

"If you hate me so much, why are you here?"

"We have a child, a little girl you never bothered to tell me about. *Vanilla*." His voice softened when he said her name.

She swallowed. "I—I tried."

"Not hard enough." His voice was savage. Leaning toward her, he grasped her shoulders so hard, his fingers dug through the thin cotton bodice.

"You wouldn't listen."

"If you'd tried to tell me about Vanilla half as hard as you tried to get me in bed, I would have heard you. Then no way in hell would I have let you marry my brother!"

"Do you think I wanted to trap you?"

"I think you wanted to trap somebody."

Suddenly his eyes were on her mouth, and just as suddenly her gaze fell to his. Unwanted heat flared inside her, and she felt the wild tremor in his hands against her damp shoulders. It didn't matter that he wore lipstick or that hideously ridiculous wig. He was all male, and she was all female. And they both knew it.

She licked her dry lips. Even dressed as he was, his physical nearness had a devastating effect on her.

She wanted to hate him, but despite his self-righteous anger, his nearness stung her into a primitive awareness of him.

Nobody had ever made her feel half so much as he did. She'd grown up knowing he'd saved her life.

Against her will she remembered how many nights she'd dreamed of him.

She was a fool. A stupid, silly little fool.

When he finally let go of her, his mouth was bitter with self-disgust and loathing.

"This is supposed to be an official visit—generously granted to a grieving mother by the corrupt police *comandante*. I'm supposed to show you pictures of your little girl and my grandchild." His drawl smoldered.

He looked so ridiculous and ill at ease in his dress and wig, she couldn't resist a teasing insult.

"Nice outfit. Way better than mine. Can I borrow it—"

His shiny, painted lips tightened. "Don't—say anything!"

Scowling, he opened his hot-pink purse and began to rummage. Finally he dragged out the same stack of photographs her mother had already shown her.

"I was just kidding. You look bizarre." She bit her lips to suppress a smile. "Your shoes and purse don't match. You—"

"Good, then maybe you won't hit on me."

"No chance of that," she whispered.

"Really?" he taunted. "I spent half my life running from you."

Her stomach lurched.

"You think I'm trash now, don't you?"

Her directness rendered him speechless.

"I didn't sleep with Tavio," she whispered, frantic for him to believe her.

"I don't care!"

"Okay. I don't know why I bothered to defend myself— to you, of all people now."

With shaking fingers, she sifted through the pictures he'd handed her but blushed as she grew too aware of Shanghai watching her.

She hated him for being able to compel her just by sitting across from her.

"I hate you," she whispered in a low, seething tone. Then she instantly regretted saying anything.

"Good."

"If it weren't for that camera, I'd slap the hell out of you!"

"Tavio's obviously taught you a lot of nasty tricks." He laughed, and the sound was a rich rumble that infuriated her so much she stomped his toes under the table.

"Ouch, damn it! I'm your beloved mother!"

"Don't you dare laugh at me!"

He smiled.

"Don't you dare smile, either!"

"You'd better not step—"

When she kicked his shin harder than she'd stomped his foot, he grabbed her leg under the table. When she squirmed to pull free, his fingers dug painfully into her flesh, and he held on.

"I wish to hell you'd figured out how much you disliked me before you seduced me and got yourself pregnant! Because—now for better or worse—we're stuck with each other!"

"You can leave for all I care!"

Spreading his fingers wide against her bare skin, he ran his powerful hand up her thigh. "Is that really what you want?"

When his hand lingered caressingly on the inner part of her leg, she grew warm.

His fingers inched up to her panties. "You like me touching you, don't you?"

Unable to deny it, she went still.

Having proved his point, he grinned and then slowly removed his hand.

"I don't ever want anything from you again," she said.

"You want out of here, don't you?"

He must have taken her silence to mean yes.

"You're not calling the shots anymore, darlin'. I am. Listen because I'm only going to say this once. You have to do exactly what I say. Exactly. Your life and *mine* depend on it."

The chopper hovered above the courtyard and then banked sharply. As guards in the gun towers sounded sirens and mounted rifles onto their shoulders, the chopper dropped like a bomb into the postage stamp-size courtyard, causing a dust storm that made dirt and rocks fly in all directions.

When Mia ran toward the helicopter, Chito suddenly appeared in the opposite corner of the courtyard and took aim at her. Her only chance was to keep running, so she did.

Somebody in the helicopter opened fire, and Chito jumped back behind a doorway. Guns blazed. Bullets ricocheted off the walls, pinging when they hit the chopper's rotors.

The pilot's eyes were enormous. She read the exact moment he decided to abort the mission.

"Shanghai! Shanghai!"

Shanghai looked down at her as she raced toward him, her arms outstretched, her eyes pleading.

They were going away! Shanghai was going away!

As the chopper began to climb, she began to scream.

"Don't leave me, Shanghai!"

The helicopter was eight feet above the ground and spiraling upward rapidly when Shanghai jumped.

Chito fired again.

Landing beside Mia, Shanghai grabbed her by the waist and rolled with her. Chito continued firing at the chopper until it disappeared over the walls. Then he ripped his empty clip out and ran. Without giving Chito time to reload, Shanghai grabbed Mia's hand and dragged her to her feet. Raising his gun, Shanghai ran right at Chito.

"What are you doing?" Mia yelled. "That's Chito! Tavio's right hand man! He's the hitman who's come to kill me!"

"He's our only way out then. The bastards have a tunnel somewhere. They're planning a break. Since your friend got in that way, he's gotta know where it is. I can't kill him till he shows us the way out!"

When Chito stopped, Shanghai dropped to his knees and fired twice, aiming high deliberately. "Make tracks, you little shit."

The tunnel was airless, and Mia had to fight against her fear of suffocation. She could hear Chito's panicked footsteps stumbling and thrashing up ahead of them as Shanghai pulled her through endless dark passages. The ceiling was so low, she bumped her head several times. The walls were so nar-

row she scraped herself against them again and again until she
felt all wet and sticky. She fell so many times, she was sure
she was going to have bruises everywhere.

As she ran, she heard little squeaking sounds at her feet.
Rats? She held on to Shanghai's hand tightly, fearing they'd
find worse at the end of the tunnel.

The tunnel grew even narrower. She felt trapped and so totally claustrophobic that she wanted to scream endlessly.

Would more of Tavio's men be waiting for them? Or would
Chito lay in wait to kill them?

Miraculously when they emerged, they found themselves
alone in a crumbling cardboard shack in the midst of many
others that served as makeshift homes for the homeless. A
plastic chair with only three legs lay toppled on its side. A
child's dusty red crocheted cap dangled from a nail. Chito was
gone.

She was gulping in fresh air when she looked at her hands
and saw that they were covered with blood.

Suppressing a scream, she held up her hands so Shanghai
could see.

"Chito's hit, I think. That's probably why he cleared out,"
Shanghai whispered, his breathing as hoarse as hers.

Dogs barked as Mia and Shanghai crouched in the shack
gasping to catch their breath. Chickens cackled outside. People were talking in the dirt street.

Cautioning her to stay down, Shanghai held a finger up to
his lips. Before she could protest his leaving her, he was on the
other side of the tarp that served as the door. When she heard
shouts and he didn't come back, she began to shake uncontrollably.

Suddenly the shack's walls seemed to close in as the tunnel's had. It was all she could do not to run out of the shack
calling for him.

Finally he stomped back inside, looking as fit and cocky
as ever. Miraculously he had a bucket of water and a rag.

"Wash your hands."

When she'd cleaned off the blood, he tossed her several dark pieces of cloth.

"Put those on."

Despite his gruff tone, she stood up and touched his forearm—just to make sure he was really okay. For a long moment, her hand refused to stop shaking as she clutched him.

"I was scared you weren't coming back."

"Don't be ridiculous! Just dress!"

When she hesitated, he drew a quick, impatient breath. Flushing darkly, he jerked his arm away from her.

As her hands began fumbling clumsily with the fabric, she felt a flare of fresh resentment. She turned the dark-colored garments over. "What—"

"A skirt and a blouse and a shawl so you'll blend in. I stole them off a clothesline. Damn it, hurry!"

Aware of his eyes glittering in the dark as he watched her, she stripped to her bra and panties. Trying not to think about him, she hurriedly pulled on the black skirt and blouse.

"Cover your hair," he said, his voice harsher and raspier now.

When she'd wrapped her hair in the shawl, he grabbed her and pulled her outside.

"We've got to get to the river," he muttered, still in that same furious tone that hurt her somehow.

"Shanghai—"

"Shh."

"Thank you," she whispered, "for jumping."

His dark face tensed.

More than anything she longed to throw herself into his arms and feel his strength. She wanted to be cradled against his chest, to be made to feel safe. But his expression was so grim, she steeled herself and pretended she felt stronger than she did.

"Feel like a swim?" he said.

* * *

The Rio Grande River felt cold. The night was dark with a thin cover of clouds. Clutching the small inflated rubber ring Shanghai had given her, Mia swam slowly and was careful not to splash.

Swimming wasn't easy. The tube was barely enough to support her with her heavy clothes weighing her down. Then she heard shouts—whether from the U.S. or Mexico, she wasn't sure. She stopped swimming, readying herself for spotlights or bullets.

The shouts died, but a damp chill quickly settled in her lungs while they paused, treading water.

"Don't stop," Shanghai muttered. "You're not a free woman till you're on the other side. If the Mexicans catch you now, they'll throw you back in prison."

Then Tavio would send Chito again. He wouldn't fail the next time.

Her muscles ached. Her right leg cramped so painfully, she couldn't kick with it. When the pain became excruciating, she fought against her panic.

Swimming with one leg soon had her exhausted. Ignoring the razor-sharp cramps that practically paralyzed her entire right side, she kicked with her left leg.

She had waited sixteen months for this. She couldn't give up.

A soft splash was followed by Shanghai's low curse.

"Damn."

"What?"

"I dropped my cell phone."

She remembered him trying to make several calls earlier that had failed.

"Wouldn't it be all wet anyway?"

"I had it in a dry pack…in case something like this happened and we had to swim and walk out. I was going to call for a ride to the Golden Spurs as soon as we made it across the river. Cole and Wolf would have come back with the chopper. I'm afraid it's going to be just you and me till daylight, darlin'…and whatever new friends we meet out here in the dark."

"Maybe we'll find an American garbage truck…."

"You have to admit it would damn sure beat walking."

Shanghai had flagged down a Mexican garbage truck after they'd left the shack and bribed the driver to take them out into the desert away from Ciudad Juarez to some remote spot where the river was narrow and shallow and easier to cross.

"The *federales* are looking for a *gringa* who escaped from El Castillo," the driver had told them as Mia had hunkered low in her seat beside Shanghai.

Shanghai had tossed a one-hundred dollar bill on the dash. "My wife and I want to cross the river tonight. We're homesick for our little girl."

The driver had snatched the bill. "I have no love for the *federales*. They steal my best truck. They fine me many times."

The road out of town had been narrow and dark. He had to swerve several times to avoid horses or cows in the road. As he'd driven, he'd told them unnerving stories about people murdered and women raped along the river.

"You be careful on the river, *mano*. *Ees* very dangerous place. Bad peoples there. Many bad peoples. Every day bodies float to the shore. Many people they all want one thing—to get out of Mexico, but they were murdered. You be careful on the river, *mano*."

Something slithered past her under water. *A snake? A body?*

"Don't stop," Shanghai said in a terse, low tone. "Swim faster!"

Even as pain shot up her paralyzed leg, she didn't argue. When they finally made it to the opposite bank, Mia thought she heard whispers in the high reeds. Shanghai must have heard them, too, because he pulled out his pistol. With his other hand he helped her climb through a stand of Carrizo cane and then up a muddy bluff. When they stepped into a little clearing, he pressed a finger to his lips, warning her to stay low and to be quiet, for there was no telling who might be around to attack them or rob them.

"Are you scared of the Border Patrol?"

"We wish. This is a no man's land. You heard our chauffeur. All sorts of thugs lie in wait for whoever swims across to steal whatever little money they have."

Mia remembered the garbage man had said most of the bodies found along the river were never identified.

"We need to head north—fast," he said.

Shoving his pistol into his waistband, Shanghai grabbed her hand.

Eleven

As the ink-black night closed in all around them Mia clamped her teeth together so they wouldn't chatter. Staring ahead at the shadowy, seemingly endless moonscape, she almost wished they hadn't left the glow of El Paso behind them.

"I feel like we've walked forever," Mia said, gasping slightly as she stumbled against a bush that was sharp and prickly.

He ignored her.

"Ouch!" She rubbed her arms. "And I'm still cold from the swim, too."

When he kept trudging silently onward, she persisted in trying to get his attention. "Stop a second, so I can dig a rock out of my shoe and get this burning thorn out of my ankle."

"Burning is it?" he asked in a smart-ass tone. But he knelt beside her and asked which ankle. Once told, his hand was warm and firm and very thorough. Before she knew what had happened, he was standing up again with the thorn in his hand. "Okay, no more burning thorns. No more excuses."

In the dark, his gaze was intense as he loomed tall and handsome above her. Just as she had as a teenager, she found him extremely sexy.

Oh, why can't I just grow up and tune this attraction out?

"Thank you," she replied, feeling angry at him suddenly as she knelt to shake the rock out of her shoe. "Where are we anyway?"

"South Texas. The middle of nowhere."

"I know that already," she snapped, still mad that she found him attractive.

"Then why'd you ask?"

She stood up and dusted her hands on her skirt. "Sorry to be such a bother."

"We'll get along better if you just keep moving."

Easy for him to say as he surged past her on his long, lean legs, clueless as well as careless of her feelings. Not wanting to be left behind, she quickened her steps. Soon she was panting in an effort to keep up.

They hadn't gone far when she heard the engine of a car right behind them. In the next moment Shanghai grabbed her hand and yanked her into a ditch hidden by a stand of prickly pear and yucca. Within seconds a pickup truck without headlights lurched past them off-road.

"Friends of yours," Shanghai said, his tone caustic.

"What?"

"Drug runners. We're lucky the sharks didn't run over us in the dark."

She sucked in a breath. His sudden anger was so unnerving, she fumed silently as she sat beside him for the next twenty minutes before he finally decided it was safe to proceed again. Once they began walking Mia's sulkiness toward him eased, and she was simply thankful she'd gotten to rest. They passed a bailout car, its doors still ajar from the fateful moment when the Border Patrol had caught up to it and its occupants had fled on foot.

"So many come from so far and fail to make it," she said in a forlorn tone.

Shanghai didn't comment, but the car must have served as

a warning to him because he picked up his pace again. The desert land was so rocky and eroded, and his strides so lengthy, it was difficult for her to keep up, therefore she had to run every few steps. For half an hour or more they climbed the gradual slope of a big hill at his relentless pace, although he did pause, if impatiently, when twice she begged him to let her rest.

The stops did little good. Soon she was so tired, she felt like she was sleepwalking. Still, Shanghai trudged on with her lagging even farther behind. When they finally reached the crest of the hill, a sliver of moon was visible through the thick clouds. All she could see for miles toward the north was more of the same rugged terrain.

"It looks like pretty empty country," he said, "but it's illusory. There's no telling how many illegal immigrants are furtively walking northward under cover of the night just as we are. Or how many drug runners or terrorists."

She shivered.

"Or criminals seeking to escape Mexico," he added, staring at her for a long moment.

"I'm not a criminal."

Without further comment, he turned and began walking faster again.

"I can't go any farther," she finally yelled after him between gulps of air. Then she stopped and dug another rock out of her shoe. "I'm hungry, cold, tired, wet and confused."

"Shh." Instead of listening to her, he was peering through a small pair of binoculars into the darkness ahead. Then he slid the binoculars into his back pocket. "You got that rock out of your shoe yet?"

"Can't we just stay here?"

He turned to her and took her hand in his. "I'm sorry you're tired. But don't give up on me now, darlin'. If we get lucky, I don't think it'll be too much longer." Gently he pulled her along, this time at a slower pace.

Soon she was shivering convulsively again. "Where are we going now? Why can't we just sit down until the sun comes up?"

"Because I have a better idea."

"What?"

"Over there." He pointed ahead.

She squinted. "I don't see anything."

"Trust me."

"That's not so easy."

His glittering gaze locked on her face. "Tell me about it."

She looked away, struggling to conceal her feelings.

When they began walking again, the landscape soon broke into endless ripples of eroded gullies that were difficult even for Shanghai, who was wearing boots instead of flimsy shoes to navigate. Another half hour passed before they finally came to the edge of the thick clump of scraggly bushes he'd pointed out to her.

"Good—I thought so. We've found a deserted cabin."

"I don't see anything but salt cedar."

"Over there. In the trees. Probably it's a hunting camp," he said.

When they got nearer, she made out a flat-roofed structure. The tiny dwelling seemed blacker than the darkness of the desert and equally uninviting. But at least she could stop walking. Then she realized they'd have to spend the night together alone in that tiny cabin.

"I don't like it," she said as they got nearer.

"Well, it's not the Ritz, I'll give you that. It's not your clean and tidy bedroom at the Golden Spurs, either. But you've been pestering me pretty steady to stop, so you should be happy."

She was about to make a smart retort, when he put his finger to his lips. Then he pulled his gun out of his waistband. Warning her to hide behind a salt cedar, he snuck up to the cabin and tapped lightly on the door. When nobody answered, he knocked louder. Then he twisted the knob. When the hinges groaned and the door swung open easily, she heard him chuckle. A match flared, and the cabin windows began to glow like faint beacons.

Not wanting to be left alone outside for another second, she raced onto the porch so fast the boards groaned noisily. She stopped before carefully crossing the threshold to join him in the moldy-smelling cabin. For a long time they were both still, listening to the quiet. She, of course, had an ear out for rats, and much to her relief, instead of the scurrying of little feet or squeaky cries, all she heard were her own frightened heartbeats.

A single candle glowed in the center of a small table. In the dim light, she made out a small bed, a couple of old quilts, several folding chairs stacked against the wall, and, of course, the table.

"Home sweet home," he said, grinning at her.

"Not exactly."

"Well, I for one hope the three bears don't come back anytime soon," Shanghai said. "Because I'm dog-tired."

"Finally. I thought you were going to walk forever."

He laughed.

On the table she saw a sheet of white paper beside the candle. Leaning down, she softly read the owner's brief note aloud, first in Spanish and then in English.

"Welcome. My house is your house. Take what you need. Clean up after yourself. There's a cattle pond right behind the house if you need water. Just leave things as you find them, and leave the note to welcome my next guest. Jimmy Morgan."

She replaced the paper.

"Sounds like Jimmy's real tired of being broken into by illegal immigrants crossing the border," Shanghai said. He moved across the cabin and kicked several empty tin cans that were piled in a corner. "See, he's had recent visitors. I see why he just leaves the doors unlocked."

"I hope we don't get any company tonight."

"What? Not in the mood to entertain?"

Two strides carried Shanghai to the crude, built-in cabinets sagging from their nails on the far wall. He opened them and pulled out several cans and pots and pans and a bar of soap.

"Pork and beans? Ravioli? Spaghetti? Fruit cocktail? Soft drinks? What'll you have tonight, darlin'?"

"We can't just eat his food."

"A while back you said you were hungry. Be grateful we don't have to live off mesquite beans and prickly pear apples. I'm not in much of a mood to shoot and clean a rabbit, either."

She was studying the narrow bed. It was just big enough for two—if they snuggled up really close.

"How can you think about food?" she whispered, suddenly feeling nervous of him in the dark.

He stared at the bed, too. "You got a better idea?"

Something in his voice made her cheeks heat, and that irritated her. Did he assume she found him so attractive she would be easy to seduce the instant it suited him?

"No. I just didn't think I should steal his food."

"I guess that means you're not going to help me gather wood so I can build a fire and cook it."

When she didn't answer, he smiled. "Okay. While I'm gathering the firewood alone, why don't you see if you can find a can opener?"

Shanghai stomped outside. After she found an opener, she heard branches and twigs snapping outside. Picking up the opener, she carried it and the cans out to him. She also brought cans of soda she'd found. After giving him a can of soda, she began breaking up the limbs he tossed her into kindling-size pieces. As always, doing something with him soon became fun.

In no time they had a fire blazing inside a circle of rocks where other fires had been lit before at a safe distance from the house. He poured the beans she'd opened into one pot, and spaghetti into another.

For a few minutes they sat together watching the orange fire dance as the branches crackled. "You've been saying you were cold all night. Move closer so it will warm you," he said.

She did, and clasping her knees to her chest like a small child, she stared into the flames and found them hypnotic.

"Think you can watch the pots so they don't scorch on the bottom while I bathe?"

The instant he said he was leaving she felt stricken, but she squared her shoulders and nodded bravely.

"Good girl." He handed her his gun. "You used to be a crack shot. Shoot first. Ask questions later."

"Right." She nodded.

When he left her and went inside again and got soap, a metal bucket, and one of the blankets, she set the gun beside her.

Five minutes later, she heard boots crashing through the scrub behind her. Since she wasn't expecting him back so fast, she whirled and aimed the gun at the sounds in the darkness.

"It's only me, darlin'. But I'm glad to see you're so alert."

Smiling despite herself because he was back, she lowered the gun. She tried to ignore her pleasure in his company. She tried not to notice how his black hair was damp and slicked back, too. Or how he'd wrapped the blanket around his lean waist and wasn't wearing anything else.

When he set the bucket in the coals her eyebrows arched questioningly. "What's that for?"

"Warm water…for you…in case you decide you want to freshen up inside the cabin before or after we eat."

"Thanks," she whispered, more touched by his thoughtfulness than she wanted to be.

He walked over to the porch and hung his wet clothes on the porch railing. Something must not have been right because after staring at them, he picked them up, one by one, and started over.

"What are you doing?"

"Trying to hang them so they won't wrinkle up so bad."

She laughed.

"I don't iron too much on the road."

Leaning forward, she dipped her hands in the lukewarm water and rubbed them together. Then she washed her arms off, too.

"I had a bath…earlier," she said when she was done.

"I know. You smelled sweet like soap in the waiting room."

So, he'd noticed something nice about her during that awful visit. She smiled and looked up at him. He was still on the porch fiddling with the way each item of clothing was laid out.

He caught her watching him and stopped dead still. Quickly she looked away. Then her stomach growled, embarrassing her further.

"Sorry," she said, blushing shyly.

He laughed. "You sound hungry."

She nodded. "Ravenous." For some reason she was unable to take her eyes off him.

"Me, too."

He returned to her side, and they spoon-fed themselves steaming spaghetti and spicy beans out of the pots without bothering with the tin plates she'd seen. Once when a noodle dribbled out of her mouth, he smiled. When she sucked it inside her lips, he laughed out loud.

As they sat together, enjoying their meal, she could feel the tension draining out of her. For so long, she'd been afraid.

No sooner had she eaten a few spoonfuls of spaghetti than exhaustion overwhelmed her.

He seemed to sense how tired she was. Leaning over, he took her spoon and set it down on a stone. Then he wrapped his big hand around hers and helped her up. When she stumbled over a rock, she felt his hand move to the small of her back to steady her. "Careful now," he said as he guided her inside the cabin.

She liked the kindly concern in his voice and manner even more than the warmth of his fingers against her spine.

"I'll get the bucket of hot water," he said as she sank onto the bed.

The promise of hot water was tantalizing.

When he returned, the water sloshed a little as he set the bucket beside her at the foot of the bed. Then he turned to go.

"But where will you sleep?" she asked.

"Outside. On the porch. That way I'll hear…"

"On the wooden boards?"

"I've slept in the rain in pickup beds when I started out rodeoing." Suddenly he leaned down and rustled through his backpack. Returning to the bed, he pressed a soft cloth into her fingers. "You can use this old T-shirt of mine as a wash rag. It's still a little damp from our swim."

Bone-weary, she took it. The thought of her bathing seemed to upset him. He turned abruptly, went outside and closed the door behind him. For a long moment she sat there. Finally she dropped the rag in the bucket and wrung it out. Again she paused before pressing the steaming cloth against her face. The heat against her skin seeped inside her and felt too delicious to believe. She closed her eyes and savored the wonder of such a simple comfort as warm water.

Hardly knowing what she did, she unbuttoned the bodice of her dress and unhooked her bra and ran the warm rag across her throat and breasts. Undoing more buttons, she bared more skin and stroked more of herself with the soothing hot rag. Slipping out of her dress, she washed herself all over. Sighing, feeling almost human again after her bath, she redressed and lay slowly down on the narrow bed.

The mattress wasn't soft, and it didn't smell too good, but unlike the prison, the cabin was quiet. There were no screams or babies crying. Slowly she became aware of the porch boards creaking as Shanghai moved about outside. A faint smile flickered across her face. Even though he could be impossible at times and think the worst of her, just knowing he was so near made the horror of Mexico recede a little.

Funny, that she hadn't heard him make a sound until she'd stopped bathing and had lain down. Suddenly he moved, and she saw his shadow clearly through a small window near the front door that she hadn't noticed before. Had he watched her?

If he had, she hoped he didn't think she'd stripped to deliberately entice him. But if he did, what could she do about it?

"Good night," she called softly, too tired to worry about anything anymore, even winning his good opinion.

"Good night."

His deep voice sounded strange and hoarse, but it was a comfort. Smiling, her last thoughts of him as she closed her eyes, she was asleep instantly.

At some point she began dreaming. She was on the yacht with Tavio. Again she was looking over the stern at the skeleton bobbing in the water. Suddenly the skeleton jumped onto the boat and chased her, bones rattling, flames shooting from its eye sockets. Then she screamed and Tavio was there.

When he grabbed her, she pushed him away and ran, screaming in terror. Desperate to elude him, she hurled her blanket off and began stumbling about the cabin, wildly bumping into things. Not knowing where she was, she crashed into the table.

"Easy darlin'."

She was still half asleep when she focused on the tall, dark shape of a man wrapped in a blanket looming in the doorway.

"Tavio?" She choked out his name, her muffled voice fearful.

"So you dream of him?" Shanghai's jealous comment bit like a snake from across the darkness.

Shanghai? Even though he sounded furious, her heart lightened.

Not trusting what she saw, she blinked and continued to stare at him. He glared at her in turn. Relief flooding her, she ran toward him and flung her arms wildly around him.

"Damn it!" He pulled back. "Don't touch me when you're dreaming of that thug."

Disoriented, she closed her eyes, and then opened them again.

"It was only a dream then?" she whispered, still not quite believing her good fortune. "You're real." She clutched him tighter even as he tried to recoil from her.

"Don't be mad at me—please. I was having a nightmare. It was so awful." Her hand slid down his chest, her splayed fingers feathering through the wiry dark matt of hair. "I was scared. Out of my mind. But now I'm okay…because you're here. Because you came…to Mexico. You saved my life…. You don't know what it was like…down there…with him… all these months."

Shanghai pulled back a fraction of an inch.

"I felt so hopeless…until you came…until you jumped from that helicopter. Chito was minutes away from killing me."

Hugging him closer, she clung to his lean waist and pressed her cheek into his bare chest. Even though he was stiff and unyielding, she heard the thundering of his heart beneath her ear. His skin was so hot, as hot as hers. With only the blanket to cover him, the bulge of his sex against her thighs told her all she needed to know.

"I feel so utterly safe with you." Her lips brushed his chest. "Like this."

"It's okay," he said on a sharp intake of breath as she nibbled at his skin.

"Because you're here." She laid her head against his chest again. "I'll never be able to repay you for this. Neither will Daddy."

He sucked in another sharp breath.

"I'm sorry I mentioned Daddy."

Shanghai cursed beneath his breath and then was silent for a long time.

"You'll be home tomorrow," he finally said, but his deep voice was tense again. "With your family. Then you'll be safe."

"But you came. They didn't."

"I wouldn't make too much of that." Again he tried to loosen her arms and lead her back to her bed.

"No…. Just hold me. Stay with me. Don't ever let me go."

"I don't think that's such a good—"

"You always reject me. Why?"

"Because, damn it…just because."

"I need you so much. I don't want to, but I do. I always have."

"It's too soon for this kind of talk between us."

"Or not soon enough. When you live day after day thinking it may be your last, you're afraid not to say the things you feel…when you feel them, because maybe you'll never get another chance. That's something I learned in Mexico. And I feel so much right now…for you."

"Mia…"

"Until you came I didn't dare to hope for any happiness ever again. I lived moment to moment. You've given me my life back."

"Cole and Wolf were in the helicopter, too."

"You jumped. Does that mean that you like me…just a little?"

His eyes blazed with an emotion that made the blood pound in her temples. He opened his lips and then stifled a gasp, and said nothing.

What did he feel for her? Why wouldn't he tell her?

"When I woke up alone in here I was so scared," she whispered.

"You'll be fine."

"But for how long? The Mexicans have brought serious charges against me. What if they try to extradite me?"

"The Kembles are too well-connected for that. How do you think I got into that prison?"

"What do you mean?"

He circled her waist with his arms, which thrilled her because he was no longer trying to push her away. "Let's just say certain people were handsomely rewarded."

She snuggled closer to him. "My family's involved with corruption in Mexico?"

His hand caressed her throat and sent waves of warm tingles everywhere. "Don't be naïve. That's the way things work a lot of the time—even up here."

"So, what are you telling me?"

"The guys in the gun towers had blanks in their rifles. Everything was going great until your friend, Chito, started shooting at us."

"You jumped."

"Anybody would have done the same thing."

"Would they? You saved me once before. You dove under Daddy's truck. Old Man Pimbley said if he hadn't hollered, Daddy would have run over your head."

"I get on bulls, remember. I'm a glutton for punishment."

His hands continued stroking her hair.

She shuddered. "Tavio saved my life, too. When I was drowning, he jumped into the gulf and risked his own life to save me. But then he thought I belonged to him. He made claims that you never made. I didn't want to belong to him. I wanted to go home. And he wouldn't let me."

"Morales took you against your will then?"

Shanghai's deep voice held such soft menace, and the dreadful question stirred such terrible memories, she began to tremble.

"N-no."

When Shanghai pushed her away, she flinched at the intensity in his gaze.

"He never touched me! Not once! I swear!"

"You swear? Well, I don't believe you, Mia!" He began to shake his head. "What kind of fool do you take me for?"

"You want to know something? Bad as he is, Tavio Morales has a better opinion of me than you do! That's why he never touched me! He wanted me! But he never touched me!"

Shanghai was still shaking his head. "Don't do this, Mia. If we have to discuss him, can't we wait till tomorrow?"

"Tomorrow? Why does everything always have to happen when you say? I think I have a better chance with you tonight!"

"Hell." He combed a lock of black hair out of his eyes. "You sense weakness and you go for it! I can't stand the thought of you with Morales!"

"Well, maybe neither can I!" Her voice softened. "I want you so much, Shanghai. I want you to believe me, too." She put her hand on his chest again, stroking his bare shoulders and then his throat. "You have to believe me!"

He was listening intently, his blue eyes filled with a fierce longing as they roamed her face slowly.

"I've always wanted you, Shanghai. There's never been anybody else for me! Not him! Not anybody!"

"Stop it!" he yelled. "Do you really expect me to believe that? I'm a lousy bull rider. You're a Kemble."

"You're the father of my only child."

He took a step back. "Look, I can't be with you like this. Not now."

"Why? Ever since you pulled me out from under Daddy's tire and I stared up into your eyes, I've wanted to be with you. Why is that so wrong when I know you want me, too?"

"It just is. Go to bed. Get some sleep. You'll know I was right in the morning."

When he took a second step back and then turned to go, she felt like her heart was breaking. They had always communicated much better physically than they did verbally. If she didn't find a way to make him stay tonight, she might never get another chance.

"Shanghai—I'm scared. Don't leave me— Please don't—"

She paused. "You know something…something crazy. Sometimes when I was really scared in Mexico, I used to cry out to you. And…and I used to think that you heard me. Sometimes I even heard your voice. It was like you were there."

Shanghai turned white. The intensity in his gaze took her breath away.

"I know it sounds crazy, but more than once you gave me the courage to hang on."

Twelve

Damn. She wasn't even touching him, and yet he felt so connected to her.

"Shanghai, I'm serious—it was like you were there…with me in Mexico," she whispered.

He'd felt it, too. He'd been sure he was crazy. But just her saying it now tugged at his heart again.

His pulse thudded so violently, he knew he should run. Instead he remained in the doorway as unable to move as if she'd turned him to stone with a spell.

"Shanghai. Don't leave me. I'm scared. I really am."

Bullshit.

And yet deep down he felt concerned about her. Why was he such a fool for her?

His gaze slid hungrily over her slim form. Too slim. Had Morales mistreated her? Shanghai hadn't wanted to think about that as he'd gazed at the rounded curve of throat and shoulders, her narrow waist and the swell of her hips. Hell. If he hadn't just seen her naked when she washed herself, he might be in better shape. Did she know how crazy she was driving him?

Yeah. She probably knew. No doubt the striptease had

been calculated. Not that he hadn't wanted her even before he'd accidentally glimpsed her bathing through the broken windowpane. That's why he'd felt such anger when he'd visited her in prison. Whether he had been manipulated or not, the memory of her breasts lit by lamplight while she'd caressed herself with his wet T-shirt would be engraved in his brain forever.

He'd willed himself to stop watching her and then had stood rooted, unable to move, until she'd dressed and had collapsed on the cot. After that he'd figured maybe he was safe for a while. Then she'd had that damn nightmare that had led to him holding her when he'd worn nothing more than this thin, scratchy blanket. After petting her and having her literally beg him for it, he was rock-hard and burning up.

He wanted her velvet skin beneath his palms; he wanted his tongue inside her so he could taste her. Being Mia, she was quick to sense his weakness.

With a wild cry, she raced across the darkness, stopping mere inches from where he stood. Then shyly she placed her hands on his chest. At first she was tentative, her light fingertips trembling as they moved upward and looped around his neck. Because of her tremors, his arms closed around her, and he pulled her close. When he whispered soothing words against the back of her neck, she clung to him, her fingers ruffling through his hair.

He was losing the battle, sinking fast. Men were weak. At least he was. Beneath her touch, his skin grew hot. When Mia buried her face in the hollow of his throat, and her hips rose to cradle him, he felt himself swell and grow harder. He squeezed her tighter, and still she couldn't seem to stop shaking. Silently, he half carried, half led her back to bed.

"Last chance," he murmured. "Go to sleep."

"No. Lie with me here."

Her soft seductive tone took his breath away as she took his hand and pulled him down beside her against the heat of her length.

"You've had an awful ordeal," he muttered, staring at the ceiling, trying to ignore the impulse to rip his blanket off and strip her so he could feel her skin against his. "But it's over."

She turned on her side. He felt her warm breath against his forearm before she kissed him there.

At the touch of her lips a jolt went through him. Numb with pleasure, he kissed her open mouth.

"Is it over? Will it ever be over? What if the authorities make me go back? What if Tavio comes after me? His people cross the border all the time. He knows about *you.*"

"Knows what?"

"That I care for you." She kissed his arm again, and the second jolt was electrifying. "I—I told him you're dead. But if he finds out I lied—"

"Hush. You're safe with me now."

"You don't know him. What he's capable of."

"He can't be worse than a smart, bad-assed bull rider, now can he?"

Just lying beside her had him on fire. Still shaking, Mia nuzzled closer and pressed her warm, seeking lips against his arm. Just his arm! If she did it again, he would explode.

"He's a murderer. He and his men have even killed women. There was this girl…Delia—" Her voice broke on a sob.

"Don't," he warned on a savage breath as he rolled over to face her. "Stop talking about him for God's sake!"

"I would if you'd kiss me."

"Oh, God." His hands began to caress her tangled hair. His lips brushed her forehead.

"Shanghai." Even as she sighed from his caresses as if in bliss, she moaned in frustration. "On the lips!"

Suddenly he couldn't take it anymore, either. Cupping her chin gently, he took her lips in a searing kiss. Mouths fused.

Tongues mated. As wildly glorious as ever, she began sucking on his tongue.

He shuddered. He felt the kiss in the pit of his stomach, in his aching groin—everywhere. *Where the hell had she learned to do that?*

In between breaths he managed a question. "Why do you have to be so damn beautiful?

"Most men wouldn't object to that," she teased.

"I don't usually."

"So it's just me."

"Yeah."

"You watched me bathe, didn't you? You wanted to touch me, didn't you?"

"You little minx."

"Well." She sounded pleased. "That's something then."

"This will end badly—like before," he warned.

"Maybe you don't know everything." She shifted so that she faced him and ripped off his blanket. He felt her eyes before her hands ran over his body. When her fingers touched his penis and began to make slow circles at the tip, the pleasure was too much.

He grabbed her hand. "My turn," he growled, "to strip you."

She sat up, and he pulled her blouse up and over her head and tossed it onto the top of his blanket. In seconds her panties, bra and skirt had joined the heat. Then he devoured her pale beautiful body with his gaze.

She twisted a little and opened her legs. Running her hands through his thick black hair, she pushed herself into him so that he lodged between her legs. Then she kissed him.

"Why do you have to be so damned sexy?" he muttered a long time later.

"Only with you."

"I wish. I think of you with other men sometimes like that thug, and it drives me crazy. How many…"

"Nobody but you."

"Like hell."

"Why is it so hard for you to think you're so special to me?"

Grabbing a fistful of her red hair, he pulled her closer. When his penis probed the wetness between her legs, she sighed.

"I see no bull's gotten the best of you yet."

He grinned. "The keyword being *yet*. A friend of mine got his privates stomped into bloody pulp."

"You've got to stop that ridiculous business, you know. You're not a kid anymore."

He hated the age difference between them as well as the thought that she might consider him old.

"I decide when I'm ready to retire."

"I just hope it's before some rank bull decides to kill you!"

He tensed.

"Okay. Okay," she murmured. "You decide. Forget I said anything. Just hold me and caress me." Her hands found him again and began to move.

He stuck two fingers inside her. "God, you're wet."

"Of course."

"Damn!" He sat bolt upright. "If we do this…"

"If—" She stroked him playfully, arching her body toward his with a playful cry.

"I've got to protect you."

Swiftly he got out of bed and stalked outside to where he'd thrown his backpack down. He ripped open a plastic packet and slid the thing on. When he returned, his hands came around her gently. Spreading her legs apart so that she straddled him, he lifted her up on top of him and pulled her down, down until their bodies snugged together and his shaft was lodged at her damp entrance. He told himself to go slowly, but suddenly, he was as frantic to have her as she was to have him.

Her long hair swished against his face as he reached up and fastened his mouth on hers, this time with a soul-devouring passion. When she opened her lips, his tongue plundered her lips.

He kissed her again and again, drinking in the taste of her.

"I want you inside me—now," she begged, sliding herself against him. "Now."

His breathing grew harsh. "You do it then."

She slid a little, and he lunged upward at the exact same moment. With a deep sigh Mia sank down, down and then with him locked inside her, she began to rock back and forth on top of him. Leaning down, clouds of her hair falling against his face and shoulders, she kissed his mouth very tenderly, and her gentle kisses drove him wild.

It had been so long, and she felt so good that soon he lost control.

As his climax began to build, she sobbed, crying out in soft rapturous moans. Happiness flooded him, the kind he'd been seeking his entire life. He wanted to stop, to hold on to the exquisite moment, to make it last, but he couldn't.

When he suddenly exploded, she screamed and clung tightly, her body shuddering.

His climax went on and on, and so did hers. Even when it was over and they were both limp, he held on to her tightly, wanting to stay inside her as he stroked her back.

In the aftermath he felt profound tenderness. At the same time his intense feelings scared him.

"You screamed Tavio's name when you slept. Did you fantasize I was him just then when we had sex?"

With a wounded cry, she jumped off him. "How can you ask that—now?"

"Is that why you were so wild?" he muttered.

"Don't ruin it," she whispered brokenly.

"I know what I heard."

"Fine. Think the worst of me—like always!" She pushed him away.

When he got up and grabbed his blanket, she let out such a howl he jumped.

"What was that about?"

"You! Why can't you be an easy guy?"

"Easy like you?"

"Get out!"

"Gladly." He strode outside.

"Where are you going?"

"I need some air." He knew he was using anger in some unfair way, but his unreasonableness only made him more furious—at her.

"Fine."

"Fine?" Feeling all mixed up, he whirled and then thought better of what he'd been about to say.

"I hate Tavio! What does it take for you to figure out I'm crazy about you?"

"Maybe—that's only 'cause I'm the one in your bed tonight, and you're horny. Did you crave him in bed, too?"

"That's the way you probably are!" She threw a can at him, and it zinged past him. The second one bounced against the wood and rolled across the cabin floor.

Feeling explosive, he slammed the door. Then he yanked his stiff, wet jeans off the railing and stepped into them.

"Shanghai—"

Ignoring Mia, he struggled into the cold denim that clung to his flesh, sticking to certain parts most unpleasantly. Then he sank down on the steps and pulled on his wet socks. It took all his strength to tug on his boots since the leather was swollen from having gotten wet in the Rio Grande.

When he heard her featherlight footsteps on the other side of the door behind him, he stiffened.

"Not more cans, I hope."

She eased the door open and crawled on her knees until she came up behind him. Cursing, he yanked even harder at his boots.

When she got so close to him that he felt her body heat, he held his breath. After a moment or two, when she deemed it was safe, she laid her head against the middle of his back.

"What are we doing?" she murmured.

Acting like a pair of lunatics.

Oh, God, she felt soft and warm, and her silken hair tickled his bare skin. It would be so easy to turn around, to melt into her sweetness and lose himself again to the pleasure only she could give him.

Too damn easy.

His need for her tenderness and love was so acute, he was an easy mark. With immense difficulty, he clung to his anger.

"I'm sorry," she whispered. "I—I shouldn't have come on so strong."

"Me, too," he said, but so roughly and with such little sincerity, she recoiled.

"I'm not like this with other men," she said in a frightened undertone.

He didn't argue this time, but maybe he should have. A few seconds later when she ran her fingers through his hair a powerful jolt made him want to kiss her so badly he hurt. Instead he jerked his head away.

"I—I don't know what to say to you," she said. "Is some of this because you're mad about me marrying Cole?"

"No! He told me all about that."

"We didn't have a real marriage."

"I said he told me. For your information he's not legally your husband anymore. He's married to Lizzy."

"What?"

"Your daddy and he had you declared dead. Leo Storm consulted teams of attorneys. The majority opinion is that Cole's second marriage is legal—not yours."

"Is this about you then? Are you mad because you're in love with somebody else?"

Abigail. Guilt hit him like a blow. He gulped in a savage

breath. He hadn't even thought about her once since he'd jumped into that courtyard.

"Hell, no!"

But Mia wasn't buying it. "Why, that's it." She sounded strange and sad.

The last thing he needed was to think about Abigail right now, and he damn sure wasn't going to talk about her to Mia. No matter how all this came out in the wash, Abby was the last person he wanted to hurt.

"I need to be alone right now," he muttered. "Okay?"

Mia made another one of those awful strangling sounds behind him that cut him up.

"Okay."

Again he heard the hurt in her wounded tone.

Damn it, he didn't want to stomp all over her feelings when she'd already been through so much. He was behaving like a jerk.

Hell.

"I'm going for a walk in the park," he said. "You stay put."

"In the park?"

"It was a joke, okay?"

"One I don't get."

Cursing silently, Shanghai sprang down the stairs. Without looking back at her for fear of succumbing to her again, he headed north into the wild desert, losing himself within seconds in the dense sagebrush and thick darkness.

He stabbed his hands through his hair. What was his hang-up with Mia Kemble? He'd spent the better part of his life determined to avoid her. Now, no sooner had he bedded her than he felt like she owned him body and soul. Hell, here he was madder at her than ever but as hard as a pike again, too.

Had Abby ever turned him on like this or made him feel half so much? Had any woman? Somehow in just a few hours, Mia had gotten under his skin so deep, he felt she was clawing out his guts.

Was this love? Whatever it was, it damn sure had him feeling twisted inside.

From the moment Cole had told him about Vanilla and his reason for marrying Mia, Shanghai had known he was in too deep and sure to sink even deeper.

Sometimes it seemed he'd been running from Mia all his life. His first impression of her in the prison visiting room came back to him. Her golden eyes had been huge and glassy; her cheeks pale and hollow. Her thinness in that awful prison uniform that had clung to her in limp, dirty tatters had terrified him.

Even though he'd been nasty, he'd felt an instant surge of protectiveness toward her. Tonight he felt those same feelings all over again, only more deeply. She had him trapped some way, just like Bad Boy had had him when his gloved hand had gotten tangled in his rope.

She was the last woman he wanted to get involved with. The very last. It wouldn't work. Sure, he had deep feelings, but he had damn good reasons for avoiding her. He needed to find a phone and call for help and rid himself of her fast before she really sank her hooks in him.

When he returned, the cabin was so quiet and dark, *that* scared the hell out of him. His pulse racing with the fear he'd find her gone, he sprinted through the door only to hear her breathing steadily.

She was asleep on the cot. As he gazed down at her, her thin face framed by clouds of hair, never had she looked so sweet and vulnerable. It was all he could do to resist the impulse to lie down beside her and cradle her in his arms.

He let out an exasperated sigh.

Was he dumb or what?

He was a bull rider.

Bull riding wasn't a career bright men chose with great regularity.

Hardly knowing what he did, he leaned down and kissed

her brow. Then he covered her with a blanket before he went back outside to sleep alone on the porch.

The tension in the library of the big house on the Golden Spurs felt as thick and heavy as a bowl of oatmeal that had sat out too long. Nobody felt more uptight than Terence Collins, especially when he stared at the poignantly happy family photos set out on several library tables, which were in stark contrast to the present mood in the library. He kept watching the phone, willing it to ring. Willing it to be *them*.

If Mia or Shanghai died, he'd feel a personal responsibility.

He needed a cigarette in the worst way. Naturally Joanne Kemble didn't allow smoking inside her house.

As a result of an acute nicotine deficiency, coupled with his gnawing guilt, the cherry walls and the tall bookcases were closing in on him. If he'd been wearing a tie, he would have been yanking at the knot. Still, ever the journalist, he couldn't help studying the white-knuckled crowd jammed too tightly onto the leather couches. He had to admit this was a helluva story.

Joanna Kemble had barely said a word to him since their brief conversation after he'd arrived and she'd coldly thanked him for arranging for protection in the prison so the helicopter could land. He'd apologized for not notifying her before the article came out. He'd said he was sorry about the hit man in the courtyard, who'd started shooting and had caused Wolf to abort the rescue.

She'd stared at him coldly. "Who knows," she'd finally said, "what's right or wrong? If Mia lives, I'll be in your debt forever. If she doesn't, I may track you down someday and kill you."

For some reason Terence found himself watching Joanne. Although she was a widow, her grief didn't show—if she'd ever even felt grief. Remembering Caesar's affair with Electra, he wondered how much Joanne had known and if she'd loved the bastard at all.

Terence was surprised at how sexy he found the aloof Joanne compared to Electra, who'd been known for her wild sex life.

Electra had been too free and too selfish and too self-absorbed. Funny, that he of all people would object to that. He eyed his daughter, Abigail. Maybe he knew better than anybody how such independent, self-serving spirits could damage those they loved most.

What an arrogant bastard he was! Me! Me! Me! Even now when maybe his cocky journalistic tactics and his desire to write something that could shock might get Mia Kemble killed, here he was at the story's center, waiting like a vulture.

You were only doing your job.

Right.

Life was always about choices and he'd made a lot of wrong ones.

Joanne was tall and regal—cool and contained. She wore her streaked, red hair in a loose chignon. He'd seen pictures of her, of course, but she was much more striking than her photographs. Her jeans were as tight as a girl's and her shape was perfect. Her boots were custom-made. Her cream silk blouse was buttoned all the way to her throat. Damn, if she didn't look like a total tight-ass.

Strangely the thought of her being prim and proper in bed turned him on. Not that a woman as rich as she would look at him. Especially when he'd been the one to write the article that had endangered her daughter—even if doing so proved to be the first step to free her.

Shanghai's half-black trainer, Wolf, who exuded excessive machismo, paced back and forth along the back wall. He was clearly very concerned about the fate of Shanghai and Mia. His frown grew deeper with the passing of each hour.

Cole and Lizzy sat hunkered together, holding hands, talking mainly to each other on a low couch near a window that looked out onto a palm grove.

Palm trees? Why did anybody bother with them? They didn't provide a lick of shade and they were hell to prune. And when they froze, the damn things died. Not that you could tell a dead palm from a living one.

He forgot the palms and watched Abigail, who'd persuaded him after much arguing to accompany her here to wait for Shanghai, her soon-to-be fiancé. Although Terence hadn't met this rodeo character, he heartily disapproved of him. The man probably screwed every buckle bunny in the West.

He'd been playing with Abby's feelings. The bastard had bought a ring and then had refused to give it to her.

Terence of all people should have understood men who couldn't settle into a life of marital routine and dull domesticity. But hell. What father wouldn't want a more reliable sort of husband for his daughter—a doctor or a lawyer maybe?

Terrence shuddered to think how the families back East would react when they learned of Shanghai's profession. They'd blame Terence, of course, for moving to south Texas, a place they still considered a godforsaken wilderness. Just as they'd blamed him when the barbarians had kidnapped Becky.

He hated the way Abigail fitted in at the ranch so well. She talked to everybody as easily as if she'd grown up here, even Leo Storm, the CEO, before he'd flown back to San Antonio.

Being a reporter Terence eavesdropped to catch tidbits of conversation. Not that he hadn't heard it all already. When there was no new news, people tended to repeat themselves, speculating uselessly. Still, there was always the chance for a new slant on the facts.

"—I told you, Knight jumped—"

"—the thug kept shooting—"

"—hit him maybe—"

"—they could be anywhere—"

"—why the hell don't they call—"

"—it's been hours—"

When everyone stopped talking after the last comment, Joanne got up and pressed her hands together. "I'm going out to my birds." Her smile was thin and controlled, but her pretty brown eyes were moist with pain.

Had he caused it? A wave of compassion hit Terence. He remembered the frantic hours after Becky had vanished…and the dull days and then the weeks and years that had become forever. Then he and Dora had turned on each other.

Mia's plane had gone down sixteen months ago. Joanne had been through a lot already—even before he'd pulled this stunt.

Joanne turned and smiled wanly to the group in general. The golden lamp lit her face and eyes, and he thought that even in this hour of sadness and uncertainty, she was as beautiful as a girl. It struck him that he hadn't thought like this about a woman in years.

He jumped to his feet. "Mind if I tag along, Joanne?" Was he insane? "Mind if I call you Joanne?" And getting more insane?

Frowning, she hesitated a fraction of a second. It was clear that she didn't want him.

He was a pushy guy. "It's a yes/no question," he said, backing off. "I'll understand—if the answer is no."

"Would you now?" Looking doubtful and yet mildly curious, Joanne's brown gaze lingered on his face in a way that gave him hope.

As the flicker of initial excitement inside him burned hotter, he forgot he wanted a cigarette. After what seemed an eternity, she lifted her chin and smiled.

The birds cooed, but Joanne wasn't thinking about her darling birds. She was trying not to be too obvious as she watched the rough-cut man who stood outside the aviary on the concrete apron—smoking.

She certainly hated cigarettes, but when he'd asked if he could smoke, she'd said okay, as long as he stayed outside.

She didn't understand her interest in him. A short time ago, she'd loathed him for writing that article. Then he'd left the hospital against doctors' orders and had gone to Mexico where he'd talked to some mysterious connection of his on Mia's behalf, and her feelings had changed.

He was brilliant—a genius. But reckless. Thoughtless, too. So thoughtless and self-absorbed.

All this she knew. She loved order and tidiness, and he dressed sloppily, almost like a homeless person. Still, she sort of liked the way his shirt and slacks and silver hair were rumpled. His body was still lean and hard, and the world-weary cynicism in his faded blue eyes intrigued her.

He had suffered as she had, and it showed. She wanted to know why and how. There were lines of bitterness beneath his eyes and beside his mouth. She knew what it was to arrive at a certain age and to be thoroughly disillusioned and brokenhearted by life.

He flipped his burning cigarette onto the ground.

God, did he have to do *that?* She grimaced when he squashed the butt out with the heel of a worn shoe that badly needed polishing. Nasty habit, she thought, smoking. And yet sometimes there were so few consolations in life.

Who did he think would pick that butt up? He didn't look rich enough to have servants. Obviously the thought of ever tidying anything never occurred to him.

He was not her type. He'd arrogantly put her child in danger without the slightest regard for that fact. He was a writer, a writer she'd admired. But he was conceited about his writing. He thought it was more important than people's lives. As a writer he would be forced to spend his life indoors with books and papers, and she was an outdoors person.

So, why had he fascinated her from the moment he'd stepped inside the library? When she'd been so determined to dislike him?

He was brave. Morales had tortured him, had nearly killed him. Even injured with hits out against his life, he'd gone back to Mexico and struck that deal to save Mia.

All day she'd felt his burning blue eyes watching her as intensely as Jack's used to. Nobody had looked at her in such a way in years. This untidy, indoor man—an intellectual, an arrogant man she could have gladly strangled a few days ago, made her feel excited, and rawly alive…and young.

It was as if during all the long, dull years of her impossible marriage, she'd been waiting for something like this to happen.

So what was she going to do about it?

Nothing. Except talk to him.

For once in her life she was going to be smart when it came to men. The wind stirred through the trees outside the aviary, and still he didn't come inside. She wondered if he was as nervous as she was. Wing Nut was barking somewhere among the trees a long way off, no doubt chasing a squirrel or a rabbit.

Mia was still gone, maybe lost forever—again. She felt the loss keenly. She should be at the house, waiting for a call. But sometimes it seemed, all she'd ever done was wait.

How could she, at her age, be here with such a man?

Simon would laugh, gloat even, if he knew about this little "incident," which he wouldn't. Not ever. Simon was her hairdresser in Corpus Christi, who'd masterminded her new look. He'd talked her into reddening her hair. He'd given her a new haircut and dyed her lashes and recommended the surgeon, who'd given her her recent minilift.

When Terence opened the door, forty of her white darlings, mad with panic, fluttered to the rafters while her own heart beat madly.

"Sorry," he whispered. "You've got a lot of birds."

"Too many some would say."

He smiled at her.

"I started with a pair."

"Sex is the most powerful force in our world."

The air between them sparked hotter.

Caught off balance, she pretended a calmness she was far from feeling. "Every time I order a new addition to the aviary, Kinky and Sy'rai joke about overpopulation."

"I'll bet they love your birds, too. Who wouldn't?"

"Then you like them?" Why did she care?

Joanne's pulse raced even faster as Terence stepped closer to her. When he didn't say yes or no, when he simply kept looking at her as if she were all that mattered to him, she wrung her hands nervously.

She caught the scent of tobacco and found it oddly pleasant on him. Her father had smoked.

"What's it like, being a reporter?" she finally managed before their silence grew really awkward.

"Like a drug addiction. I write about what I care about. I don't make much money. Making money is the thing my family does best, so they think I'm a failure. I find myself fighting losing battles. It's difficult, too…because you sway opinion by what you say or don't say. Then sometimes it's difficult because you write about things that can hurt people. Like my story about your daughter. I scared the hell out of you. You're still scared, and I have to live with that. I'm sorry. If anything happens—"

She held up her hand. "If you hadn't written it, she'd still be with Morales."

His blue eyes flashed. "Hold that thought while you endure the hell of waiting." He swallowed a long breath. "Mostly I've been a champion of lost causes. It cost me my wife, and one of my daughters."

"So you lost a daughter?"

"Kidnapped in Mexico."

"Because of something you wrote?"

"Maybe. But maybe because my family is so rich."

"And still you keep on being a reporter?"

"I'm not the type to learn from my mistakes."

Neither was she, apparently, or she wouldn't be here right now with him.

"Or maybe you believe in what you do." She looked away, through the screen walls at the new barn. "I lost that in my own life a long time ago."

"How?"

"The man I loved died. I married his brother. I settled, you see. And I paid for it. And so did Caesar. So did our children. We lived a lie."

"Don't most parents try to keep their secrets?"

"Then it all came out when Caesar made such a fool of himself over Cherry."

"Ah, the stripper. That must have been hell for you."

"It's over now."

"When we're young we think we can have it all, but we always pay for our sins, don't we?" he said.

"And then some."

When he reached for her, she wasn't surprised. His hands were smoother than Caesar's and Jack's, and oddly she liked that.

She should have moved away. Yet, somehow she couldn't.

What surprised her was the explosive tumult his kiss caused inside her. The moment his lips touched hers, she was a stranger to herself. She forgot that her duties lay with the family and the ranch. She forgot Mia entirely, and her long-starved body made its own demands. Her mouth clung to his. She opened her lips, wanting to taste him despite the cigarettes.

He was the car wreck that alters ordinary life in a single blinding heartbeat, the telephone call in the middle of the night that destroys a world.

When he'd asked if he could join her, she should have screamed no and fled. He was flagrant temptation, and she was an utter fool.

But she didn't care. One taste of him, and it was too late. She'd come alive in his arms. She could no more have resisted him than a moth can the flame. She had been bored, crushingly bored with the sameness of her existence for far too long. And too tense from worrying so long about Mia.

She was tired of waking in the dead of night and lying in her bed until dawn, her heart filled with despair, knowing that she was getting older and feeling lonelier. No, it was much better to make love in the sunshine with her birds cooing in her aviary.

The taste of cigarettes was not as repulsive as she would have imagined. The roughness of his unshaved chin was somehow erotic. The touch of his hands, which were surprisingly big and flexible and powerful as they gripped her or caressed her, aroused and compelled her. When he ripped pins from her hair so that it cascaded about her face and shoulders, her blood began to hum.

She knew she shouldn't let him pull her skirt up and her panties down in the aviary, that the phone might ring, and that Cole or Lizzy might come. But for the life of her, she couldn't stop him. Were those her fingers on his zipper?

When he cupped her butt in his hands and opened her legs so he could fit himself to her, she stood perfectly still.

On some level the thinking Joanne Kemble couldn't be letting this rough, rude man she didn't even know, a man who'd played God with her child's life, screw her in her own aviary where anybody could walk up and see them. But she wanted this—him—too badly.

When he plunged inside her, she knew an insane, reckless joy. She was a kid on a circus ride, thrilled beyond belief.

"How very strange this is," he muttered in a voice that was thick with passion as he drove into her.

"Yes. Yes!"

When he finished a few moments later, he stayed inside her and kissed her feverish brow. For a full five minutes he held her before he pulled her panties up and her dress down. "I'm going now."

"Slam bam," she teased.

He didn't laugh. "Anyone could come and find you. Then you'd really hate me."

"I don't know about that."

He cast a warm glance at her upturned face. "This isn't over, for me, either, you know."

His blue eyes seemed to stare straight through her. Caesar had ignored her. With this stranger she felt connected and alive.

"I've never done anything like this before," she confessed, savoring the way the balmy air caressed her face.

"I know. This is new for me, too."

"I don't believe you."

"Your choice."

"Nobody can know about this," she said.

"All right. You know I think I'd promise you anything." He kissed her again. "I won't tell anybody you're so wicked and wild." Then he opened the door and was gone.

She leaned back against the wall and began to struggle with her hair. Somehow she had to get back to the house without anybody seeing her.

For another long moment she stayed. She closed her eyes and listened to her birds coo.

Thirteen

A new, red sun burned away the desert haze and glinted off Shanghai's black hair as he cooked their breakfast. Mia stared at him in anguish, her need for one kind word or one tender glance tearing at her.

Why couldn't he smile? Just a little smile? What would that cost him? Instead his dark, unshaven jaw was set in a stubborn line, and his hard face was as stern as death.

What had she done that was so wrong? Other than love him?

Why had he come to Mexico and saved her? Why had he been so passionate and tender? Had the sex merely been a wild, lustful act for him?

If only she'd been that lucky.

When he'd stalked out angrily into the dark, she'd lain down on the bed and hugged herself tightly. The familiar nocturnal sounds of cicadas singing and coyotes yelping had terrified her. The blackness had closed in upon her until she'd felt she was suffocating. And still he hadn't come back. Lying there for what had seemed like hours, she'd never felt more lonely or abandoned.

What had she done to deserve such treatment other than love him?

YOUR PARTICIPATION IS REQUESTED!

Dear Reader,

Since you are a lover of fiction – we would like to get to know you!

Inside you will find a short Reader's Survey. Sharing your answers with us will help our editorial staff understand who you are and what activities you enjoy.

To thank you for your participation, we would like to send you 2 books and a gift – **ABSOLUTELY FREE**!

Enjoy your gifts with our appreciation,

Pam Powers

SEE INSIDE FOR READER'S SURVEY

What's Your Reading Pleasure...
ROMANCE? _OR_ SUSPENSE?

Do you prefer spine-tingling page turners OR heart-stirring stories about love and relationships? Tell us which books you enjoy – and you'll get **2 FREE "ROMANCE" BOOKS or 2 FREE "SUSPENSE" BOOKS** with no **obligation to purchase anything.**

Choose **"ROMANCE"** and get **2 FREE BOOKS** that will fuel your imagination with intensely moving stories about life, love and relationships.

FREE!

Choose **"SUSPENSE"** and you'll get **2 FREE BOOKS** that will thrill you with a spine-tingling blend of suspense and mystery.

FREE!

Whichever category you select, your 2 free books have a combined cover price of $11.98 or more in the U.S. and $13.98 or more in Canada.

And remember... just for accepting the Editor's Free Gift Offer, we'll send you 2 books and a gift, ABSOLUTELY FREE!

YOURS FREE! We'll send you a *fabulous surprise gift absolutely FREE, just for trying "Romance" or "Suspense"!*

® and ™ are trademarks owned and used by the trademark owner and/or its licensee.

Visit us online at
www.FreeBooksandGift.com

Offer limited to one per household and not valid to current subscribers of MIRA, Romance, Suspense or "The Best of the Best." All orders subject to approval. Books received may vary. Credit or debit balances in a customer's account(s) may be offset by any other outstanding balance owed by or to the customer.

YOUR READER'S SURVEY
"THANK YOU" FREE GIFTS INCLUDE:

▶ 2 Romance OR 2 Suspense books

▶ A lovely surprise gift

PLEASE FILL IN THE CIRCLES COMPLETELY TO RESPOND

1) What type of fiction books do you enjoy reading? (Check all that apply)
○ Suspense/Thrillers ○ Action/Adventure ○ Modern-day Romances
○ Historical Romance ○ Humour ○ Science fiction

2) What attracted you most to the last fiction book you purchased on impulse?
○ The Title ○ The Cover ○ The Author ○ The Story

3) What is usually the greatest influencer when you <u>plan</u> to buy a book?
○ Advertising ○ Referral from a friend
○ Book Review ○ Like the author

4) Approximately how many fiction books do you read in a year?
○ 1 to 6 ○ 7 to 19 ○ 20 or more

5) How often do you access the internet?
○ Daily ○ Weekly ○ Monthly ○ Rarely or never

6) To which of the following age groups do you belong?
○ Under 18 ○ 18 to 34 ○ 35 to 64 ○ over 65

YES! I have completed the Reader's Survey. Please send me the 2 FREE books and gift for which I qualify. I understand that I am under no obligation to purchase any books, as explained on the back and on the opposite page.

Check one:

| **ROMANCE** |
| 193 MDL D37C   393 MDL D37D |

| **SUSPENSE** |
| 192 MDL D37E   392 MDL D37F |

FIRST NAME   LAST NAME

ADDRESS

APT.#   CITY

STATE/PROV.   ZIP/POSTAL CODE

▶ DETACH AND MAIL CARD TODAY! ▶

(SUR-MI-05) © 1998 MIRA BOOKS

The Reader Service — Here's How It Works:

Accepting your 2 free books and gift places you under no obligation to buy anything. You may keep the books and gift and return the shipping statement marked "cancel." If you do not cancel, about a month later we'll send you 3 additional books and bill you just $4.99 each in the U.S., or $5.49 each in Canada, plus 25¢ shipping & handling per book and applicable taxes if any.* That's the complete price and — compared to cover prices starting from $5.99 each in the U.S. and $6.99 each in Canada — it's quite a bargain! You may cancel at any time, but if you choose to continue, every month we'll send you 3 more books, which you may either purchase at the discount price or return to us and cancel your subscription.

*Terms and prices subject to change without notice. Sales tax applicable in N.Y. Canadian residents will be charged applicable provincial taxes and GST.

If offer card is missing write to: The Reader Service, 3010 Walden Ave., P.O. Box 1867, Buffalo, NY 14240-1867

BUSINESS REPLY MAIL

FIRST-CLASS MAIL   PERMIT NO. 717-003   BUFFALO, NY

POSTAGE WILL BE PAID BY ADDRESSEE

THE READER SERVICE
3010 WALDEN AVE
PO BOX 1341
BUFFALO NY 14240-8571

NO POSTAGE
NECESSARY
IF MAILED
IN THE
UNITED STATES

Only when she'd heard his footsteps on the stairs had she closed her eyes. When he'd come inside, he'd stared at her for such a long time. Why?

His lips against her brow had been sweet and tender, soothing her worst fears. Maybe he didn't hate her after all. Only now after that kiss, she was more uncertain than ever.

What was going on with him? Did he even know? As she stared at him, the silence between them grew excruciating.

When he kept staring stubbornly into the pot of beans, she finally had had enough. Why did he always get to control everything between them?

"S-so—where did you go that awful, rainy night when my daddy ran you off fifteen years ago?"

For a second or two he looked startled, like a wild animal caught without cover. Then he turned away and kept stirring the beans.

"I said where—"

"Lots of places," he muttered off-handedly. "What difference does it make to you?"

"I guess you don't know an answer like that is the same as saying nothing."

"I guess I do. Maybe I prefer silence." He pierced her with a look.

"Why? Do you have to be so rude to me?"

He sucked in a breath. "You don't quit, do you, darlin'?"

"That used to be the thing you liked about me the most."

"Things have changed." He subjected her to a thorough, intimate appraisal. When she felt his insulting gaze on her breasts, her nipples peaked against the thin fabric of her blouse.

He frowned and turned back to the beans.

"So, back then what was…your favorite thing about me?"

Again he let his dark glance drift from her face, down her body, lingering on her breasts too long. When his gaze returned to her mouth, she bit her lip. Quickly he yanked his eyes away again.

"You were nice to me," he muttered. "You were a sweet kid."

"And now that I'm all grown up—"

"The beans are bubbling," he said.

What was he really thinking? Did he want her again? Did he hate her for that? Himself? For months in Mexico she hadn't wanted to be touched. Now she craved to have Shanghai's arms around her. She wanted his kindness again, but if all he would give her was sex, she'd probably settle. But that wasn't new. That was her curse.

He poured her some beans. Then he slammed the spoon down in the tin bowl, which he handed to her.

"That looks good," she said. "Thanks for letting me sleep until I woke up…and for building the fire and for cooking and for everything."

"You've got nothing to thank me for. But since you're so dead set on pestering me with conversation, darlin'— When I left Spur County, I wanted to ranch, of course."

So now, to avoid her more intimate question about his feelings for her, he would deign to answer her first question.

"But the pay was too low for even a hand like me to live on. If there hadn't been room and board, I would have starved. I couldn't save a dime. I felt like I was nothin' workin' like that, livin' day-to-day. I felt even worse than I had back at Black Oaks working our land with Cole and Daddy. But you wouldn't know how it feels to know you're nothin', being a rich Kemble, now would you?"

It was on the tip of her tongue to lash back that that was how she'd felt the whole time she'd been powerless in Tavio's compound.

"It sounds miserable," she whispered, her low voice compassionate.

"You Kembles always strutted around like you thought you were better than everybody else, like no matter what we did, we couldn't measure up."

"No, that's not how… That's not how I ever felt. You have to know that."

He looked at her again, his stare intense and searching. "Well, one day I collected my pay and hitched a ride to the nearest rodeo, which was in Abilene, Texas. I paid the entry fees, and to my surprise I won more than my investment, so to speak. So, that's how I got my start rodeoing. After that, I never looked back."

She winced. She'd thought about him all the time. "What about Cole?"

"I was too wrapped up in surviving to think much about anything else. I pretty much focused on riding well and staying alive."

"You get hurt much?"

"Sooner or later everybody who rides bulls gets hurt, darlin'. At first you think you're invincible."

"Did you break bones?"

"A few. I've got an injured arm right now. I mainly just ignore it. What hurt worse was burying one of my best friends."

"What was his name?"

"Hank. He was twenty-six and the best damn bull rider that ever lived."

"I'm sorry."

"It was a few years ago." He paused. "Five to be exact. Since then I've seen a lot of country. I used to tell myself I kept ridin' for him. Did you know they have dizzying, razor-walled canyons in Utah?"

"I don't think I've ever been to Utah."

"It's beautiful. The plateaus of the Sangre de Cristo Mountains of New Mexico are mystical. You feel taller, and your shadow's longer. You think the world is endless. The Painted Desert in Arizona is really somethin' to see, too."

"What was your favorite place of all?"

His mouth thinned. "I'm not much of a tourist. I don't guess I think like that."

"So—you were all het up to sue Daddy the night you left. You forget all about that?"

He glowered at her, and she almost wished she hadn't asked that question.

"You goin' to badger me all mornin'?" he snapped. "Or are you going to eat? Your beans are getting cold." He grabbed a bowl for himself and spooned himself some.

"About the lawsuit…"

"Okay. I'll admit I festered a while. For quite a while. I even reassembled some of the old documents. But then rode-oing kind of took me over. You can't ride bulls or broncs and be halfhearted about it. Otherwise you can't make a living. You work out and train all the time to stay in shape. When you're not doing that, you're on the road, driving nights or sleeping in back seats while your buddies drive. Some years I traveled one hundred thousand miles and rode in more than one hundred rodeos. That's lots of lonely highways, truck stops, dried-out burritos and crummy motels, when you're flush—pickup beds when you're broke. In the beginning it was mostly pickup beds."

Guilt washed over her that it was her father who'd driven him away from his home.

He must have read her feelings because he smiled sheep-ishly, and said. "Aw, hell. Don't feel sorry for me. Your daddy did me a favor. Like I said, I've been luckier than most. If I'd stayed in Spur County I'd still be broke. I'm a world cham-pion several times over, and I've bought a ranch with my prize money. I'm addin' to it and stockin' it with rough stock all the time. Things are looking up for me, darling!"

"So, you never even think about maybe coming *home?*"

His dark face went still. "After a few years, it didn't seem like there was anything worth going back to Spur County for."

"Oh." She felt faint, sick almost.

"Black Oaks is a part of the Golden Spurs now."

"What about me?"

What a naïvely romantic little fool she'd been. And still was. Last night had meant nothing to him.

Her throat tightened. Suddenly she found conversation with him as tiresome as he apparently did.

Struggling to regain her breath and remain cool and collected, she set her spoon down with a clatter and stood up. "I think I'll take a short bath in the cattle tank after all."

"What? We need to head north. The sooner I get you back to your family, the better I'll feel."

The sooner I scrub every place you touched me last night, I'll feel better!

"I won't be long. I promise," she said sweetly.

Shanghai stared at the dove-gray sky and then at the ashes of the fire as he paced the porch while he waited for her. He was done boiling water and packing the canteens in his backpack. He'd straightened the cabin as best he could.

I won't be long. Famous last words.

At first Shanghai was annoyed by the wait. Then when he yelled her name, and she didn't answer, he grew alarmed as he thought about all the sorts of critters, even the two-legged variety that were attracted to watering-holes. Especially when there was a naked lady involved.

He pulled his gun out of his waistband, and took off at a brisk trot for the pond. When he reached the thick sage and salt cedar that edged the water, he crouched low and held the gun high.

Then he saw her.

Fully dressed, she was standing perfectly still beside the pond watching a golden cougar drink on the opposite side. She didn't seem the least bit afraid of the huge predator. Her eyes sparkled when several deer loped by. His attention on the cat, even though deer, its natural prey, seemed plentiful enough, Shanghai kept his gun out as he stole carefully up to stand beside her.

She smiled when she saw him. "I was hoping you'd come and see this. It's like the Garden of Eden."

The image of a man and a woman naked in a wild kingdom flickered on the edges of his testosterone-charged mind.

"We've got to go," he said in a low, abrupt tone.

"I didn't want to turn my back on him."

He aimed his gun toward the cat.

"No— Don't shoot him—"

He fired two rapid shots. The bullets pinged off rocks a yard or two to the left of the cougar. Instantly the cat leapt into the sage, vanishing as quickly as a shadow when the sun goes away. Soon there were only faint rustlings in the brush as the big animal moved through it.

"Why—"

"It's best not to get too familiar with them. Best for them, too."

He thought she would argue. Instead she said, "It's so beautiful here, I'm sort of sorry to leave."

Her whiskey-dark eyes devoured him, forcing him to remember last night. He'd had fun here, too, with her. More than he should have. The memories were still eating him up.

"It's so beautiful, isn't it?"

The childlike wonder in her eyes aroused all the emotions he didn't want to feel.

A lot of people would have seen only rough hills dotted with prickly pear and a few scrawny mesquite trees. He, too, found the land too beautiful—especially this morning with her beside him.

"I used to watch the birds fly over the hacienda and long to be free. Now here I am. Free. Because of you. I can never repay you, Shanghai."

Nor I you, he thought.

Shanghai couldn't stop staring at her. She was so close he could see every individual eyelash and every pore of her glowing, creamy skin. Her red hair was damp and curly, and unruly tendrils blew about her flushed cheeks. Her throat glistened with dewy moisture from her recent bath. He remembered watching her bathe herself last night. He remembered how she'd writhed on top of him. She was driving him crazy.

As he glared at her, she looked uncertain for a moment—until her pretty mouth quirked with flirtatious mischief. Sensing her power over him, she shot him an innocent, wide-eyed stare. Then she quickly lowered her lashes.

He couldn't take his eyes off her. His head pounded as he fought an inner civil war to deny his desire for her.

Failing, he moved closer, close enough to touch her. "This doesn't make any sense."

"What?"

"You and me," he said. "We're natural-born enemies."

"Really? Is that what we are?" She began to laugh.

"Don't tease me."

"Sometimes I can't help myself."

"You always were a brat." He put his arm around her.

"You said I was a sweet kid."

"*Very* sweet," he whispered, touching her cheek with the pad of his thumb. "God, I've been a rude bastard, haven't I?"

"Well, at least you know. So, are you going to apologize?"

"I'm sorry. So damn sorry."

"Saying so isn't enough. Let's kiss and make up."

Cupping the back of her head, he lifted her face to his. When his lips touched hers, she opened her mouth. His tongue slid inside, and he pulled her closer. Instantly he was made dizzy by the taste of her and by the feel of her breasts against his chest. Without thinking, his hands caressed their fullness until her nipples ripened in his palms.

Awareness of the exact spot where her pelvis arched against his fly, made desire race through his body like an electric shock.

God.

"You're asking for it—again," he muttered.

"Is that what I'm doing?" She laughed at him. "I thought you were doing the asking."

"Not in a million."

"Okay then. Fine. Let me go!"

When she pushed at his chest, he swung her into his arms.

"Not in a million." He carried her back to the cabin, stopping on the porch to kiss her again.

He'd thought to make the kiss brief before taking her inside, but when his mouth seared hers and she moaned, he shuddered. All his anger and uncertainty dissolved in the excitement of that kiss. Her response was instantaneous and instinctive, and it heightened his own passion. When she kissed him with a ravening hunger, matching each thrust of his tongue, he knew he was lost.

They never made it to the bed. He let her go, but just to unzip his jeans. He yanked her skirt up and her panties down as she stroked him down there. Then he grabbed her and pushed her against the wall of the cabin.

When he touched her between her legs, she was wetter than last night. He thrust into her urgently. Then he seized her legs and pulled them around his waist. She squeezed him with her legs. She felt so good—hot and tight and slick, so tight. Perfect. He loved being inside her, loved holding her, kissing her. Loved every second he was with her even when she drove him crazy. He grew huge, ready to burst at any second.

His heart began to slam against his rib cage as he forced himself to move slowly.

She gasped and moaned and screamed his name. Her hands wound frantically around his neck, her fingers threading through his hair.

"Now," she begged. "Now. Please…"

His hands gripped her bottom pulling her to him with a bruising strength.

"Am I hurting you, darlin'?"

She clung, sobbing in between soft little cries, her body surging in the same wild rhythm as his.

Nobody ever had felt as wonderful as she did. Not even close.

His body shuddered, exploded. For a long time he stayed inside her, wanting to hold on to her and stay with her forever.

This was where he belonged. With her. Forever.

Gently he smoothed her hair from her flushed face and eased out of her a little. He felt a blast of cool air gust between his burning body and hers and instantly pulled her back. She opened her eyes, and he felt himself drowning in their sated, whiskey-colored depths.

Her heart in her eyes, she smiled dreamily. "You'll probably hate me again. But right now, I'm too happy to care." She looked away, shy of him suddenly.

Without meeting his eyes, she reached for his hand and brought it to her cheek. She let it rest there for a while. "I thought about you in Mexico…every day. Every night." Then she began kissing each finger, one at a time.

He swallowed a breath. She was so sweet. So precious to him. And he'd been such a bastard to her last night. The pain in his heart was as sharp as a knife.

She leaned into him and traced the jagged scar on his shoulder with her fingertips. Next she kissed him there. When she looked up at him again, her face radiated a compassionate emotion too powerful to name.

"I think you've been hurt a lot more than you'd ever admit."

Oh, God. He clenched his hands into tight fists. He felt so choked up, his breath all but stopped.

"Bull riders have to be able to take pain."

"But do they ever get to let it out?"

"Oh, darlin'…" He pulled her closer, wanting to hold on to her and this moment forever.

He'd never felt like this—not in his whole life. He was drowning, dying, and it scared the hell out of him, rocked him, and shook him to his core.

What the hell? So, he'd gotten laid a couple of times. So, she was the best damn woman he'd ever had. So, she had a pretty smile. So, she looked daffy after their incredible sex.

It was just sex.

Liar. She's more than that and you know it.

She'd been more than that for a long, long time. An image of himself strutting into arenas packed with fans flashed in his mind. He saw his imaginary self throwing his Stetson high in the air as he strode back and forth in his jingly spurs and jauntily pretended he was brave enough to ride the devil himself. Before this moment he'd thought he could never feel so loved as when the fans applauded him.

His mouth tightened. Here he was, brought to his knees by this woman. It was bad enough that he'd betrayed Abigail, but Mia had to be a Kemble, too. Caesar's daughter.

Her family had robbed him of his birthright. She'd stolen his daughter and lied to him; she'd married his brother. Worst of all because of her last name, he could never measure up to her, never be good enough for her to be proud of him. By all that he held sacred, he should despise her.

Instead he felt as clueless and guileless as a baby who found himself in a strange new world. All the rules he'd lived by and could have stubbornly died by had suddenly changed because they had been based on lies he'd fed himself.

What the hell was he going to do about it?

What the hell was he going to do about her?

Nothing—that's what!

Fourteen

Mia fumed as she stared impatiently up and down the asphalt road. She'd had it with Mr. Shanghai Knight. After incredible sex, he'd been sweet to her afterwards—for maybe a minute or two. Then he'd closed up on her again, as tight as a clam. He was all business—determined to get her home as quickly as possible so he could be shed of her for good. His cheerfulness toward her was due entirely to this goal.

Well, she was fed up with his on-again, off-again brand of romancing.

Maddened, she thumped her right foot as she stared down the road. Why couldn't somebody just come and put them both out of their misery? But no! The desert was as ornery as her cowboy companion. There wasn't a single vehicle on that narrow black ribbon that cut through sage and cacti for miles in either direction and shimmered against the far horizon.

"Somebody will come along," Shanghai said in such a deep, matter-of-fact, know-it-all voice she wanted to kick him. "You wanna place a bet on how long it'll be? I say no more than five minutes."

Everything he'd done, said, or not said since they'd made love and left the cabin had annoyed her.

"No, I don't want to place a bet! I'm hot and I'm thirsty and I'm tired. You walk too fast, and my feet hurt."

"All you have to say is more or less than five minutes and we'll have a bet."

At his good-humored tone, she hissed in a breath. The handsome jerk was enjoying her bad mood way too much.

"I said I'm not betting you!" Her foot thumped harder.

The sun blazed down on them from a cloudless blue sky that acted like a mirror, magnifying its intensity. Her black skirt and blouse and the shawl that covered her hair soaked in the heat rays.

Being hot made her feel grumpier. Not that she could blame that on him. But then again, why couldn't she? "How far do you think we walked?" she demanded.

"Only three or four miles."

"Only?" The tender places between her legs felt raw from walking. *That* was definitely his fault.

"Lucky thing we hit a road so fast," he said smugly, looking entirely too pleased.

"Lucky? We might as well be on the moon!"

"Simmer down. Somebody will come along, and you'll be rid of me."

"I can't wait. But you said that five minutes ago!"

"You're exaggerating."

"Not by much." She kicked at a rock.

He chuckled. "You got another rock in your shoe, darlin'?"

"No, I don't have a rock! Thank you very much! And don't call me darlin'!"

"All right—Missy *Ethel* Mia Kemble. There, is that better?"

"No! It isn't better! I hate being called Ethel, which everybody in Spur County knows. Even you."

When he laughed, she stared down the asphalt road again. She was spitting mad. That's what she was. He'd made love to her like he was crazed for her. Then he hadn't said so much as a single nice word afterward. What was she—a mere sex object? A human doll to play with and discard once he'd had his fun?

Quit thinking about it.

"Sometimes I hate cowboys."

He laughed at that, too.

"That wasn't supposed to be funny!"

"What's eatin' you anyway? You've been madder than a hornet ever since we left the cabin."

So, the thickheaded idiot had actually noticed! She sucked in a breath and crossed her arms over her chest.

"Great! I nearly get myself killed for you—and all I get is the silent treatment!"

Was he really that clueless? "Would you just leave me alone?"

"Gladly."

His obliging her so readily set a match to her temper.

He'd barely said a single word afterward! He'd simply zipped his jeans up in silence after he'd finished his business, grabbed his backpack, stomped down the steps and headed north, hollering, without looking back, "You comin'?"

He'd expected her to yank up her panties and follow him like a well-trained puppy. And she hated herself because she had. After she'd climaxed once again, she'd felt joined to him on a soul-deep level. When she'd come down from that mystical mountain, she'd felt soft and shy and tender, and she'd wanted to know what he felt, too. He'd been so sweet at first.

She remembered holding his hand against her cheek because he'd seemed so dear, and the memory scalded her with shame.

Where he was concerned she was such a dope.

Well, two could play the not-speaking, not-caring game. From now on, she'd ignore him, too. She'd be as quiet as an oyster. As silent as a tomb.

And no more sex. No more being jerked around by the torment of her emotions afterward.

As she watched the road, she covertly glanced at him. His Stetson shaded the top part of his face. His mouth was set in a hard, straight line. Even so she remembered how it had felt on hers. His wide shoulders made him seem powerful. His jeans rode low on his hips, covering his muscular thighs and legs like a second skin.

He was handsome, the sexiest man alive—at least to her—even now when she was mad enough to bash his head in with a boiling pot. He didn't seem the least bit upset by their lovemaking or by the fact she was irritated with him.

Did he start every morning with a bit of wild sex and then proceed with his day like nothing important had happened? She began to wonder again about his regular girl.

Her curiosity about the girl grew to a fearsome level. She itched to ask him.

Of course, she couldn't, not right now anyway—since she wasn't speaking to him. She tapped her foot with a vengeance.

Suddenly he swooped down to his knees beside her. Before she could react, he wrapped a big brown hand around the foot that had been restlessly thumping the asphalt. Instead of hollering or kicking at him, she froze at his touch as a million shock waves raced up her leg.

Her pulled her shoe off and shook it out for her.

Then he looked up at her, beaming fit to be tied. "You're right, darlin'. No rock. Nothin' but a little sand." When he slipped her shoe back over her toes and heel, his large hand gave her a wonderful foot massage.

"I said don't call me darlin'."

"I reckon it's a habit."

"Well, break it."

"Old habits die hard…er…sweetheart."

She could tell by his tone his mind was on sex.

She pressed her lips tightly together. *"Tell me about it."*

He arose, smiling at her. "Hey, we're startin' to fuss like an old married couple."

She lunged at him then and poked a single fingertip into his hard, wide chest. "Well, we're not! Maybe we slept with each other a time or two…"

"Three times. Or have you forgotten Vegas?"

"I tried! Believe me I tried! Which means you're the last man I'd ever marry, Shanghai Knight! The very last!"

"Well, ditto—darlin'! Ditto!"

His words cut—even though they were a jovial response to her angry remark.

To her horror, her eyes began to sting.

She swallowed three times and silently counted backward from ten. She'd never live it down if she cried in front of him right now.

"There! I see a truck," he hollered, shielding his eyes as he looked past her. "Six minutes was all it took."

"You bet five."

"Lucky for you, you didn't take my bet."

"Lucky me," she whispered.

Shanghai stepped into the middle of the road and held out his thumb. "Maybe you should get out here with me and hike your skirt or something."

"What?"

"You said your feet hurt. You want a ride, don't you? Or do you prefer to stand out here all day in that black widow outfit giving me hell?"

A black, three-quarter-ton Dodge pickup pulling a trailer overloaded with hay was barreling toward them as Mia stepped into the road. She pulled the shawl off her hair and fluffed it about her shoulders. Then she held out her thumb, too.

When she pulled a sleeve off her shoulder, the driver slammed on his brakes so hard he skidded off the road, into a clump of prickly pear, coming to a stop as bits of the un-lucky shrub blew about in whorls of dust.

She started coughing, and the driver started hollering.

"Well, I'll be danged. I cain't believe it—Shanghai Knight! Everybody in ten counties is searching for you and I hit the jackpot. What in tarnation are you two doing out here in the middle of nowhere?"

"We'd sure be obliged for a ride, mister. The little lady's feet are killin' her."

"Get in then!" The man beamed at Mia. "Bless your heart, ma'am." His white smile was pleasant even though he was missing a front tooth.

"Lionel Williams," he said, extending a beefy hand.

"Howdy, Lionel."

Mia nodded and smiled as the men shook hands. Then Lionel leaned across the cab and opened the door.

"I seen you ride, Shanghai. Lots of times. I'm a great big fan."

"Thanks."

Shanghai hung back and helped Mia climb up into the truck. Then she felt his gaze on her butt, and her skin heated.

"And you must be that Kemble gal I read about, who everybody gave up for dead?"

Mia was about to nod when he said, "What was it like—hanging out with the drug lord?"

When she froze, Shanghai put both hands on her butt and gave her such a shove, she fell into the middle seat.

"Did you know they've got at least a hundred posses out looking for you two? The Border Patrol is stoppin' ever single car at the border. All the big bridges are backed up for miles. It's a real international incident. Made the national news even."

"We swam the Rio Grande," Shanghai said. "Then we walked."

"You're kidding. We're close to twenty miles from the border."

"No wonder my feet hurt."

"Well, I'll be damned. I cain't wait to tell Cathy. That's my wife. She's always complainin' 'cause she don't get enough excitement on the ranch. My cell don't work out here too good, or I'd call her right now. We'll call your folks at the Golden Spurs, too, just as soon as we git to Two Nails."

"How far is it?"

"Not far. I reckon no more than thirty miles."

Mia felt herself begin to relax. It was wonderful being in a truck—driving north, away from Mexico.

"Two Nails Ranch?" Shanghai asked a few minutes later.

Lionel nodded.

"You know Stewart Lowrey?"

"Grew up with him. Rode a few bulls with him when we were kids. He was good. Not as good as you, though. He's got him a place five miles down the road from Two Nails. He's doin' good."

Mia watched the road, saying nothing, just feeling glad she wasn't walking. When the men on either side of her fell silent, Lionel flipped the radio on to his favorite station, which naturally was Country and Western.

As the truck lurched along the deserted road lined with prickly pear and yucca, singers whined about lost love. Mia wished he'd change stations. Not that she said so. But the familiar laments began to make her long again for a certain impossible man's love.

"Somethin' sure smells good," Shanghai said as he and Mia tromped into Lionel's kitchen. "Homemade biscuits, I bet."

The small dark woman with black hair and glasses looked up from the pot she was stirring and smiled at Mia. "You bet right, mister."

"There's no better smell on earth," Shanghai said. "I always wished I had a mama to make biscuits for me."

"That's certainly what my Lionel thinks. I make them for him every day. Maybe you should get married."

Shanghai glanced at Mia. His stricken expression was somehow so compelling, her throat tightened. Maybe he wasn't quite as set against her as she'd thought.

His idle comment about his mama spurred memories. The gossip in Spur County had been that Shanghai's mama had run off because his daddy had been so mean to her. Cole had told her that after their mother had left, Old Man Knight had been so mean to Shanghai he'd finally run off, too.

Mr. Knight had seemed easygoing in public, and apparently he'd been nicer to Cole after Shanghai left. Maybe because he'd learned his lesson from having teamed up with her father to drive Shanghai away.

Mrs. Williams's gingham apron and wisps of her raven hair were smeared with flour. There was even a dab of the white stuff on her nose. Mountain "oysters" were sizzling in a frying pan beside a pot of simmering pinto beans. A rolling pin lay on her countertop on a pile of raw dough and flour.

"You must be Cathy," Shanghai said, his deep voice as gentle as the one he used to use with Mia when she'd been a kid.

More memories tugged at Mia's heart. When she'd been five, a big rat had bitten her in the attic. When she'd told Shanghai, he'd tattled to her daddy. As a result, she'd been forced to get rabies shots. Shanghai had probably saved her life again, but she'd hated the shots and had gotten spitting mad at him.

When she was over the shots, he'd sought her out one day with a present. She'd been thrilled by the silver ribbon and paper, of course. Inside she'd found a toy horse and a cowgirl. She'd loved them. She still had them.

The screen door slammed. "Cathy—you're never going to believe who…"

Lionel gave his wife a big bear hug and then introduced everybody quickly. "So, the whole state of Texas is looking for this pair, and I find them. Meet Shanghai and Mia."

"Howdy. Welcome."

"They've got to call people to pick them up," Lionel said.

"You must be starved." Cathy's brown eyes filled with concern.

"No," Mia began. "We don't want to trouble…"

"We are for a fact, ma'am," Shanghai said.

"Then we'll have lunch first—before you call all those folks. It's not quite ready. And Mia, you look to be about my size. Why don't I lend you some clean jeans and a shirt. You could send them back to me when you get home. You could have a bath, too."

"I really…"

"Follow me." Cathy paused. "Oh, and Lionel, why don't you lend Shanghai a razor, so his friends will recognize him?"

"Do I look that fierce?"

"Pretty fierce."

"You're too kind, ma'am," Shanghai said, again in that deep, gentle tone that turned Mia's insides to mush.

Damn his hide for making her feel tenderness. She wanted to be furious at him for the rest of her life.

Mia felt wonderful to be so clean and to be wearing normal ranch attire—jeans and a checkered blouse. She'd put her shining hair up in a ponytail, too.

They ate in the kitchen as if they were family. Shanghai gobbled down more biscuits than Mia would have believed possible for one man to eat, and all the time he talked constantly of their adventures, much to the amusement of their gracious hosts.

It was infuriating to know he had so much talk in him— for other people. From time to time, he would glance at Mia across the table and smile, as if inviting her to add something, but she was too annoyed since he'd taken charge of the conversation. Still, as she listened, she kept thinking about what had happened at the cabin.

Soon Shanghai would make those calls to the Golden

Spurs. Strangely she was no longer in a hurry to get home. It was pleasant being in this kitchen with the Williamses. Pleasant being with Shanghai in such normal surroundings with them as a buffer.

They weren't rich, but they seemed happily married. What would it be like to have a real husband? To spend the rest of her life with the man she loved? To know he loved her back and that he wanted her for more than sex?

The next time Shanghai looked at her, a lump formed in Mia's throat.

Would he disappear from her life as he always had before? She wished she still felt as angry at him as she had earlier. Anger was a protection of sorts. Too bad it never lasted—at least as far as he was concerned.

If he vanished again, this time she would have to find a way to put him out of her mind and heart forever.

But how? Every time she stared into Vanilla's eyes, she would find him there.

Fifteen

From the pulsating darkness of the prison, Tavio stared through the bars and fixed his unwavering black gaze on the slim girl standing across the street. Not that she noticed or even looked up. Because of Mia Kemble, he was a nobody now.

He clenched the bars, his hands tight as claws. Angelita probably never gave him a thought.

It galled him that she had escaped and he was still locked up, that Chito was hurt, maybe dying. Tavio sweated all the time as if he had a fever. His crack-laced cigarettes and booze were in short supply in this hellhole.

His flesh was burning up. His nerves felt as taut as guitar strings. Surely he'd go mad if he didn't get out of here.

Because of Angelita, Octavio Morales was the laughing-stock of Mexico. She had escaped, and here he was, caged like a wild beast with rats and other vermin. Her friends had broken her out and shot his right-hand man.

Where were his good friends now, those who had taken his money and gold watches and his stolen trucks for so long? Why didn't any of them visit him in prison? Why didn't they show respect? His grip tightened on the bars. He could do with a little respect.

"Be patient, Tavio. When things cool down, we help you," Guillermo had said on the phone yesterday.

Guillermo! That bastard! He was famous in all the newspapers for his surprise raid on the compound. The press was making him out to be a hero.

Little did they know. Guillermo was a corrupt, ball-less bastard who fantasized he was a tough guy. He fed this fantasy by watching gangster movies constantly and by hanging out with Tavio, pretending he was as tough as he was.

Tavio lived for the day he could strangle Guillermo with his bare hands.

Tavio squinted until the girl's face blurred. He could almost imagine she was Angelita.

He remembered Angelita's red hair, her long legs, her white creamy skin. She'd felt like warm satin. *Dios*, he'd wanted her. He should have raped her—again and again. Maybe now he wouldn't still burn for her. Maybe none of this would have happened.

Fury gripped him in a vise. For more than a minute, his chest was so tight, he couldn't breathe.

He'd tried so hard to please his father. Then his father had thrown him out like he was so much rotting *basura*. He'd tried to please Angelita, and what had she done—the same.

Like Guillermo, she deserved to die.

But more slowly.

First he would teach her a lesson she would never forget. When he thought about what he would do to her, he got hard, and his face dripped with even more perspiration.

He would rape her. When he was done, he would give her to Chito, if he survived, and watch while Chito and his men played with her. When they finished, he would personally break every bone in her body, stroking her hair and her face after each bone shattered.

Then he would throw her out in a dirty street like so much

basura. He would kiss her one last time and whisper, "Think of me while you die."

But first he had to get out.

Sixteen

The wind off the bay was blowing so hard the six flags of Texas, which flew along the familiar, red roofline of the Golden Spurs headquarters, stood straight out, like soldiers at attention.

Wolf was flying the helicopter and Shanghai sat beside him as they hovered above the house. Thus, Mia had the back seat all to herself. The flight from the border had been relaxing thus far, but as she stared down at the three-story, white stucco house and saw all the trucks and cars, she froze.

"Looks like you've drawn a full house down there!" Shanghai yelled above the roar of the rotors. Grinning at her, he turned back around.

At the thought of facing the hordes of people, new fears mushroomed inside her, but before they could get a grip, a powerful gust slammed the helicopter, causing it to plummet at a sharp angle straight for the ground. As the big oak trees and rocky earth rushed up to meet her, Mia forgot to breathe.

Wolf screamed something unintelligible at Shanghai. Surely she was about to die. Surely instead of Mother and her baby, the last things she would see were the palm fronds blowing crazily and the men and women racing away from the whirls of white caliche dust the helicopter was kicking up. Mia gripped the edges of her seat and held on for dear life.

Biting back a scream, she tore her gaze from the rapidly approaching ground and stared at Shanghai's solid, broad back. He was looking down, too, but other than a slight frown, he didn't seem the least bit unnerved. Wolf was fiddling with the controls and talking over the radio without the slightest hint of alarm.

At the last moment Wolf leveled the helicopter and landed it so gently, every butterfly in her stomach stilled. She didn't realize they were on the ground until she saw her mother running toward her with outstretched arms.

Wolf cut the engine. As the rotors stopped, Shanghai unsnapped his seat belt and turned around to check on her again.

"You okay?"

Breathless, she managed a quick nod.

"You're white as a sheet darlin'. You want me to pinch your cheeks?"

She stuck out her tongue.

"Smile. You're the belle of the ball, darlin'."

"I just want to be home. Inside the house with my mother and my little girl…and Daddy."

At the mention of her father, Shanghai's gaze narrowed. Then he jumped onto the ground before she could say anything else. Taking her hand, he helped her out. Instantly she was torn from his arms and embraced by her mother, who hugged her and petted her cheeks and then embraced her again with a ferocious, maternal zeal.

"I was so scared when I heard about the hit man in the prison," Joanne said when she was able to speak.

"Me, too."

"And then for a day and a half we heard nothing."

"Where's Vanilla?" Mia whispered, feeling nervous as she scanned all the faces for a little girl's.

"Since the press is here, I left her inside with Sy'rai. They're playing with blocks in the nursery. I didn't think—"

"Good. It's going to be confusing enough when a brand-new person with so much invested in her shows up."

"You're her mother. She'll feel your love."

When Mia saw people pointing cameras at her in the distance, she covered her face with her hands. "Who are all those people?"

"Pack journalism, Terence calls it," her mother said without explaining her connection to Terence. "They're like wolves wanting to feed the gossip mongers, but they sell themselves as newsmen."

Her mother took her hand. "The press is allowed only to photograph today…and from a distance. There won't be any interviews. They can't come up close, either."

Joanne smiled at the clump of reporters, who stood near the buildings that housed the offices. Then she led Mia over to Lizzy and Cole and Walker and Hawk, who were standing in the deep shade of an oak tree near the antique dinner bell on the front lawn. One by one, Mia embraced them all, hugging each of them as if she'd never let them go. There were tears and whispers of love on all sides. When Mia finally let go of Walker, who had wet eyes, she began searching the crowd of relatives who stood nearer the house for her father.

"Where's Daddy?" she asked. But her question was ignored.

Uncle B.B. was standing beside his beautiful, fashionable wife, Aunt Mona, who was still as gorgeous as she'd been as a girl. Mia's flamboyant Aunt Nannette was talking to her son, Bobby Joe, while batting her false lashes at a handsome, young cowboy.

Where was Sam, Bobby Joe's older brother and her favorite cousin?

Jim Jones, the top lawyer for the ranch, and Leo Storm, the ranch's CEO, stood apart from the family, their backs to each other. They wore dark suits and were talking rapidly on their cell phones. No doubt both their conversations had to do with the chaos her rescue had caused the ranch. No doubt, her return from the grave was both a PR and legal nightmare for them.

After all, the Golden Spurs was more than a ranch. It was an immense global agribusiness corporation with interests in the thoroughbred horse industry, the oil and gas industry, recreational game hunting, farming, and, last but not least, cattle ranching.

But Daddy? Still searching for him, Mia breathed in the smell of grass and the sea as the wind whipped her hair, for the bay was less than ten miles away. She looked up at the tall house. For a second the realization that she was home and surrounded by family, that she was free, calmed her.

Even with so many people gathered to celebrate her homecoming, the ranch seemed as quiet and vast as she remembered. She couldn't wait for the excitement to die down, so she could live here peacefully again and raise her daughter and work with her horses. Against a distant fence line, deer nibbled at green grasses. Nearer a herd of pedigreed red cattle grazed lazily in the afternoon sun.

Daddy? Where was he? Didn't he care that she was home?

When she didn't find him, a strange desperation built inside her until suddenly she felt unbearably afraid. *Where was he?* All these months, she'd half expected him to tear into Tavio's compound with his six-shooters raised and an army of cowboys and rescue her. Was he rejecting her again?

"Where's Daddy?"

Neither Lizzy, nor her brothers, nor her mother, nor any of them said a word. Instead they seemed frozen.

"Where's Daddy?" she finally whispered on a strangled breath.

Lizzy was very white as she placed a hand on Mia's arm. "Didn't Shanghai tell you?"

"Tell me what?"

Lizzy's eyes were widened with dread.

"Where is he?" Mia's voice was shrill. "What happened to him?"

Joanne came forward. "He had a stroke. He's…"

"And Sam? Where's Sam? Is he dead, too? What else has happened?"

"Sam's in prison. It's a long, complicated story. I know your father's death is a shock, but you wouldn't have wanted him to live the way he was. His ashes are under the spur tree."

Grief numbed Mia as she turned blindly toward the spur tree. Knowing his were among the many spurs that hung there glistening in the sunlight, her eyes began to burn. "I— I was so stupid. I thought I'd come home…and everything would be the same as always. But nothing ever is, is it?"

"A few things have changed," Cole said, "but we'll get into all that later."

"I know about you and Lizzy being married."

"I—I thought you were…dead," Cole said. "We'll get the lawyers to straighten it all out. Your inheritance, I mean."

"I'm glad you're together. You and Lizzy always belonged together."

Mia wiped her eyes as she studied Lizzy. Her platinum curls were shorter than she remembered. Her sister's cheeks were radiant as she stood beside Cole. Even though Lizzy wore an unflattering white poncho and a long ethnic skirt, she'd never been more beautiful. Not that Mia felt the slightest jealousy. Lizzy and Cole looked so right together.

"I'm glad you're happy," Mia reassured her. "So glad."

"Well, at least Shanghai found the time to tell you about us," Cole said. "Good. That's a start."

"On what?"

"He knows the truth about Vanilla, too," Cole added.

"He's furious at me about that. Not that we've had much time to delve…"

She stopped talking. Remembering what they'd done instead of talking, she blushed. Then her attention was caught by a pretty girl with warm, golden hair. The girl had been talking to Terence Collins and to Leo Storm. When she saw Shanghai, her face lit up, and she dashed toward him, hurtling straight into Shanghai's arms.

"Who's that over there with Shanghai now?" Mia whispered.

"His trainer, Wolf." As if sensing dangerous ground, Cole shifted his weight from one foot to the other.

"I mean the girl with the pretty gold hair and the big smile, who's in his arms."

"Abigail Collins," Lizzy said.

"His girlfriend?"

"She owns the ranch next to his," Cole added. "It's south of Austin. Apparently Leo's recently bought some property that he expects to appreciate that is near theirs, too."

"She's been such a comfort while we've been waiting for you two," Joanne said. "She's Terence Collins's daughter."

As Mia watched Shanghai and Abigail, something inside her shattered. For a second or two the pain in her chest was so great she could barely breathe.

Suddenly Leo, who'd been watching the pair, too, pivoted and walked away abruptly.

Too much had happened too fast. Suddenly Mia felt too fragile to endure any more excitement or surprises. Unable to talk to anyone or to watch the happily reunited couple, Mia made her excuses and then ran up the stairs of the house.

Once inside she scanned the large paintings, the oriental carpets and the carved staircase. At least she was home. Funny, she'd thought she'd be so happy here.

When she shut the front door, she sank into the nearest chair and covered her eyes. Why was everything always so hard?

It was all pretty overwhelming. Here she was, home at last, but her father was gone forever. And Shanghai, who'd made wild violent love to her only this morning, was holding a beautiful woman in his arms.

Tears ran unheeded down her cheeks, anyway, even as she wiped them away. She looked up, hoping to distract herself and found herself staring at the faded portraits of her pioneer ancestors. They looked fierce and stern. They would have despised her.

She didn't care. The house felt so big and alien, and she felt as lost and alone as she had in Mexico. Would she ever fit in here again? What was she going to do with the rest of her life? Cole, who'd become her main confidant before the crash, was now married to her sister, with whom she'd always had a competitive relationship.

Suddenly her gaze focused on the faded portrait of the original Caesar Kemble, the ranch's indomitable founder. He'd fought Indians, Mexican raiders. He'd stolen land, bought it, ranched it, endured droughts and fought pitched battles to find water. He must have gone through far worse than she.

His blood flowed inside her. She lifted her head, her gaze drifting over the other portraits again.

Think solution. Think survival. What were the first steps she needed to take to put her life back together?

She had a child to raise. Just the thought gave her a faint sense of purpose and stiffened her resolve to get past this weak moment. Clearly she couldn't moon over Shanghai.

The front door opened softly.

"What's wrong?" Joanne whispered from the doorway.

"Daddy…and other stuff." Mia sat up straighter and rubbed her cheeks with the back of her hands. "Give me a minute, please. I need to be alone."

Her mother's eyes filled with sympathy. "I'll go down to the kitchen then," she said, disappearing soundlessly.

A few minutes later when Mia felt stronger, she stood up and wiped her eyes again. Thinking she was alone, she turned only to receive a jolt when she saw Shanghai's wide-shoul-dered body framed in the open doorway. He must have been there a while.

At the mere sight of him, her heart seemed to stop. "I didn't hear… What are you doing here?" She turned away from him so he wouldn't see that her eyes were red.

"You've been crying?" He tensed. ,

"The shock of it all I guess. Daddy…"

"I'm sorry. I wish I could make it easier for you." He paused. "I don't want to intrude on your grief, but I couldn't leave you without saying goodbye." His deep voice was in-finitely gentle.

She needed his strength so much. It was all she could do not to fling herself in his arms.

"Why didn't you tell me about him?"

"Maybe I should have. I thought only of getting you here safely. I'm sorry if my not telling you caused you unneces-sary hurt. If I can help in any way before I go—"

She swallowed. "You're going now?"

"I missed a couple of key rodeos. I'll have to work pretty hard to play catch-up."

"Are you serious about Abigail Collins?"

"She thinks so."

"And you?"

"Tell you the truth I've been sort of torn."

"What about us?"

He clenched his teeth and notched his jaw higher as he glanced past her. He drew a long breath and still didn't an-swer.

For the first time she saw the shadows under his eyes. He looked exhausted both mentally and physically. She saw a few gray hairs at his temple that she hadn't noticed before.

"I put you through a lot, didn't I?" she said, figuring it was best to change the subject. She was done with begging him to love her.

"You're safe. That's the main thing. About us. I don't know." He looked away.

"You look tired."

"It's hit me all of a sudden. I could use a good night's sleep." He was watching her closely again. "And so could you. You'll feel better tomorrow. Being home will get easier."

"I sure hope so."

He smiled.

"Don't you want to see Vanilla?"

"Yes. I want to see her so bad it's killin' me."

"Then let's go up together." She pointed toward the stairs. "That's where I was going before my grief hit me."

Flushing darkly, he shook his head. Then his face closed down completely. "Not today," he muttered, backing toward the door. "I wouldn't know what to say to her. I'd probably scare her half to death and screw everything up."

"But—"

"I expect meeting you for the first time is enough for her right now. I want to buy her a present first. Maybe clean up. You know—look my best, prepare myself. You've only got one chance to make a good first impression."

She nodded. He seemed so vulnerable all of a sudden. Was he as scared...of their little girl as she was?

"Look, I've got to go," he said. "My ride's waitin'."

"Abigail?"

His face shut down again, but he nodded.

"I just wanted to make sure you're going to be all right."

When he turned to go, she ran after him, feeling more desperate than ever.

"Shanghai—"

When he stopped, her throat tightened.

Blue eyes stared straight at her and held her motionless. Suddenly it was difficult to breathe. Did she only imagine she saw a wasteland of pain in his eyes? Was it possible he felt terrible, too? Long seconds passed while their gazes clung.

"Thank you…for jumping…for everything else, too," she finally managed in a hoarse whisper.

"I'm just glad you're safe. You tell Vanilla about me—you hear. Good things. Tell her I'll be coming to see her—real soon."

"Promise?"

Again he looked directly into her eyes.

"Yes."

She could hardly speak for the lump in her throat. She wanted so much more from him.

"I gave Leo my cell-phone number in case you ever want to call me," he said. "That's the best way to reach me since I travel so much."

"All right."

When he turned and went to the door, she flung herself after him. The door would have slammed if she hadn't caught it. Holding on to it, she watched him stomp down the stairs into the brilliant Texas sunshine. She held up her hand, ready to wave had he ever looked back.

But he didn't. Lingering in the doorway, she watched him lope across the lawn toward Abigail, who hugged him. When he let her go, he opened the passenger door of her white Lincoln to let her in. Then he ran around the back, got in, too, and hit the gas pedal. When they sped off, the big car slid all over the caliche road as he made a fast getaway.

Leo, who had been watching them, too, had turned to observe her just as she sagged against the door. Not that she cared if he saw her despair.

"Timber," shrieked the little girl as she charged up to the tall castle just as Sy'rai crowned it with a final, yellow block.

Vanilla was swiping at the blocks with both arms, giggling as they fell when Mia and her mother entered. The little girl was so intent on kicking and scattering the blocks all over the beige carpet that at first she didn't notice her new fans.

The nursery was much as Mia remembered—pink walls and the pink crib she'd picked out. Only the darling mobile over the crib was gone and there were way more toys in the toy box and stacked on the shelves. Books with cardboard pages lay all over the carpet, too.

"Vanilla loves to be read to," Joanne said. "She's a real little bookworm. Like Lizzy was. Lizzy reads to her all the time."

Always Lizzy.

Awestruck, Mia sank to her knees so she would be on eye level with the little girl. Vanilla had elfin ears, big blue eyes, wispy brown hair and a pixie smile. She seemed a whirlwind of energy as she kicked another pile of blocks over and then ran up to Sy'rai and smilingly said, "Timber."

Sy'rai petted her head. "You little stinker. You kicked over my castle. Don't you dare kick over any more blocks."

Vanilla charged the last remaining tower, shrieking, "Timber" again as it fell. Then she clapped. Whirling around and clapping, she saw Joanne and Mia and grew perfectly still. Then she ran to Sy'rai, shut her eyes and hugged her.

"She can be shy…of strangers," Joanne warned Mia.

I'm not a stranger. I'm her mother. I've thought of her every single day.

"She's so big," Mia said, blinking against tears, trying to act calm and composed. "She's grown so tall. And she's beautiful. So incredibly beautiful."

"She'll get used to you in no time. Soon, probably by tomorrow, you'll be the best of friends."

From behind Sy'rai's ample bosom, Vanilla was slanting her eyes coyly at Mia when Kinky came into the nursery carrying a walk-around phone.

"For you," he said, handing the phone to Mia.

"Who is it?"

"*He* wouldn't say."

As she clutched it tightly, her heart stopped because she so longed for it to be Shanghai.

"Hello," she finally whispered in a husky tone.

"Angelita?"

Tavio?

The sound of his voice hit her like a fist to her stomach. There was a long moment of horrible silence. She went numb as she continued to watch her daughter play.

"Who is this?" Mia whispered. "Say something."

But she knew.

"You give me no choice, Angelita. You say this Shanghai is dead. I save you. But you lie. Then you run away with him. Because of you, Delia is dead."

"Delia. Oh, God, no!"

"Guillermo, he use her and he let his men use her while he watch. He kill her because I tell him to. Just like I tell Chito to kill you."

"You monster!" A sob broke from Mia. "Delia…oh, Delia…" She would never forgive herself for dear, sweet Delia's fate.

"Your friend, Shanghai, he shoot Chito. My men, they laugh at me. My business no good now. For these many things you and Shanghai must die. First, your lover Shanghai—to break your heart."

Mia froze. He stopped talking and inhaled deeply, probably on one of his crack-laced cigarettes.

"You're insane."

Holding the phone against her ear, she sank against a wall for support. Vanilla was smiling at her now. She tried to smile back, but her mouth was trembling too much.

"Please, just leave me alone. Please, Tavio—"

He began to laugh. "I like it when women beg me."

Fear coiled inside her.

Tavio stopped laughing.

"Please…please, Tavio. There is goodness in you. I felt it."

"You killed it!"

"Please…"

"Shut up! If it's the last thing I do, I come to Texas and kill all your family."

Then the line went dead.

Through a film of horror she stared at her beautiful little girl.

Seventeen

Early morning.

Wearing dark sunglasses, her red hair bundled into a base-ball cap to disguise her appearance, Mia stepped out of the elevator into the lobby of her fashionable River Walk hotel.

Leo was on his feet and beside her instantly. She noted his heavy briefcase and the short, stocky man beside him with thick white hair.

"Meet Gus. He'll be your bodyguard," Leo said, "until this Morales thing is under control and the press settles down."

She would have liked to have argued, but she'd learned to pick her battles since she'd been home. Other people made a lot of the decisions at the Golden Spurs. It had always been that way.

As CEO of the Golden Spurs, Leo always had too much on his plate. There were several ongoing lawsuits involving the corporation. At present certain family members wanted a larger share of the oil and gas royalties.

"I suppose I could use some help fending off reporters."

"Has Morales called you again?" Leo demanded.

She shook her head.

"Good. With any luck, the Mexicans will keep him locked up and throw away the key."

"I wish I believed that."

Gus extended his hand and after the briefest hesitation, she took it. He was shorter than she was, but burly. His round face was flushed, pugnosed and belligerent. His green eyes were shrewd and suspicious, and they darted everywhere.

But his smile was nice. "It's good to meet you, miss." Then he bowed with surprising gracefulness and stepped to the background.

He would do.

After that, she didn't see much of him. Even so, she knew he was there.

"How about breakfast before we get down to business?" Leo patted his briefcase.

She nodded.

"Your hotel café has the best omelets in town. But we could go wherever you like."

When she said the hotel was fine, they walked outside and ordered breakfast under colorful umbrellas that shaded the little tables on a limestone terrace that overlooked the San Antonio River. The service was quick and efficient.

"You're right about the omelets." Finishing hers, she set her fork down.

Without comment he lifted his coffee cup.

"If I were home, I'd be at the barn at this hour."

"Ah, with the horses." He smiled. "I'm glad you're back at that. How's that going?"

"Like a lot of things—slow at first."

"It's hard to start over," he said, as if he knew. "You were doing such a great job before the plane crash."

Before Mexico, one of her passions had been her involvement with the gentling of the ranch's cutting horses.

"I've been going out to the barn every day to help with the foals and the yearlings."

He continued to sip, waiting patiently for her to continue. Leo was a bulldozer at times, but then he had to be, to deal with certain members of her family, such as her Uncle B.B. Still, like now, Leo could be the best listener in the world.

"Oh, it's not difficult work. Not like what you do."

"Hey, you have a gift. Don't belittle it."

She smiled.

"So, what are you doing exactly?"

"I catch the foals with a rope and then gently teach them to be led. Once they've got that, I kneel and teach them to yield their feet to me, first the front ones and then the hind ones." She stopped, feeling a little shy about her enthusiasm. "I—I don't know why I love doing it so much."

"I think sometimes we're simply born to do certain things. Unfortunately some of us never find what those things are."

"When I'm with the horses, I feel complete, happy even, hopeful. I forget about Octavio Morales and all the horrible stories that are being written about me and him."

Since her family was so famous, at least in Texas, every day there was a fresh story in some newspaper about the charges made against Mia in Mexico or about the fact that Cole had married both sisters. Detailed articles with legal arguments were constantly printed about which sister was really Cole's wife. Then there were the more salacious news stories that speculated she'd had a torrid love affair with Tavio.

"I keep worrying that some of my friends and family will believe I did those awful things."

"You can't control what other people think, so don't torture yourself trying to."

"Tell that to the talking heads on the television and the reporters besieging the ranch and jamming our phone lines."

He frowned. "I know it's hard now, but it will die down."

"I just hate the thought of people reading and listening to those stories and believing I'm such an evil person."

"Fortunately most people have short memories and an even shorter attention span."

Although his eyes were kind and his voice reassuring, she knew he'd been working overtime because of all the problems her homecoming had caused him. He had the ranch's PR machine in high gear. He'd made himself available to be interviewed for countless articles and shows, and his quotes and appearances were usually the only rational defense of her conduct in the scandalous pieces written or broadcast about her.

"Thank you for all you've done," she said.

"You ready to sign some papers?" Leo pulled his glasses out of his pocket and put them on.

"That's why I flew up."

He leaned down and opened his briefcase.

"Being alive again is turning out to be more incredibly complicated than I ever would have believed possible."

"We'll get over these hurdles. Luckily Cole is being very fair about the inheritance issues."

Her will had been read over a year ago, and her properties had passed to others, mainly to Cole. Since then, Cole had sold and bought both land and stock. Thus, all sorts of legal compromises were being worked out between them. Documents, which would return legal title to most of her former holdings to her, were being drawn up. The whole process would take months to sort out. Cole would keep the stock she'd given him as part of the arrangement they'd worked out when he'd agreed to marry her.

"I won't work for Caesar Kemble without at least owning some stock in the Golden Spurs," Cole had said before agreeing to marry her.

Caesar had been apoplectic when he'd discovered a Knight owned stock in the Golden Spurs. Her relationship had been strained with her father until the plane crash. Now she would never know if he would have ever forgiven her.

Leo set a fat stack of documents with little yellow tags on certain pages and a blue pen in front of her.

"Flip to the tagged pages and sign at the red arrows," he said. "It won't take long."

"What about that awful Comandante Guillermo Gonzales? Can he really extradite me and make me stand trial in Mexico the way he brags in the newspapers?"

"In his dreams."

They'd had this conversation several times because she tended to panic every time she read any of Gonzales's threats.

"Not unless he kidnaps you," Leo continued. "I told you we've got a legal team in Juarez. But the main thing is for you to stay out of Mexico."

"I have no wish to go back other than the fact I keep wondering what happened to this girl I befriended...Delia. I got her into trouble, and I keep worrying...." She remembered Tavio saying Delia was dead.

"Well, worry all you want to in the States. You'd just get yourself in trouble if you went down there."

She fell silent at that, so she tackled the pages with the blue pen. Leo was right. Signing the papers didn't take long.

When she was done, Leo said, "Good. I'd better get to the office." He slid his glasses off and put them in his pocket. "When you're ready, we'll drive you and Gus to the airport."

Dallas, Texas

As he climbed onto Hurricane, Shanghai's riding hand hurt so bad he was afraid it was broken. Because of Mia, he'd lost his temper and rammed his fist full-force into his motel-room door this morning.

Shanghai nodded. When the chute banged open, Hurricane jumped and then immediately started spinning and bucking.

Ignoring his pain, Shanghai moved with the plunging bull as gracefully as a dancer. Not that every twist of the monster didn't send white-hot darts of agony up his riding arm. But hell, he preferred physical misery to what he'd felt at breakfast when he'd read all about Mia and Morales.

At the end of eight seconds, when the horn blared, Shanghai raised a leg and jumped off easily, landing on his feet. Then he turned his back on the bull, daring the bull to charge him and walked toward the rails. As bullfighters ran toward the infuriated bull, the crowd erupted in thundering applause.

He stopped to wait for the score, hoping their approval would revitalize him.

"You're not gonna see a ride any better than that in this century!" The announcer's voice was shrill with excitement. "Shanghai's score is 92, which puts him ahead of everybody. He's either the best! Or he's one lucky son-of-a-gun!"

The crowd screamed and hooted for Shanghai.

Looking up from the thousands of faces to the scoreboard, he felt nothing—no emotion, absolutely nothing—except maybe gratitude that he'd gotten off another monster with all his favorite body parts intact.

Even the little kids and the pretty girls gazing out at him tonight from the stands with their wide, awe-filled eyes did nothing to fill the emptiness inside him.

What was wrong with him? He'd felt dead ever since he'd left Mia at the Golden Spurs.

The fans kept on clapping and yelling, but the only thing screaming in his head were the damning words he'd read about Mia and her drug lord.

Smiling, a cowgirl ran up to him and pressed a business card, that probably had her phone number, in his shirt pocket. She winked coyly. In disgust, he held his injured riding hand against his chest and headed for the locker rooms.

He was thirty-nine. Too old for the same old games he'd always played.

When he strode into the locker room, his buddies all shut up. Looking sullen, Zach grabbed his rigging bag and headed past him, slamming out the door without bothering to even meet his gaze or speak.

Ever since Shanghai had lost his temper yesterday, his buddies were wary around him. For a second or two they all just stared. Then they looked away, not knowing what to do or say.

Shanghai heaved in a thick breath. Things had started to get awkward in the locker room ever since he and Mia and Morales had become big stars on television and in the newspapers. Finally yesterday Zach had made the mistake of asking why anybody cared how many times a no-good bastard like Morales had screwed the rich-bitch heiress during her captivity.

Shanghai had jumped him and had slammed him into a locker, yelling at him not to talk like that about her.

"What's she to you?"

"Nothing. I just don't like hearing lies about her. That's all."

It had taken four of their friends, including Wolf, to pull him off and calm him down.

Wolf grabbed a beer out of the cooler and walked up to him.

"Great ride, cowboy."

Shanghai shrugged. "I got lucky."

"What else matters?" Dakota's glum tone reminded Shanghai that the kid had been suffering a run of bad luck for the past two years.

"Where you goin' next, Shanghai?" Robby wanted to know.

"Nebraska," he replied, feeling strangely bleak at the thought.

Dakota hunched lower over his beer, not drinking or talking to the rest of them.

"Nebraska's an awful long way from Texas," Wolf said, sidling closer. He lowered his voice. "Have you been back to see your little girl yet?"

Shanghai squinted as he stared down at the beer bubbles racing up the side of his brown bottle. Then he hunched lower.

"You *ever* going to see her?"

"You know what our problem is, Wolf?"

Wolf glanced at him questioningly. "Didn't know we had one—other than you being a wuss sometimes."

"You're not a cowboy. You don't follow the rules."

"Which are?"

"Cowboys don't pry. And they don't give unwanted advice."

"You don't say? They probably don't complain, either, but on another tack—you know that truck you sold me last week—"

"That was an as-is deal."

"The transmission's slipping."

"You knew it had over two hundred thousand miles on it. I said no guarantees. So it's your baby now. Look, I'm not in the mood for this! Like you said, Nebraska's a long way, so I'd better hustle." Shanghai stuffed his chaps and rope in his riggin' bag and waved goodbye.

"Not so fast," Wolf said, following him. "What are you going to do about your kid?"

"I started sending Mia a check. Not that it's any of *your* business."

"That's it? That's all you think there is to being a daddy?"

No, he didn't think that was it! That's just what was eating at him! "Would you shut up about her?"

"Man, if you don't quit being a wuss and go down and meet her, you're gonna be sorry—"

"Mia and Vanilla...they're not my family." Shanghai spoke through tight lips. "Not really. I've been giving this a lot of thought. I'd best let them go."

"You've been giving this a lot of thought…and this is the best you can do? Jesus! I knew you bull riders had to be a dumb bunch, but this takes the cake!"

"I'm outta here! Like I said, I don't have to take this! You're a trainer! Not a therapist! You're fired!"

"Which means I'll see you in Nebraska. Only I'm flying, buddy."

Shanghai was too furious to reply. He kicked a bench out of his way, and headed for the door. When he reached it, Dakota Post was there first, to open it for him.

"Thanks."

"I know I already owe you plenty, Shanghai," he muttered in a low voice meant only for Shanghai's ears when they were alone in the corridor.

"I told you not to worry about it."

"But Melly… She's pregnant again."

"Congratulations."

"And the bank's going to repossess the trailer…"

Dakota had had a bad wreck on a rank bull two months ago and hadn't won any prize money since.

"I know you lent me all that money toward my hospital bills and I haven't paid—"

"How much do you need?"

"A few hundred I guess."

Shanghai threw his gear down and pulled his wallet out of his back pocket. Quickly he counted out five one hundred dollar bills and laid them across Dakota's palm.

"You hang in there. Your luck'll turn. Sooner or later it always does."

"Thanks. I'll repay you…as soon as I can."

"Sure." Shanghai patted him on the shoulder. Then he picked up his gear and started for the parking lot, but no sooner was Shanghai outside the locker room, than a small voice stopped him.

"Can I have your autograph?"

Another kid came up to join his friend, and Shanghai knelt in the dust, signing their programs until the last skinny kid in a belt buckle and hat too big for him ran off, waving his program.

At last Shanghai stood up. Instead of picking up his gear, he pulled Vanilla's picture out of his pocket and studied it. It was the one where she was halfway down her red slide, and her blue eyes were alight with excitement.

She was so damn cute she tore his heart out.

Carefully, so as not to bend it, he replaced the picture. Then feeling lonelier than ever, he headed for the parking lot.

When he got to his truck and started the engine, Mia started haunting him. He shrugged, hating the way he'd been obsessing about her lately. But just like always, she refused to let him go.

He remembered how her skin had glowed golden in the lamplight as she'd bathed herself in the cabin. She'd felt so good on top of him, too. He remembered the feel of her pulse beating soundlessly against his skin. She'd been so soft and hot, so sinfully lush and wet with her legs wide-open to him. She'd been so tight when he'd been inside her, too. And, oh how sassily she'd pestered him when they'd been trying to hitch a ride the next day because she'd felt so ashamed of herself for being so sexy.

Images of her as a kid consumed him, as well. He saw her bright head under the wheel of her daddy's truck right before he'd jumped to save her. He'd been so scared, he'd thought he'd die. He saw her laughing up at him as she petted Spot. He remembered her huge, whiskey-colored eyes shining with concern for him as he lay sprawled underneath her dining-room table after Caesar had slugged him.

But it was funny—how most of all he remembered how good he'd felt filling up on homemade biscuits while sitting across the Williamses' kitchen table from her.

What would it be like to wake up every morning and know

they'd share breakfast together? At their own kitchen table? Or talk about the day they planned to have together? Maybe they'd sit on one of the swings on his shady porches and drink iced tea on a summer day. What would it be like to have a normal life and settle down with a family?

So far this season, he'd driven ninety thousand miles. The underside of his left wrist was callused because he mainly drove with his left hand. Maybe Wolf had a slight point about the mental acuity of those who wore Stetsons. His life was passing him by.

Mia hadn't phoned him once since he'd left with Abby. He knew because he checked his cell phone for messages at least twice a day. Maybe she was as dead-set on forgetting him as he was on forgetting her.

"Maybe that's for the best!" he yelled.

Not that anybody heard him.

If you're not careful, you'll end up all alone.

"Maybe that's for the best, too!"

Closing his eyes, he clenched the steering wheel harder, but it was impossible to stop the sudden surge of regret. Mia had always adored him and chased him, and he'd taken it as his due. Never had he appreciated her.

Hell. Had he ever asked her to love him? He didn't owe her a damn thing.

You owe the kid, though.

Shanghai caught himself.

What was he doing sitting here in a Dallas parking lot wasting his time thinking about Mia or the kid when he had a rodeo to get to in Nebraska?

As Wolf sprinted for his truck, he passed a rusted-out pickup parked in a lonely spot and instantly got a bad vibe. He stopped to look around. Not that he saw anything to worry about other than the lights being out in this section of the lot.

A full moon hung from a starless, black sky. Not that he

was one for views, or art, or pretty sights of any sort. He wouldn't have noticed the moon tonight except he felt spooked, and paying attention was a defense strategy.

When he reached his truck, which was parked in a lonely spot and got out his keys, two men rushed him from behind. They blew into him so hard and fast, he was thrown into the gravel gasping. He managed only a single, well-placed kick into one of the bastard's balls.

The man groaned and dropped a machine gun. As Wolf grabbed the gun, a flashlight beamed into his face. He aimed the gun at the light, which went out instantly. Blinded, he heard frantic Spanish curses and caught Morales's name.

This was a hit. The bastards had deliberately staked out his truck.

Scrambling backward, Wolf punched his panic button, causing his truck alarm to blare. At the blast of noise the bastards took off. Wolf sprang to his feet and raced after them. He was built like a barrel, all muscle, but short legs. They were skinnier, lighter and way faster.

Within seconds he heard their squealing tires.

Cowards.

His hand tightened around the machine gun as he walked back to his new truck. Who the hell were those slimeballs? Why him?

"The whole thing is simply incredible." Mia shut the scrapbook.

She meant the scandal about Cherry and her father and Cherry's murder as well as her father's murder. She still couldn't believe that Uncle Jack and not Caesar was her real biological father.

"I can't believe Sam, of all people, could kill anybody. And believe me, I should be a judge of murderers after this past year."

Joanne didn't smile. "He burned down the barn and the old

aviary. I lost a few of my darlings. Fortunately Cole went in and slashed the screens and drove most of them out. He saved the horses, too."

They were sitting across a library table by the window that overlooked the playground Cole had built for Vanilla. Between reading the newspaper clippings that had to do with last year's scandals and thumbing through old photographs of Uncle Jack, Mia and her mother had watched Vanilla run about the lawn and swing with Sy'rai.

At the moment Sy'rai was pushing her in a swing and Vanilla was yelling, *"Wheeeeee!"*

"She's got so much energy," Mia said.

"Oh, she's a handful. Just like you were. It's just a matter of channeling the energy in the right direction."

They were silent for a little while. Then her mother took her hand. "It's been so difficult trying to make you understand about Jack. I grew up loving him and admiring him. Then he was gone. You're so much like him. I think that's why I've always loved you so much. You're all I have left of him."

Mia pressed her mother's hand tightly.

"Just as I think it's why Caesar always resented your talents at riding and shooting and ranching because Jack was your father. There was such an intense rivalry between Jack and Caesar. Jack excelled at everything, you see. Caesar could see Jack in you, just as I could. With Jack dead, he was king. Only you reminded him of the old days when he'd been second."

"Even knowing the truth, it still hurts that Daddy never… I mean that…Caesar…rejected me."

"I know."

"He was the only father I ever knew."

"I'm sure he did his best."

"I have to get over it."

"You will."

"Why couldn't you have told me about Uncle Jack before? When you knew I was always so jealous of Lizzy?"

"I thought the truth would divide us as a family and some-how cause more problems. I gave you all my love. I thought I could make up to you for what Caesar couldn't give you."

"But there was always something missing. And it was ter-rible to feel so…rejected."

"Lizzy's been hurt, too. You see, I couldn't love her as I loved you. I think at least Caesar tried to love you equally. I'm not sure how hard I tried. I hurt Lizzy terribly. We've talked, and there's a new understanding between us, but I think I'll regret that always."

Oh, Mother…

What was the use of wishing things had been different when one couldn't change the past? Mia stared out at her ex-uberant child, who was running up the slide backward.

"I think I'll go outside, Mother. Would you like to come?"

Vanilla grew friendlier with her by the day. Every time Mia played with her, she told her stories about Shanghai. She'd created a storybook with photographs of Vanilla. She'd drawn pictures of Shanghai riding bulls. She'd left the final pages of Vanilla's little book blank and told Vanilla that was because she didn't know the ending yet.

"Where are the pictures, Mia? Does the little girl's daddy ever come home?" Vanilla would demand when they got to the white pages.

"We don't know yet, sweetheart. What do you think?"

Her mother nodded and they went out together. Glad to have more adoring playmates, Vanilla clapped and ran up to them eagerly.

"Slide. Slide," she said. Then she turned, a whirlwind as usual, and darted toward the slide.

Laughing, Mia ran after her.

Vanilla climbed the stairs and then cocked her head and flashed Mia a smile to make sure she was coming.

"Come on, Mia!"

"You never stop, do you, precious? And you think it's perfectly normal for a big person to slide down a little person's slide."

"My slide," Vanilla said.

"Yes, your slide."

Mia spent most of her free time with Vanilla. Having missed so much with her little girl, she couldn't get enough of her. Vanilla loved to read and to play on her slide and swing outdoors. She loved to explore the flower beds or go swimming at the beach.

Laughing, Vanilla slid down the slide first. Mia got stuck halfway down and had to scoot herself. Then they both ran around to the stairs to do it again.

And always when Mia was with her like this, she wondered how Shanghai could bear to stay away from their darling child.

So far, he had neither called nor come.

Don't think about him.

What's the use? Why was she the least bit surprised that a man who'd left his father and brother and the only home he'd ever known would turn his back on his daughter, too?

That was simply how he was.

At the top of the slide, Vanilla turned around, her blue eyes brilliant with joyous excitement.

Shanghai's eyes.

As always they stole her heart.

Eighteen

The road cut through the flat boring plains of Oklahoma. His left hand on the wheel, Shanghai felt on edge as he whipped down the seemingly endless asphalt highway.

He barely knew what he was doing when he swerved off onto a county road thirty miles south of Oklahoma City. He caught the next county road on his left. Twenty minutes later, he rolled up to a sagging trailer resting on concrete blocks in a yard full of junk. The weeds around the rusty hulk were waist high.

He sprang out of his truck, yelling, "Dirk!"

Not that Dirk answered.

Not that Shanghai was expecting him to. The door groaned on its hinges as he let himself inside.

The tiny living room with its threadbare couch was dank and cluttered, a little worse than his last visit. The black-and-white television was blaring a little louder, too. Newspapers lay on the floor as did whiskey bottles, boots and grimy socks, as well as a mountain of soiled underwear. Dirty dishes overflowed in the sink.

The trailer reeked so badly of rot-gut whiskey and sour food, Shanghai breathed through his mouth like he used to do when he was a kid and his daddy was on a tear. Dirk was nowhere in sight. Not good.

"Dirk! It's me—Shanghai!"

Before clomping toward the back bedroom, Shanghai paused for a second to study the yellowing newspaper clippings of Dirk's former glories that were tacked to the paneled walls. There were pictures of Dirk riding bulls and magnificent horses. In one giant photograph he wore chaps and his Stetson and stood beside other rodeo greats. There were pictures of Dirk with Roy Rogers and other Western movie stars.

Dirk had won seven gold medals. He'd been the best. The greatest. As charismatic as a movie star, he'd been Shanghai's idol. Then Dirk's luck had turned on him.

Had it been the drinking? Or his age? He'd started having wrecks, and each injury had taken longer to recover from. He'd gone through a lot of women. Slowly his addiction to booze had ground him down. The corner shelf, which had once held his trophies, was empty now, all the trophies having been pawned years ago.

Bills were stacked on the kitchen table beside the plastic shells of empty TV dinners. Shanghai thumbed through a few of the bills. All the utilities were way past due. Grabbing a fistful, Shanghai stuffed them into his back pocket. He'd pay them later as he had in the past. If he left the cash, Dirk would spend it on booze.

Shanghai stomped down the hall. When he cracked the bedroom door, he found Dirk's long, bony body sprawled across a filthy mattress. The hollows beneath his eyes were black. The rest of his face was gray. His mouth seemed to have shrunk, and his buckteeth protruded more than usual. He wore a stained, tank-style undershirt and briefs. If he hadn't been snoring, Shanghai would have thought he was dead.

"Dirk!"

Dirk blinked and smiled and then shut his eyes and rolled over. At least he wasn't a mean drunk, Shanghai thought as he knelt and picked up the blanket on the floor. Without a word he laid it across his former idol.

Dirk began to snore again.

"Sleep well. Enjoy," he whispered.

Dirk Campbell was one of the reasons Shanghai had gone into the rodeo.

Dirk had been a big star once.

Just like me now, Shanghai thought.

Way better than me.

When Shanghai passed back through the living room a few minutes later, the news was blaring. Octavio Morales's swarthily handsome mug shot filled the screen.

"Seven people are dead in a Ciudad Juarez break, and the gun battle is ongoing."

Shanghai went still as he listened.

"Early this morning seven guards were killed in a prison break attempt by Octavio Morales, notorious drug lord. It is feared Morales has escaped. Authorities say that this man is responsible, either directly or indirectly for more than twenty murders on both sides of the border. A reward is offered for his capture or information leading to his arrest."

Clips of blood-soaked bodies on stretchers filled the screen. "Morales is armed and dangerous," the newsman said.

There were pictures of Mia getting out of the helicopter. Then the reporter blabbed that she'd lived with Morales a year.

In disgust, Shanghai turned off the television.

Would the bastard come after Vanilla and Mia?

Adrenaline coursed through Shanghai. Despite his sudden hurry to get back on the road, Shanghai dug a one-hundred-dollar bill out of his pocket and slapped it in the center of the kitchen table where Dirk's past-due notices had lain.

Then he started running.

"No! I won't do it!" Mia said, pushing her teacup away.

Brave words. Hart, the man sitting opposite her, was with

the DEA. How did one fight the DEA? Still, why had she offered him tea on the porch?

"You want to know something, Mr. Hart? You make me
feel even more cornered than Tavio Morales ever did."

John Hart smiled slightly as he scooted his chair back
from the table. He had a plump, boyish face, a kinky beard
and spiky red hair. Even though he had his good-ole-boy per-
sona down pat, something about him made her uneasy.

"You're very lucky to be alive. Tavio Morales must have
formed a profound attachment to you." He smiled again, his
friendly blue eyes damning her for things she'd never done.

She felt her cheeks heat. "What exactly do you mean by
that?"

"Nothing."

Yet he did. She drew a tense breath. When he'd called her
this morning, he'd said that it was urgent, pushing her until
she'd agreed to meet him today. Now she wished she'd said
no.

"I'm hoping I can make you agree to my plan," he said,
"once you know the facts about Morales. He may have been
nice to you and seemed dashing, but he is a very dangerous
man."

"Do you think I don't know that? I barely escaped with my
life! I still feel afraid all the time. I wake up in the dark and
think…"

"Do you want to be scared all your life? Or do you want
to finish this? We can help you, Ms. Kemble."

Longing to flee the porch for the safety of the barn and the
comfort of her horses, she clenched her fingers together in her
lap. Since her captivity, she hated feeling trapped more than
anything. She was glad that they were sitting outside at least,
that there were no walls closing her in with this man.

Still, the longer Mia sat across from Hart, the worse she
felt. What was it about him?

Her mood was in sharp contrast with the peaceful, bucolic

setting. A recent norther had brought rain. The air was cool
for this time of year, and the pastures greener than usual. Fat
black bumblebees droned in the flower beds. Farther out on
the lawn, wild turkeys roamed. There were two shy-looking
deer on the fringes of the mesquite trees, too.

Hart began to recite a litany of facts about Tavio's prison
break and trafficking operation, all of which she already knew.

"I—I don't see how any of this affects me now."

"He threatened you over the phone."

"Once."

"He's out of prison!"

She didn't want to think about Octavio Morales or what
his escape might mean to her personally.

"Look, I told you no. I don't know why we're still talking." She got up. "I have work to do in the barn and a little
girl to see about."

"Morales has to be stopped."

"You want to use us as bait to catch Octavio Morales, and
I said no."

"If you cooperated, you'd help us put a large dent in his
organization." John sipped his hot tea. "He's an evil man."

"When I left Mexico, I just wanted to start my life over.
That alone has been hard."

"I know."

"My father was murdered while I was gone."

"I'm sorry." Hart set his teacup in its saucer. "Ma'am, Morales operates in Chihuahua and Sonora, Mexico."

"He's been in prison. Surely…"

"It'll take more than a few weeks in the can to bring him
down. He's still in business."

"I didn't realize…." She sank back into her chair.

"On this side of the border, his tentacles reach from Texas
and New Mexico into Kansas, Colorado, Oklahoma, Califor-
nia, New Jersey, Idaho, North Carolina, New Jersey, Michi-
gan and no telling where else. He has up to five hundred

individuals who are associates of his. He trades drugs for firearms, which is why his escape from the penitentiary down there went off like a well-planned military assault."

"None of this really matters as far as my decision. I want to forget him. I want to get on with my normal life."

"There's more. He's put up five hundred thousand dollars to have you kidnapped and brought back to Mexico."

"Oh, my God."

"What do you think your chances are down there with him or the Mexican judicial system?"

She stared at him.

"He's got a hit out on Shanghai Knight's life, too. The DEA is putting pressure on the Mexican government and on all those who have contacts with the Morales-Garza drug cartel to get those hits rescinded. Certain officials have helped us make several new seizures recently, but despite our best efforts, Morales's offer for you and the contract on Shanghai's life still stand."

"I can't believe…"

"Morales seems to be beyond even the Mexicans' laws. He's pissed at a lot of people, probably because his trafficking operation has suffered gigantic losses. But his number one target seems to be you. As I see it, you have no choice but to work with us."

"And Shanghai?"

"We're trying to find him. Morales sent a couple of goons to Dallas to kill him. Lucky for him, he sold his truck to a friend who knew how to take care of himself."

"And Shanghai?"

"Supposedly he was headed to a rodeo in Nebraska. Only he never got there."

Cold fear lodged in the pit of her stomach.

Mia's tightly knotted hands in her lap ached. "I—I thought when I came home it was over."

"Believe me, Ms. Kemble, Morales won't quit until we get him. You've got to help us."

"I—I don't want any part of this."

"You're already part of it. Just read the newspapers. If we get him and put him away where he belongs, the public will lose interest. We have a lot of information on Morales and you. If you press…"

"Are you blackmailing me?"

"Why, no ma'am! I think you're an innocent victim!"

"But you're willing to use me…."

"We seem to have gotten off to the wrong start."

"We certainly have." Mia jumped to her feet to signal that their interview was over, at least as far as she was concerned.

He stood up more slowly. "I'm going to be away for the weekend, but you can reach me on my cell phone. If you change your mind, or if you need me or the agency for anything—don't hesitate to call."

John held out his card. When she didn't take it, he set it on the table. "My pager number is on the back. Call!"

John Hart leaned back on the sofa of his camper smoking. He didn't like having to scare the hell out of a woman like Mia Kemble. But what choice did he have? So he had to twist a few screws. He'd learned a long time ago if you were too nice to people like her, his job took longer.

She'd come around. *They* always did.

If she didn't, she might blow two years of hard work. He was mortally sick of Operation Mex-Tex-Zero, the International Organized Crime Drug Enforcement Task Force investigation into cocaine, marijuana and methamphetamine trafficking on the border. He was sick of trying to coordinate with agents and analysts in the FBI, the IRS, other big agencies and various U.S. Attorneys' offices. They were all assholes.

The whole thing was bullshit as far as he was concerned. What the hell had they accomplished? Victory over the drug lords? More drugs crossed the border than ever before.

He wanted Morales. Mia Kemble could give him Morales if she wanted to. It was his job to motivate her.

But for the occasional flare of his cigarette, his camper was dark. He'd parked off a lonely road in the middle of the desert in Big Bend National Park. He'd kayaked during the daylight hours, but now the kayak was out of the river and tied securely on its rack on top his truck. He'd eaten a couple of peanut butter sandwiches and had drunk three or four beers. He would have preferred to cook a steak, but he hadn't wanted to risk a fire. Not out here all alone in the park away from everybody. Nighttime the park belonged to the smugglers. Not that he couldn't handle a smuggler or two. He patted his big gun that lay beside him.

He was feeling good. Real good. The danger added just enough of an edge to keep him from feeling bored.

He bored easily. That's why he'd gone to work for the DEA in the first place. He'd wanted to be a cowboy, a good guy who killed the bad guys. Nobody had told him that life wasn't always that simple.

He didn't like people much anymore—not the bad guys and not the good guys, either. Maybe there weren't any heroes in the real world. After two divorces, his favorite thing to do was to come out here in his camper where he could look up at the stars and lose himself in the darkness and forget about the mess humans were making of the world.

He needed to make a change in his life—but what? No ready answer came to Hart as he smoked. Finally, without bothering to grab a pillow, he squashed out his cigarette and lay back on the sofa, his hand on his gun.

Within minutes, he was asleep. His fingers relaxed, and the gun slipped onto the floor. He didn't hear it any more than he heard the smugglers' horses' hooves clanging on the rocks.

The handle of his trailer jiggled, and then flashlights blinded him. He jumped for his gun, but a booted foot kicked it across the floor.

A hard hand pushed him back down. Before he could cry out, Octavio Morales's soft, husky voice detonated the cozy trailer like a bomb blast. "Sit down!"

The outlaw's gold-plated handgun was aimed straight at his heart. When Octavio's men lifted their machine guns eloquently and then began hollering at him in Spanish, Hart was sure he had seconds to live.

The men yanked his clothes out of the closet and emptied all his drawers on the floor. Then much to Hart's surprise, Octavio waved them back.

"We talk alone!" Glowering, the smuggler threw himself down on the sofa beside him. "Tequila!"

"All I've got is a lousy can of light beer."

"Light? Forget it then." Octavio stuffed a pillow behind his glossy, black head and stretched out his dirty cowboy boots across a scarred table.

"Let's talk," he snarled as he ran a scarred, brown hand through his hair.

Hart was dizzy with fear.

"You and me—we can accomplish much—if we work together."

"W—what do you want?"

"I need to clean up my operation. When I was in prison, bad people betray me. They must pay. You have cases you want to make, no? You want to make a big name for yourself up here in Disneylandia, no?"

Hart had been on the border ten years. "I wanted that in the beginning when I was young and idealistic." He'd given up on it a long time ago.

"If I let you bring these big men in my organization down—" he held up ten fingers "—will you give me Mia Kemble?"

"I need specifics."

Octavio listed ten men in his operation on both sides of the border he was willing to surrender for Mia.

"An American federal judge? You're shitting me."

"I want the woman. Think about it, no? You want to make big name for yourself, no? You want to be somebody?"

Hart said nothing.

"If you give her to me, I give you cops' names. Big buyers' names in the States. Judges. Attorneys."

"If I hand her over, what happens to *her?*"

"None of your fucking business."

Murder? He thought about those bodies on the stretchers after Tavio's prison break. What was one more bloody body? This was war. There were always casualties in war.

Then he thought about her little girl.

The drug war is already lost, asshole. What are you doing?

"I can't deny it's what I've always wanted," he said.

When Octavio held out his hand, Hart took it.

"I will make all our dreams come true, no? And next time when I visit you, we drink tequila, no?"

The morning was soft and gray as Mia walked along the beach holding one of Vanilla's small hands while Lizzy held on to the other. Joanne had declined to come with them because she was driving to the border on a shopping trip. She'd been going to El Paso a lot lately, which seemed odd.

At Cole's insistence, Kinky had come with them today, since he couldn't come himself. The ranch's coastline that edged the bay was remote. Occasionally thieves, vandals or rustlers roared across the water, beached their speedboats and made all sorts of mischief in distant pastures. Mostly they were kids. Still, now more than ever, Cole had said they needed to be cautious.

Thus Kinky stood beside Gus in the shade of the beach house. Both men had guns tucked inside the waistbands of their jeans. Mia was aware of them scanning the crescent-shaped beach, the bay and the road for any sign of strangers.

Not that anyone had bothered them so far. Still, Mia felt

tense that such precautions were necessary. She kept worrying about Shanghai, who didn't have a bodyguard. At least he'd finally called Cole from the road, so she knew he was alive. When Cole had told him to call his friend, Wolf, Shanghai had said he was on his way to Texas—south Texas. That had been two days ago.

"Swim!" Vanilla said, staring out at the waves and then up at Lizzy.

Even now Vanilla still favored Lizzy over Mia, and it hurt.

Understanding her sister's feelings, Lizzy shook her head. "Mia will take you swimming."

"Okay, but first I've got to take off my jeans," Mia said gaily.

She kicked off her shoes and then her jeans and tossed them onto the sand. She wore a bikini under her clothes. At the sound of an engine, she looked up. A truck braked at the beach house, and a tall dark man alighted. The light was behind him, so she couldn't see him all that clearly.

Shanghai? Ever since Cole had said he was on his way here, she'd kept thinking he might turn up any minute. Filled with hope, her heart soared when the man turned and waved at them.

As he ran down the sandy slope toward them, she felt a pang of acute longing. When he got closer, he didn't look quite as wide across the chest as she'd first imagined.

"Cole!" Vanilla yelled.

Lizzy turned and waved wildly to her husband.

Mia's chest ached, but she forced a smile as Cole joined them.

"Swim, Cole!" Vanilla held her hands up to him, preferring him now over Mia.

He tugged off his boots and socks and then swooped the little girl high in his arms. Settling her on his shoulders, he stomped out into the waves, not caring when the saltwater soaked his jeans.

The sisters stayed on the beach, watching them.

"I know it's been hard…coming back," Lizzy said.

"Yes."

"It was difficult for me when I left Manhattan. But you've had to deal with all the bad publicity, not to mention the real threat that Morales might show up at any moment. What a mess it all is. Cole and Leo already had their hands full trying to run the ranch. There's been so many family problems. It'll all settle down. You'll see." She paused. "Did I tell you I'm writing a novel?"

"No."

"It's hard. Harder than I expected. Stories pop in my head, but when I try to write them down, it's awkward getting words on a page."

"You'll figure it out." Mia stared at Lizzy. Her face was softer and lovelier than ever before. Maybe because she finally had Cole and had begun writing. "You always loved to write."

Lizzy nodded. Her platinum hair was tied with a pink ribbon at her nape in a ponytail that blew about in the sea breeze. Strangely today Mia felt no jealousy for her sister's beauty and happiness. In fact she felt guilt that she'd ever caused her pain.

"I should have talked to you before I asked Cole to marry me. I was so upset about Shanghai, I was selfish. I thought you and he were through, but you weren't."

"No. Apparently not."

"I made you unhappy, didn't I?"

"In the short run, but you made me realize how I truly felt about him."

"I'm glad something came out of my idiotic behavior. I feel like I've lost so much," Mia said.

"Did I ever tell you that Sam got a hold of a diary that my mother, I mean…Electra, wrote?"

"Mother said something about that, but I'm eager to hear your slant."

Lizzy had told her all about Electra, the world-famous photojournalist, being her biological mother and how difficult that had been for her to comprehend at first. It still was. Just like thinking about Uncle Jack as being her own biological father felt strange.

Lizzy was watching Cole in the surf and seemed distracted.

"A diary you say?" Mia prompted.

Lizzy turned to face her again. "A journal, really. Mother... er...Electra must've written it during her travels. We think Sam stole it when he murdered her in Nicaragua. He sent a copy of it to Mother to blackmail her. Then he stole it back, but we found the original in his truck. Mother...er, Joanne... gave it to me. I read it, several times. In fact, I read it again not too long ago."

"And?"

"Electra and Daddy had two other daughters."

"What?"

"I guess Mother skipped that part. I think she thought you were on overload."

"If so, she was right."

"Mia, I've got sisters. Twins. They're a little younger than we are."

Mia held her breath.

"Electra got into some kind of trouble, and Daddy went and saved her, but he got her pregnant again. And she wrote all about it. Right before I got married, I gave the journal to Leo and asked him to hire a detective to find my sisters."

"What will that mean for the ranch?"

"Who knows? Still, if I have sisters out there, I want to find them."

"But they won't be my sisters," Mia said. "Since your father and my father were brothers, we're cousins."

"I hadn't thought it all out. You'll always feel like a sister."

"But biologically these twins are my cousins, not my sisters," Mia said.

Lizzy sighed. "It's complicated. Apparently Electra regretted giving me away, so she kept them. But then there came a time when she must've realized she simply wasn't cut out to be a full-time mother."

"And where are they now?"

"Nobody knows. Leo told me recently that his detective has made no progress."

"Well, it will be exciting when he does." Mia watched Cole and Vanilla jumping in the waves. "Imagine that."

"Yes. It's too incredible, isn't it?" Lizzy said.

Vanilla turned and smiled at Lizzy as she was held high against Cole's broad shoulder. Lizzy laughed and blew the little girl kisses with both hands in a dramatic show of affection.

When Cole returned, stomping back through the waves toward them, Lizzy ran out into the water to them. Watching them as she waited alone on the beach, Mia fought the fear that she'd never be first with her daughter.

When Cole reached Mia, he smiled. "I almost forgot... No, hell. To be honest, I've just been working up my nerve to tell you."

"What?"

"Shanghai's back."

"You played in the water all this time and didn't tell—"

"I just had coffee with him in Chaparral. He's here to see Vanilla. He told me he was going to call you."

A bittersweet pain twisting her heart, Mia tossed her head and glanced down at the beach. "Well, frankly, I don't care if he never calls."

"I think he's scared to call."

"I don't care about your brother, okay! He's got a girlfriend, remember?"

"He didn't bring her along."

Mia made a fist behind her back and dug her fingernails into her palm.

"What if I told you that he got himself thrown and that he broke every bone in his body? Would you care then?"

"What? He's hurt? Where is he?"

"And that he's hurting so bad, he's limpin' around like an old man twice his age?"

"Dear God! Where is he? You've got to tell me!"

"I thought you didn't care." Cole grinned. "He's fine."

"You mean he didn't get thrown?" Her throat was still tight with fear.

"I was just fooling."

"You snake!"

Vanilla wriggled out of Cole's arms to the ground and began toddling back to play in the surf.

Forgetting Shanghai, Mia chased after her daughter. Catching her, she lifted her into her arms and ran with her into the warm water.

As Vanilla laughed and splashed the water happily, she looked up every second or two to make sure Mia was still watching.

Mia smiled down at her daughter every time. Only the tightness between her shoulder blades told her how tense she was about Shanghai.

Nineteen

Terence raced up the stairs after Joanne. She looked stunning in a blue sundress of such stark simplicity that one noticed only her, her face and her body and not the dress at all.

He unlocked the door to the new apartment he'd rented on the edge of the desert just so he'd have someplace to bring her. Flicking on the light, he then swung her up into his arms and swept her across the threshold as if she were his bride. He was making a total ass of himself, and there wasn't a damn thing he could do about it.

"All day I've wanted this, to be with you, alone," he said, his voice low and deep, as he let her go in such a way that her body slid against his on the way down.

"Me, too," she whispered. "The whole time I was buying Mexican pots and pottery." When she smiled he noted the rapid pulse in the hollow of her throat.

"I can't believe you made me go shopping and then to lunch," he grumbled, "when you knew what I wanted. You even made me tell you all about my suspicions regarding Hart's sudden fame since Operation Mex-Tex-Zero."

"It'll be better since we waited," she said.

"Hunger being the best sauce?"

"Something like that," she replied breathlessly.

When he was sure she was standing on both feet and had her balance, he crushed her lips with his mouth. At the same moment, he shoved his hands under her thin silk sweater.

"You damn sure took your time eating lunch," he muttered. "Two glasses of wine."

"The merlot was excellent, you must admit," she teased.

"Dessert even?"

She laughed. "I thought we should get acquainted. You know—converse."

"I felt I was going to go wild every time you smiled and flirted and touched my leg or thigh under the table. Then you unzipped me...but only halfway. You knew what you were doing, didn't you?"

Again she laughed. "I'm not sure I've ever had more fun."

She was braless, which he'd known by her jiggle when she'd walked ahead of him through the flea markets of El Paso.

She didn't do a thing to stop him when he cupped her breasts and caressed her nipples until they peaked between his fingers.

Several, long, wet kisses later, her hose and panties were on the flax carpet. He clasped her around the waist and lifted her higher. She wrapped her legs around his hips, and he walked with her toward his dining-room table. With a single swipe of his arm, he sent papers and books flying. With infinite care he laid her down on the smooth, ebony surface and rubbed his swollen penis against the soft dampness between her thighs, making sure she was ready.

"How come you didn't wear a bra today?"

"I did. But on the outskirts of El Paso, I thought about you and ripped it off and threw it out on the highway."

It was his turn to laugh.

He kissed her throat and caught her musky scent, which sent him over some edge. When she arched into him, he drove inside her with a fierceness that had been beyond him, until her. Moaning, she clung. As always the first time was too fast.

When they made love in the shower, he took his time until she was screaming and pounding the tiles as her climaxes went on and on.

"You can't get enough," he said afterward. "As a small boy I used to fantasize about meeting a nymphomaniac."

"I have a lifetime of doing without to make up for."

Terence didn't want to ruin the few hours they had together by asking about her loveless marriage to Caesar. *Later.* Still, he was curious. She seemed so untouched in some ways, like an innocent young girl. She was as thrilled with him as a virgin having her first affair.

He knew it wouldn't last.

But he intended to enjoy every minute of it.

He bound her to the bed with ribbons, and when she struggled frantically against them, he turned her over on her back and took her. Afterward when they were exhausted, they slept for hours.

When she got up, she dressed again and redid her makeup in his bathroom. Once again, she looked regal and untouched in a simple blue sundress—cold even. Then, like a queen, she began wandering about his apartment, looking at everything. She thumbed through a stack of newspapers on his coffee table, sifted through the papers he'd pitched off his table. He felt on edge, as if his privacy were being invaded.

"I see John Hart is making more headlines," she mused.

"All that hoopla about Operation Mex-Tex-Zero?"

"They make it sound like he alone is responsible for the seizure of those two thousand kilograms of cocaine at the border," she said.

"Worth umpteen millions. What I want to know is where's he getting his information. It just seems…"

"What?"

"Too pat. Odd. He's had a fairly average career until now."

"What are you saying?" she asked.

"Nothing. I'm talking out of hand. All I know is that lots of bodies have been turning up in Ciudad Juarez lately. They've all been tortured. Rumor has it Morales is on a rampage. I'm glad Mia has a bodyguard."

She laid the newspaper down.

"Life is tough for a lot of people here in El Paso, but it's ten times worse in Ciudad Juarez," he said.

She sighed. "I never imagined you in a cozy apartment like this."

He saw no reason to inform her he'd rented it just for her.

When she pushed the door to his office open, a prickle of alarm shot through him.

"Joanne—"

Ignoring him, she slipped inside his office.

"There's nothing of you in the rest of the apartment," she said as she fingered his computer, his books and then the pictures of Abby and Becky. "The furniture is so new, it reminds me of a hotel room."

She lifted the photograph of Abby on her golden horse and set it down. Then she picked up the picture of the twins when they were three and still in pigtails. For a long moment she held the photograph up to the light. Despite the fact that it wasn't heavy, her hand began to shake.

He thought he heard her whisper, "Oh, no."

Then he could do nothing but stand paralyzed for several more long seconds, willing her to put the picture back down. Did she know? Had she somehow learned about the twins? Electra's girls? His? Had Caesar known?

No. She couldn't know any more than Caesar could have known. Electra had been very specific on that point. She'd told him she'd taken great pains to insure the adoption arrangements between them would be totally confidential.

Finally Joanne put the picture down, and he was able to

breathe again. Without looking at him, she said, "They are lovely. Children are so much fun, especially little girls, aren't they?" Her tone was perfectly neutral.

He nodded and was glad when she came out of the room. Quickly he shut the door.

"I'm thirsty," she said, moving past him, careful to avoid his touch.

He dashed into the kitchen and found her a bottle of water.

She took it. "I have to go," she said without opening the bottle.

"I thought you were going to spend the night."

"I'm feeling tired all of a sudden. It's a long drive."

"You could rest here. There's a bed."

She laughed, but not lightly as before. The atmosphere was different suddenly—charged.

Without another word, she went to the door. He opened it, intending to follow her.

She held up her hand. "You know how I hate goodbyes."

"But this isn't—"

"No. Of course not." She smiled ever so tenderly. "We'll see each other soon. I'll call you...tonight as soon as I get home."

Then why was her voice so strange and sad?

It was over. She was ending their affair before it had hardly begun.

"Joanne—"

"Don't worry so—"

"Why are you going?" he whispered, frantic to change her mind.

"Because I love you."

"Don't then!"

"I can't explain. Don't ask me to. We've got to stop this—before we're in too deep."

"We already are," he thought, but it was too late.

She was gone.

* * *

It was a picture-perfect spring morning. Sunlight filtered through the mesquite trees and the cottonwood that shaded the new barn as Mia brushed and talked soothingly to Renegade, the troubled gelding, a thickset sorrel, Cole had bought on a whim two weeks ago. Except for Gus, who was lurking just out of sight somewhere in the trees, watching the barn, she was alone.

"Why did you buy him?" she'd asked Cole as Kinky had unloaded Renegade from the horse trailer.

"This beautiful beast was on his way to the slaughterhouse," Kinky had said. "Cole's gotten softhearted."

Despite his narrow escape, the gelding had exuded such quiet confidence when he'd stared into Mia's eyes before he was led to the barn. She'd thought of Shabol.

"I thought you said this horse was crazy," she'd said. "He doesn't look crazy."

"Just you try to ride him," Cole had muttered, stroking the animal.

"He rolls over on them," Kinky had said. "Or slams them into a railing."

"Somebody must've abused you mighty bad," Mia had murmured to the big darling.

He'd become her pet project. Every morning and afternoon she brought him a coffee can full of oats and then slipped a hackamore on him when he was done eating and led him about the corral for half an hour or more. By the third morning he'd been standing at the gate waiting for her.

Wing Nut usually followed Mia to the barn, dog tags jingling, toenails scraping wildly on the concrete floor of the barn while he dashed about eating some oats, too, and, unfortunately, gobbling any horse apples he managed to find.

Now Renegade was her soul mate. The tacit understanding and affection they shared were truly remarkable. Not that she'd ridden him.

She loved getting up early and working with him and then all the other horses in the barn. She'd pick up any stray rocks she found in the barn so they wouldn't break up the horses' feet.

When she was done in the barn, she always felt stronger. Slowly, surely, with their help, she was getting past Mexico. This morning while she'd been sweeping and feeding everybody and mucking their stalls, she'd seen a spotted fawn and its mother, and an armadillo and a jackrabbit on the edge of the lawn. Such sightings rooted her in her real life. This was home, where she belonged. Mexico was a bad dream. One day soon, she'd feel safe again.

The day was heating up. Glancing at her watch she realized it was time for Vanilla to get up and have her breakfast. Quickly Mia put the brushes away and led Renegade outside the barn so he could roam and explore. She removed the halter and stepped back. Hesitating, he gave her a long look, which she took to be both affectionate and euphoric. Then with a final goodbye snicker, he turned. After pawing the earth, he exploded, racing away on galloping hooves toward the trees where the deer had been.

Laughing, she packed up her things, closed the door to the tack room and then headed to get her purse, which she'd left by the sink.

The moment she stepped into the little room, she stopped, her attention caught by a splash of red beside her purse. For a second she rocked back on her heels. Then she saw that it was a beautiful rose; a single, long-stemmed, bloodred rose.

Puzzled and yet enchanted, and somewhat worried, she ran to it and picked it up and twirled it beneath her nose. Wondering about the identity of her mysterious admirer, she went to the doorway and stared at the trees where Renegade had vanished.

The horse was gone. If Gus were out there, he was invisible. The wind sighed in the oak trees, and she wondered who her secret admirer was.

* * *

Indecision and procrastination were driving Shanghai crazy. It was shortly after eleven, and he was in a lousy mood as he drove down the ranch road with all his windows open.

What to do? What to say? How to approach her? What would *she* do?

The air was balmy now, but it would get hot later in the afternoon. He'd rolled up his sleeves. He'd thought he'd hate everything about being back in Spur County and was surprised how much he liked the feel of the wind in his hair just as he liked the dry scent of the grass and cacti and the earthier smells of cattle and horses. Odd, he didn't long for the scent of pine.

Shanghai had been staying at a cheap roadside motel outside Chaparral for the past three days and nights and he still hadn't worked up his nerve to confront Mia.

Today. He punched her cell-phone number into his cell and put his phone to his ear. But, hell, no sooner had it started ringing than he flipped his phone shut—again. Maybe he needed to ride the back roads a while longer, thinking about his past, and about his future, too. Thinking about her.

A man didn't have much time on earth, so he couldn't afford to waste it. What the hell did he want to do with the rest of his life?

What really mattered? Fame? Fortune? Cheap thrills and cheap women who made a man feel momentarily alive?

Or just settling down to a comfortable, ordinary life with somebody special you got a real kick out of being with? A relationship like that would take work. He'd have to reveal himself. He couldn't hide.

When he was a kid, he'd been a smart-ass with all the answers. He'd wanted to be somebody. He'd wanted his name to mean something, the way the Kemble name meant something if only to the rodeo crowd. Back then he'd been determined on hating all Kembles forever—even Mia.

Well, he wasn't a kid anymore, and the notions that had served him then weren't working all that well now. Hate was a mighty poor companion.

Hardly knowing what he did, he made first one turn and then a few more. Before he knew it he hit the blacktop road that wound through unimproved pastures to Black Oaks. Its hard surface was cracked and laced with tall weeds. Nobody came this way much anymore. In some places the asphalt was no more than a broken path that cut through the dense thickets of mesquite and live oak and *huisache*. As he observed the ranch land he'd once worked, he saw that thousands of mesquite-choked acres needed to be chained.

Black Oaks didn't really matter to the Kembles. Caesar had just wanted the Knights gone and Black Oaks forgotten. So, he'd let it go wild.

Well, Caesar was the one who was gone now. Death and time damn sure had a way of leveling things. Cole was in charge now.

Shanghai rounded the last bend. When he saw the ancient Knight homestead, which had once served as the headquarters for a vast ranch that had taken a century to build and far less than that to crumble into nothing, he stopped.

The house was dark. It looked lost and as shapeless as a shadow in the pools of purple beneath the trees. At least when his mother had been here, she'd had red gardenias and purple petunias in the window boxes this time of year. She would have had baskets dripping with plump ferns hanging from every eve, too.

Just looking at the sagging roofline knotted his stomach. If something wasn't done, the place would fall down upon itself in a few years. Frowning, he hit the gas again and drove closer, but when he braked again in front of the one-story, frame house, a peculiar kind of dread filled him. For a second or two he became the lost, frightened little boy who'd grown up here. Then he shook himself.

It was funny how the place seemed to have shrunk since he'd left. Away on the road, he'd remembered it bigger.

He stared at the unpainted, warped boards for quite a spell before he worked up the guts to open his door and climb out.

After his mother had gone, he'd felt so small here, so ashamed. The Kemble name had been so big it had dwarfed him. Maybe things would have been different if his mother hadn't run off. But his daddy had gotten a whole lot meaner after she'd left. All Shanghai had wanted during the last years he'd lived here was to escape.

Why hadn't she taken Cole and him with her? That question had tortured him for years. Deep down he was still afraid to really love a woman.

Even though Shanghai wanted nothing to do with the house and its pain or his mother's betrayal, he felt this place in his bones as he felt no other place he'd ever visited. Maybe he had unfinished business here.

Staring at the drooping porch, he remembered how his mother used to swing him on the porch swing. She'd had the prettiest voice, and he'd sung along with her. His favorite song had been "You Are My Sunshine."

He'd never been able to carry a tune, so he'd probably sounded like a lunatic, but, oh, how merrily she'd clapped when she'd praised him.

A brunette with blue eyes, she'd been so sweet, too sweet for his daddy, he supposed. Shanghai remembered her soft voice in the darkness, too, when she used to whisper good-night to Cole and him. When she'd run off, he'd lain in his bed and had closed his eyes and had pretended he heard her voice saying good-night to him. Then one night, he'd forgotten how she'd sounded. Oh, how he'd cried then.

A breeze gusted through the trees, causing a shutter to bang around back. He felt a sharp stab of loneliness as he climbed the steps.

He didn't need this. He had no business here. He should

have stayed away forever. Maybe he would have if John Hart hadn't called him and told him about the hit out on Mia's life. Then Wolf had told him about two hit men who'd attacked him.

As he opened the sagging screen door and let himself inside, Shanghai's gut clenched. His footsteps sounded hollow as he stomped about, but the three tiny bedrooms and the small bath were just as he remembered them.

Not that he wanted to remember the nights he'd cowered under his bed when their daddy had brought home a woman and the two of them had hit the bottle. Shanghai had hated the loud sounds from that bedroom, the bed banging against the thin wall.

When he'd been sober, his daddy had been as quiet as a scared bird. In town he'd been easygoing with everybody and always ready for a game of cards. But Shanghai had never trusted the quiet weakling or the easygoing man everybody else knew. He'd always known the mean drunk was there, just waiting to come out—at least when it was just the two of them.

Shanghai remembered the last time he'd seen his father and the words that had kept him away all these years, even after his father had died.

You're not mine!

Your mother married me with a no good bastard in her belly.

Shanghai had really felt like a nobody when his father had screamed that. Was it true? Did it matter anymore?

Shanghai was still lost in his thoughts a few minutes later, when he heard an engine being revved outside before the driver turned it off. Looking out, he saw a woman get out of a bright red pickup. She was wearing a pink T-shirt and tight jeans that hugged her butt in all the right places. She had long red hair that rippled halfway down her back. In the distance he saw another pickup stop. A man with white hair was watching her.

It was Mia.

Cole had told him they'd hired a bodyguard.

Conflicting emotions crowded his mind—pleasure, a visceral thrill, fear, protectiveness. Hell, Shanghai still didn't know what he'd say to her.

When she opened the back door of her pickup, she waved to her bodyguard. Then she freed a little girl, who was also wearing a pink T-shirt, from her car seat. The child wriggled to get loose.

"House," Vanilla shouted, running forward, pointing.

When Shanghai strode outside, the little girl turned back and held out her hands to Mia, who swiftly picked her up. Then she ducked her head, hiding from Shanghai.

"She's shy," said Mia, whose smile was almost as shy. "She's barely used to me."

Suddenly he was so glad to see them he felt like an utter fool. What the hell had taken him so long? Even so, his jaw went taut, and he couldn't seem to smile.

Mia was beautiful with the sunlight filtering through the trees and gleaming in her bright hair. He'd never seen anybody so beautiful in his whole life. His chest tightened painfully.

"Hello, Vanilla," he murmured, trying to sound casual as he descended the stairs.

"I heard you'd come home," Mia said. "I kept thinking—"

She probably thought he was a complete idiot.

"I've been meaning to come by."

"Shouldn't you be at some big name rodeo?"

"I used to think so." In spite of himself he grinned. As if in response, her face softened, too. "I used to think I should be anywhere else," he said.

"But you're here. Why?"

"You heard anything from your friend Morales lately?" He tensed again as he wondered if she'd slept with the bastard.

She went paler. "You still with that girl you drove off with?"

"Abigail?" He shook his head. "We broke up. A few days ago."

"Because of me?"

"Well, I didn't see how I could come back here and leave her wonderin'. She took it real hard. I hurt her pretty bad. I'm sorry about that. But I guess some things can't be helped." He nodded toward the pick up. "Your bodyguard?"

"Gus."

Mia's eyes tugged at him, lured him. He swallowed the bait and moved in closer. Vanilla peeped over her mother's shoulder and shot him a flirtatious glance. When he smiled, she buried her face against her mother's plump bosom again. Lucky her.

The kid with her elfin ears and bright blue eyes was cute. Really cute. Much cuter than in her pictures. And she'd grown.

"When you didn't call, I figured you weren't ever coming back," Mia said, bouncing Vanilla on her hip. Her voice was pleasant enough, but her pretty, whiskey-colored eyes were haunted.

He sighed and shifted his weight from one booted foot to the other. "Well, I'm here now."

"Why?"

"When I heard Morales was loose, I was on my way to Nebraska," he said. "At some point I just did a U-turn and headed here. Hell, I don't know why I do half the things I do. That's why I get in so much trouble."

Mia's smile was slow and warm, and it did funny things to Shanghai's insides. He felt all mixed up.

"I didn't sleep with him. I told you that already."

"Right." His throat felt so tight he could barely swallow. "I've tried to quit thinking about you and Morales." His gaze drifted over her. "But Cole said he called you."

"Once."

For a long time they just stood there. "Okay." He fought to get a grip.

When Vanilla peeked at him again, he smiled. Vanilla laughed, causing the tension between Mia and him to ease.

"I stopped at one of those great big toy stores and bought her a present," he began, his voice gentle. "I didn't know what she'd like, so I just got her somethin' that struck me."

He loped past Mia to his car and pulled a stuffed white-and-black dog out of the back.

"Why, that's precious," Mia said when he held it up.

Vanilla squealed in delight.

"Look what I've got, little darlin'," he said, bending close to Vanilla and waving the stuffed toy so that its ears flopped as he pretended to play peep-eye. "It's a dog. His name is Spot."

"What do dogs say, Vanilla?" Mia asked.

Vanilla's head popped up. When she saw the dog again, she broke into a slow grin. "Arf! Arf!"

The stuffed dog had a huge black-and-white head with enormous dark eyes.

Mia bit her lip. "He does look a little like our Spot."

"Only cuter." Shanghai heaved in a deep breath. "I bought him because we both loved that mutt so damn much."

Mia's sparkling eyes were lifted to his as Vanilla held out her hand to take the stuffed dog. "Mine!"

"Yes, little darlin'. He's all yours."

When Shanghai handed her the stuffed toy, she wrapped her arms around it and laid her head on top of its head. "Arf!"

Shanghai stared past them. "When I left, I made a pact with myself I was never coming back here. Not for anything."

"And now?"

His gaze fell on Vanilla. "I'll stay until this Morales situation is sorted out. That's for sure. As for the rest, we'll take it one day at a time." He paused. "I think for starters, you and me—we need to talk."

Vanilla began to kick and wriggle to get down.

"Talking is not so easy when she's around. She's never still a minute."

"When?"

"You hungry?" she murmured.

"What?"

"It's lunchtime at the Golden Spurs. Sy'rai has cooked fried chicken and all the stuff that goes with it."

"Cream gravy?"

"And mashed potatoes. Green beans and iced tea, too. Oh, and a salad. She always makes a fresh green salad out of her garden."

"Pie!" Vanilla chirped, grinning bashfully up at Shanghai.

"Cherry pie today," Mia said. "Vanilla likes to sit in her chair and eat."

"Chair! Eat!" Vanilla chirped, pointing to the truck.

"Mia, I brought you something, too." Shanghai felt his face get hot.

Quickly, in order to get the embarrassing moment over with, he pulled a box of chocolates in a golden box out of his truck and gave it to her.

"Aw, hell," he said. "Might as well go for broke." He grabbed a long-stemmed, bloodred rose off his seat and handed it to her, too.

"I know it's kinda corny," he said, aware of the slight huskiness in his voice. "A red rose and all."

"I don't care," she whispered, smelling the delicate red petals.

Their eyes locked. Hers were warm and sparkling. "I wondered about that other rose this morning. That was sweet."

He felt his cheeks heat again. "Corny."

"Sweet."

He wanted to kiss her so bad he hurt. But he knew it was too soon.

"I'm not real good at giving girls flowers," he said. "I remembered how you threw that rose at me and how nasty I was about it at first. I thought maybe you liked red roses."

"Thank you," she whispered.

"I wanted to forget you." His voice was low and faintly hoarse.

"You were doing real good until you said that."

"Do you want me to lie?"

"No, but maybe you'd better stop while you're ahead because of the roses and the chocolate and Spot."

"But how could I forget, when I couldn't get the good times with you out of my mind, darlin'? No matter how I tried, I kept reliving them over and over in my mind."

"Me, too," she whispered. "Maybe that's a start then. We both have a lot to forgive each other for."

"Do you think you can? It seems to me I'm the one who needs the most forgiving," he said.

"I hope so, but I'm still afraid, Shanghai."

"That makes two of us."

When she smiled, his heart brimmed with intense emotions, some good and some bad, but the strongest of them all was hope.

BOOK THREE

Smart Cowboy Saying:

Good judgment comes from experience
And a lotta that comes from bad judgment.

—Anonymous

Twenty

As Mia heaped fried chicken and mashed potatoes onto Shanghai's plate, she warned herself not to read too much into his return. She mustn't be too eager or too *easy*, she told herself. Bottom line—she mustn't let herself fall into bed with him as soon as he snapped his fingers.

Now that he was in the Golden Spurs kitchen, eating in enemy territory in the same room with the Golden Spurs ranch hands, he seemed much more wary of her than he had at Black Oaks. She had to be careful. He'd broken her heart when she was a girl. After all they'd shared in the cabin, when he'd gone off with Abigail, he'd bruised it again. After years of rejection, how could she ever trust him?

Looking tense and dark, he sat alone hunched over his coffee. He'd chosen a table in an alcove that was usually vacant except during roundup when they hired extra hands and lots of family showed up to help. When she came to the table with his plate, he got up and pulled out her chair.

After they sat down again, they ate in silence at first. He kept his gaze on his plate as if to avoid hers. She was conscious of the hands turning to stare from time to time, and she imagined he was aware of them, too, because of the way he half glanced at them over his shoulder from time to time.

"It's hard coming back," he finally said to her. "You'd think at my age I could shrug off something that happened so long ago."

"Your dad?"

"Yes."

She nodded sympathetically. Cole had told her that his father had always been hard on Shanghai.

"When you're a kid, you think when you're grown, you'll be so big and tough none of the kid stuff will ever hurt you again."

"You ride bulls for goodness' sakes."

"When I was at Black Oaks I kept remembering my mother and how everything changed after she left. It wasn't losing the ranch to your daddy that was the end of everything. It was losing her. I went to Mexico for you because of her. I'm here now mostly for the same reason. I didn't want Vanilla to lose you. I still don't."

"When you jumped, you did more for me than you'll ever know. If I live to be a very old lady and I said thank you every day, I could never repay you."

"That's hardly necessary."

"I will never forget it. Being a prisoner is humiliating and degrading. You're helpless. You never know who'll do what to you or what you'll be forced to do. You have to be nice to people you hate…to survive. So you feel like you're selling yourself out. It's very demeaning and compromising. You probably can't imagine—"

His dark face tensed. He leaned closer, listening to her with rapt attention.

"You have to fight back, too," she said. "I was scared all the time. I don't know how much more I could have taken even if Chito hadn't been sent to murder me in that prison. I—I'd reached a point…where I could feel myself withdrawing from reality in order not to deal with it because I was just so scared all the time. I don't want to live that way ever again."

When she took a deep shuddering breath, he laid a hand on her forearm. "You're home. You're safe."

"But for how long? John Hart says Tavio wants me kidnapped and brought to Mexico."

"I know. Cole filled me in as to all the latest developments."

"Hart wants to use me as bait."

He nodded. "Could be that would be for the best. He's been responsible for numerous seizures on both sides of the border. Maybe he knows what he's doing."

"I don't like him." She took a head-clearing breath. "I'm tired of other people telling me what to do all the time. That's the way it was in Mexico."

"I hate to tell you this, darlin', but that's the way it is everywhere."

"I don't trust John Hart."

"He's all we've got."

"Tavio bought off all kinds of people. Why not an ambitious DEA agent?"

"You can't just sit here, waiting for Tavio to make his move. I say we work with Hart."

"Then you're on his side."

"No, darlin', I'm on yours."

"Then you won't make me act as bait."

He sucked in a breath. "Okay, we'll do it your way. We'll wait on Morales."

I'm not going to have sex with him the minute we get away from the house! I'm not! Mia told herself as they headed out of the barn on Renegade and Sundance. Other than being a little skittish, Renegade was behaving himself and responding to her every command.

Except for the clatter of their horses' hooves on the rocky earth, there was a stillness about the range that evening that awed Mia. The lavender sky was an immense dome above them, and the eight-thousand-square-acre pasture seemed endless.

"It's my favorite time of year," Mia said, feeling proud because Renegade was being so responsive and docile. She'd ridden him for the first time just yesterday evening.

Shanghai nodded agreeably but made no comment. He sat tall on Sundance. She couldn't help but admire how well he rode. But then he would.

Yellow and violet colored wildflowers blazed in the tall grasses. Five deer stood in a carpet of yellow against the fringed edge of an oak mott, their eyes alert as the riders passed them. When Renegade slipped on a hidden rock and lurched to one side, Shanghai shot her a concerned glance. But Renegade recovered himself and continued to plod along like a well-mannered horse.

"I'll race you to the creek," she shouted out of the blue and took off.

Shanghai galloped behind her, keeping up easily.

Truly proud of Renegade, she slowed down when they reached the creek and dismounted. Holding on to their reins they walked toward the grass to the creek. Large live oak trees with thick spreading branches grew on both sides of the trickling water. A low dam had been built to enlarge a natural swimming pool that existed there. The water was green and clear in the pool. Frogs croaked. Dragonflies swooped low over the water. Many varieties of colorful butterflies fluttered.

"Snakes?" Shanghai murmured dryly.

"We've never seen one here, but that doesn't mean…"

"There was a snake in paradise."

"Why did God make snakes…or rats?"

He smiled. "I guess they make the good things seem better."

She felt mesmerized by the feelings unfolding within her. Moss hung in swaying gray draperies from the trees. The fact that they were alone in this wild, beautiful place made both of them nervous. Her pulse skittered too fast, and she could see the apprehension in his quick smiles. Suddenly they were like strangers, who'd just met at a party and had run out of small talk.

He knelt. Picking up a flat rock, he skipped it across the glistening surface of the water. "Nine skips," he said, frowning. "I read somewhere that the record's around forty."

"Not even close," she teased, knowing how competitive he was.

He turned back to her. "You're driving me crazy. You know that, of course."

"How?" she asked with a little catch in her voice.

"Did you wear those skintight jeans to make me want you? Did you race ahead of me, so I'd watch you?"

His blue eyes were so dark and glazed with desire, her mouth went dry.

"I'm not going to fall into your arms every time you look at me with those hot eyes of yours or say provocative things like that…just because you've got me alone out here in the wild."

"I've got you?" His voice was like a soft caress. "You were the one who suggested we go riding to talk."

"We haven't talked yet."

"Later." He pitched his Stetson onto a rock. Then he un-snapped the top two snaps of his Western shirt, revealing bronze skin and black swirls of hair.

"Don't—" Her voice sounded fainter than air.

Renegade whinnied.

"It's hot," he said, but he let his hands fall to his sides. "Maybe you're right, though. We should talk first."

She parted her lips but could think of nothing to say or do. "You start."

"Somehow I feel too distracted."

Her heart slowed at the husky intimacy in his deep voice. The longer she held his gaze, the more she felt herself weakening on the sex issue. The yearning she felt for him was so acute it nearly made her sick. Wasn't she shutting the barn door after she'd already let the horse out?

Life was short. She'd learned that in Mexico when she'd never known in any given hour if she'd live until the next.

"We can always talk," she said.

Without realizing what she was about to do, she stepped into the circle of his arms and clung to him. He was so hard and solid, so strong and warm. He felt wonderful.

"I don't know what you want me to do," he whispered as his arms tightened at the back of her waist. "One minute you say no sex. Then you put your arms around me." His gaze dropped to her lips. He pulled her closer so that she was flush against his body.

"You drive me wild," he rasped, his eyes still fixed on her lips.

"I don't know what I want, either. Just hold me."

Suddenly an intense wave of bittersweet emotion that she was at a loss to understand broke over her, and she began to cry.

"What's wrong?" he whispered.

"I don't know. I don't know," she sobbed, clutching at his collar, threading her hand through his hair. "I guess I'm afraid. I loved you for so long, and it never came to anything."

"You got pregnant."

"I mean… For us." She was quiet for a while. Then she drew a long, fortifying breath. "But you saved me. And you're here now. And yet…"

"I'm here. That's a big step—for me."

He looked so serious, so off balance somehow as a wayward smile touched his lips.

"I know."

Then he lifted her chin and began kissing her with a tenderness that was so exquisite it broke her heart. First his lips caressed her cheek and then her nape and only finally her mouth again.

"I'm afraid to love you, you see. Afraid it won't end happily," she confessed, even as she couldn't stop kissing him.

"I understand. I'm sorry I've made you unhappy in the past. Maybe we'd better stop this for now."

When he began to withdraw, she clung. "No," she said, pressing her mouth to his. "I know the risks. I'm not the innocent little girl who threw herself at you. I know you're a man with a man's needs just as I know sex probably doesn't mean the same thing to you as it does to me. With you it's a physical act and a need. With me, it's more."

She began to tremble and drew a shaky breath. "I shouldn't have run on so. What I'm trying to say is that I know the risks."

"Maybe I don't want you taking them. A man has the right to say no, too, doesn't he?"

"But you're just being noble for my sake."

"Nobility's damn sure a new character trait for me. Why don't let you let me enjoy it a spell?"

"Because it's driving me crazy."

He caught her face between his hands and brushed his mouth against her cheek. "Me, too. But then that's all part of being noble."

"Shanghai...please—" She slid her hands up his chest and around his neck.

"Sit down," he whispered. "You and me we did the teasin'-brat thing. We've done the sex. Seems to me, we skipped the courtin'."

When she sat down on a big flat rock, he took her hand and knelt before her.

"What?"

"Shh. Let a noble cowboy serenade you."

"You can't sing."

"I know. I don't buy girls flowers, either. But you're not just any girl."

That said he began to sing to her in a deep, gentle voice that made her heart race, "You are my sunshine..."

He gazed down into her eyes.

"You can't be serious—"

"My only sun…"

She closed her eyes and let his deep voice wrap her. She smiled dreamily. At some point during the years, he'd learned to carry a tune. He slid his hand around her nape and massaged her with his thumb.

Never in her whole life had she felt this close to love.

San Antonio

Western music whined in the popular Western bar called Ride 'Em that was located on San Antonio's River Walk. Cowboys and their dates danced past Abigail and Kelly's circular table that was jammed with plates of cheese-glazed nachos sprinkled with jalapeños and a pitcher of beer and two mugs.

Watching the dancers made Abby's heart ache with a renewed vengeance for Shanghai. She should go! No matter what she'd promised Kel.

Although a tall cowboy at the bar with a black ponytail was tapping his toe in time with the infectious rhythm and ogling her while he smoked, nobody had asked either Kel or her to dance. Which was good.

Abby was wearing a spandex denim skirt a size too small that rode up her knees, exposing way too much leg. The red jersey top that stretched across her breasts was too snug, as well. The chunks of turquoise jewelry at her throat, ears and wrists were way too flashy. Maybe because Kel had picked them out with that idea in mind.

The hokey cowboy hat that was ringed with a headband made of conchos and fake turquoise sat on Abby's golden head at a pert, comehither angle.

"It's the costume. It's way too corny," Abby said to Kel, who was her secretary as well as a friend.

"Smile at the guy. He looks raunchy, which means he's your type."

"Stop it. You're my secretary. You're not supposed to know all about my love life."

"I read your mail and keep up with your e-mail, remember. You're messy as hell. You always go for the wild guys. That's why they don't pan out."

"I don't *just* go for the wild guys."

"You're neat and organized and brilliant, but I guess deep down you're a mess like the rest of us."

"I didn't come here to get analyzed. Not by my secretary."

"Hey, secretaries rule the world."

She was so right.

"If you want him, smile at him. Lick your lips. Make him think about the dirty, fun things you can do to him with your tongue."

The cowboy wrapped his mouth around his cigarette and sucked really hard. Then he blew a smoke ring at them.

"Gross. Besides I'm too tired. I've been smiling at people all day."

"He'll be way more fun. He's got one of those skinny bull rider butts you like so much."

The last thing she needed was another bull rider.

"I wish I hadn't let you talk me into this."

"Two for the price of one," Kel said, meaning the nachos were supper and the beer was entertainment and consolation.

Abby and Kel had been working in San Antonio all day and were spending the night in the city because Abby had an early appointment tomorrow with an important client, who wanted her to come up with marketing strategies for his latest jewelry collection. After that she had nonstop meetings that included a dinner meeting and an after-dinner meeting.

"This is the only cure for a broken heart," Kel said, picking up a nacho. "Cross my heart."

"Beer and nachos?" Abby munched a nacho, which was so sinfully hot and fattening, she could almost feel her thighs swell and the denim stretch.

"No. A new stud."

"I'm not here to pick up some stranger."

"He won't be a stranger after a few dances and a beer or two. By morning, you'll feel like you've known him forever."

The cowboy took another drag and ate her with his eyes. *Nope. Not him.* She wasn't *that* desperate.

Even as Abigail shook her dark, golden head, she found herself scanning the crowd for other tall men in Stetsons and jeans. A few possibilities were leaning over the pool tables, but not one of them could hold a candle to Shanghai, who was tough and wild and haunted and yet incredibly gentle, too. Oh, why couldn't he have loved her?

Was it only two nights ago that he'd dropped by with flowers and told her it was over? He'd been so sad and sweet about it, he'd made her cry.

"There's this girl," he'd said as he'd fumbled in her kitchen cabinets for a vase for the daisies he'd brought her.

"Mia Kemble?"

He'd nodded. "She's loved me and chased me her whole life."

"I saw the way she looked at you the other day."

"Maybe she got me when my back was turned, and I was too dumb to figure it out."

"So you love her?"

He hadn't answered for a while, which probably meant he did, only maybe he was still too dumb to know it or too stubborn to admit it…or too proud. Mia was from a rich family, and he wasn't as sure of himself as he wanted people to think.

Finally he'd said, "I got her pregnant. Maybe I'd better find out if I can love her. Even if I can't, I…"

"Pregnant?" That reality had hit her like a thunderbolt.

"A little girl…with big blue eyes. Her name's Vanilla. I just found out about her."

What could she have said after that except goodbye?

He was gone—forever. That was all that mattered. So here

she was in a joint like this, pretending she was having fun when she felt so raw and vulnerable.

If she was smart—she'd run from cowboys. Only here she was, throwing herself at temptation.

I'm a moth, she thought. *A stupid, horny, brokenhearted moth.*

"I don't know why you're so sad," Kel said. "It's not like Shanghai was ever around. Or like he ever called you much."

Fool that she was, Abby had lived on hope.

"I don't want to talk about him."

"I don't blame you. We need to be concentrating on your future. On that happy note—" Kel held up their empty pitcher and waved it at a waiter.

"Did we already drink all—"

"The night is young. We haven't even…"

"I wish I'd driven home to the ranch."

A deep voice behind them that was somehow familiar cut into Kel's pep talk. "Do you want to dance—Abby?"

At the sound of her name, she spun on her spandex-clad bottom. The man who stood over her was tall and dark. He wore an expensive-looking, three-piece, gray, silk suit and wire-rimmed glasses that flashed with so much neon glare she couldn't see his eyes. If she had seen them, she might not have been so quick to slot him. But she didn't, so she thought— typical suit, who reeks of money and thinks that's enough.

The man looked smart and elegant and corporate—way too smart and rich as far as she was concerned. Money did something to men. They were boring robots who didn't know how to have fun. Thinking about money all the time, dealing with it, investing it—it made them weak. It tamed them. It took the beast, all the grrrrrr out of the man. She didn't do tame men.

"I don't think so," she said, tipping her hat back and shaking her head.

"Sure she wants to," Kel said. "She's been sitting here driving me crazy tapping her toes and fingernails to the beat."

"My feet hurt," she lied.

"I'm sorry to hear that, Abby. Could I get you something?"

"Hey, you called me by my name—again. Do we know each other or something?"

"Or something." He moved out of the shadows, so she could see him better.

"Leo?"

He smiled. He had nice, white teeth—due to expensive dental care no doubt.

"Leo Storm?"

"Right. I own the ranch next to yours."

"Oh, my gosh. What a coincidence." She tapped her forehead. "How could I forget you—again? The light's bad.... I—I didn't realize you wore glasses."

"Only sometimes."

"I can't believe we keep meeting.... You must think I'm really stupid."

"Sorry I didn't do something brilliant to amaze you the other times we met so you'd remember me." He reddened and looked away.

She blushed, too. "Long day," she said. "All day I remember everybody's name. Then at five, I go blank."

"You brought a casserole over the first time we met, which was delicious, by the way. I was on the phone when you came, remember? So we didn't talk much."

"Oh, right. Actually I—I met your brother, Connor. He almost ran me off the road when I was driving home one night. When he stopped and said he owned the ranch next to mine and had been dying to meet me, I bought him a casserole at a deli. But you..."

Leo's expression darkened. "My younger brother. He drives too damn fast. I'm glad he didn't hurt you."

Just the thought of beautiful, golden, rugged Connor Storm brightened her spirits a little. "Your brother was very nice."

"I'm sure."

"So when I knocked on the door, expecting Connor, I didn't know what to think when you answered, so I just gave you the casserole."

Leo had seemed so dull compared to his younger brother. Leo had been on a business call on his mobile, talking big money numbers, frowning, his voice sounding cold and pressured.

She did business with his type all day long. Was it a crime that she avoided them when it came to her personal life?

"When we met again at the Golden Spurs, you were there to pick up your bull rider friend, Shanghai Knight," Leo prompted.

She'd been so scared that he was in love with Mia, she'd been in a fog.

"So, since we're neighbors and have mutual acquaintances, do you mind if I sit down?" he said.

Without waiting for her answer, he plopped himself in a chair across from them and began chomping down on a nacho. When the waiter came, he paid for their beer, added an impressive tip and ordered a third mug and more nachos.

"No time for supper," he said and polished off two more nachos.

To avoid talking to him, she drank her beer too fast. As a result, Leo's dark face began to blur.

He leaned closer. "How's the famous bull rider?"

"He dumped me."

"For Mia?"

She nodded.

For some reason she found herself thinking that maybe he'd already known that. *Crazy thought.*

"I'm sorry. I know now is not the time to say this. But maybe someday, you'll see this as a good thing."

"You're right about now not being a good time. But Mia and he…they go back a long way."

He tilted his dark face back, causing the lenses of his

glasses to glint. She could almost feel him filing that tidbit away.

"Don't tell anybody about this," she whispered.

When he put a sympathetic hand over hers a minute later, she was surprised that he had large, rough, working-man's hands.

"You should go chase some other girl," she said, but she didn't pull her hand away. "I'm a mess."

"One dance, and I'll scram."

"Promise?" she whispered.

As soon as she stood up, his big hand slid around her and imprisoned her at the waist. Before she knew it, she was molded against him, and he had her all to himself in the darkest corner on the dance floor.

Normal cowboys glided around the floor in a big circle like skaters at a rink with their dates. Not him. Much to her surprise, she felt better in his arms than she could have ever believed. Her grief over Shanghai lessened. She closed her eyes and tried to imagine Connor.

Leo danced like a dream. Born rich, his mommy had probably paid for lots of dancing lessons at some country club. He was tall. At least height was one thing he couldn't fake or buy. She liked tall.

Through the smooth silk of his suit, she could feel the ripple of his hard muscles as he moved, and his big hands were hot wherever they touched her. His suit, which was probably padded, gave him "pretend" linebacker shoulders. He seemed big, and he exuded power. Somehow he made her realize how vulnerable she was, but instead of being threatened, she felt protected.

Then the beer really hit her, and she found her body was plastered against his. When his legs brushed hers, the effect heated every sense in her being.

How could she feel horny when her heart was broken?

The next song was faster. They were already dancing before she remembered that after one dance he was supposed to be history.

The music was hot, sweet and wild. He pulled her against his body, and pushed his silk-clad leg between her thighs. Leaning back, she rocked up and down on his leg. He shimmied with her, shook with her, whirled with her, brought her close to his body again. Pressing her against his thigh again, he swayed with her to the jungle beat until she felt primitive and wild.

She was way past telling him to stop. How could she have ever thought he was dull? Shanghai was forgotten. She wanted only one thing now—to dance and dance and dance…with Leo Storm, the dullest man she'd ever known.

Many fast songs later, when they were both gasping for breath, he held her so close she realized his heart sounded like thunder.

"I—I'm not attracted to you," she said. "Connor, maybe, you—no."

"Connor! What is this?" he grumbled. "Confession time again?"

"Seriously—I like cowboys. I always have. You don't have a chance with me."

"I manage a ranch—one of the biggest in Texas. Does that count?"

"Maybe a little. But it won't for long."

"I'm not looking for a lifetime commitment. It's late. What do you say we go somewhere?"

"Kiss me first."

"I'm not a cowboy, remember? You prefer Connor."

"Don't remind me."

She took off her hat and placed it on his head. It didn't quite fit, but he looked better than she'd thought he would.

"Kiss me, cowboy."

"Just one time," he said. "We'll call it a teaser."

She puckered her lips and pretended to close her eyes. He

took off his glasses and slipped them in his pocket. As his dark, tanned face lowered toward hers, she saw a brilliant black flame light up his gorgeous, dark eyes so that they burned with an incredible intensity. Even before his mouth touched hers, and she felt as if a volcanic heat scorched her bones, she was thrilled by the passion in his gaze.

He was *that* hot.

He ended the kiss almost immediately and let her go.

Some teaser.

Her heart had speeded up, and it had become difficult to breathe.

"Not bad for a guy who's not a cowboy," she admitted. Without knowing what she did, her fingertips touched his cheek. "Who are you really, Leo Storm?"

"Why don't you come home with me tonight and find out?"

"I don't think so."

"I guess one more kiss won't hurt," he murmured.

"Another teaser?"

"No. I'm going for broke on this one."

Twenty-One

What am I doing here?

When Shanghai pulled up at his motel, Mia was awash in second thoughts again. She knew better than to trust herself to get out and go in with him. And yet…

I will lose him if I do this. I've been too eager too long.

He shut off the engine and turned toward her in the darkening twilight. His face was carved into hard lines. He looked as uncertain as she felt.

Long minutes passed while they sat in silence, neither touching nor speaking. Cars whizzed past on the highway behind them. Soon the air between them was thick and heavy.

He took her hand in his and drew it to his lips. When his mouth blew warm air between her fingers, she shuddered. The whole time she had been married to Cole and had slept alone, she had dreamed of this. In Mexico, she had dreamed of Shanghai, too. All her life, when he'd been away, she'd thought of him. He'd been with her always, if only in her imagination. There had been times when she'd felt like his spirit had called to hers; times she'd thought maybe he'd missed her a little, too. Not that she'd ever let herself believe that he was willing her to think of him as she'd willed him to remember her.

Now he was here, *really here,* for what might be a brief time. She knew how foolhardy it was to give her body and risk her heart, but she didn't want to spend another day without him.

He kissed each of her palms, causing her flesh to tingle beneath his mouth. In a hush she turned toward him, feeling more alive and hopeful than she'd ever believed she'd feel again.

All he'd ever had to do to add meaning and depth to who she was, was to look at her or touch her or speak to her. Theirs wasn't just a sexual attraction. The emotional bond was equally intense, at least, for her.

She didn't know why he mattered so much to her. She only knew that if he left again, he would take a big part of herself with him, and she wouldn't feel whole. But such was the risk of loving him.

She clenched her hands for the briefest moment. Not to love him was to refuse life itself.

Hardly knowing what she did, she began to unsnap the top buttons of his Western shirt.

He sucked in a swift breath.

Ripping the edges apart, she buried her lips against the corded hot skin at his waist.

"Darlin'," he growled in a low guttural tone as she began to kiss him, her fingers sliding inside his belt an inch.

Faster than lightning, he slammed out of the truck and hauled her out with him. Bringing her close against his body, he moved his cheek across hers. Then he pressed her into the back truck door and held her against his long, lean body for an infinite time, his heat burning into her.

"I thought you were never coming back," she whispered against his throat, her voice low and desperate.

"I was a fool." His hands were in her hair. His leg moved between hers, parting them.

A maid came out of a room and stood perfectly still, watching them as she clutched a large bundle of sheets.

"You comin' in with me or am I driving you home?" he whispered raggedly.

She giggled and clung tighter to him.

"That's a yes, I guess." His grin lit her heart.

Then they were inside the motel room, both frantic the moment he bolted the door. He tossed his keys on the dresser, and as if that were a signal they began tearing off their clothes and throwing them into a heap until they were both naked with a rumpled mountain of garments pooled between them.

He stepped over the clothes. Gathering her in his arms, he carried her to the bed. Lowering her onto the mattress, he kissed her again, feasting on her mouth and nipples with his lips like a man who'd been starved. Soon her skin was wet all over from his tongue. He worked his way down her belly, licking and kissing her everywhere until he parted her legs and began to stroke her.

Her body heated when she felt his eyes looking at her. She went wild when his tongue finally delved inside her. Even when she tugged his head closer and started screaming, he kept licking her, stopping only when she'd climaxed several times and finally lay limp. Still clutching his head against herself, she shook until she was so utterly exhausted she could barely breathe. Then she flung her arms out and didn't move. Not even when he covered her with the sheets and blanket and pulled her into his arms and held her quietly.

A long time later, she got up and took a shower. Drained, but happier than she'd ever been and yet scared, too, she leaned against the wet tiles and let the warm water stream over her.

Maybe she should be ashamed to let him do that the first day she'd seen him, but she wasn't. Not really. He'd made her feel beautiful and adored in the most intimate way possible. She'd always felt ashamed of that part of her body, always wanted to keep it hidden. If she never had him again, at least she would have the memory of these fleeting moments when he had worshiped her and made her feel so absolutely feminine and gorgeous even there.

"You okay?" he called when the hot water had grown so cold that she'd turned off the faucet.

"I think so."

He laughed. "Don't use up all the hot water."

She giggled. "I already have."

"Come out then. I have something for you."

"I don't think I can walk."

"Then I'll carry you."

Two seconds later he opened the shower door and wrapped her hair in a towel. Stepping out, she wrapped herself in the other towel and tiptoed back to the bed.

"You used all my towels, too," he said.

"I'll bet management has more."

"I'm not complaining." He pulled her into his arms. "Besides, I want you to make yourself at home."

"So much for not being easy where you're concerned," she said.

"You can't help yourself, apparently."

She blushed. His words were too true.

"You're too conceited for words," she said.

"A failing of most famous bull riders, I'm afraid. We're a flawed bunch of arrogant, foolhardy idiots."

She licked her lips, reveling in the warmth and affection in his low tone.

"Marry me," he said, sliding a black velvet box across the sheet toward her. When she just stared at it and then at him, he opened the lid. "I know I should go down on bended knee, but the mood to ask you right now just hit me."

The large diamond twinkling at her made her gasp.

"I already bought the ring...before we had sex. Or rather you had sex."

"Me?"

"Yeah, you. You owe me one, darlin'. But the point is, I was already going to ask you...."

When she didn't say no, he lifted the ring out and pushed it over the knuckle of her ring finger.

She shook her hand and made it flash. "I can't believe you just went out and bought this without even asking me."

"I'm asking you."

When she tried to tug it off, it was so tight, it wouldn't slide back over her knuckle.

"Looks like a yes to me." He grinned. "I guess we're stuck with each other."

"Is that how you feel? Like you're stuck? Do you have any *other* feelings?"

Such as *love,* she thought, her heart aching to hear such words from him.

"I told you about those men who tried to kill Wolf in Dallas. Well, Wolf told me they had machine guns. They were like sharks, hunting their prey in a pack. All I've been able to think about ever since is that I want to be here if more guys like that come after you."

"You're afraid for Vanilla?"

"And for you." He kissed her forehead lightly. "I want to marry you. Sometimes guys like Tavio lose interest if a woman's married because then they see her as another man's possession."

"I won't be your possession—or his or any other man's—not ever. I'm still struggling to find myself after being held as Tavio's prisoner in Mexico. Really, I'm not over that experience. In fact, I don't think I'm in any shape to marry anybody."

"I want you to sign papers that Vanilla's legally my child."

Was he thinking that Tavio might succeed in killing her?

Clearly he wanted Vanilla, and he didn't want to fight her family for custody if she died. She couldn't really blame him for that. He was Vanilla's father. His request was both understandable and legitimate—no matter how much it hurt.

He hadn't mentioned love, but if she married him, he'd stay…at least for a while, and Mia could pretend they were a real family. Vanilla would get to know him.

But then he'd leave them all over again, and they'd all have to deal with that. She was too confused to know what was best.

"I'll give you a divorce when this is over," he said, not looking at her now as he traced her hand with a fingertip. "If that's what you want."

"Is that what you want—a divorce?"

"No. I'm just saying this doesn't have to be permanent. I won't use this to try to own you or control you."

She nodded, feeling strange and sad even as she wondered how he really felt.

"It just has to look permanent. I'm not after the Golden Spurs anymore. So don't worry about that, either. This marriage is about protecting you."

"And Vanilla?"

"Of course. I went to Mexico to make you safe. Why would I want you both at his mercy now?"

When he looked up and smiled at her, she clenched the sheets.

She wanted more. So much more. Was that wrong?

"I never thought I'd even consider marrying a man who doesn't love me."

"What about Cole? You married him fast enough, didn't you?"

She inhaled a sharp breath. Cole was different because she'd never imagined herself in love with him, never considered theirs a real marriage.

As if Shanghai sensed her disappointment in his proposal his voice softened. "It's hard for me to make promises when nobody I counted on ever kept theirs to me."

She nodded, struggling to understand.

"My mother ran away. My father was a drunk." There was

a wealth of pain in his low voice. "Hell, maybe he wasn't even my father."

"I know how that feels. I'm sorry about all that. But I'm not going to treat you the way they did."

"I'm trying to explain why this is the best I can do right now. I don't want you building false hopes about me or this marriage."

She knotted the sheets even more tightly.

"I don't want to build up false hopes, either," she said, remembering how she'd chased her father and then him, always longing for them to love her.

"Good."

Too bad for her she'd already built up false hopes. It was the way she was. She couldn't seem to stop herself from chasing men who were doomed to run. His lovemaking had left her feeling cherished and awed and now he was speaking in such cool, practical terms, asking her to marry him because he wanted to protect her, and yet offering to divorce her as soon as possible.

"I still don't want to marry a man who doesn't love me."

"Fair enough. You decide."

She stared straight in front of her for a long while. Finally she said, "If I marry you, I won't sleep with you again."

When he moved his leg against hers, she jumped. "You wanna bet?" he murmured dryly.

"I'm warning you, don't marry me because you think you'll get a lot of easy sex."

"That's your rule. Not mine, darlin'. How can you dream up a scheme to torture me when you know how crazy I am about you that way?"

Before she realized what he was about, he'd grabbed her, cupped her head between his hands and kissed her.

"Stop it right now. I'm warning you—"

His mouth was so searingly hot, his kisses soon had her breathless.

"We're not married yet, so I guess the rule's not in force yet," he teased.

When he angled her head to one side, she sighed and quit fighting him.

His hand closed over one of her breasts and reshaped it to fit his brown, callused palm. Deftly he began caressing her nipple.

The blood began to roar in her ears. "Oh, Shanghai."

"Do you want me to stop?"

"I wish."

He laughed. "You're so damn sexy."

"But not easy."

"No, definitely not easy," he agreed as he leaned over and she licked her way down his abdomen to his shaft. "No other woman has ever been more trouble, I assure you."

After her lips circled him, it wasn't long before he was breathing too hard and too fast to debate the issue.

Feeling strangely jumpy because the dogs had stopped barking, Guillermo hurried a sleepily yawning Marisol across his tiny living room. Because he hadn't wanted anybody outside to see a light and be warned they were up, they'd dressed in total darkness in his bedroom that had wall-to-wall mattresses as flooring. She was carrying her shoes because she hadn't been able to stand up on one foot on the mattresses to put them on.

"Put on your shoes and hurry," he whispered, his voice tight with impatience as he cracked the front door an inch. "We've got to leave before the sun comes up and my neighbors begin to stir."

"I don't care about the neighbors. I'm sleepy—" Her voice was cross from having been awakened.

Clamping his fingers around her wrist tighter, Guillermo slipped his gun out of his shoulder holster and stared down the street for a long time. The houses were quiet and dark, the unpaved road dusty and barren except for Paco, the skinny black dog, napping in the middle of it.

Paco always barked at strangers. So did the dogs on the roofs of the other houses. Still, the utter soundlessness of the street bothered him.

He reholstered his gun, telling himself there was nothing to worry about. Tavio's escape simply had him spooked.

Tavio couldn't possibly know about this stylish casita where he brought all his young loves. At the thought of his house, Guillermo's mind turned to happier thoughts.

How many *comandantes* had taste like he did? He'd studied pictures in fancy magazines. Thus, the small rooms of his small house were decorated with oriental rugs, and the walls hung with eastern tapestries. Sometimes he imagined himself an Arab sheikh or an ancient chieftain when he brought a new girl here.

Here he seduced, treating his women to beer or wine and to delicacies like thick juicy steaks. And *siempre*, always, he was very careful not to be followed when he drove them here.

Marisol fought to tug her hand loose. "I said I'm sleepy. Why can't we stay all night?"

"Shh."

"What are we waiting for?"

He didn't like whiny women. "Be quiet, *puta.*"

"*Puta?* You never called me that before."

"That's what you are, *mi amor.*"

She hissed in a breath.

Tonight he'd gotten her very drunk. He'd taken pictures of her dancing naked, of her butt cheeks spread wide with various objects inserted inside her, frontal shots as well with the pouting lips of her vulva spread, too.

She was only sixteen. She'd been a virgin. Still, he'd taken her every way a man could take a woman, causing her to weep several times.

Por supuesto, after tonight she was a *puta.* Turning virgins into whores had long been a favorite sport of his.

"You think you are a big man, but now I know better."

He swung around violently. "What do you know?"

"You're scared because everybody says Octavio Morales is going to kill you. That's why I had to stroke you so long with the jelly. That's why you wake me in the dark."

He slapped her twice. When she fell down screaming he grabbed her and shook her until her eyes grew huge. Then his hand closed around her mouth. Still she fought him, biting at his fingers.

"Don't make me really hurt you," he growled and was gratified when she went limp.

A minute or two passed while she gasped for every breath and stared at him with those big dark eyes of hers like a paralyzed mouse about to be scratched to pieces by a long-clawed cat. He felt his cock grow big. Who needed a hand job or a pill to get hard now? If it wasn't so late, he'd rape her right here.

When she was still and silent for a long time, and he finally released her, she fell to the floor.

"A man in my position can't be too careful."

She stared up at him with bruised, dark eyes that had sparkled and flirted with him earlier. Both cheeks were scarlet where he'd struck her. Skin like hers bruised easily.

Something to remember him by.

Good. Now she knew how tough he was. He could be nice to her again. Until their final fuck. He would celebrate that by branding her left butt cheek with the tip of his cigar.

"It's just that I want to protect you, *querida.*"

"From Morales?"

"Shut up about him, and be quiet when we go outside to my car."

He opened the door wider. "Go! Now!"

Like a child she sprinted ahead of him. He watched her, delighted with the way her hips moved in the tight red dress. She was a *puta,* and there were many pretty putas in Ciudad

Juarez. Usually he passed his used whores on to Enrique and treated himself to a new one.

Dios, but he was hard again because of her cowering. He would keep her for a while. Sex after such a spat always held an added thrill. He knew that she would be submitting, that he'd taken something from her she'd never get back.

He would give her flowers tomorrow, maybe a shawl and a pretty silver ring. And some cash. Fifty dollars cash.

Putas loved money. She'd be all giggles and jiggles again tomorrow night.

As Marisol ran toward his car, he saw the adobe house and the dusty street as if they were part of a scene in a movie. A terrible premonition hit him. Suddenly she was Apollonia in *The Godfather,* and he was his favorite film star, Al Pacino, playing Michael Corleone when he'd been hiding out from his enemies in Sicily.

With a scream in his throat, Guillermo turned. Horrified, he yelled to her to stop, but it was too late.

He was already running away from the car when his Toyota exploded and the black sky became flame and shards of flying glass and burning metal.

Oblivious to the greasy feel of taco juice dribbling down his chin, Guillermo grabbed a stale tortilla only to stare at the splatter of cold, yellow egg on his plate. The stench from his armpits was spoiling his appetite. He smelled worse than a well-used whore. When he lifted a napkin to his jaw, the bristle from his three-day stubble tore the flimsy paper.

He hadn't slept since the explosion, nor eaten since noon yesterday. For three days, Enrique had been moving him from safe house to safe house if you could call this squalid, eroding sandbox at the end of a dirty street in a bad neighborhood safe.

One minute Guillermo was wrapping his flour tortilla around a glob of cold egg and greasy chorizo. In the next he saw a big black van barreling up the dirt road so fast, chickens and dogs and brown-legged children went flying before it.

Morales.

The *pendejo* had found him.

Guillermo got up so fast his chair fell over backward. Still clutching the tortilla with dribbles of egg falling out of it, he ran out the back door in his bare feet.

Behind him men in uniforms shouted.

"Stop! Or we'll shoot!"

Despite the hard rocks and thorns cutting into his feet, he ran for many blocks, weaving in and out of the narrow streets until finally he found himself breathless, trapped like a rat in a maze. His street had dead-ended into a wall of dank-looking adobe shacks jammed together.

Seeing a narrow, corrugated drainage pipe filled with garbage beneath the dirt road, he dove for it, yanking out handfuls of shitty diapers and rotting food and a dead rat. Then he jumped into the pipe backward, pulling the rotten fruit and dirty pampers back in front of himself.

He shut his eyes and prayed.

Ten men ran up and down the street. Knocking on doors with the butts of their guns, they quickly entered and searched the houses. When the people didn't answer, they kicked the doors in and searched them anyway. When one man argued, Guillermo cringed at his cries when he heard them beat him nearly to death.

"He's got to be here!" Tavio's voice rang in the street. "What's that over there?"

Men ran over to Guillermo's hiding place. One of them stood so close, Guillermo could have grabbed the man by the ankle of his boot.

"Nothing, Tavio. We find nothing!"

"Pull this shit out of this pipe!"

When one of the bastards reached inside the pipe with his hand, Guillermo bit his finger halfway off.

The man screamed and drew back, but another one came up and sprayed the pipe with bullets. After that Guillermo couldn't feel anything from the neck down. They dragged him out by the hair, and he was helpless to resist them.

"Tie his legs to the back of my Silverado!" Tavio yelled, while big-eyed people from the houses watched from behind their windows. "If there's anything left of him when we get to the desert, we'll finish him off there."

"Tavio...please..."

"I trust you. You attack me at my rancho in front of my women. You put me in prison. You ruin my business. You drink with me. You take my presents, but you are not my friend. You know what is wrong. You show me no respect. Today I teach you respect."

Ten miles outside of Ciudad Juarez, when Tavio's men finally cut him loose in a dusty area filled with low mesquite and grease-wood bushes, Guillermo was barely conscious when Tavio spoke to him again.

"Too bad the ladies can't see you now, eh, Guillermo. You like to brand women with your cigar, no? You like fire? You like to hear them scream?"

Guillermo tried to move his hands. He strained to make nerves and muscles work. His heart pounded. His blood pumped.

Nothing. Nothing except Tavio's laughter.

Tavio grabbed a bottle of tequila and took a long pull. Guillermo squinted but he couldn't bring him into sharp focus. Still, he could see his dark hand lift one of his crack-laced cigarettes to his nose and then put it back in his shirt pocket.

"Dig a shallow ditch around him," Tavio ordered. "Then get out the drums of gasoline."

"No... Please..." Guillermo begged, his voice a pitiful squeak.

Tavio strode closer and leaned down. "You think you're a tough gangster now?"

"No… Please…" Frantically Guillermo tried to move.

Tavio's men dumped armfuls of branches on top of him, and Guillermo was helpless to stop them. Next they emptied two drums of gasoline into the pit where he lay soaked in the foul-smelling stuff.

"No…." *Don't burn me alive!*

Tavio struck a match. He stared at him for a long moment. "I thought you were my friend," he whispered. Then he leaned down. "I will tell you a little secret. I do not like to kill or to rape or to burn women." His dark eyes full of regret, he stood up again. "I like you." Then almost carelessly he flicked the match toward Guillermo.

Guillermo began to scream even before the explosion that shot sparks and flame and roared so loud none of the men standing around the fire could hear his cries.

The last thing he saw through the flickering orange glow was Tavio's grim face as he smoked his crack-laced cigarette.

"I'll see you in hell!" Guillermo screamed as Tavio's face blackened and was lost in darkness.

Twenty-Two

When Abby woke up, her mouth was sour with the taste of beer and onions and beans as she struggled to push the naked man off herself. The long, lean stranger with the wide shoulders, who had her pinned beneath him on the mattress, felt as heavy as lead.

What? Oh, my God!

Who was he? For a minute or two, she didn't know where she was let alone who *he* was.

Then it all came back to her. The bar. Dull Leo Storm. Her neighbor.

She was in Leo's loft apartment in downtown San Antonio. As easily as some cheap slut, she'd fallen into bed with him.

How long had she been here? What had they actually done? How many times?

This was a new experience for her. She had only the haziest memories, and none of them went past her striptease act when she'd stood on his table and stripped to The Song—the anthem of the rodeo world.

How had dull Leo Storm known to play "Wild Thing"?

Rugged and pulsating and sexual, the music had made her remember dancing with Shanghai. Crazy with heartbreak, she'd let go of all her inhibitions. Encouraging her, Leo had stood beneath her, chanting the words while she'd pretended he was Shanghai. On shaky knees, she'd undulated to the mad beat, ripping off her clothes and throwing them at him. When she'd finished, he'd grabbed her, slung her over his wide shoulder and hauled her across his apartment to his bed, cowboy style.

She'd closed her eyes to shut out his suit and shorter haircut and had gone on pretending he was Shanghai.

Leo had been very good at sex, at least the kissing part, which she remembered vividly, maybe because he'd been so enthusiastic about her. Not that she could remember all that much of the evening once he'd stripped. Oh, dear—she did remember playfully pulling his tie off with her mouth. But after the initial foreplay, hard as she fought for details, fortunately, everything got blurry.

Maybe because I don't want to remember.

I'm a slut, she thought, hating herself and him. What kind of lowlife took advantage of a brokenhearted girl and ravished her?

What man wouldn't when she behaved like a slut?

He would have no respect for her now. He'd probably tell his brother and all their neighbors. Maybe he'd even brag to Shanghai.

They would all think she was easy.

Easy was too kind a word.

Slut was more accurate. If he turned out to be a big mouth, she'd never live this down. Why had she gone out when she was feeling so low and vulnerable?

Because staying home alone had terrified her.

She had to get out of here before he woke up!

After much wriggling and shoving at his hatefully broad shoulders, she managed to get free of the handsome jerk. As she grabbed her clothes, he began to snore lightly until he rolled over. After that he began to sleep more quietly.

Mortified as she studied his sprawled, muscular body in the moonlight, she fastened her bra with only one hook. He was good-looking in the buff, she'd give him that.

But what if she got pregnant? Had he even used a condom? If only she could remember. On the other hand, maybe it was just as well that she didn't. Now she'd have no embarrassing details to haunt her.

As she pulled on her red jersey top, memories of his lips on her nipples as he'd suckled and caressed them assaulted her. Her face did a slow burn as she pulled on her skirt and began to search the floor for her red satin thong panties.

When she couldn't find them, she wanted to wake him up and scream at him. But there was no telling what he might do, or what she might do if he kissed her again as he had in the bar, so she gave up the search. He was a good kisser.

Too good.

Grabbing his keys, she ran out the door without her panties. She'd call him later and tell him where he could find his truck.

When she called him, should she ask him to mail her her panties?

No. Hell, no!

On second thought she wouldn't bother calling him about his damn truck. He'd have to find it on his own.

Joanne took a deep breath against the panic that threatened to overwhelm her as she clutched the phone to her ear in a death grip.

"I'm afraid I'm busy on that date, too," Joanne said.

She wasn't looking at her calendar, but she didn't need to.

"Every time I call, you say you're busy," Terence said in a mild tone. "I guess a smarter guy would take a hint."

Joanne said nothing as she strode across the living room and then went outside to stand on her veranda. She hated his calls now because she wanted to say yes to him so badly.

She drew another deep breath and stared across the pastures. The sky was gray and the wind was blowing, causing the palm fronds to clatter so noisily she had to go back inside.

"I—I guess I don't think this…us…our seeing each other is…is such a great idea," she said.

"Why the hell not?"

"It should be obvious."

"To whom?"

"We're so different."

"So?"

"There's no future."

"Do people like us really need a future? What's wrong with us just seeing each other until we get tired of each other?"

Nothing—if you weren't who you are and I wasn't who I am.

"Someone's bound to find out," she said.

"So what? We're not committing a crime."

"It would be embarrassing."

"And that's your final answer?"

"Goodbye, Terence."

"What is it really?"

Again she saw the picture in his office of his twin blond daughters. "Please, don't call again."

Quickly, without saying anything else, she hung up on him.

Maybe her abruptness this time would convince him that his calls were useless. Hopefully he'd give up soon. Because every time he called, his deep, gravelly voice cut her to pieces.

She couldn't care about him. Not seriously. It was just that she'd so little happiness of the kind he provided.

So little good sex, too.

God, she missed the sex. Just talking to him had her wet and shaky and feeling half her age.

On an impulse, partially to distract herself, she dialed Leo and was relieved when he answered.

"I know it's early..."

"I was just on my way out."

At least she hadn't awakened him. "It's me. Joanne," she said without further preamble. "Did you find anything out?"

"About what?" He sounded confused.

"The twins. Electra's missing twins. I know Lizzy gave you Electra's journal and asked you to hire a detective."

He drew a long breath.

"Not yet." His deep tone had sharpened.

"But you're still working on it?"

"Yes. I'll let you and Lizzy know when I find out something."

He said goodbye. When he hung up, she felt even more dissatisfied than ever.

Usually she had the utmost confidence in Leo. But he hadn't sounded like himself. There had definitely been something strained and odd in his tone.

It's not Leo. It's me. I'm overly sensitive because I'm so rattled about Terence. That's all.

Leo would call when he knew more.

Why hadn't she told him what she knew?

"Get married at the end of this week?" Mia whispered, stunned.

Gripping the wheel, Shanghai stared down the road, swerving to avoid a pothole. "I don't see why not."

"Plan a wedding? That fast? You can't be serious!"

He shot her a quick, impatient glance. "I'm here. I popped the question, and you said yes. We have to get some blood tests and a license, wait a few days. And then—why the hell not?"

"This isn't something as easy to set up as a doctor's appointment or a haircut."

"All we need is a preacher and a few people in the chapel to stand up with us. You could pull it off if you wanted to."

"So now the ball is squarely in my court."

"People spend way too much time and money on weddings these days. Like I said—you could do it."

"So our wedding is no big deal? You just want something thrown together?"

"Your words. Not mine. I don't see what's wrong with my idea."

"A man would think like that."

"We have other more important things to deal with," he said gravely. "Life and death matters for one thing." His voice took on an edge. "I wouldn't mind shutting the press up on the subject of your sex life, either. They've damn sure gone to town on Cole having two wives at the same time—the Kemble sisters. You know I hate the hell out of all the bullshit stories about that year you spent in Mexico with Morales."

"All right," she whispered tightly. "Whatever you say. But it doesn't seem very romantic."

"Why not? Why won't people just think your bridegroom is simply eager to have you?"

"Are you?"

Looking annoyed now, he kept staring at the road. When he didn't confirm his eagerness, her confidence after the wonderful time they'd shared in bed began to erode.

"Is this just a marriage of convenience to you?" she prodded.

He frowned and withdrew his arm from around her shoulders. "Is it to you?"

"I asked first."

"You're in a lousy mood all of a sudden." He placed both hands on the wheel and stared ahead without smiling or bothering to answer.

"So is it?" she choked out.

His mouth thinned. "Women—you're all the same about stuff like this. Once you get goin', you don't stop till you corner a guy."

"You still haven't answered me."

"'Cause I..."

His mobile phone rang. He shot her a glance and seemed relieved for an excuse to answer it and to talk to whoever it was instead of to her.

"What?" he said, his brows drawing together. "Oh God—"

"What's wrong?" she whispered, frantic suddenly.

His eyes narrowed as he concentrated on whatever his caller was saying. All she caught were clipped words and phrases.

"Where...dead rats...a girl...unconscious...gotcha. We'll be there."

When he ended the call, he stomped a toe on the accelerator of his truck.

"Well?" she demanded, wild to know what was going on.

"It's begun," he said in a grim, low tone without explaining.

"What?"

"Your friend—Morales."

"Don't call him that. What's happened?"

"That was Cole. There's been a plane crash about eight miles south of the ranch's headquarters. Not really a crash exactly. A rough emergency landing. A single engine Cessna Skyhawk."

"Cole *would* know the exact kind of plane."

Shanghai smiled tightly. "There was a girl inside."

"Who?"

"She's groggy, almost unconscious. Can't say much... other than your name."

"She knows me?"

"She's said your name over and over again. She's been drugged probably. Kinky and Cole think she's fine, though. They're bringing her to the house."

"Were there drugs on board?"

He hesitated. "No. The back seats had been ripped out to make room for larger cargoes, but the hold was full of..."

"Tell me!"

"You're not going to like this." He studied her. "Huge dead rats."

She gasped.

"How'd he find out you're so scared of rats?"

"I had nightmares. He heard me screaming about rats and came to check on me."

"The lousy bastard came to comfort you when you were in bed?" he exploded. "How the hell did you reward him?"

"I didn't!"

One glance at her, and his hard face softened. She shut her eyes and buried her face in her hands.

"Please—don't keep doing this! It was bad enough...then. I—I don't know how I got off so lightly. I really don't, but when you accuse me of stuff I never did and he never did over and over again, it makes the fear come back, and I feel terrible, dirty even, just like I did then."

"I'm sorry. I'm being a real shit again."

Shanghai pulled off the road and shut off the engine. He leaned back in his seat and closed his eyes. Then he removed his Stetson and ran his finger along the tattered turkey feather.

"I'm sorry, darlin'. I've gotta get a grip on this jealousy monster. Sometimes it damn near eats me alive."

"Yes, you do. I care about you, not him. I did then, as well. Deep inside I think I always hoped someday I might have another chance with you. One of the biggest reasons I didn't want to sleep with him was that I didn't want to have to come to you feeling unclean."

He swallowed and pressed his lips together. "All right. I believe you." For the first time, since their conversation had begun, he opened his eyes and stared straight into hers. "I do."

She felt his inner turmoil. He was trying hard to believe her.

"Kinky says that the rats in the plane are African Gambian

Pouch rats from the Florida Keys." His tone sounded stilted and awkward. "How the hell would he know that?"

She nodded. "Kinky's something of an amateur zoologist."

"I remember when you came to me and told me how you locked yourself in the attic and that rat bit your ankle. I didn't think you were ever going to forgive me for tellin' Caesar, who made you get all those awful shots."

"Morales is sending me a message. Maybe he flew the plane here. Maybe he's already on the ranch. Maybe…"

"Don't drive yourself crazy." Shanghai's arm came back around her, and she leaned into his solid warmth.

"Chito could be with him. Or he could have flown the plane."

"Stop it."

"I'd rather it be Tavio than Chito."

Shanghai scowled.

"You're right. I'll stop." She snuggled closer against him, needing his strength. But he was tense and angry again. Even so, she was sure now that she wanted to marry him. She wanted him near, all the time, even if he didn't love her. Even if he didn't totally believe her about Tavio. Just the thought of Tavio brought back too many memories of Mexico and how helpless she'd felt.

She wanted Shanghai and their little girl. She wanted to be safe and happy and to trust in tomorrow. Maybe she couldn't have forever. Right now tomorrow would be enough.

"Angelita!"

"Delia!"

Mia stared at the slim, olive-skinned girl sitting on the sofa of the living room surrounded by Cole, Lizzy, Sy'rai, Kinky and her mother with amazement.

"Tu no eres muerta," Mia began in Spanish. *You're not dead.* "Tavio told me…"

"He and Chito—they tell me they're going to kill us both—

together," Delia said, her voice shaking. "That's why he brought me here."

Mia ran to Delia and sank to her knees on the floor beside the sofa. "I haven't been able to forgive myself for letting you get in that truck. Tavio told me all the horrible things Guillermo...

Delia shuddered at the terrible memories. "He rape me and he burn me with his cigar."

Mia took her hand. "You're safe now. Are you hungry?"

"They're heating some soup for me."

Cole came up to Mia and spoke in English. "She doesn't want us to alert the authorities. She's terrified of anybody finding out where she is."

"After what she's been through, do you blame her?" Mia said. "Can't we wait on that?"

"I don't like it," Cole said. "Hart..."

"I don't trust Hart."

"I know you don't," Shanghai said. "Still..." He leaned closer to Delia to question her in Spanish. "Who flew the plane?"

"I don't know. Guillermo's man maybe. Enrique, he give me something. I was asleep."

"Why don't we leave her alone for now?" Mia said, sitting down beside her. "Can't you see she needs to rest and to feel safe."

"But—"

"Just for a few days," Mia pleaded.

"I think we should call John," Cole said.

"Not yet," Mia protested.

"So much for Homeland Security," Shanghai said.

"What does one, young desperate woman matter?" Mia whispered. "She's not a terrorist."

"I know you think she's your friend, darlin', but she is associated with a vicious drug cartel."

"You've both made valid points," Cole said.

"She could be a terrorist or a murderess," Shanghai persisted.

Even though she didn't speak English, Delia's eyes grew huge.

"She's not!" Mia circled the girl with her arms and shot Shanghai a smoldering glance. "I know her! Shanghai, you've got to trust me on this!"

He frowned. "I don't like it."

When Shanghai cautiously drove up to the high-winged, white-and-blue Cessna Skyhawk with Mia at his side, a flock of black buzzards took flight, their wings flapping clumsily.

"Buzzards?" Mia whispered.

"You should be happy. They'll make quick work of the rats. Kinky and Cole kicked all the long-tailed suckers in the plane out so they wouldn't stink it up."

Suddenly she was glad that he'd braked fifty yards away from the plane.

"So Cole intends to keep the plane if they can't find the registered owner?" Mia queried.

Shanghai nodded as he opened his door and jumped into the high grass. When he came around to her side to help her out, she shook her head.

"I can see from here."

From the truck, she watched him lope toward the plane, sidestepping round the objects she imagined to be the dead rats before he climbed inside the plane.

When he jumped out, he hurried toward her with a plastic box. When he came closer, he held the box up, and a black cat with huge yellow eyes yowled at her and then began clawing at the grill door.

"*Negra?*"

The cat meowed frantically when she touched its nose. Then Negra licked her fingertips.

"You two know each other."

"Tavio's men were going to kill her. He let me have her."

"So he's giving you a gift to please you." Though the statement was spoken softly, it was deadly.

They were tense on the way back to the ranch house. Still, Mia held the cat carrier in her lap and crooned to the animal. Negra's howls to be let out grew louder as Mia continued to stroke her nose through the grill.

"No telling when she last ate or drank anything," Mia said.

"Morales is definitely sending you a message."

"I don't like the way your thoughts revolve around Tavio."

"I don't like it, either," Shanghai said. "He put up five hundred thousand dollars to have you kidnapped. Where you're concerned, he's obsessed. I wouldn't be too surprised if he wants to take you down himself. He could be here!"

She gulped in a strangled breath.

"I'm not going to let you out of my sight for a minute." After a moment's silence, he slid his arm around the back of her seat and pulled her closer.

"I'm not going to let anything happen to you," he whispered.

The sky was a magical lavender color above the pine and oak woods. Unfortunately twilight didn't last long in central Texas. It would soon be dark.

Astride Coco, Abby watched the egrets swooping in low, one at a time, each settling in the high branches of their favorite oak tree amidst the pines. White feathers littered the grass beneath the tree. Already there were more than forty egrets above her in the branches. There would be a few more stragglers, even after night fell.

Still, she wanted to get home before dark, so she nudged Coco with her heels and they headed across the old plank bridge that rumbled and echoed pleasantly with the sounds of the mare's hooves. When Abby's low-lying ranch house came into view, she saw an all-too-familiar black truck parked in front.

The door on the driver's side sprang open, and a tall, swarthy man in a beautifully cut dark suit climbed down.

Leo Storm.

Every muscle in her body tensed. She should have answered her damn phone and ended it.

Fighting to ignore him, she avoided the house and rode straight toward her barn without waving or smiling. Even so, she was disturbingly aware of his eyes following her.

Dismounting outside the barn, she pressed her face into Coco's muzzle for a long moment and prayed for strength.

When she heard his footsteps crunching into the gravel as his long strides carried him to her, she winced even as Coco nickered encouragement.

"I believe these are yours." Leo's amused voice sounded dry.

She turned. When she saw a pair of red satin panties dangling from his brown fingertips, she felt her cheeks heat.

He grinned, and her body grew hotter. Irritated, she snatched her panties and stuffed them into the back pocket of her jeans.

"Okay. Waving my panties at me like a flag had to be fun. Now please go!"

"It wasn't nearly as much fun as you were the other night."

Without another word, she turned her back on him and led Coco inside her barn, which smelled of hay, leather, sweet feed and saddle soap. Normally such smells would have relaxed her. Not tonight, not with the clamor of Leo's boots clanging on the concrete behind her.

Still, for the mare's sake, she pretended she didn't feel edgy. With steady, sure hands, she went about the business of unsaddling Coco, removing her bridle, grooming and feeding her.

Leo sat down on a pile of feed sacks and watched.

"I asked you to go."

He didn't budge.

When she was done and headed past him with the mare on the way to Coco's stall, he said, "Sorry…about the panties. That was a dirty trick."

"To say the least," she muttered as she locked Coco inside her stall.

"If you'd answered your phone…"

She turned and glared at him. "Why are men always so arrogant? You don't own me, you know…just because…"

He shot to his feet.

Dear God, he was tall. And powerfully built, too.

"I know that. I just wanted to talk to you. To make sense out of…"

"Maybe you should have just taken the hint." She took a deep breath. "I don't want to talk to you."

"You could have saved me a lot of time if you'd simply called back and left a message telling me where my truck was."

"Okay, I'm sorry about that."

"By the time I found it, it had about several hundred dollars in parking tickets."

"I'll pay—"

He grinned at her. "I don't care about the truck…or the tickets. All I care about is finding out why you won't even talk to me."

"I—I hope you won't tell…any of our neighbors…or your brother…about what happened the other night."

"Is that what you think of me?"

"Clearly I wasn't thinking or I never would have gone to your loft that night." She flushed again at the memory of his body tangled with hers.

"Have you had dinner?" he murmured in a deep low tone.

"No, but I don't want to go out."

"Tomorrow night then?"

"I wish you wouldn't push."

"Give it to me straight."

"You're a nice guy...probably." She spoke slowly, distinctly. "But you're not my type."

"You could have fooled me."

She gave a brittle little laugh and felt furious at him again. "I'm going through a rough time."

"So am I." The lines around his mouth deepened as he studied her.

"I want to forget that night ever happened."

"That's asking a lot."

"Can we just be neighbors?"

"Why are you so dead set against me?"

"Because I'm in love with somebody else. There!"

"Hello! He dumped you."

"I'm still in love with him, so I've decided it wouldn't be fair to me or to anybody else for me to date right now. The whole time I was with you, I was pretending you were him. How does that make you feel?"

"Lousy." He scowled down at her, his thick black brows nearly meeting over the bridge of his straight nose.

"Okay. So, now you know. I need some time—to get my head straight."

"All right." His eyes were bleak and dark as he turned to go.

"Leo—"

His raven head snapped around.

"I don't remember much that happened at your place Did we—"

"Do it?" he whispered helpfully, his good humor instantly restored by the awful memory. He grinned.

They had. At the thought, her knees turned into jelly.

"Don't worry. You were great! Which is why I want to see you again. So, when you get your head on straight again, call me. But if you want all the delightful details, don't delay. I might forget some of them."

"I wish you the worst case of amnesia ever."

He grinned again. "We'll have dinner. I'll cook steaks. I'll tell you everything."

"Leo! Swear you won't tell anybody else!"

He put his hand on his heart. "I can't wait for you to call."

"Don't hold your breath. No! On second thought *do!*"

She turned and raced toward her house.

Twenty-Three

Awash in sunlight, the ranch chapel brimmed with sweetly smelling, south Texas wildflowers—mock bishop's weed, daisies, dandelions, bluebonnets and purple thistles.

"Who gives this woman to be married to this man?" the preacher asked.

"I do," Joanne replied with quiet reverence.

Her mother's soft voice brought tears to Mia's eyes because she couldn't help thinking of her father, both fathers, who weren't there.

"Wherever you are, be happy for me, Daddy," Mia whispered under her breath, thinking of Caesar. "Or at least, please try."

Standing beside Shanghai, she wore a white lace sundress and a wreath of wild daisies in her plaited hair. Despite the simplicity of her attire, she'd taken great pains to be beautiful for him.

Shanghai wore a black suit. It looked good on him. This was the first time she'd ever seen him not dressed in jeans.

Even though Mia hadn't had time to do invitations, she'd called a lot of people. The chapel pews overflowed with ranch hands, family and dozens of local ranchers and their families.

Near the doors at the back Gus sat with two plainclothes FBI and DEA agents, who were posing as ranchers and standing guard, in case Tavio should make an appearance.

Directly behind Mia in the front pew, Joanne and Delia were struggling to hold Vanilla still. When they could no longer contain the little whirlwind in pink satin, Shanghai winked at Joanne, and she let the toddler go. With a little cry of joy, the child erupted out of her grandmother's arms and began to skip shyly up and down the aisle, smiling at guests she knew. Finally when she returned to the altar, she came to a standstill beside Shanghai and Cole. When she grinned up at Shanghai, he knelt and lifted her into his arms where she remained, playing peep-eye over her daddy's shoulder with her grandmother throughout the rest of the ceremony.

When it was time to say their vows, Shanghai offered Mia his arm before they moved toward the altar. When he said the words in his deep, strong voice, Mia fought to ignore the nervous knot in her stomach.

All her life she'd dreamed of Shanghai loving her some day and marrying her. Was today a dream come true? Or was he going through the motions? Would he leave her as easily as he always had before?

Then his warm, dark hand was on hers, and she shivered when she felt him slide her wedding ring onto her finger. She clenched her hand tightly for a long moment, to make sure it was real. As if he stood a great distance from her, she heard the minister tell Shanghai he could kiss her.

Shanghai tipped her chin, and the warmth of his mouth grazed hers.

From the fifth pew Benjamin Kemble, who was ten, let out a shudder. "Yuck. Kissing." Then his mother told him to be quiet.

Several guests laughed.

When the kiss ended, Shanghai held Mia close.

As Vanilla began to clap, Shanghai looked into Mia's eyes

so long and lingeringly, she wondered if he was searching to find his future there, too.

She smiled.

Covering her hand with his, and squeezing it hard, he smiled back.

"Mrs. Knight," he said, his deep voice ringing forcefully in the hushed chapel.

After that, the rest of the preacher's words floated over her. The only reality was Shanghai's tall, dark body beside hers, their locked hands and Vanilla wriggling beside her in his arms as the child pointed out various fixtures in the church to her parents.

Maybe their marriage wouldn't last, but she and Vanilla were safe so long as he was near, Mia thought.

Shanghai was here beside them now.

She pressed his hand.

If only…

The reception at the big house was in full swing. With the ceremony over, Mia felt lonely and a little let down as she stood apart from Shanghai but among her laughing friends and family.

There hadn't been time to plan a fancy reception, but Sy'rai and the wives of the neighboring ranchers had prepared a feast, even if most of the food was casual. There were mountains of fried chicken, mashed potatoes and gravy. Another table overflowed with barbecue and still another with fresh gulf seafood.

Since Mia hadn't had time to hire a photographer, either, she'd bought disposable cameras for her guests. All her young cousins had seized them and were racing around taking pictures.

"Phone call. For Shanghai," Sy'rai said rushing up to Mia with Shanghai's cell phone. "Do you know where he is?"

"Over by the cake, but I'll take it to him."

"It's Mr. Hart."

Mia's hand tightened on the cell phone. "Not now, Mr. Hart," she wanted to say.

She was lifting the phone when William shouted to little Benjamin to go stand by Cousin Mia so he could snap their picture. When Ben hurtled recklessly up to stand beside her, he knocked the phone out of her hand.

He picked it up and flipped it shut before she could tell him not to and jammed it into her hand.

Well, so much for Mr. John Hart.

William was squinting as he peered at them through his yellow camera.

"Tell Ben not to make a bad face, Cousin Mia!" he shouted.

Benjamin was pulling at his ears and sticking his tongue out at his cousin.

"Stop that, Benjamin," Mia said, hiding the phone behind her back so it wouldn't show in the photograph. "How will a face like that look in my wedding album?"

"Funny!" He giggled. "Watch this! I can touch my nose with my tongue! See!"

Just as Benjamin's tongue curved fiendishly upward, William's flash blinded them.

"You'd better be careful, Ben, making those faces. Your face could freeze."

He laughed. "No, it can't!" But he sucked in his tongue before he ran off.

"Mia! It's time to cut the cake!" Lizzy was waving at her from across the room.

Mia headed through the throng toward the table that held the cake, but slowly, for she stopped to chat frequently. On such short notice, they certainly had a huge turnout.

All the happy faces made her feel joyous that so many people she loved were here to share this special moment in her life. Oh, if only her mother could have agreed with her that Terence Collins should be invited. If it weren't for him, she might still be in Mexico.

Mia still couldn't get over how upset her mother had gotten when Mia had suggested calling him. Her mother had been washing a big terra-cotta pot in the sink at her greenhouse at the time.

"No! Absolutely not! I will not call that man!"

"Such passion," Mia had teased aloud. "From you. I wonder why. You're usually so controlled."

Her mother's cheeks had become blotchy and stained with flags of red. She'd set the pot down in the sink and had dashed off with the water running.

"I'll never forgive him for writing that awful piece that could have so easily backfired and gotten you killed…. The brute didn't even think to ask my permission."

"He's a journalist. And if he hadn't written it, we might not be having a wedding. We went through so much, he and I. I like him so much."

"I simply can't stand the man."

"You said he was brilliant."

Her mother began fiddling with the stacks of gardening gloves on a shelf.

"I'm sure you're mistaken. He's an egotist. Besides…he smokes. But, dear, it's your wedding. Of course, I'll invite him—if it's that important to you." She threw a glove down. "I really can't abide smoking, though."

"I had the strongest impression that you two liked each other very much right after I came home."

"I—I can't imagine how you formed it," Joanne had sputtered before she'd whirled out of the greenhouse without remembering to turn off the water.

The whole discussion had seemed false and strange. It wasn't like her stern mother to love or hate anyone with such vehemence, especially a man she barely knew.

On the opposite side of the library, she heard Shanghai. He and Wolf and several of his rodeo buddies stood near the cake. When their eyes met, he shot her a quick, white grin that was so sheepishly endearing, she wanted nothing more than to rush across the library into his arms. For an instant the madhouse grew silent and there was only Shanghai looking at her, only her heart pounding in her ears with the hope that maybe today was the beginning of a whole lifetime of such secret, meaningful glances between them.

Just as she was about to run to him, Shanghai's phone vibrated in her hand. She looked down and read the name, John Hart.

Carefully she flipped the phone open. "Hello. John? It's Mia."

"Finally."

"It's my wedding day. Busy day, you know." Her voice had sharpened as it sometimes did when she spoke to him.

"Rumor has it Morales has crossed the border. Put Shanghai on."

"We're about to cut the cake."

"Okay, but tell him to call me back! And fast! I'll be in a dead area soon."

She hissed in a breath. "All right. Whatever you say."

She was about to hang up when he added, "If you're smart, you'll start cooperating with me, Mia. I'm not the bad guy, you know. Morales is. He wants to kidnap you, remember?"

She hung up.

She chewed her bottom lip. Hart had made several big seizures lately. He was supposed to be a top agent.

It didn't matter. She didn't trust him.

To heck with John Hart. Why should he spoil her wedding day? With a frozen smile she went to Shanghai and handed him the phone.

"Sy'rai said you left it in the kitchen."

Shanghai kissed her rather fiercely on the lips.

"Yuck," Benjamin yelled, and everybody laughed as if he were very witty. Thus inspired, he had to say yuck over and over.

After the laughter died, everyone gathered around to watch

the bride and groom. Shanghai slipped the phone into his pocket and handed Mia the heavy, silver cake knife. Slicing into the white cake, she smiled up at him again.

His hand touched her waist. Suddenly she felt so radiantly happy to be with him, to be married to him. All her life she had dreamed of this. Cutting a small piece of cake, she lifted it to his lips. Then he did the same, placing a lush bite thick with sugary icing on the tip of her tongue.

When she licked her lips, he said, "That looks like fun," and licked her and kissed her again.

Giggling with embarrassment, Benjamin covered his eyes and repeated his favorite Y word.

Not wanting to spoil the precious moment, Mia decided to postpone telling Shanghai about Hart's call indefinitely.

What difference could it possibly make?

Twenty-Four

"Oh, it's beautiful," Mia said when they drove around the bend and she saw the newly painted house Shanghai had grown up in peeping through the mesquite and oak trees.

If it weren't nearly dusk, the white house would have gleamed.

"You totally remodeled it without telling me."

"I wanted to surprise you, but there's still a lot to be done," Shanghai said as he parked in the deep shade near the house. "Leo and Cole helped a lot."

He yanked the knot of his tie loose and ripped it through his collar. Then he shrugged out of his jacket and laid both items on the back seat.

The wind sighed in the trees. Despite the renovations, she felt strangely uneasy. Was it bridal jitters—she'd been running on nerves all week—or the lateness of the hour, or Hart's call about Morales that had her so spooked? She needed to tell Shanghai about Hart, but didn't feel like facing such a conversation.

Long, purple shadows wrapped the tiny white house so that it seemed lost in the gloom.

She scanned the darkening trees. Where was Gus? As usual, he kept himself well-hidden.

"I thought the reception would never end," Shanghai said. "I wanted to be with you here alone so much."

"Me, too. But everybody else was having such a good time."

"They're all so thrilled you're alive."

She stared in awe at the house that a mere week of hard work had transformed. "How did you do it?"

"Why? would be a better question," he said. "When I lived here, I was so damn determined to run from this place. I used to think it seemed evil. I can't believe I spent all week fixing it up so we could honeymoon here. Believe me it took teams of people. And it isn't near finished. I got all the utilities turned on. The phone people are coming on Tuesday. There was a lot to do, but the foundation and the substructure of the roof were as sound as was the plumbing."

"We'll have to plant flowers," she said, seeking to dispel her alarm about all the shadows. "It's too dark and shady under the trees. If you weren't here, I'd be scared."

His smile vanished as he eyed the dense trees. "Because of Tavio?"

"Don't be jealous of him."

"His undying passion for you makes me seethe."

"It's not reciprocated. I—I just blame myself for putting you and Vanilla and everybody else in danger because I was so unlucky to cross paths with him."

"I hate that you knew him, and that everybody knows you lived with him a year. And yet I want him to come. I want to end this thing—one way or the other so you'll never have to be afraid of him again."

She thought about Hart's call, but she hated the idea of Shanghai talking to the man.

"I wish it wasn't so dark here," she said. "I remember your mother used to have flowers beneath every window."

His smile gentled his tanned face as he leaned across the cab. She lifted her mouth, expecting his kiss, but to her surprise his lips teasingly grazed the tip of her nose instead. Then he got out and went around to her side of the truck. Lifting her out, he swung her into his strong arms.

"Put me down." She kicked her feet in the air. "I can walk on my own."

"Be still, darlin'. I'm going to carry you over the threshold. You're my bride, remember."

"This isn't a real marriage." She only said that because deep down, she was so afraid.

"Says who? I said my vows. I heard you say yours."

"But—"

"Didn't you mean them?"

"I did."

"So did I."

She stared up into his eyes, wanting to believe him so much it hurt. But her father hadn't loved her. Not really. And she'd chased Shanghai for so long, it would be a while before she could feel sure of his love.

"We'll take it one day at a time," he whispered. "Who knows? Maybe you'll fall madly in love with me all over again."

"Or vice versa," she murmured, casting a shy glance at him.

Not that he was looking at her. As he stared at the house, his face gave her no clue as to his feelings. Swiftly he carried her across the grass and up the stairs. When he reached the door, he stood before it a long moment. Turning and scanning the fringe of trees, he signaled Gus and the two agents who'd stepped out of the trees for a brief moment.

As if he were satisfied, Shanghai glanced at her again. "Well?"

"What?" She hesitated. "What are you waiting for?"

"Turn the knob, darlin'. My hands are full. You weigh more than a feather or two."

"Oh."

She blushed, and he laughed. Then she turned the knob and he nudged the door wider with his shoulder before stalking inside. The carpets weren't down yet, so his boots rang on the glossy hardwood floors.

"It's wonderful," she said. "I can't believe all you've done—"

"It's small. But big enough for the three of us when we're here."

"What do you mean?"

"We'll have to spend a lot of time at my ranch, too. The Buckaroo Ranch. I told you about my place."

She smiled. "A time or two." He always swelled with pride when he mentioned it.

She felt giddy that he was talking as if they had a future beyond Tavio Morales and his threats.

"Did I tell you I've retired from bull riding?" Shanghai murmured almost offhandedly as he set her down.

"No! You certainly did not! Really? When?"

Her heart raced eagerly. She was that thrilled. The thought of him being trampled or gored had always been a constant terror.

"I don't want to risk my neck if I have you to come home to. I'm going to settle down and raise rough stock."

"Just like that? It's the middle of the season. You were doing so well. What about all that prize money?"

"With Tavio's bunch hell-bent on kidnapping you, I don't think I'd be much good on a bull. I'd get gored for sure. Hank bled out in ten seconds while I held him in my arms. I didn't used to care much about dyin'. All of a sudden I do."

"But you said you weren't going to retire any—"

"Later on I may get some sort of job in the administrative side of rodeoing. I don't know what I'll do for sure."

Clearly he would make his own decisions about his future. He left her, and while he bolted the door and checked every window, pulling the shades down after a final wave to her bodyguard and agents, she ran about, examining the three bedrooms.

"I know they're small," he said, following her into the second bedroom that contained an antique bed with a beautiful quilt on top it. She opened the closet and was startled to find it filled with her clothes. The next one contained his.

When she whirled, he pulled her into his arms.

"Small closets, I know. At least by Kemble standards."

"My last name is Knight now. Are you going to throw the Kemble name up at me for the rest of our lives?"

He ignored her question. "But we'll add on—a big master bedroom and bath with walk-in closets bigger than this bedroom. We'll turn the garage into a den and build a new garage. I think it'll be suitable for a Kemble princess."

"I don't need big! I could be happy in this house...just with you."

"Could you? Is it really good enough?"

He seemed so human, so vulnerable, and suddenly so anxious to please her. Didn't he know that all she cared about was being with him?

She felt his hand drift across her bare back and shivered involuntarily. Suddenly she wasn't the least little bit interested in closet space or impressive additions.

Placing a hand in the center of his wide chest, she said, "Remember what I said about no sex...that I'm not going to be easy..." Even as she said it, she caught the teasing note in her light tone.

"You think marryin' was easy for me, darlin'? Retirin'? Givin' up bull riding, which up until now has been my passion?"

"Not to mention the buckle bunnies."

"And then marryin' a Kemble? In the Kemble chapel?" His expression was tender. "Darlin', I did it all just for you." He was watching her face, his low voice filled with soft urgency.

Against his white dress shirt, his skin looked even darker.

"I didn't ask you to, now did—"

"I won't ask you to do anything you don't want to do, either," he murmured, tugging her closer. "Morales or not, this is our honeymoon, you know."

"We're not going on a…"

"Who says we have to travel to honeymoon? This is better in a way. We won't have to wear ourselves out on the road. The refrigerator is stocked with every delicacy. Strawberries, salmon, boiled shrimp, crunchy vegetables. Even caviar."

Sensing that she wasn't hungry for food, especially not raw munchies, his big hands caressed the small of her back for several seconds before one of them drifted lower to cup her bottom and pull her snugly against him.

"I know I should tell you to stop," she whispered.

"Then why don't you—Mrs. Knight?" His husky voice rang in fierce possession. Then his lips found hers, and his tongue moved inside her parted lips to mate with hers.

Mrs. Knight. She rather liked the sound of it this time around.

Mrs. Shanghai Knight.

Instead of pushing him away, her arms circled his neck, and she arched herself closer. Feeling his male bulge against her pelvis through her dress, she squeezed her eyes shut, and let her feelings take over.

The moment she wriggled against him, his rough, expert hands were all over her. She heard a zipper, felt hooks being unfastened. Her hands raced down the front of his dress shirt, undoing each button. Next creamy white fabric swished down her naked skin and pooled at her feet. In seconds she was standing before him naked, shivering a little in the air-conditioning.

They stared at each other for a long moment. He was gorgeous. Hunky. Incredible. But then she knew that already.

"Cold?" he murmured, leaning his dark head toward her breasts.

"Not for long, I'll bet."

He laughed as he lowered his black head. Then his warm mouth and tongue were teasing and sucking and rasping across her sensitive nipples until she was so excited and nervy, she wasn't cold at all. Soon at every light tweak of his tongue and every molten breath, she felt lightning bolts of sensation flash through her—in the pit of her stomach, in between her trembling legs. Within seconds she was hotter than he was, burning up, dying for more. And still he lapped at her satiny skin with soft, luscious strokes, kissing his way all over her body.

Her eyes snapped open. "This isn't supposed to happen."

He laughed conceitedly and then nibbled an earlobe. "You knew it would." He plucked the earlobe with his teeth. "'Cause it always does."

When liquid warmth enveloped her, she sighed. "I hate being so predictable."

"'Cause you're so sexy."

"You planned this."

He kissed her lips lightly, but it was a kiss she felt everywhere.

"Who me? Be honest—you want this just as much as I do. All day long I could see it in your eyes."

Fleetingly she thought of Hart. She should tell Shanghai.

No. Not when she could barely breathe. Was it so wrong to want to savor being like this with her new husband? Oh, how she preferred this tender, loving side of him to the dark jealousy that could consume him when he thought about Tavio wanting to kidnap her.

"More kisses, please," she whispered.

"There's iced champagne in the kitchen, too," Shanghai said. "Do you want anything else? Strawberries?"

"Only if you do. I'm okay with kisses."

"I'm better than okay," he murmured. Licking behind her ear, he pushed her gently against the wall and cradled her close to his body.

Then he lifted her a little, and his hips rubbed against hers so expertly his penis was soon lodged between her damp thighs and poised at the tight, damp opening. At the slightest pressure, he'd be deep inside her.

Where she wanted him.

With a smile, he slid up and down against her sensitive tender wetness, not entering her more than a centimeter. Pausing there, he would then pull out and make her gasp. Then he'd do it again, each teasing stroke sending shock waves of erotic heat through out her nervous system. When she was totally limp and yet dying for more, he stopped, his penis lodged at the entrance, his triumphant gaze locked with hers. With almost no effort, he brought her to the edge of something so momentous she could barely breathe.

"Your call, darlin'. You said no sex. And I'm willing to abide by your rule."

"Bastard," she moaned playfully on a ragged gasp. "You did this on purpose."

He chuckled. "Guilty as charged. But then you tempted me."

"That part was easy."

"I feel as deliciously tortured as you do, my love."

"Then if I'm nice, I'll put you out of your misery, won't I?" On a shudder, she seized his wide, bare shoulders and pressed her pelvis closer, wiggling against the tip, her purpose clear as he pushed into her.

She let out a breath when he filled her completely. Her hands clasped his neck. She laid her cheek against his warmly furred chest. With his hands he ground her hips against his, and she felt him swell inside her.

The wonder of being with him like this was too great to trust. She must hold back something of herself. Then he began to thrust. Lifting her hips to his, hugging him, kissing him, clinging to him, she went wild—and held back nothing.

"Easy," he murmured huskily.

But she couldn't stop the explosion that washed her with heat and love.

So much love.

Her climax made her convulse and cry out and cling. Afterward, as she held on to him and fought to regain her breath still again, he tried to wait, but he had no more control than she. Plunging inside her a final time, his passion shook him. Clutching her closer, his powerful body was racked with spasms that went on and on. He held her tightly, their bodies joined, and pushed himself even harder against her welcoming softness.

"God, oh God, you feel good."

Finally he carried her to the bed. They collapsed onto the mattress and lay still, but after only after no more than a few minutes' rest, he made love to her again, only more slowly and more tenderly, lingering over every kiss and every touch.

Later when they were sated and in his bed with the quilt pulled up to their chests, drinking champagne and eating strawberries, she sighed as she nibbled the luscious red tip of a berry. "And I so wanted to play hard to get."

He chuckled. "I like the real you better." He plopped a berry into his mouth whole.

"You do?"

"Yeah. You always chased me. Maybe I ran, but I think I got hooked on it." He clinked his flute against hers. "I wish I'd let you catch me a long time ago. I should have followed you back to the Golden Spurs after Vegas."

"You really think so?"

"I know so. We've wasted a lot of time." He stroked her hair. "Bull riders aren't known for their brains, darlin'."

"What are they known for?"

"I think you know."

She set her champagne glass down. "Why don't you show me again."

"Any time, darlin'."

Instead of kissing her or pulling her close, he got out of bed, went to the closet and tugged on a pair of jeans. He turned all the lights in the house out. When he went to each window and raised the shade and looked outside, she felt renewed pressure to tell him about Hart's call.

"What are you doing?" she asked.

"Just checking."

"Come back to bed."

"I don't see your bodyguard."

She ignored the faint prickle of alarm she felt. "It's too dark probably. Come back to bed."

When he returned, he shrugged out of his jeans and held her close for a long time. "You know I never thought I'd have anything like this…anybody like you…I mean. Growing up, after my mother left, I felt like nothin'. I felt worthless."

"I love you."

"That means everything to me darlin'. I think…I think I feel like I've finally got a real home to come home to."

He began to kiss her then, and she returned his kisses, wondering if maybe tonight really might be the beginning of forever.

Mia awoke sometime before dawn to the faint creaking of a floor board inside the house. Listening, she tensed a little. All old house made noises didn't they? Another board creaked, near the kitchen, and then another. Outside the birds had begun to twitter.

Her head lay pillowed across Shanghai's broad shoulder. His eyes were closed, his powerful arms wrapping her. Her thoughts grew hazy as she savored Shanghai's warmth. He was still asleep. Would she wake up like this for many mornings in the future? For the rest of her life?

She would. He'd been just as insecure and afraid as she was. That's why he'd run from her in the past.

Sitting up a little, she leaned away from him and studied

his thickly curling black lashes. If he'd been a girl, he would
have been a beauty, too. Not that there was anything feminine
about him—other than those lashes, which she, as a redhead,
who had to use mascara, could only envy.

The poor darling. Fondly she stroked the black lock of hair
that sometimes tumbled across his brow. He'd been such an
enthusiastic lover, as if now that he'd finally found what he
needed to make his life whole he couldn't get enough of her.

When she inched away from him to her side of the bed, he
didn't stir. Nor did he move when she stood up and dressed
hurriedly, slipping into the first pair of jeans and T-shirt she
found in her closet.

Sleepily, thinking to make him coffee and drink it with him
in bed as the sun came up, she padded softly into the kitchen.

One step through the doorway, and a hard hand that reeked
of crack-laced cigarettes closed over her mouth. Her stomach turned over. A golden barrel flashed. Then Tavio jammed
his gun against her temple.

"If you make a sound, Angelita, your husband will come,
and I'll kill him."

When she shuddered, his grip loosened, and in the dim
morning light, she looked at him.

Tavio's carved face was paler and thinner, more haggard
than she remembered. His black hair was shaggy and unkempt, his eyes bloodshot with exhaustion.

"I watch the house for hours. I know he is making love to
you. I imagine you in a sexy nightgown, and I want to kill
him with my bare hands."

"What do you want?"

He ground himself against her hips.

"Then take me. Just me. Take me anywhere. I'll go with
you. Just leave him… Don't hurt him."

She thought of Shanghai sleeping so trustingly in the next
room. He'd been so passionate and tender and protective.

"Please…don't hurt him."

"You love him that much?" Tavio's hand moved down to her throat, stroking her satin-smooth skin with a reverence that chilled her. "You betray me—for him."

"No. I always wanted my freedom. You knew that."

"I have to kill him."

"Why? Just take me. I'll do whatever you want."

"You'll sleep with me? You'll come back to Mexico. You'll give up your precious freedom for him?"

She nodded.

"You give this man everything I want. You love him. You give him your heart and your body. In my country women's bodies are cheap. You will always think of him. Not of me. He has to die. Then you will belong to me."

Frantic, she shook her head wildly.

"I watch you and him for days. I see him leave the rose in the barn. I see you kiss him. I nearly kill him then… I hate him so much."

"Tavio, *escúcheme.*" *Listen to me.* "I grew up with him. I always loved him…since I was a little girl. He saved my life twice. I was practically a baby the first time. My father hated him, but that only made me love him more. He rejected me always, but I loved him anyway. If you kill him, do you think that will change what has always been in my heart? We have a child. If you kill him, you'd better kill me, too, because I will hate you as I've never hated anybody before. I will want only one thing—revenge."

"Brave words." He paused, his tired face set in harsh lines. "Anyway, I have to kill him. Otherwise, he will come after you."

"Not if he thinks I want to go with you. He is half mad with jealousy over you already."

"He is?" Tavio grinned.

"If he thought I cared for you…even a little bit, it would be worse for him than dying."

His grin broadened. "And you will make him think this?"

"Yes."

"You will make love to me now in his kitchen."

"Y-yes."

A closed look came to his face as he held up his gun and examined it thoughtfully. "All night I think I kill him. So much has happened. Prison. I lose much money. Because of you, I kill Guillermo. I am full of hate. I need to kill somebody so much. But maybe it is good to make love to you first."

His gaze returned to hers, his black eyes glowing like a devil's. "So be it. I will take what I should have taken so long ago."

He traced her cheek almost carelessly with a callused thumb, but she stiffened at the hint of possession in his touch. To have his rough hand on her skin so soon after Shanghai's having made love to her was unbearable.

She recoiled.

Sensing her resistance, he wound her hair in his fist and snapped her head back cruelly. "Damn it. You will not think of him now! Not when you make love to Tavio."

She shuddered. A single tear rolled down her cheek.

"Say you love me. Say it over and over as I kiss you."

"I...love you."

"Say it louder."

"He will hear."

"If he comes, I will kill him."

His hands ruffled her silken hair as he caught her closer and with his hips pressed her buttocks into the counter. Behind her, she heard the faint clatter of his gun against the tile countertop as he set it down.

Could she get it?

Reading her mind, he laughed. Then he gripped the hand that would have gone for the gun and placed it on his thigh.

She flinched at such intimacy. When she would have drawn her fingers back, he whispered, "Keep it there. Open your fingers. Stroke me. And say it. Tell me you love me. Tell me over and over again."

His lips caressed her throat tenderly.

"I love you," she whispered, closing her eyes as she felt herself twisting and dying inside.

"Again!"

"I love you."

His mouth moved across her cheek toward her lips. When he pressed his body into hers, she felt so sick at her stomach bitter bile surged up her throat, threatening to strangle her.

Frantic that she was about to vomit, she opened her eyes. They locked on Shanghai's hard, dark face. Bare-chested, he stood in the doorway. He looked lost, as bewildered as a child who'd been punished unfairly by a loving parent.

Her eyes widening, she gasped in horror.

Then Hart stepped up behind Shanghai and aimed his gun straight at her heart.

Twenty-Five

"Freeze! Both of you!" Hart yelled.

For a second or two, time seemed to flow in slow motion as Shanghai's cold gaze remained on hers.

His handsome, dark face was ashen. Wearing only a pair of jeans with the knees ripped out, his sculpted, brown body was rigid.

A knot of fear tightened in Mia's stomach.

Then Hart and his agents began screaming commands, and her brain kicked into overdrive.

Hart's gun was still aimed at her. When she tried to push free of Tavio, Hart yelled, "Freeze!" again.

Lunging for his golden gun, Tavio pushed her out of the way. "*Bastardos!* Don't shoot her!"

Tavio's hand hit the gun at an angle and sent it flying across the tile at her as she fell. When she tried to grab it, she shoved it across the tiles onto the floor at her feet.

Hart's men burst inside and blew into Tavio.

Tavio rolled, grabbing wildly for the gun as four agents tackled him. Almost as an afterthought she picked up the gun and then scooted backward to a far corner of the kitchen.

Tavio snarled, bit and kicked like a savage animal. The

fight seemed to be going his way until Hart strode up and kicked him in the jaw. When Tavio's head hit the floor like a rock, Hart sat down on his chest and grabbed him by the throat.

"You're dirty, Hart. I tell everybody how…"

Hart turned purple. "Bastard!" He slammed the butt of his gun against his jaw. When Tavio's head crashed to the floor again, Hart stood up, holstered his gun and told his men to cuff him.

"You don't know how long I waited to get that bastard." He glared at Mia. "Thanks for giving Shanghai the message, honey. But then I guess we all know why you didn't."

She stood up slowly. As Hart's men dragged Tavio's limp body out of the kitchen, Tavio's golden gun glittered darkly in her hand.

Shanghai was still looking at her, his blue eyes ablaze with hatred.

"Shanghai—"

Light and shadow played across his carved cheekbones and stern mouth.

"Why didn't you tell me Hart called? Didn't you know I'd eventually check for my calls?"

Guilt washed her. He thought the worst of her—as always. "I—I was going to."

"When—for God's sakes? Were you going to leave me a note…after you ran off with Morales?"

Dead silence after that.

"You wanted him to come for you, didn't you?"

"No! Of course not!" She was so upset from everything that had happened, she began to shake uncontrollably. She could barely stand, let alone speak coherently, especially now when all her dreams were going up in smoke.

Why was it that the men she loved never believed in her?

"Why would I want Tavio?" she whispered. "We've been through this so many times."

"Shut up. Don't say anything. You'll only make it worse."

"Shanghai, you have to believe me—"

"I don't *have to* anything."

What was the use? She was a Kemble. He'd always been dead set against her. She was tired of chasing him. She wanted to be chased and cherished and trusted.

"I'm done with your lies," he said. "I heard you tell him you loved him."

"I love you. I've always loved you!"

At those words, Shanghai's eyes flashed with a mixture of longing and fury.

She wanted to go up to him, to touch him, but what was the use?

When she lifted her chin, his body went rigid, his face tightening. "I won't let you manipulate me with your clever lies ever again!"

When she moved toward him then, he slammed his fist into the door so violently, the wood splintered. Then he yelled in agony, and his face went white with pain as he cupped his injured hand in his good one.

"Shanghai, your hand—"

"As if you give a damn—"

She ran to him then, panicked that he'd broken a bone. "But I do! Of course, I do!"

He jerked away from her.

For a long moment she simply stared at him, drinking in his features, memorizing the line of his throat and the hard lines of his jaw, and the curve of his mouth that had brought her such ecstasy.

"What are you looking at? Don't pretend you care! Because we're done, you and me! You're safe from Tavio. You don't need my protection anymore. I'm out of here, darlin'."

"I need your love."

"Go to hell."

Sucking in a breath, holding his injured hand close to his chest, he bolted past her out of the house.

She sank to her knees. "Don't leave me," she whispered. "Please don't leave me."

She let out a breath and forced herself to stand up.

I can do this, she thought. I can do whatever I have to do.

She'd survived her father's rejection and Shanghai's rejection after they'd made love in Vegas and Mexico. She'd survived Tavio.

She could survive this.

She wouldn't chase him. She wouldn't beg him. Not ever again.

A buzzard soared low over the trees.

Tavio saw it and flinched.

Something was wrong. Tavio felt the wrongness of it in his bones.

"You all go on," Hart was saying to somebody, probably one of his agents. "I'll bring him in."

When the front door of Hart's truck opened and then clanged shut, Tavio groaned. For some reason Hart had sent all his men in the other vehicle. Something worried him about that, but his ribs were cutting into his lungs so badly every time he gasped for air, he couldn't think.

His jaw burned as if someone had used a dull knife to peel his flesh off the bone. Raw nerves shot sparks down his neck and spine.

Despite the pain, he sat up a little. Through the tinted windows he caught a glimpse of Angelita's red hair as she was being led by the hand into the big house by her husband.

Angelita! She was still in danger.

He cracked a bruised eyelid wider, hoping to see more of her. But she had vanished into the house. Instead he saw a single buzzard perched on the chimney of the big white ranch house with its wings spread wide. The truck was parked under a live oak. The windows were cracked a little, so he could hear the roar of the cicadas.

Even though it was a balmy spring morning, when Hart turned the key and started the big engine, Tavio sensed doom.

His mother had been a famous witch. *Curandera* was the nicer word. Tavio had inherited her talent. Long ago he'd learned to trust his dark instincts.

"It's just you and me now, Morales," Hart said as he tossed his cigarette butt out the window into the weeds.

At the hint of malice in the agent's voice, Tavio struggled to sit up. Then a loose rib stabbed his lung. When the pain cut off his breath, Hart laughed.

"Angelita… You've got to go back…."

"She must be one hot bitch!" Hart turned around and leered. His feral gaze gripped the trafficker with icy fear.

Tavio knew well how to inspire terror. Now it was his turn to be on the receiving end of a sadistic bully.

Tavio's throat tightened.

"You haven't booked me," Tavio snarled. "You haven't read me my rights."

"You watch too much television, ignorant *bastardo*. Who are you to tell me what to do now? I call the shots now."

Hart laughed as he roared away from the ranch house, his truck spewing dust and diesel fumes.

Tavio's heart thudded more violently when after only a few miles, Hart turned onto a washboard road that led into a thicket of oak smothered with wild grapevines so dense the truck would be completely hidden from the road.

Again Hart parked the truck in the deepest shade. Without a word, the agent got out. He took his time before opening Tavio's door, but when he did, he smiled. Grabbing Tavio's belt buckle, he yanked him out so roughly, Tavio screamed even before he threw him on the ground where he began to puke blood all over himself.

Hart laughed, then fell on him and socked him in the temple so hard, everything blurred.

Tavio had always known he would die violently, but he had dreamed of going down in a gun battle with a machine gun in each hand, taking ten *bastardos* with him at least, before dying himself.

Not like this—with his hands cuffed behind his back.

"I didn't come here to kill her," he muttered. "I came here…"

"Shut up!"

"Listen to me…."

Hart put a boot to his head and ground his face in the dirt and rocks so hard he bled. "No, you listen…. Look at me! I want you to see this coming!"

Tavio looked up, but the blood in his eyes made it difficult to focus.

Hart's hand was lightning quick when he yanked his gun out of his holster. Jumping back, he aimed it at Tavio's face.

"You're not one of the good guys anymore," Tavio said.

Hart laughed, but a little nervously.

"You're just like me. A drug whore. I bought you, paid for you. I made you famous. You're killing me to shut me up."

Hart went purple. A vein began to throb along his brow.

"I'm accomplishing what a huge, dumb-ass task force made up of more than half a dozen agencies couldn't do. I'll be a hero. The newspapers will love me. Terence Collins will love me."

"I didn't come here to kill her."

"Right. You came here to fuck her, and she damn sure had a taste for it, didn't she? Maybe I'll have to do her myself to see what all the fuss is about."

Hart moved in closer and laughed. He was still laughing when he pulled the trigger.

The bullet felt like a sledgehammer slamming between Tavio's eyes and hurling him backward into the dirt. Stunned, his life blood pooling beside his head, Tavio lay on the ground staring up through the branches and vines to the dazzling patches of blue.

Only vaguely was he aware of Hart standing over him now, his legs spread wide like a conquering hero's.

"Your britches are wet," the *bastardo* said.

Tavio didn't care anymore. He was thinking of the dream he'd had when he'd started out as a young trafficker. He'd always thought he'd retire and buy himself a big cattle ranch in northern Mexico some day. He'd thought he'd be a big *hacendado,* somebody important like his white father. More important than Federico with all his factories and newspapers.

He'd imagined a beautiful white woman like Angelita as his wife. He'd chosen Angelita because she was prettier and more elegant than his father's wife or Federico's. When he'd found her, he'd imagined the house they would have lived in, the children they would have had.

Dreams... Did all dreams end badly? Were there no happy endings? Only fleeting moments of abandon, adventure and glory?

Federico had won. It was all over.

Now he was only a hunk of bleeding meat that would soon rot.

His last thought was of Angelita and her long white legs and her satiny, flowing red curls. He remembered how wonderful she'd felt when he'd pulled her from the water and held her in his arms after he'd saved her. She'd nestled close to him then, seeking his protection. Her body had been ice cold at first, but slowly he'd warmed her with his.

"Angelita," he whispered.

Hart lit a cigarette and smiled down at him.

"Hart...Angelita...danger..."

Hart leaned down and blew a smoke ring. "Speak up. I can't hear you."

Tavio tried to speak but choked on the smoke. Then blood bubbled up from his throat.

"Go back to the house," he whispered. "Angelita…"

As Hart shook his head in confusion, Tavio tried again to speak. But he was too weak. His body began to twitch, his cuffed hands clawing the dirt.

He died with his eyes wide open. His last thoughts were agonized because he knew she'd die, too.

"Shot while trying to escape? Something's wrong," Mia said in a neutral tone so she wouldn't alarm Vanilla. "His hands were cuffed when Hart drove off."

Shanghai had been throwing his suitcases in his truck while Mia watched with Vanilla in her arms.

"I'll tell you what's wrong—your lover's dead." He, too, spoke calmly.

"Doesn't it strike you as odd that Hart insisted on taking Tavio in alone?"

"He wanted the glory, I guess."

"Or no witnesses," she countered.

"Why don't we keep things simple? Hart's the good guy. Morales is the bad guy. Personally, I'm glad the bastard's dead, and you and Vanilla are safe."

Shanghai threw his camera and a couple of maps into the front seat. His Stetson with the lucky turkey feather was sitting in the driver's seat.

Feeling numb about Shanghai's leaving her, Mia hadn't been able to think. All morning she'd felt dazed.

Even so she'd been stunned when Hart had returned with Tavio's body and had asked if he could use their bathroom because he had a nasty cut on his cheek that was oozing blood all over his uniform.

"What happened?" she'd asked.

"I stopped to check a tire. Morales said he needed to urinate, so I let him. When I was unzipping him, the bastard tried to strangle me."

"But his hands—"

"Somehow he got loose. I went for my gun and shot him."

"Good shot," Shanghai had said after he'd inspected the body.

"He was all over me. I had no choice."

She'd stared at Tavio's body that had lain so quiet and still at her feet on the lawn for a long time, remembering how vital and terrifyingly unpredictable he'd once been.

"Right between the eyes, too. Wouldn't that be hard to manage in a life-and-death struggle?" she'd asked.

Hart had turned an ugly shade of purple. "It was self-defense. The bastard was trying to kill me!"

She'd stared at Tavio for a long time. He'd held her life in his hands for a year.

Even now, hours after Hart had driven away and she stood beside Shanghai, it was difficult for her to realize that Tavio was really dead, that there was nothing left of him but a body to bury.

Would anything really change on the border? Another drug lord would take over. Life would go on, maybe a little worse than before.

Except for me. The danger is over for me. I'm free to choose what I want to do with the rest of my life again. Maybe when Shanghai is gone and I'm my normal self again, even brokenhearted, I will appreciate having that kind of freedom.

Now she could feel nothing because Shanghai was driving away again and wouldn't return.

She loved him so much. Why couldn't she feel anything? Or say anything?

He, too, had been silent for the most part since their parting argument. It was as if he were in a tortured haze all his own.

They'd been civil, conducting themselves as if they were polite strangers as they said their goodbyes in full view of the big house and anyone who might be watching them.

After Hart had bagged Tavio's body, Shanghai had told the

family there was an emergency at his ranch, and that he had to leave.

"But you just got married yesterday," Joanne had said, trying to reason with him. "I'm sure Mia needs you right now."

"With Tavio dead, she's safe."

"But—"

"It can't be helped."

Playing the part of eager bridegroom, he'd pulled Mia to him and kissed her on the lips for her mother's benefit. Instead of thrilling Mia, his cool, dry lips had stung more cruelly than ice ripping soft, wet skin.

"Well—" Shanghai slung a final suitcase into the back seat of his truck as Vanilla clung sleepily to Mia's neck.

She turned to face him again.

"I'll come back for the rest of my stuff later," he said, not looking at Mia, keeping his eyes on Vanilla.

"Wave goodbye to Daddy," Mia murmured listlessly, hating the hideous calm that gripped them both.

Shanghai grabbed his hat out of the front seat and put it on.

"No!" Suddenly Vanilla rubbed her eyes and twisted violently only to bury her face against Mia's shoulder.

"Practicing to be a terrible-two?" Shanghai whispered gently, stepping closer so that he could pet her soft, fine hair.

"No! No go!" As if Vanilla sensed the dark undercurrents between the adults, she fisted her tiny hands and refused to look at him.

When Shanghai and she had cooled down enough to consider the consequences of divorcing each other now with the ranch and their own lives under such intense scrutiny from the press, they'd decided to wait. Wanting to keep their relationship private, they'd agreed to tell no one, not even the family about their plans to separate.

For the next month Shanghai would stay at the Buckaroo and run his ranch. He would put in an occasional appearance

at the Golden Spurs. To silence the gossips, she would spend
a weekend or two at the Buckaroo. No one need know that
Shanghai would be absent from the Buckaroo when she was
there.

Suddenly Mia wanted him gone. To endure him now, to
watch his handsome face and know that he felt no tenderness
for her, was sheer torture.

If he couldn't love her wholeheartedly and believe in her,
she didn't want to spend the rest of her life begging him to
forgive her for something she'd never done in the first place.
She was done with pleading for his love. Although she knew
she would be unhappy for a long time, she would go on.
Somehow she'd find her way.

But step one toward recovering from all that she'd been
through was his departure.

Still, all of a sudden, he seemed reluctant. For interminable minutes, he stood beside his truck staring at her. Finally
he moved closer. Opening her fingers, he placed something
cold and hard inside her hand.

"Hang these on that damn tree—right along beside Caesar's!"

Then he climbed into his truck and slammed the door so
hard the entire vehicle shook.

She stepped back as he sped away. Turning toward the
house, she didn't watch him drive away. When she opened her
hand, she found his spurs gleaming inside her palm.

Shanghai's spurs jingled like wind chimes along with the
others. Mia touched them one last time and then pulled her
hand away from the tree.

The sky was blood-red above the fringe of oak to the west.
Mia shivered a little as she stood all by herself beneath the
spur tree amidst a sea of yellow wild flowers.

The cowboys were superstitious about the tree. Caesar
had never liked it because it had made him feel mortal and

less powerful as a man. Some of the hands called it the death tree because the spurs of the cowboys and the family who'd worked or lived on the Golden Spurs Ranch were always hung there when they left or died. If they didn't come back, their spurs stayed there for good.

The wind brought the scent of grass as it stirred her hair. As she tilted her chin upward, she smiled, savoring the glorious sunset and the infinite peace and quiet. With or without Shanghai, she was home to stay.

Maybe someday someone would think to hang her spurs by his, but if she were lucky that wouldn't be for a very long time.

Caesar's spurs glinted in the rosy light.

"I'm home, Daddy. I guess you're glad about Shanghai's going. I guess you won't consider his spurs hanging alongside yours that big a punishment as long as he's gone for good."

She sighed. Life was not always what one wanted. What would she make of her life without Shanghai?

She thought of her mother and her father. Her mother had loved Uncle Jack, and her father had loved Electra.

Would she settle for something less than what she wanted and go on? Is that what most people did? Or would her heart heal and mature? Would she choose more appropriately next time? Or would she find some meaningful cause to work for? The horse program would take a lot of her time for now. She had a child to raise and a future, with or without a man. But Vanilla would grow up.

The shadows were long and deep beneath the spur tree.

Suddenly a terrible bleakness at the thought of the years without Shanghai consumed her. Against her will she wanted him—just as stubbornly as she always had.

Clutching her own spurs so tightly in her hand that they cut into her palm, she headed for the house. The devastation she felt was so great, she didn't smile when Delia, who'd stayed hidden from Hart and his agents and Tavio until now, rushed down the stairs of the big house and seized her by the hand.

Poor thing, she was trembling. Her eyes were huge and wild. Had she seen Tavio's corpse? Maybe she didn't know he was dead and that she was safe.

"They're serving dinner downstairs," Delia said in Spanish. "Your mother told me to come find you."

"Tell them I'm not hungry. I want to be alone. Will you help Sy'rai with Vanilla?"

"Of course."

"I'll stay at Black Oaks tonight."

"Is Tavio really dead?"

So, she did know.

"Yes. He's dead. You're safe."

"Estás segura?"

"I made Mr. Hart unzip the body bag. I saw him."

"His mother was a witch."

"He wasn't breathing. I touched him. His skin was cold. Don't be afraid. Not anymore."

"Sometimes witches come back to life."

Mia wrapped Delia in her arms. "Hush, *querida*. There aren't any witches here. Now run along and help Sy'rai. Don't think about Tavio anymore unless it is to pray for his soul. Tomorrow after a good night's sleep you'll feel better. We'll all feel better."

"And Mr. Shanghai? He's not coming back?"

"Please…I can't talk about it right now. Just go inside. Tomorrow we'll talk. Tonight…tonight I'm too tired."

Shanghai raced through the dark night, accelerating way above the speed limit. He was popping Bufferin like candy. Even so his right hand throbbed from where he'd slammed his fist into the door.

He stomped harder on the gas peddle, telling himself that the faster he went, the faster he'd be free of Mia and the agony of giving her up.

He'd driven like a madman for hours, only stopping once for gas. He'd thought he'd feel better as soon as he was rid of her. So how come he felt worse?

If he drove straight through, he'd be home before daylight. Maybe with some sleep…

Suddenly red lights flashed behind him. Then he heard the shrill scream of a siren.

"Damn."

When the trooper, who pulled him over, recognized him as Shanghai Knight, he started acting as shy and awed as a little kid wanting his autograph, which softened Shanghai's dark mood considerably.

"Hey, you were goin' pretty fast back there. If I give you a warning, could you slow it down?"

"Sure. Thanks."

The officer handed him the ticket. "My son's a big fan. He'd sure be tickled if you'd autograph something."

"Sure thing. I've got a rodeo program in the back seat."

Shanghai turned around and grabbed it. As he signed his name under his picture, even more tension eased out of Shanghai.

"Thanks! Thanks a lot!"

After the officer drove away, Shanghai reached for the key in the ignition and then let his hand fall to his thigh. Then he just sat in the dark for a while, his thoughts eating him. Why couldn't he stop worrying about her?

She'd betrayed him. In the worst possible way. He'd seen her kissing that bastard. He'd heard her telling him she loved him even.

Then he'd gone insane.

Only now, maybe because of the trooper's friendliness, maybe because of the drive, his jealousy was easing up a bit. And now that he was sane enough to think, something was worrying him.

If she loved that sick bastard, why had she married him,

Shanghai, and made love to him with such wild abandon?
Why hadn't he at least let her explain why she hadn't told him
about Hart's call? Why had she looked so heartbroken when
he'd slammed his fist into the door and hurt himself?

Hell! He'd condemned her without even trying to understand.

You dumb-ass cowboy!

Maybe it wasn't such a smart thing to make one of the biggest decisions in your life when you were too furious to think
straight. He'd married her to protect her. When Tavio had
shown up, he'd turned on her.

Kicking himself for being a damn fool and so full of his
own pain he'd had no regard for hers, he restarted his engine.
Without really thinking things through, he made a savage U-
turn. Then he hit the gas and shot forward so fast he burned
rubber.

He was probably a sucker. But he couldn't walk out on her
the way his mother had walked out on him without first hearing her side.

He pulled out his flip-phone and dialed the ranch, but the
lines were busy. He dialed Mia's cell, only to have a robotic
voice say the customer had turned it off.

Sh-Shanghai— Mia's voice haunting him, called to him.

Suddenly he could feel her right beside him, and he could
hear her choking whimper. She was terrified, and he felt her
fear as he'd felt it when she'd been in Mexico, and he'd believed she'd been a ghost haunting him.

What could possibly be wrong? Tavio was dead.

Again he remembered the gaping hole right between
Tavio's eyes. Mia had marveled at the perfection of that shot.

Now that he thought about it, it was a bit strange. What if
Hart worked for Morales? Would he come back to settle the
score with Mia? Or was there some other missing piece to the
puzzle?

Shanghai…. Help!

Mia's voice cried out to him again and again, and the urgency in the frantic sounds was like a fist in his solar plexus.

Damn it. Was he crazy? What had he been thinking of to leave her? When she was the best damn thing in his whole life?

He yanked the warning ticket out of his pocket, wadded it up and pitched it on the floorboard.

Sh-Shanghai!

He stomped down harder on the accelerator.

Hold on! I'm comin', darlin'!

He felt her terror, and it became his own.

Twenty-Six

Why did everything always seem worse at night?

Bone weary, Mia pulled the chain of the lamp beside her bed, and the tiny bedroom at Black Oaks melted into darkness. She sank down onto the bed and closed her eyes.

Negra hopped up onto the bed, purring. Mia felt so tired and so depressed over losing Shanghai, she hadn't wanted to face her mother or Sy'rai or deal with Vanilla. Thus, she was grateful for the quiet and the darkness that surrounded the secluded house.

Relaxing as she stroked Negra, her mind drifted to her wedding and then to her brief honeymoon night. She'd been right to fear happiness.

Shanghai. Oh, Shanghai.

She ached for his body to be next to hers. Was it only last night that they'd lain in this very same bed together, talking and drinking champagne after making love, and she'd believed her dreams would come true?

Slowly her eyes closed. Still purring, Negra curled up beside her. Before she knew it, she was falling, slipping into sleep like a black ghost. For hours she tossed back and forth, dreaming of golden champagne sparkling in flutes that clinked together, of a white silk dress sliding against her bare skin, of a bull rider's rough hands caressing the smoothness of her satiny flesh. Of Shanghai's lips lingering and caressing her everywhere.

Then abruptly her dreams darkened, and she was running for her life with Shanghai through a shadowy tunnel with small furry rodents squealing and nipping at her feet. She awakened in utter blackness and sat up shaking, one hand fisting her sheets, the other covering her mouth to prevent her screams.

"It's only a dream," she said aloud to reassure herself. But her echoing voice sounded so hollow in the empty house, she grew more nervous.

A board creaked and then another. She tensed.

Tavio?

Staring wildly at the shadowy shapes the furniture made against the white walls, she covered her lips. Then in the next moment she heard the front doorknob jiggle. She sat bolt upright, and Negra hopped onto the floor and raced under the bed.

Where was her cell phone?

Remembering that it hadn't been in her purse earlier, she wondered where she could have put it.

Then a key turned in the lock, and she told herself to relax. *Shanghai! He'd come back!*

The thought that he was outside and that he might be regretting their misunderstanding as much as she was brought a rush of hot tears to eyes. Filled with hope, she blinked back her tears and scooted to the edge of the bed.

The door opened, and she ran to greet him.

"Shanghai—"

"It's only me," Delia said in Spanish, her tone low and concerned as she shut the door quietly.

Delia's shadow was huge and dark as it leapt against the living room wall.

"What is it, Delia? Are you all right. You seem...tense."

"Never better."

The tightness in Delia's odd, rusty voice triggered a warning. Some sixth sense made the hair along the back of Mia's neck stand up.

"What time is it?" Mia asked, feeling bewildered and off balance.

"I—I don't know. Late." Delia's black eyes glowed in the dark.

"What are you doing here? Why are you looking at me like that?"

Delia pulled something from her pocket and whirled on her. Tavio's golden barrel glinted in the darkness.

"Where did you get that?"

"I steal it."

"But—"

"Enrique, Chito's brother. He fly me here so I can kill you. Tavio, he don't want me to kill you. He come here and he tell me to go home."

"Tavio?"

"You make him weak."

"What? I thought you were my friend. I taught you to read."

The gun shook as if Delia were conflicted. "You nice American women," she sobbed. "You think you understand everything, but you don't. You change Tavio. He big man before you come. He protect us. You come and ruin everything."

"Chito beat you."

"He protect me, too!"

"I don't believe this! He beat you!"

"But he protect me. When the other men want me, he don't share me like he did his other women. He fight them. In his way he was loyal to me. He got shot when you escape from prison, and he die later in my arms. Because of you."

"You're learning to read. You're smart. If you keep learning, someday you can get a good job."

"You think you're my friend because you taught me to read. You don't know nothing. Estela, Tavio's wife, was my friend. I grew up in the house next door to hers. She was like my sister. Now Tavio is dead. What will happen to her? *You don't know nothin' about my life!*"

Her hand that held the gun was shaking more violently than ever but she raised it higher.

Mia—

Shanghai's voice in the room, all around her!

He loves me.

The certainty filled Mia with the will to live.

Feeling Shanghai calling to her with love in his heart, Mia sprang to the left at the exact moment Delia pulled the trigger. The bullet hit the wall behind her, shattering the Sheetrock.

"Hold on! I'm comin', darlin'!" Shanghai yelled as he stomped up the porch stairs.

The front door crashed open.

As fast as a rattler, Delia spun on her heel to shoot him.

"No!" Mia screamed, lunging at her, grabbing her by the ankle, pulling at her, dragging her to the floor. "You won't kill him! I won't be abandoned again. I won't be!"

Trying to wrench free of her hand, Delia stared down the length of the gun barrel at Mia. Her eyes glittered in the dark like a cat's as she fired.

Even as pain stung her shoulder and made her yelp, Mia's hand tightened on Delia's ankle. Then she whipped her to the floor. The gun went skittering out of their reach. Delia turned into a wild woman. Using her long nails as weapons, she began clawing at Mia viciously, on the arms and her throat, struggling to reach her eyes.

As suddenly as she'd attacked her, Delia was gone. Her body was dropped onto the floor, hard, a few feet behind Mia. Then Delia began bawling.

"*Bastardo!*" In between pleading to be released, Delia cursed viciously. "Let me go! You're breaking my arms!"

"If I do, it'll be your fault! Quit fightin' me!"

Hazily Mia opened her eyes. Gripping her bloody shoulder, she scrambled to her knees. Delia was on the floor, kicking and trying to roll over. Shanghai was kneeling on top her, straddling her, holding her hands behind her back in a death grip.

"You okay?" he muttered.

"I think so."

"Get out to my truck! I've got some rope in the back seat!"

Mia staggered to her feet, blood dripping down her arm. When she returned with the rope, he tied Delia's hands and then her feet.

During his deft maneuvers, Delia cursed him roundly.

"Damn you, girl, but you've got a foul mouth! Those aren't words fit for ladies. I'm going to get me a couple of dish towels."

"If you knew what she'd been through, you'd understand," Mia said.

He turned to Mia. "Don't be a sap. She would've killed you. Watch her, okay?" Then he strode to the kitchen and she heard him whipping towels off the racks.

When he returned and knelt over Delia, he gagged her. After that, Delia's spitting and cursing began to sound more like muted grunts. He stood up, his expression tender with concern for Mia. Slowly, hesitating to believe he really wanted her, she went into his arms.

Holding her tightly, he led her to a light switch and flipped it on. For a long moment he inspected her shoulder, moving her arm, holding the wound up to the light. Then he placed a dish towel on the wound.

"You got lucky. It's just a nick. Maybe you'll need a stitch or two. Or maybe one of those fancy bandages that works like a stitch will do."

"You came back," Mia whispered, still not quite believing he had.

"If you'll take me back."

"If?" Relieved to be alive and in his arms, she rested her cheek against his strong chest. "You didn't leave me this time."

"I was a damn fool to think I could live without you ten seconds much less a lifetime. *No matter what you did.* And you didn't do anything wrong. It was me…crazy jealous all the time… I don't have an excuse really. If you told me to get lost now, I wouldn't blame you."

"I'm not giving you any excuse."

"I don't want to mistreat you like I was mistreated as a kid, and that's what I was doin' when I drove off. Not listening, not trying, just walking out. Then it struck me—hell, darlin', what kind of crazy guy thinks a classy gal like you would sink even lower than a Knight and want a certified lunatic bastard like Morales?

"And there's something else…something that doesn't make any sense at all. The whole time I was driving, I felt your pain. It's like you're a part of me or something…like you were calling to me."

"I was."

He stared at her in wonder. "The farther I got from you, I could feel you crying out to me to come back."

"Because I was. I was terrified."

"I felt the same thing after you left me in Vegas," he whispered.

"I think I was…calling out to you then, too. For years and years, I willed you to come back. I—I can't believe you heard me."

"I was too stubborn to really listen and believe what I was hearin'. But you were always there like a ghost haunting me."

"I've always wanted you. You know that."

"Someday I hope I'll be the man you deserve."

"You already are. You always have been. It's you who must learn to believe that."

"I left you and you nearly got killed."

"But you came back."

"I thought I needed to be rich and famous to deserve you."

"What do those things matter when you're at home with the person you love? In bed with him or her? Or playing with your children? Or simply sharing a meal together? Other things matter in the quiet times, don't they?"

"I think I was scared of loving you. My mother left me, you know? Deep down I was afraid you'd leave, too."

"So you had to leave first?"

"Maybe."

Shanghai wrapped her more tightly against his body. "I don't want to be like her, either. I don't want to do what she did to me to anybody else. She made me love her and then she walked out on me when I needed her the most. I don't want to do that to you—ever."

Gently Shanghai kissed her, and she felt her fears of abandonment and loneliness start to dissolve.

He wasn't leaving. He was staying. He loved her. He really loved her. Just like she'd always dreamed he would. His arms around her were real and solid, just as his warm mouth was real.

When his lips finally left hers, she stared at him for a long moment. Then Delia began butting her head into the wooden floor and spoiled the mood.

"If she keeps doing that, she's going to hurt herself," Mia said. "Hadn't we better do something about her? Call somebody maybe?"

"I'll have to carry her out to the truck. Then we'll drive her up to the big house. The ranch phone lines are all busy, and nobody's cell phones will answer, either. I know because I tried to call the ranch and Cole and you the whole time I was driving back."

"My cell phone disappeared hours ago."

"I'd bet a bundle Delia took it. I told you we should have turned her in to the authorities."

"I was so naïve to think anyone in Tavio's compound was my friend."

Negra strolled into the living room and meowed.

"Except for you, precious," Mia said.

"That Cessna Skyhawk Cole's so crazy about was a real Trojan horse."

"Except for Negra."

"That cat is utterly useless."

"No, she isn't. She loves me. Cats don't lie. But a lot of things between human beings aren't what they seem," she said.

"I love you, more than that damn cat does. I know that's real at least."

"At last," she murmured, not in the least worried that he could be jealous of her cat.

His mouth slanted across hers again. His kiss was long and deep, and she felt it all the way to her bones.

Watching them, Negra went over and sniffed a golden object that lay forgotten on the floor. Shaking her head, she lay down and rolled over on her back beside the gun. She stretched languidly and began to purr.

As her people continued to kiss, her purr turned into a roar as if she sensed that all was finally right in her world.

Epilogue

Mia flipped through the little book, which started off with drawings and photographs of Shanghai riding bulls, that she'd begun for Vanilla when she'd first come home.

"Why, it's lovely. I love that picture of you and Vanilla and me underneath the spur tree when you handed her your spurs. Vanilla will love it, too, when she's older and understands. Why, you've even put in some wedding pictures. I can't believe you took the time to get all these pictures printed."

"Do you like the one of Benjamin sticking out his tongue?"

"Yes." She laughed.

"I thought Vanilla's story needed a happy ending," he said.

"She'll love it." Mia closed the little book and set it on the dresser. "I can't wait for the two of us to sit down with Vanilla and read it to her."

"Me, either."

"But if we don't hurry we're going to be late for the barbecue." She blushed, remembering how they'd spent the afternoon. "What will everybody think?"

"The truth," Shanghai replied quietly.

The truth was they'd made love all afternoon while Sy'rai

had supervised a hired sitter to care for Vanilla at the big house.

"We're newlyweds," he said. "They'll understand."

She put her hands on her waist and spun before the mirror in their bedroom at Black Oaks to make sure she looked all right.

"You're beautiful," Shanghai breathed.

Mia laughed at her reflection and his. He was standing behind her, buttoning his long-sleeved shirt and jamming it inside the waistband of his jeans. His movements were jerky; his dark face tense again at the thought of facing her family.

The annual Kemble family reunion was this Saturday, which was Memorial Day weekend. Thus, the Golden Spurs was jammed with more than a hundred Kembles or descendants of Kembles. Private planes and jets lined the family airstrip. SUVs and luxury cars jammed the big parking lot behind the house.

Some of her cousins would stay a whole week for what the family called Summer Camp and enjoy ranch life. Some had flown or driven in for a day or two.

"Too many Kembles for one lone Knight without armor to fend off," Shanghai had said earlier.

"What about Cole? He'll be there."

"Since he's the main guy running the ranching operation, I'd say he's one of you now."

"So are you."

Now as she watched a muscle tick along his jawline, she wished he could relax tonight. Her family would like him if he'd only be himself.

"Am I as beautiful as Lizzy?" she whispered, determined to distract him.

"I see all your old demons are wide-awake and on the attack," he teased.

"Yours, too."

His gaze met hers in the mirror. "Mine, too," he admitted. Then he grimaced. "Old habits die hard."

"My family won't attack you, you know," she murmured.

"But they'll think things."

"So?"

"You're right. After all the headlines, we should be used to people thinking all sorts of things."

"Leo told me we'd better settle down and become an old boring married couple. He says he gets in a bad mood every morning when he opens his paper and sees the Kemble name or the Golden Spurs Ranch mentioned unless he sees Terence Collins's byline."

"Terence has been wonderful. He's called several times to make sure I'm all right."

There'd been stories about Tavio being captured at Black Oaks. About Shanghai's retirement, too. Recently there had been some extremely disturbing stories about John Hart, as well.

Delia, who was still in custody, had accused Hart of murdering Tavio to stop him from telling the authorities that the agent had been working for Morales. Hart had been suspended without pay pending an investigation into Tavio's death and the drug busts Hart had been involved in during the last few months.

Mia spun again, causing her pale-green dress, which was made of a light silky fabric, to float above her thighs and show off her legs.

"Do I really look okay?" She fluffed her hair and then let it spill over her shoulders like a flame.

"I'd rather take you to bed again than go to that damn barbecue."

Her cheeks flushed a deeper shade of pink as she remembered all the things he'd just done to her in bed. Her eyes glowed. "So you do think I'm pretty?"

"If you were any prettier I'd be lying on that bed with a sheet over my face dead of a heart attack."

Fire raced through her veins as he came up behind her and circled her waist with his large, wide hands. Then he eased her bottom closer so that it nestled against his fly, which was swollen with need for her again. "To me, you are the most beautiful woman in the world. But then you know that." He swatted her derriere affectionately and let her go.

"Not so fast! Who put you in charge?"

She squirmed against the bulge in his jeans—just to torture him, too.

"Tease!" he rasped.

She turned around and cupped his dark face between her palms. Basking in his love, she sighed happily. "I can't believe this."

"Sometimes I still can't believe you love me, either," he said. "Being with you like this is everything. Because it feels true."

"For me, too," she whispered.

"The fans in the arenas, they may scream and clap, but they're strangers. The truth is you've always been special, and you've always made me feel special. Fans can't begin to touch the way you're looking at me right now."

"With my heart in my eyes?"

He leaned forward and brushed his lips across her brow.

"You gave me that same look when you were ten, when you came over to Black Oaks to find out about Spot and he ran up to you wagging his tail. For years I tried to forget that look on your face. You had it in Vegas the next morning after we made love. It scared the hell out of me. I thought I knew where I was going. I wanted to be a big rodeo star. Somebody in my own right. With a name as big as Kemble. Then you came along and derailed me. I was such a big fool I hid from the truth."

"You seemed so cold."

"'Cause I was afraid. 'Cause I was bumbling through life with my heart and mind set on all the wrong prizes. I was like a blind man. Snorting-mad, just like a big, dumb bull that has to charge everything that moves."

"I felt so lost…like something was wrong…like nobody would ever love me. My daddy…"

"Your daddy wasn't your real daddy as you well know by now. Caesar Kemble was a hardheaded cuss, darlin'. Same as my daddy was. Maybe worse. They did a number on us. The sooner we forget that, the better. I'm going to spend the rest of my life making you know how special you are."

"Oh, Shanghai."

He kissed her lips softly. "I am yours. Believe it. I'll always be yours."

The grounds around the big house were all lit up with thousands of white twinkling lights in the trees. Sy'rai and Kinky and the rest of the hands along with the family had been working a week to get the place cleaned up. Three immense yellow-and-white tents had been set up on the front lawns along with a dance floor and a Western band. Banquet tables brimmed with barbecue and all the fixings.

Guitars and banjos were whining. The barbecue and dance were in full swing by the time Mia managed to drag Shanghai to the party. When they walked inside the tent where the food was, Shanghai's mouth thinned. Beneath Mia's hand his forearm felt tense. Then Cole came up and handed him a beer and led him over to a group of Kembles from Colorado. Before long, Shanghai was surrounded by Mia's relatives from Montana and Utah and Nevada, all of them asking about his bull riding career.

She drifted away to talk to family she hadn't seen since before Cole's plane had gone down, and she'd been lost in the gulf. They hugged her and told her how glad they all were she was alive and happy. Tears were shed on all sides. Heartfelt stories were shared.

Soon she realized that the whole time she'd felt so alone and frightened in Mexico, her family had been hoping and praying for her to come back home. She hadn't been forgotten or abandoned. She'd just thought she was.

Separated from her, Shanghai looked uneasy about his

popularity at first. Every so often his eyes searched the throng for her, and when he found her circled by her distant cousins, he flashed her a wide grin that made her heart quicken. Confidence would flood her then, and she'd enjoy her family all the more.

Leo Storm came late and without a date. Despite the heat, he wore a three-piece suit. He pocketed his glasses upon entering the tent, but he looked tired even when he smiled at her mother, who rushed to greet him. Lizzy and Mia joined them.

"Why didn't you bring a date?" Lizzy demanded.

Leo flushed.

"Oh, Lizzy, you know Leo works too hard to find time for romance," Joanne chided. "Or even to change into something more comfortable to come to our party."

"I asked somebody," Leo countered defensively. "She said no. So here I am, glad to be here. And glad that the Morales crisis is over. Pretty soon it'll be back to business as usual."

"Settling family squabbles and fending off lawsuits?" Joanne said.

"I didn't know when I had it easy."

Shanghai joined them and circled Mia's waist with his arm.

"Why didn't you bring a date? You never take no for an answer when you want something for the ranch," Lizzy persisted.

Leo shot Shanghai a dark glance before shaking his hand.

"Lizzy!" Joanne's brows drew together.

"My mother used to say I was stubborn," Leo said. "Bad trait. Well, the lady in question won't date me because she's got a thing for cowboys. I know I should give up, but so far I haven't."

"Lizzy, why don't you quit pestering Leo about his mystery girl and ask him what he'd like to drink?" her mother said.

"An ice cold beer," Leo replied as a woman in an apron with a silver tray loaded with drinks arrived.

Leo lifted a mug and saluted Lizzy. "Cheers."

"Your brother tells me you're in the market for an Arabian stallion," Shanghai said.

Leo's slow smile lacked warmth. "Connor talks too much."

"What about the twins?" Lizzy said. "Has your detective made any progress at all on finding my missing sisters?"

Leo shot her a dark look before he forced a smile. Was it only Mia's imagination, or was he uncomfortable with her sister's question?

"It's complicated," he said, hedging. "I think we may have located one of them. I'm checking it out—*personally*."

"Leo!" Joanne went pale. "Why didn't you call us and tell us this first thing?"

"I think it's best to be cautious, not to raise false hopes…on either side. Electra took great pains to be secretive so Caesar would never know."

"Still, you've been awfully secretive as well about telling us you might have found one of them," Joanne said. "And now your attitude…"

"Merely cautious, I assure you." Once again his face was stiff before he caught himself and forced a smile. "Hopefully I will have good news soon."

Mia was excited about the thought of stepsisters or cousins, and yet maybe Leo was right to be a little guarded and warn them not to get their hopes up until the detective had checked all the facts. There was the danger that if anyone knew that the Kembles were looking for Caesar's long-lost daughters, a fortune hunter might turn up instead of the genuine daughter.

Under his breath Shanghai whispered in Mia's ear, "Have I socialized with your family long enough?"

"You get an A+."

"I'd rather get a reward."

"Like what?"

"Come with me to the barn."

"What for?"

He grinned at her shamelessly. "You know."

"Shouldn't we go check on Vanilla?"

He nodded. "After the barn. After we've kissed for a spell."

Kissed? She knew what he really meant.

Giggling, she practically ran ahead of him down the wide paths that had been cut through the mesquite and cacti for the golf cart her mother used to do her chores at different locations on the ranch. Shanghai chased after Mia the whole way.

Inside the dark tack room, he gave a low growl, hooked his arm around her and brought her close against his body. When he'd pinned her to the wall and raised her skirt and pulled her panties down, he gently inserted a finger inside her.

"You don't waste time," she teased. "What is this slam, bam, thank…"

His only answer was to move his finger inside her slowly, caressing slick vulnerable surfaces until she forgot about talking and simply moaned in delicious delight.

"What about your jeans?" she said in a husky tone a long time later. "I want to touch you, too."

He held still while she slid his zipper down so that his erection could be freed of the denim. Circling him with her hand, she squeezed before she began to stroke him.

"I want to be inside you," he whispered, his voice suddenly fierce with urgency. "Now."

With a broken cry, she let go of him. He shifted his weight, opened her legs wider, stroked her gently for a long moment and then lunged between them. Then that was the last of his gentleness. He was rough and wild, plunging into her again and again until he finally exploded.

When she came seconds after he did, emotions cascaded over her and she wept.

Struggling for his own breath, he held her close.

"I'll never get enough of you," came his hoarse whisper in the dark.

"That's what marriage is all about."

"Then life is good. Damn good. Sweet. I never knew it could be this way."

She kissed his feverish cheek and then his sweaty throat where his pulse beat madly. "We'd better go see about Vanilla before we go home."

He pulled her against him even tighter. "I want more children."

"Then I have good news for you." Her voice held a lilting note.

"What?"

"Yes." She paused. "Maybe we'll have a little boy this time."

He nuzzled her throat. "Did I ever tell you I love you?"

"A few times, I believe. But I'll never tire of hearing it. Not even when I'm a very old lady with dozens of grandchildren and you're sitting in a rocker on the porch right beside me."

"Funny thing, I used to dread the thought of growing old. If you're with me, a rocker doesn't sound half bad."

"Just goes to show you how your perspective can change."

He placed his hand on her stomach, and then he kissed her one final time before they left together to see about Vanilla.

"A little boy," she said. "I hope he has blue eyes, and looks exactly like you."

Two classic holiday stories from
New York Times bestselling author

DEBBIE MACOMBER

Everyone wants to be home for the holidays…

The Forgetful Bride

Caitlin Marshall's trying to
go home to Minnesota, but
at the last minute she gives
her airline ticket to a
stranded soldier. So Cait
spends Christmas with
Joe Rockwell.…

When Christmas Comes

When Faith comes to visit
her friend in Washington,
she finds Charles, a complete
stranger and a curmudgeon
to boot. Then his brother,
Ray, shows up…

HOME
FOR THE
Holidays

Through all the mix-ups
and misunderstandings,
among the chaos and
confusion, romance
begins to emerge…

*Available the first week of
November 2005,
wherever paperbacks are sold!*

MIRA®

www.MIRABooks.com

MDM2239

New York Times bestselling author

SHARON SALA

One man
murdered.

One more dug
from his grave.

Twelve others missing.

This is no coincidence.

Respected Washington, D.C., journalist January DeLena is positive
the threads of each victim's disappearance are intertwined. All
signs point to the man who calls himself The Sinner—a disturbed
homeless man who lures victims into his fanatical world of
salvation and redemption.

January can't keep her suspicions private. And soon she's got the
ear—and the interest—of homicide detective Benjamin North.
But January has a secret. One that places her directly in the path
of the twisted, self-proclaimed messiah's rage. Suddenly, getting
this story has January and Benjamin headed to hell and back.

THE
CHOSEN

"An emotional roller-coaster ride....
Sala's storytelling gifts are unquestionable."
—*Romantic Times* on *Missing*

*Available the first week of November 2005,
wherever paperbacks are sold!*

MIRA®

www.MIRABooks.com

MSS2220

New York Times
bestselling author

MAGGIE SHAYNE

**Some people will do anything—and
kill anyone—to keep their secrets.**

Michael "River" Corbett—River cannot
remember what truly happened the night he
was arrested for the murder of his wife. But
now someone is trying to kill him, and
he is forced to run for his life.

Cassandra "Jax" Jackson—The
uncompromising police lieutenant knows
she's putting her career on the line when
she encounters this desperate stranger and
doesn't turn him in.

Dawn Jones—The daughter of a madman,
Jax's young friend is haunted by voices she
doesn't want to hear. And unless she listens
to what the dead are telling her, Jax might
be doomed to join them.

DARKER THAN MIDNIGHT

*"Tense…frightening…a page-turner
in the best sense."*
—*Romantic Times* on *Colder Than Ice*

*Available the first week of November 2005
wherever paperbacks are sold!*

www.MIRABooks.com

MMS2229

USA TODAY
bestselling author

MERLINE LOVELACE

It's been months since that horrible day USAF captain Miranda Morgan flew her C-130 Hercules into lethal cross fire in Afghanistan. But Randi still can't believe that Ty, her best friend, is really gone.

Now back in southeastern Oklahoma, Randi knows she did all she could to get Ty out safely, but his billionaire father is convinced there's blood on Randi's hands and, through his fog of hatred, will stop at nothing to punish her.

eye
of the
beholder

"Readers who enjoy military thrillers by such authors as... Suzanne Brockmann will be riveted."
—*Booklist* on *After Midnight*

Available the first week of November 2005, wherever paperbacks are sold!

www.MIRABooks.com

MML2230

The colder the winter, the sweeter the blackberries will be once spring arrives.

Will the Kimball women discover the promise of a beautiful spring?

Blackberry
WINTER
Cheryl REAVIS

HARLEQUIN

Available December 2005
TheNextNovel.com

HN22

If you enjoyed what you just read,
then we've got an offer you can't resist!

Take 2 bestselling novels FREE!
Plus get a FREE surprise gift!

Clip this page and mail it to MIRA®

IN U.S.A.
3010 Walden Ave.
P.O. Box 1867
Buffalo, N.Y. 14240-1867

IN CANADA
P.O. Box 609
Fort Erie, Ontario
L2A 5X3

YES! Please send me 2 free MIRA® novels and my free surprise gift. After receiving them, if I don't wish to receive anymore, I can return the shipping statement marked cancel. If I don't cancel, I will receive 4 brand-new novels every month, before they're available in stores! In the U.S.A., bill me at the bargain price of $4.99 plus 25¢ shipping and handling per book and applicable sales tax, if any*. In Canada, bill me at the bargain price of $5.49 plus 25¢ shipping and handling per book and applicable taxes**. That's the complete price and a savings of over 20% off the cover prices—what a great deal! I understand that accepting the 2 free books and gift places me under no obligation ever to buy any books. I can always return a shipment and cancel at any time. Even if I never buy another The Best of the Best™ book, the 2 free books and gift are mine to keep forever.

185 MDN DZ7J
385 MDN DZ7K

Name	(PLEASE PRINT)	
Address	Apt.#	
City	State/Prov.	Zip/Postal Code

*Not valid to current The Best of the Best™, Mira®,
suspense and romance subscribers.*

*Want to try two free books from another series?
Call 1-800-873-8635 or visit www.morefreebooks.com.*

* Terms and prices subject to change without notice. Sales tax applicable in N.Y.
** Canadian residents will be charged applicable provincial taxes and GST.
All orders subject to approval. Offer limited to one per household.
® and ™are registered trademarks owned and used by the trademark owner and or its licensee.

BOB04R   ©2004 Harlequin Enterprises Limited

MIRABooks.com

We've got the lowdown on your favorite author!

☆ Read an excerpt of your favorite author's newest book

☆ Check out her bio

☆ Talk to her in our Discussion Forums

☆ Read interviews, diaries, and more

☆ Find her current bestseller, and even her backlist titles

All this and more available at

www.MiraBooks.com

MEAUT1R3

ANN MAJOR

32088	THE GIRL WITH THE GOLDEN SPURS	___ $6.50 U.S.	___ $7.99 CAN.
66956	MARRY A MAN WHO WILL DANCE	___ $6.50 U.S.	___ $7.99 CAN.
66741	THE HOT LADIES MURDER CLUB	___ $6.50 U.S.	___ $7.99 CAN.

(limited quantities available)

TOTAL AMOUNT	$ _____
POSTAGE & HANDLING	$ _____
($1.00 FOR 1 BOOK, 50¢ for each additional)	
APPLICABLE TAXES*	$ _____
TOTAL PAYABLE	$ _____

(check or money order—please do not send cash)

To order, complete this form and send it, along with a check or money order for the total above, payable to MIRA Books, to: **In the U.S.:** 3010 Walden Avenue, P.O. Box 9077, Buffalo, NY 14269-9077; **In Canada:** P.O. Box 636, Fort Erie, Ontario, L2A 5X3.

Name: _____
Address: _____ City: _____
State/Prov.: _____ Zip/Postal Code: _____
Account Number (if applicable): _____

075 CSAS

*New York residents remit applicable sales taxes.
*Canadian residents remit applicable GST and provincial taxes.

MIRA®

www.MIRABooks.com

MAM1105BL